Garry Kilworth has spent much of his life abroad, but his family roots (part gypsy) are in rural Essex, where he now lives. Although he left school aged fifteen to join the RAF, later in life he obtained an Honours Degree in English at King's College, London. He became a full-time author when his children left home, and has written numerous novels and short stories, several of which have won prizes. His most recent novel *House of Tribes* is also published by Corgi.

Critical acclaim for *House of Tribes*:

'A wonderful, witty tale of mice – thrilling, savage, philosophical, and literary in turn. Read it, and never buy a mousetrap again'
William Horwood

'I enjoyed *House of Tribes* immensely – intelligent, funny, well told and more humane than a few books about humans I could name'
Iain Banks

'Kilworth makes mouse mythology into mythic ethology as never before. It's a rodent ratatouille which knocks the pants off Mickey Mouse!'
Brian Aldiss

'Garry thrilled with his Story of Foxes, enchanted with the Story of Hares, and now delights with his *House of Tribes* – by turns tragic and hilarious, always compellin̲   ̲h – with one or tw   to have inhabitin
Robert Hol

D1369105

Also by Garry Kilworth

HOUSE OF TRIBES

and published by Corgi Books

GARRY KILWORTH
A MIDSUMMER'S NIGHTMARE

CORGI BOOKS

A MIDSUMMER'S NIGHTMARE
A CORGI BOOK : 0 552 14464 9

Originally published in Great Britain by Bantam Press,
a division of Transworld Publishers Ltd

PRINTING HISTORY
Bantam Press edition published 1996
Corgi edition published 1997

Set in New Baskerville by Falcon Oast Graphic Art

Corgi Books are published by Transworld Publishers Ltd,
61-63 Uxbridge Road, London W5 5SA
in Australia by Transworld Publishers (Australia) Pty Ltd,
15-25 Helles Avenue, Moorebank, NSW 2170
and in New Zealand by Transworld Publishers (NZ) Ltd,
3 William Pickering Drive, Albany, Auckland.

Reproduced, printed and bound in Great Britain by
Cox & Wyman Ltd, Reading, Berks.

This one is for Birgit.

'Up and down, up and down,
I will lead them up and down,
I am feared in field and town,
Goblin, lead them up and down.'

Puck in *A Midsummer Night's Dream*
by William Shakespeare

ACKNOWLEDGEMENTS

My thanks to Janet and Colin Bord for the useful *Atlas of Magical Britain* (Bracken Books), *Gardener's Magic and Other Old Wives' Lore* by Bridget Boland (Bodley Head) and the *Encyclopedia of Things That Never Were* by Michael Page and Robert Ingpen (Paper Tiger). Also for the Fairy Clock of Flowers, from *The Dictionary of Phrase and Fable* by Rev E. Cobham Brewer (Avenel Books, 1978).

Fairy Clock of Flowers

One am   – scandinavian sowthistle closes.
Two am   – yellow goat's beard opens.
Three am   – common oxtongue opens.
Four am   – hawkweed, late-flowering dandelion, wild
                 succory open.
Five am   – white water-lily, naked-stalked poppy, smooth
                 sowthistle open.
Six am   – shrubby hawkweed, spotted cat's ear open.
Seven am   – garden lettuce, African marigold open/night-
                 flowering catch-fly closes.
Eight am   – scarlet pimpernel, mouse-ear hawkweed,
                 proliferous pink open/evening primrose closes.
Nine .am.   – field marigold opens/purple bindweed closes.
Ten am   – red sandwort opens/yellow goat's beard closes.
Eleven am   – star of Bethlehem opens.
Noon   – ice plant opens/field sowthistle closes.
One pm   – common purslane opens/proliferous pink closes.
Two pm   – purple sandwort closes.
Three pm   – dandelion closes.\
Four pm   – white spiderwort, field bindwort close.
Five pm   – julap opens/common cat's ear closes.
Six pm   – dark crane's bill opens/white water-lily closes.
Seven pm   – naked-stalked poppy closes.
Eight pm   – orange day-lily, wild succory close.
Nine pm   – cactus oruntia opens/convolvulus linaeus,
                 chickweed close.
Ten pm   – purple bindweed opens/common nipple-
                 wort closes.
Eleven pm   – night-blooming catch-fly opens/smooth
                 sowthistle closes.
Midnight   – late-flowering dandelion opens, creeping
                 mallow close.

ONE

Common Oxtongue Opens

OBERON, KING OF THE FAIRIES, STOOD IN A GLADE OF Sherwood Forest and stared around him at the discarded Coke cans, sweet wrappers and crisp packets. He sighed deeply. Although he knew that in the morning the litter would be gathered up by cleaners, the sight still depressed him. He hated the intrusion of mortals upon his world. These ugly mortal effects, their property, were tainted with human touch and scent: to a fairy's sensitive nose the odour of human sweat filled the glade. It could not be more offensive if the area was strewn with human remains, arms and legs, internal organs, toes and fingers, eyes and lips.

'What untidy creatures these mortals be,' he murmured to himself.

He sighed again, then spoke to the woodland around him at large, the small creatures who stared at this powerful fairy king in awe.

'Now is the midsummer when we fairies must depart our ancient woodland home. The lofty colonnade of trees which once supported our entablature the sky, has shrunk and closed about us to become these prison bars; the vast arena of our early years has since become a dungeon cell from which we must escape, or perish. Our magic upon which we do rely, is diminished and so with every passing moon becomes more dim and unpredictable. We can no longer make ourselves invisible at whim, nor cast our spells upon the midnight air to bring unhappy lovers to each other's arms. We must seek another wood in which the light might filter down, through flickering tresses of high poplar trees, between the widespread cedar's hands, to fern and mossy floor below, where tread the feet of fairies and their forest friends.'

At that moment the moon was caught in the crazed branches of the Major Oak standing in the centre of the shrivelled forest. As the wind shook the tree it was as if the old oak were trying to shake the moon from its hair. The light from the heavenly body danced upon the forest floor and once more Oberon took heart in nature. The moon looked bright and shiny: untouched by human foot.

'At least those slipshod mortals cannot soil the moon,' he said to himself with satisfaction. 'The moon is safe at least.'

Sid, a young car mechanic captured by the fairies only a week ago, came into the glade and interrupted the musing king at this point.

'They've been there too,' he said, in a melancholy

voice. 'Neil Armstrong and Buzz Aldrin.'

King Oberon, small in stature but a giant in personality, whirled on the only other person in the glade.

'What?' he cried. 'Mortals on the moon?'

Sid nodded his head. 'Went there and came away. Shouldn't be surprised if there's a Coke can on the moon. Or bubble gum stuck to one of the rocks. Even astronauts might be messy. They're only people.'

Infuriated, Oberon looked up at the moon again. Tainted! Even the very moonbeams in which he was bathed were tainted. He'd better not tell Titania about this. The moon meant more to her than it did to him and goodness knows it was precious enough to a male fairy.

'Keep that to yourself, Sid,' Oberon warned the rude mechanical, 'or there'll be trouble in fairyland.'

When mortals were present the fairies spoke in modern tongue, in the way an adult who is uncomfortable around children will speak down to the younger generation. It was only on their own, amongst themselves, that they spiced their language with an older form of speech.

By this time the other fairies were beginning to drift into the glade. Puck was one of the first. The most mischievous of fairies looked at Oberon quizzically.

'Keep what to himself?' asked the curious Puck.

'Never mind, you wouldn't like it if you knew,' Oberon said.

'Then don't tell me,' Puck said. 'I hate knowing things I don't like. There's too much knowledge in the world already. We would be much happier knowing less. Look at mortals – how much less sad they would be if they didn't know they were going to die! Look how miserable the knowledge of death makes them. The more they learn, the less they love life.'

King Oberon was hardly listening by this time. Puck, the most worldly of all the fairies, did tend to twitter on like a blackbird once he had a subject. The subject didn't need to be very substantial either, to keep Puck in full flow.

Titania made an entrance into the glade next, on the back of her tame screech-owl. Once she alighted, she took on the less comfortable height of four feet from the forest floor, which was exactly the same height as Oberon. The fairies had been practising with this size for some time, knowing that they had to go out into the world of mortals, and recognizing the need not to be too different from its inhabitants. Sid had suggested they might be even taller, but fairy revulsion at big clumsy bodies would not allow them to go above a certain height, though sometimes Oberon sneakily added just half an inch to his stature, in order to be a little loftier than the Queen of the Fairies. It never took long for Titania's spies to inform her of his deviousness, and she and her favourite fairies would shrink themselves to about two feet high, in order to make him look ridiculously large.

'How now, my lord?' Titania said. 'Time for your speech?'

'Indeed,' replied Oberon. 'I shall need your support tonight, my queen.'

Titania smiled encouragingly, no doubt realizing that Oberon was feeling upset at what he had to do. A smile from the pretty Titania, whose radiance could flood a woodland glade with light, was a precious gift. Oberon was grateful for that smile. He plucked a garland of white bryony from a nearby shrub and hung it about his queen's pale slender neck.

'This for the most beautiful of all fairies,' he

4

murmured, and she smiled again.

Sometimes, when Oberon stared into her small, heart-shaped face, framed by wild, tangled hair as black as the spaces between the stars, a lump formed in his throat. Those times when her gossamer dress glittered like a thousand insects as she stood with the moonlight behind her, and he could see her lithe slim form through the folds, he choked on her beauty. He would look up into the dragonfly-blue eyes and whisper her name, offering his kingship at the altar of her being. His magic was more powerful than hers, but her presence held him in thrall and made him vulnerable.

He shook himself from his reverie. It was time to speak. There was chattering amongst the audience.

'Cobweb, settle down. You too, Moth,' ordered Oberon.

The king stood under the massive Major Oak, now weak in limb and bole, supported by poles and wires. The ancient tree was like some old giant endowed with life eternal, gradually coming apart at the joints.

'I've called you here,' said Oberon, 'because it's time to consider leaving Sherwood Forest . . .'

A murmur went through the gathered fairies.

'. . . it's a sad thing,' continued the king, 'but Sherwood has shrunk now to a small wood – a copse – and it will soon be unable to support our magic. As the forest diminishes, so do our powers. We must leave here, or be discovered, for we will soon be unable to hide ourselves away from the eyes of mortals. Four hundred years ago, when we were better known to the outside world, a mortal named William Shakespeare used us in one of his plays – sympathetically, I think – but he aroused for all time an interest in our presence.

'The bard of Stratford-upon-Avon disguised our whereabouts by putting us in some foreign forest, over the oceans, and his forethought has served to protect our home from common knowledge. Over the centuries Sherwood has been whittled away to almost nothing. Our beloved Major Oak is failing in health. Gone are the mossy banks, the nut-bearing trees. We must go out into the world for a brief time in order to find another forest.'

A fairy called Mist asked in a frightened voice, 'Where will we go?'

Oberon held up a hand. 'Puck, who used to girdle the earth many times a night when his magic was strong, tells us there is a woodland called the New Forest far south of here. The New Forest is larger, surrounded by heathland, and there we shall be able to regenerate our art.'

'How will we get there?' asked Peaseblossom. 'Will our magic carry us through the night?'

Oberon shook his head. 'It's too late for that. We must go by road.'

'*Walk*?' cried a horrified Moth. 'How many leagues?'

Oberon pointed to the enthralled Sid, who was sitting nearby playing with a blade of grass.

'The youth you see before you is what is termed a "motor mechanic". Sid is going to get us one of those box things on wheels – what's it called, Sid?'

'A bus,' Sid replied.

'Yes, a *bus*. A new shiny bus . . .'

'An old, battered bus,' corrected Sid. 'I only had my rusty Ford Escort to put in part exchange.'

'Old, new, it doesn't matter,' said Oberon, hastily. 'So long as it transports us across the English landscape. We shall set out tomorrow evening, which as you all know is midsummer eve, and arrive before the dawn.'

'We hope,' said Sid.

Oberon ignored the interruption from the rude mechanical.

'It will not be a pleasant journey, I'll grant you, for we will have to cram ourselves into a foul-smelling vehicle of the modern age, but unfortunately it's necessary. The residue of our magic, weak as it is, we believe will work a little in the outside world. Now, any questions?'

'Can we take our animals?' asked Cobweb. 'I've got my weasel to consider.'

'No animals or birds,' said Oberon. 'No *room*.'

'Except my owl,' stated Titania. 'My owl comes.'

Oberon gritted his teeth. 'No exceptions. Your owl can fly down to the New Forest.'

Titania's face set. 'My owl goes *everywhere* with me. My owl is coming on the bus.'

Oberon knew better than to do battle with Titania on such issues.

'Perhaps Queen Titania's owl is the exception . . .?'

'If her owl goes, so does my weasel,' cried Cobweb.

'And my rabbit.'

'And my stoat!'

'And my fitchew!'

('What's a fitchew?' asked Sid.)

The cries went up from the band of fairies surrounding the Major Oak. Moonlight filtered through the canopy and washed the faces of the supernatural creatures, making them shine. Oberon studied these faces with annoyance.

'What? Will we have a menagerie on board? Stoat chasing rabbit, weasel at the throat of mouse? Will we have fitchews stealing Sid's provisions? I tell you that anyone who tries to smuggle another creature on board, apart from Titania's owl, will be left behind – banished – is that understood?'

(Sid asked, 'Puck, what's a fitchew?')

This terrible threat had the right effect, though Cobweb still looked resentful. This was no Greek democracy, here in the glade, despite the fact that the playwright had put the fairies in a wood outside Athens. The most powerful fairy ruled virtually absolutely, and that fairy was Oberon. He was lord of the forest, despite his failing magic.

Whether Oberon's power was right or wrong was not a consideration amongst the fairies, since he had come by it naturally and had possessed it always. Whether he used it corruptly or not was also outside the concern of fairies, since they operated under their own code of morality. It was true he used it to get his own way at times, but any other fairy would have done the same in his position. Oberon was Oberon, there was no other forest fairy king, there never had been, there never would be, and therefore his power was unquestioned.

'What the hell is a bloody fitchew?' yelled the frustrated Sid.

'A polecat!' several of the fairies yelled back at him. 'Now be quiet.'

Here was a good example of why the old speech should not be used in front of mortals: their knowledge of language was extremely limited, their vocabulary small, yet their curiosity was as vast as the span of space.

'This bus thing,' said Cobweb, attacking on another front, 'I've seen them bring humans to the Visitors' Centre. Somebody's got to work them. They need someone in the front seat to make them go.'

'True,' replied Oberon. 'It's called a *driver*. You have to *drive* a bus.'

'Who's going to do that? Sid?' asked Moth.

'Sid cannot drive us,' Oberon explained, 'for we have to do this thing ourselves. What sort of achievement would it be if we allowed a mortal to take control of our movements and carry us to our destination? One of us will drive.'

'And who will that be?' asked Cobweb, sarcastically, obviously expecting the answer to be 'Oberon', since *driving* sounded like fun.

'Titania,' replied Oberon, unexpectedly. 'Sid has been teaching her secretly. Our rude mechanical had to make adjustments to the bus seat, so that Queen Titania's pretty little feet . . .', he beamed at his queen and was rewarded with a reciprocal smile, '. . . could reach the operating parts. Sid says she will make a fine fairy driver.'

Sid looked up and raised his eyebrows, but said nothing.

Oberon continued, 'We shall also need a navigator to help Titania to find the way and I was going to ask Cobweb to do that, but since he's been so obstructive I'm appointing Moth as the navigator instead. Sid will show you some things called *maps*, Moth, and instruct you on how to use them.'

Cobweb scowled sulkily, but was wise enough not to argue any further with Oberon on the subject.

'Now, all the unpleasant bits are over,' said Oberon, 'time to get on with the witenagemot.'

A witenagemot was of course once a Saxon parliament, but those political meetings were such riotous affairs that fairies adopted the name for their all-night parties.

Peaseblossom said, 'Sid, can I drive the vehicle?'

'That's already been decided,' muttered Sid. 'I'm not driving and nor are you.'

'Stop chuntering, Sid, and break open the bonny-clabber!' cried Puck. 'It's our last night in the forest.'

Sid was responsible, among other things, for providing the fairies with beer and buttermilk from the outside world, which they mixed together to make their favourite beverage. The motor mechanic was not the first youth to be enchanted and enslaved by the Sherwood fairies: there had been many others over the centuries. And during that time they had developed selected tastes for Outworldly things. One of those desires was for bonny-clabber, a jugful of which an Irish pedlar, who had fallen into a drunken sleep under the Major Oak one night, had by his side when the fairies found him.

'I brought some lager for me,' said Sid, opening the box he had by his side. 'I can't drink that muck you lot swig down your throats. Too sickly.'

'You drink what you like, my lad,' Puck said, reaching for the cans of bitter ale and supermarket full-cream milk, 'so long as you bring our favourite tipple.'

The dancing began.

As always, Sid became very excited when the fairies danced. And oh, how they loved to dance. They were so fast and furious in their movements he could hardly follow an individual, weaving through the others with his or her tiny feet flashing back and forth. It was truly a miraculous sight, the light playing fanciful games around their delicate bodies, the old leaves swirling in the little whirlwinds they created. It was such a *passionate* affair, that had the urgency of death about it, as well as enjoyment. It was as if there were an irresistible *need* to dance, which had to be answered, or some brownie might wither away like a thistle at the end of summer, and vanish on the wind.

The music came from strange little instruments fashioned from pond-water reeds and hollowed wood:

flutes, strings and drums. The first time Sid heard it, the sound had chilled his blood, because he knew it to be pre-Christian, pagan music, woven from the eerie tunes of an ancient Otherworld's time. If lizards could sing, thought Sid, they would make such a sound with their blunt mouths and keen nostrils. The wind had never managed to make such shrill tones, nor running water copy the low notes, yet there was something of both the wind and rushing brook within the primitive airs.

The best amongst the musicians was Peaseblossom, on his flute.

'Come on, Sid, get up and dance,' cried Titania, breathlessly, taking him by the hand.

Sid could not resist the Queen of the Fairies, any more than Lord Oberon could, and he was soon on his feet and jigging like mad to the swirling sound. He yelled when Puck yelled. He jumped higher than Swallowtail. He threw himself into a frenzied whirl to outspin Oberon.

He fell into an exhausted heap as the garden lettuce and African marigold opened and the night-flowering catch-fly closed.

He awoke as usual to the sound of the birds and remembered that this was the day he was going to the New Forest. On the surface it appeared a simple task, to transport a bus load of little people from Sherwood to the south coast. A few hours driving at the most. But then Sid had lived long enough with Oberon's fairies to know that no task was simple when it involved fairy planning. The planners were by their very nature quirky, unpredictable beings, given to adding unnecessary elaborate and intricate twists and turns to any scheme, thereby complicating the easiest of plans.

Before they set forth, however, the rebellion occurred.

TWO

Dark Crane's Bill Opens and White Water-lily Closes

OBERON WAS AWARE THAT THERE WAS A REBELLION amongst the fairies, with Cobweb at its head. He had heard that Puck was dealing with the situation, so he decided to keep well clear. The fairy king knew that if he intervened he would most probably lose his temper and make things worse. Oberon was aware of his weaknesses: he had the failings of most fairies – doubled. Mainly he owned a quick and terrible temper, an envious nature, and a determination to have his own way.

'I have many fardels to bear,' he sighed, 'but this hugger-mugger must cease if we are to survive.'

It was of course still light and the fairies had only just woken up, having risen disgustingly early in the evening at Oberon's command in order to be on the road before the closing of the orange day-lily. Disgruntled and irritable, Cobweb had gathered around him others who were afraid of leaving Sherwood.

'This is our ancient home,' cried Cobweb, 'why should we leave it just because Oberon tells us to? He says the wood will shrink to nought. Well I for one don't believe him. There's still enough magic around for me . . .'

'And what will you eat, Cobweb?' asked Puck, who had heard the commotion in a small clearing behind a black-berry bush. 'There are few enough toadstools on the ground, blackberry bushes like that one yonder are being cleared for new paths for the visitors, the elderberries are only in season for a short while and the nuts that get us through the winter are in short supply. I could go on, but I won't, because I'd just be repeating myself.'

'We'll . . . we'll grow our own,' muttered Cobweb, 'won't we?' he appealed to the mob.

The other fairies were not to be drawn in front of the Puck, Robin Goodfellow, whose mischief might be turned on them rather than the mortals he normally harassed.

'Will you?' grinned Puck. 'I'd like to see that – fairies toiling in the meadow. I've never yet seen a fairy working for the common weal. We're lazy creatures, too fond of a petal bed. We would rather play hoodman blind than cut straws in a cornfield. It's in our certain nature. We're not humans. We don't have to sweat and labour to feed our-selves and we don't want material wealth. In the New Forest there'll be succulent berries, dry nuts and juicy toadstools for everyone. There'll be sweet wild honey to steal from hives. There'll be cuckoo pints in plenty from which to drink before going to bed in some mossy hollow. The New Forest is big enough to keep us all – and it's growing bigger – while this place is dying.'

There was a lot of sense in what Puck was saying. Fairies didn't work, *couldn't* work, it wasn't in their make up. A fairy wouldn't know how to plant a seed, water it, nurture it, harvest its crop. A fairy picked what was on a bush if it was there and if it wasn't he or she went to another bush. They took mouth-drying sloes, chestnuts, acorns, stinging-nettle flowers. From the ground, or growing out of bark, the delicious toadstools: grisette, dryad's saddle, fairy ring mushrooms, velvet shank, chanterelle, and many more. A fairy wouldn't know how to grow a toadstool if the instructions were printed on the top in purple letters.

Mist, another of the rebels, looked at the ground, and said, 'Puck's right. Food is getting short. We can send out woodland creatures looking for us, but there's only so much around and the squirrels and birds need to find food enough for themselves. If they start to starve they'll move on to other places. We've got no choice, really.'

At that moment they heard a roaring sound from the car-park outside the Visitors' Centre.

'There's Sid with our chariot,' Puck said. 'So what shall be your answer – are you all to remain incarcerate in this shrunken wood, or shall you join me in an adventure?'

'Coming,' cried Mist, without further hesitation, and flew through the shrubbery towards the car-park, her feet barely touching the ground.

Others followed, until only Cobweb and Puck were left standing in the clearing.

Cobweb's nutmeg-brown face screwed itself in the resemblance of a prune.

'What say, Cobweb?' said Puck. 'It won't be the same without you.'

'I'm staying,' grunted Cobweb. 'You'll be back – you'll

see. There's no place like our fine Sherwood out there. You'll all be back.'

Puck sighed and turned and left the clearing, heading towards the car-park himself. On the way, Puck found a stone in the roots of a tree. It was shaped roughly like a heart and fitted easily into the palm of his hand. He kept the stone as a kind of talisman and to remind him of Sherwood Forest, which had been his home for six hundred years.

When he reached the car-park, there was Sid's bus, chugging away through a rusty exhaust, sending out dark choking fumes into the atmosphere. The vehicle had been hand-painted a sort of purply-brown at some time, one of its headlights was cracked, and it seemed loose in all its joints and fittings – but its engine rattled away merrily. Sid was a good mechanic, so Puck understood, and only needed bits of string and tree gum to keep the motor running.

The mortals that ran the Visitors' Centre had closed up for the night, so there was no-one around to question the presence of the bus.

Titania was already in her driver's seat. Sid had fitted blocks to the pedals so that her short but shapely legs could reach them. She had been taught well, but Sid had never cured her of the disconcerting habit of releasing the steering-wheel in order to change gear with two hands. Since she was fast – much faster than a human – the operation took but a fleeting moment, but Sid's heart always skipped when it happened, knowing that it required only a second for the bus to career off course and crash into a brick wall.

Oberon climbed gingerly aboard the bus, clutching his oak knobkerrie tightly: the smooth, worn stick had been fashioned from a branch of the Major Oak. It was the symbol of his kingship and very precious to him.

This was the first time he had been up the steps and entered any kind of bus. It was a frightening experience. His stomach was already queasy with the smell of diesel fumes and the vibrations of the bus were upsetting to him.

'When does it stop quivering?' he asked Sid. 'It seems to be trembling for some reason.'

Sid, occupying the front passenger's seat, shook his head.

'Shakes like this all the time,' he said. 'Got to put up with it.'

Oberon gripped the shiny rail by the door and called out to the fairies.

'All aboard,' he shouted. 'We're on our way.'

One by one the fairies came up the steps and began to fill the seats in the bus. Like Oberon, none of them had been on a modern vehicle before now. Like Oberon they all clutched some kind of good luck charm: an acorn, a flint, a blackthorn stick. Blewit even had an old bird's nest.

Mustardseed had his tunic pockets full of wood mice, who kept poking their whiskery noses out for a quick look, then vanishing again. Tails hung like short pieces of string from his pocket flaps. Muffled squealings came from various parts of Mustardseed's body, as wood mice fought for the most comfortable positions in the dark recesses of his clothing. Clearly Mustardseed had ignored Oberon's order not to bring any live creatures, but then Oberon knew that the gentle fairy had never been without his mice for more than a few moments the whole of his existence.

'How many mice have you got?' asked Oberon, sternly.

16

'Two thousand one hundred and twenty,' replied Mustardseed, without hesitation.

'That's all right then,' muttered the king, turning away. 'If Titania insists on taking her owl, I'll allow a few dozen mice in the pockets of a responsible fairy.'

'I wasn't allowed to bring my stoat!' cried Mist. 'It's not fair.'

'It's not fair – but it's fairy,' cried Oberon. 'Now hold your tongue. I want to hear no more about it – from any-one. It's only a few mice, after all – two thousand one hundred and twenty. A paltry amount.'

Sid, overhearing this conversation, might have been surprised had he not known that fairies have no under-standing of numbers, but would never admit to this fail-ing. Neither Oberon or Mustardseed had any idea what 2,120 mice looked like, any more than they did a dozen mice. They played these games of bluff with one another, fooling no-one but themselves.

Sid also knew why Oberon was not making a fuss over the mice. The king was preoccupied with the fact that he was on a vehicle with its engine running. He had none of his wits left for argument. The other fairies shared his fears. Some of the fairies had ridden horses out in the meadows, and Puck had even been in a horse-drawn coach, but none of them had any experience with engines. They sat in their seats, white-faced, waiting for the world to end.

Titania had grown used to the smell and sound of the bus during her lessons in the çar-park at night. Noticing the apprehension amongst the others she herself had felt when she had first encountered the bus, she revved the engine savagely. She was a fairy after all, with a fairy's penchant for tormenting her companions.

17

At least three fairies leapt from their seats in fright, heading down the aisle for the doorway.

Sid jumped up.

'Whoa, steady on, steady on,' he said, calming them, holding up his hands. 'It's not going anywhere yet. Go back to your seats. I'll tell you when to panic.'

The fairies were persuaded back into their seats, while Titania turned to grin at Oberon.

'That's not funny,' he warned her. He looked round. 'By the way, where's your owl?'

'Outside,' Titania told him, 'sitting on the roof. She doesn't like it in here.'

'Can't say that I blame her,' muttered Oberon. Then in a louder voice, he cried, 'Everyone on board?'

Puck said, 'Everyone but Cobweb. He refuses to come.'

Oberon raised his bushy eyebrows. It was a gesture which would have had forest creatures scuttling for dens, nests and dreys. 'Not coming?' he said, severely.

Puck shrugged. 'That's what he said.'

King Oberon went to the door of the bus and looked out. Peering from the shrubbery on the corner of the Visitors' Centre was a forlorn-looking brown face with small pointed ears. Oberon stared at Cobweb and narrowed his eyes.

'Not coming, eh?' he murmured to himself. Then loudly, 'Start the bus moving . . .'

Titania let out the clutch sharply and the bus lurched forward throwing Oberon off his feet. There was, as Sid had anticipated, a general scramble for the doorway. He reached over by Titania and shut the door. The bus rumbled forward, across the car-park, heading for the entrance to Sherwood Forest in fits and starts. Fairies fell down the stairwell and piled up against the door. Oberon was at the bottom of this pile and he roared in rage. Small fists began flying, elbows began digging in ribs, feet began kicking.

Sid started pulling fairies off the king and sending them back to their seats.

'I don't want to leave Sherwood! I don't want to go!' screamed a terrified Peaseblossom, fighting back when Sid wrenched him from the stairwell. 'I'm not going, I'm not going . . .'

Swallowtail, sitting near the front, regarded Peaseblossom in disgust. 'Pull yourself together,' she said. 'Have you no trust in our queen's driving skills?'

The bus rolled from side to side, skidding on the gravel as it headed down the driveway to the park.

'Is it supposed to do this?' asked Peaseblossom, looking green and sickly.

'Of course,' replied Swallowtail, knowing little more than the male fairy, 'otherwise it wouldn't be doing it, would it?'

Peaseblossom was guided gently back to his seat.

Oberon was at last allowed to get up from his crushed, undignified position on the stairs. He looked ruffled and angry. His large handsome head, with its tall hair standing six inches straight up from his scalp, looked out of sorts on his stocky body. He had been humiliated and he showed it.

The bus crunched to a halt at the exit to the centre.

'Some fairies are going to end this trip with two heads and a set of toad's legs,' he thundered.

Oberon was interrupted by a frantic tapping at the door. When he looked down, there was a terrified Cobweb looking up at him. Sid used the handle to open the door.

'Yes?' asked Oberon, patronizingly. 'Did you want something?'

'I got lonely,' said the agitated Cobweb. 'I got very lonely.'

'You were only there for a few moments,' Oberon said.

'It seemed like a long time,' Cobweb argued. 'Can I come in now?'

'Let's leave him behind,' cried Titania, and shot the bus forward a couple of yards.

'Please!' yelled Cobweb, racing up alongside again. 'Don't leave me!'

'Will you behave?' Oberon questioned.

'Yes, yes. I'll be good.'

Satisfied, Oberon stood aside and let the frightened Cobweb on board.

'Mind you do,' he warned the wayward fairy, 'or you'll be cast out into the night, wherever we are, and left to find your way there by yourself.'

Whether the king was serious or not, the threat was so terrible Cobweb shook at the knees. He crept along the aisle until he found his seat and then sat down. Someone reached forward and patted his shoulder to comfort him.

Before the door was closed, Oberon took a last lingering look at the forest which had been their home since the Dark Ages. Titania, aware of the solemnity of the moment, turned in her seat and stared too. The rest of the fairies peered out of the windows at the woodland, purple in the soft light of a midsummer evening. The midges hovered over favourite shrubs, while swallows and swifts dipped and weaved through their clouds. One lone weasel stood tall on its hind legs, a small sentry, watching the bus intently. A band of rabbits played at the corner of the forest, unaware of the exodus.

King Oberon let out a small sigh and then turned and nodded to Titania. The bus moved off, out through the exit, into the lane beyond. Soon trees were zipping by the windows and the forest became a part of the past.

Sid advised Moth, the navigator, sitting next to him.

'I should take the A6075 towards Mansfield – we can then take the A38 to meet the M1 at junction 28.'

He showed the map book, open at the relevant page, to Moth.

Moth hardly glanced down at the red- and blue-veined page which looked like a mortal's circulatory system.

'I shall navigate not by strange charts drawn by humans, but by tried and tested fairy methods,' he told Sid. 'My way is to guide us by the moon and stars, by the scent of fern leaves on the breezes, by the call of the pine tree in the wind. I follow moondust and apple pollen. I am advised by the redstart's piping and the nightjar's cry!'

The only word Sid really latched on to, amongst those gabbled by Moth, was 'stars'.

'You want to do it by the stars,' he said, 'that's up to you. Personally I would've thought this was a bus, not a bloody yacht out in the Atlantic Ocean, but far be it from me to question one of you lot. So long as we get there by morning and I'm set free by Oberon, once and for all, I couldn't give a monkey's how we do it.'

Moth, who was talking about an emotional attraction for the Milky Way and certain constellations, rather than a technical use of fixed star points, nodded in satisfaction.

'So be it, Sid,' he said, 'but not by monkeys. Monkeys are silly creatures who know little of fairy navigation.' Then to Titania, 'We go that way.'

Moth pointed out into the fields, reddened by the gentle evening sun. Titania obediently turned the bus to enter the field by a farmer's gate, smashing through it and sending splintered wood flying through the air. The bus bumped and jolted over the meadow, frightening the resident cows into a stampede in the far west corner, where they tried to escape through a dense blackthorn hedge.

'Where to now?' cried Titania, the juddering rattling the words in her throat. 'Do I go through cow pats, or around them? There's a stile at the end of the field, but it looks a bit small for the bus. What shall I do?'

Sid shouted, 'Buses aren't made to go over fields. You have to use the roads. Fields – fields aren't smooth or hard enough. We might get stuck in a ditch or something.'

Moth, shaken to his very bones, grumbled, 'Well why didn't you say so? Back to the highway, Titania.'

'Make up your mind,' said the fairy queen, turning the bus in a great arc and narrowly missing a water trough. 'The cow pats are making me skid . . .'

They got back to the road and Sid was relieved to find they were going in a westerly direction. That way lay the M1 and once on the motorway, provided he could get Moth to go south, he felt they would be well on their way to the New Forest.

'This is better,' said Oberon, as the bus sped along the highway. 'This is much better.'

The fairies began to settle themselves, wondering why they had made that fuss in the first place. The smell of mortals and engines was still ghastly, but the motion was less terrible than anticipated: no worse than sleeping in a squirrel's drey at the top of a pine on a windy day. This was easy and they would be in the New Forest before long. Then, above the grumbling note of the engine, they heard music. It seemed to be coming to them on the evening breezes.

'Is that music for the maypole dancing?' asked Peaseblossom of Sid, excitedly. 'Shall we go a-Maying? Will the chimney-sweeps be leading about a Jack-i'-the-green while the May-queen dances?'

Puck said, 'It's midsummer, not May-time, Peaseblossom.'

Sid nodded. 'That'll be a village midsummer fête. There aren't any chimney-sweeps now, Peaseblossom. At least, not enough to make a dance.'

At that moment they were using a road which passed through the middle of the village green. There were tents and stalls on the side where the church stood. On the other side of the road was a pub called The Robin Hood, and morris men were prancing up and down, waving handkerchiefs and wielding staves. The bells jingled on their legs as a mortal with an accordion played a tune which made the fairies' feet tap on the floor. Children were carrying pink floss on sticks, or ice creams in their hands, while adults wandered around supping ale. A hog was roasting on a spit outside a tent where a man was sell-ing slices of the meat between two halves of a bun. There was a carnival atmosphere in the air and the fairies' eyes shone with excitement and dance-fever.

'We've got plenty of time to get to the New Forest,' said Titania. 'Loads and loads of time.'

'Hold on,' cried Sid, alarmed at the lights in their eyes. 'We don't have that much time. It's best we keep on the road until we know what the traffic . . .'

But he was wasting his breath. No-one was listening to him. All eyes and ears were on the colourful scene out-side. Titania slowed the bus down to a crawl. A man stepped out in the road in front of her and signalled for her to drive to the back of the green, which had been turned into a car-park.

Titania followed the man's gestures obediently, letting the bus come to rest in the long shadow of the church spire.

THREE

Naked-stalked Poppy Closes

THE VILLAGERS ENJOYING THEIR ANNUAL FÊTE WERE NOT especially surprised to see over two dozen small people alight from a coach and begin to participate in the fun. Some thought vaguely that these might be circus dwarfs on an outing – or rather 'vertically disadvantaged people' as the politically correct amongst them would have it – but the majority believed that a crowd of schoolchildren had arrived. It was true the faces of the fairies were childlike. So in point of fact no-one paid much attention to them in the hustle-bustle of the evening's activities. The fête was so well known that people from far and wide came to see it.

Some of the fairies went straight to the dancing, which at first they were content to watch, while jigging a little in time to the music. Others, like Titania and Puck, wandered around the stands, peering at junk on the white elephant stall. Puck noticed a Buddha figure which had been painted black, but which was actually solid gold underneath. Puck's eyes were able to see beneath the paint and he recognized the precious metal immediately. He picked up the object and showed it to Titania, who also recognized its worth.

'Nice little statue, that,' said the stall-minder, a woman in her late fifties. 'Two pounds. Make a nice birthday present for your mother, young man.'

Puck weighed it in his hands.

'Heavy, I know,' the stall-minder said. 'Probably lead or some such – but a good solid mantelpiece will hold it. Or a window-sill, if you've got a bay window like mine. I could probably let you have it for one pound fifty.'

Puck smiled at Titania and said, 'Lead?' before replacing it carefully back on the stall. As the pair of them walked away, they heard the woman calling, 'All right, a pound then? It's for a good cause, you know . . .'

Mustardseed went to the hoopla stall and threw nine hoops over nine prizes before he was ordered to go away. Mist threw darts at a board and scored a dozen bull's-eyes in a row. Blewit unseated several coconuts at the shy before the woman in charge realized the thrower had paid no money. Swallowtail announced where the pirate treasure was hidden on a map of a coral island, and was glared at by the vicar's wife because she had not paid the necessary fee. Moth and some other fairies would have won the lucky dip, if they had given the barrel-minder the requisite twenty pence.

All over the fête there were penniless fairies having a go at things without paying and revealing the secrets of the stall-minders to the crowds. Their efforts were astonishingly skilful and accurate. A certain amount of chaos was created, the vicar was sent for, and suspicious stall-minders began accusing helpers of corruption.

Titania found herself wandering away from the rest of the fairies, drawn to a certain section of the fête by a subtle but powerful magnetism. Puck followed her closely and she knew he was puzzled by her need to break away from the group and follow some instinctive urge. She eventually found herself stopping to admire a beautiful chubby little baby in a pram. The child looked up and smiled.

When she looked into the baby's eyes, Titania found herself mesmerized by the infant's stare. There was some instant and compelling attraction about the baby, which touched a chord in Titania's breast. It was almost as if Titania had been drawn by the baby to its side. This was a magical suckling, whose aura was almost as strong as that of a fairy.

She pinched the baby's cheeks, making it giggle, until a woman told her to go away. Titania's doll-like face looked up into the mortal's eyes and generated enough malice in her expression to frighten the mortal.

'I don't m-m-mind you *looking* at the baby,' stammered the woman, 'but you mustn't touch.'

'Why not?' asked Titania, before Puck could pull her away. 'Is it yours?'

'I'm looking after the child. I'm the family's nanny. The infant is my responsibility.'

'Where did you purchase it?' persisted Titania, ignoring Puck's tugging of her sleeve, and looking around at the bring-and-by stalls. 'How many pennies did you pay? Was it more than tuppence? I'll give you a silver thre'penny bit for it,' promised the fairy queen, taking the coin from the hem of her gossamer dress. 'It's all I have in coin. I was paid it as toll from a tooth fairy passing through Sherwood Forest over a century ago. It's genuine.'

The nanny looked horrified. '*Purchase* this baby? Young lady, where do you get such terrible ideas from? Go away, you little monster. Go away.'

This time Titania allowed herself to be pulled away from the confrontation by Puck.

'I ought to change her into a slug,' muttered Titania, her normally pale cheeks a rosy red with annoyance. 'I ought to turn her into a toad and wish her under a slab of stone for the next forty years.'

'Later,' said Puck, 'let's go to the dancing.'

By the time Puck and Titania reached the place where the morris dancers had been giving their demonstration of a death and fertility rite turned entertainment, the fairies had taken over. They had taken some staves from a pile by the man playing the accordion and were dancing and leaping as much as three feet high in the air. On each small face was an expression of sheer joy. Even the bewildered morris men had stopped in order to watch this exhibition of athleticism.

The morris men's fool was rushing up and down, striking the fairies on their bottoms with his inflated pig's bladder tied to a stick: an action which seemed to add fuel to the fairies' dancing. Cobweb, Peaseblossom, Mist and a dozen other fairies pranced up and down, clashing the staves, performing a very ancient morris dance unsullied by the passing of time or the modifications of modern men. It was pure Moorish – Morisco with no alterations – and full of archaic canters, trots and jumps, strange even to the watching morris dancers themselves – movements that had been edited out over the centuries.

Mustardseed, as energetic as the rest of his fellows, was continually losing mice from his pockets as he leapt up and down, but the creatures immediately ran up his legs again, looking for their nests. It gave the impression of a constant flow of bodies up and down Mustardseed's legs and torso, and was a source of alarm to some of the watchers.

'You kids push off,' said a morris man, weakly. 'Alf, stop playing.'

The accordion player did as he was told, but Peaseblossom grabbed his instrument and struck up a tune that was only vaguely familiar to the morris men. The music as well as the dance was now exclusively for genuine Moriscos and the gambolling fairies responded even more energetically than they had before. Every fairy present joined in the frolic and their cavorting was so rapid it was difficult for the watchers to follow them with human eyes.

'You be the Mad Morion,' cried a breathless Oberon to Titania. 'I'll be the Moor!' and with that his skin turned black, and he leapt and whirled as wildly as any dervish dancer whose head had been turned by fasting and praying in the wilderness.

The fairy antics pulled people from the pub, from the surrounding houses, and from the stalls, as well as the patrons of the fête. Every human for two miles around was soon crowded around the dancing area, watching with bewildered eyes the flashing arms and legs, the springing bodies, that performed miraculous feats on the village green. The only mortal that was not witness to the dancing was Sid, who had fallen asleep in the bus waiting for the fairies to return.

The fairies danced for an hour, during which time all the humans either fell asleep, exhausted by proxy, or went into a staring trance.

Eventually Puck realized they would have to be on their way and called for a halt. 'King of Shadows,' he cried, 'we must away!' Oberon was jerked out of his high excitement by the more worldly Puck and managed to collect himself before ordering the fairies back to the bus.

'That was wonderful,' cried Blewit, as she smoothed down her ruffled dress. 'Can't we have any more?'

But Oberon knew they had wasted a great deal of time and that they had to be back on the road.

'No, it's time to leave these entranced mortals and be on the road to the New Forest.'

He led the way through human-like-statues, to the bus, where they woke Sid. Titania was one of the last on board and she hurried to her driver's seat, carrying a small bundle, which she placed on the seat beside her. Then she started the engine and backed out to the road. Soon they were speeding along the highway towards the motor-way.

After a few minutes Sid's curiosity got the better of him.

'What's this?' he asked, pointing to the bundle on the seat beside him. 'You buy some tat at the fête?'

'Didn't buy it,' said Titania. 'I took it.'

Sid shook his head, wearily. 'You fairies – you'll be in real trouble before we get to the New Forest, stealing things. It's against the law in the real world, you know.'

He reached over and casually lifted the edge of a piece of blanket which was wrapped around the object. His eyes widened in disbelief as he saw what was underneath. Two little blue orbs regarded him. Below these wide, enquiring organs was a pert button nose. Under the nose was a small rosebud mouth. A further investigation revealed a pudgy body with arms and legs, swaddled by the blanket.

'A baby!' Sid yelled in shock. 'You took a *baby*.'

None of the fairies, including Oberon, seemed the least bit alarmed. The king got out of his own seat and went to look at the infant. His eyes widened when he looked down and Titania knew he had recognized the specialness of this particular infant mortal. Its uniqueness shone like a solitary lamp in the darkness of a bleak moorland.

Oberon looked up at Titania. 'This child reminds me of the one you stole from the Indian king.'

'Different,' Titania said, shaking her head. 'Far more precious than the Indian child.'

Oberon nodded and then bent down and tickled the baby's chin with his finger.

One by one the other fairies came forward, looked at the child, and returned quietly to their seats.

'Pretty little boy,' Oberon murmured.

Titania flashed, 'You're not having *this* one.'

Oberon looked huffy. 'I was only admiring it, my queen. If it's yours, it's yours. One day I'll find my own baby – much more exotic than this one – and you'll have to be a silent witness while I turn him into my henchman.'

'You do what you please with your own infants, my king, for this one is mine and mine alone.'

'It's not yours,' choked Sid, 'either of you. This baby belongs with its mother. You can't just steal a baby. You must be crazy. We'll have every police force in the land after us. We'll be thrown in prison for life. We don't even have the excuse that we're unbalanced – at least, I don't. Don't you know they put out emotional appeals on TV and half the nation will be looking out for the mite? Anyway, it's cruel – let's take it back now,' he pleaded.

Titania looked at the rude mechanical as if *he* were the mad one.

'Take it back? My beautiful little human baby? Never. Besides, I left a changeling. What's cruel about it? Look, it's smiling at me. My baby loves me.'

Sid groaned. 'What did you change it for?'

Puck said, mildly, 'One usually leaves a sickly elf – or an enchanted piece of wood carved into a figure.'

'I didn't have either of those,' said Titania, 'so I left a goldfish.'

'A GOLDFISH?' yelled Sid.

Titania shrugged. 'It was the nearest thing I could find on one of the stalls. There were some dolls further up, but I didn't have time to go for one. So I left the goldfish.'

Sid moaned deeply. 'Even the goldfish wasn't yours.'

'Not really,' smiled Titania, 'but fairies don't really recognize owning things – except babies,' she added, quickly, with a glance back at Oberon in the rear-view mirror.

'Just so long as it doesn't jeopardize our journey,' said Oberon, generously. 'Otherwise I see no reason why my sweet queen should not keep the pretty child.'

'No reason,' murmured Sid, looking out of the window in despair. 'No reason at all.'

The baby began to complain about something and Sid suggested it was the tightness of the blanket. He loosened its folds under the critical eye of Titania and sure enough the baby stopped yelling and began kicking and waving its arms. It was simply asking to be released. It smiled and gurgled at Sid, but when Titania looked down on it, the child opened its mouth and stared as if mesmerized.

'My baby likes you, Sid.'

'It's not *your* baby – look, why don't you have one of

your own if you're that keen on them?'

Titania and the rest of the fairies looked at Sid as if he had suddenly changed into a loathsome bug. He quickly checked his anatomy to make very sure he *hadn't*. Then he raised his eyebrows. 'What did I say?'

'Fairies can't have babies, Sid,' explained Puck. 'That's why they take them.'

'Oh, you admit it's stealing, do you?'

'It would be, if we were mortals, but we're not – we're fairies,' Puck said. 'Fairies can't steal things because they don't recognize the principle of ownership.'

Sid said, 'Look, I'm sorry you lot are impotent, or not fertile, or something, but that doesn't give you the right to take things that don't belong to you, especially people like me and that baby. If you don't recognize the principle of ownership, how come she keeps saying it's *her* baby?'

'Who's she, the cat's mother?' snapped Titania.

Puck said, 'You still don't understand, do you, Sid? We don't believe in owning *things* – but people aren't things, are they? They're people. Fairies can own people, all right. It's objects – *things* – that they can't own. Not outright. That's Oberon's knobkerrie there, but if someone took it, he wouldn't call it stealing. It'd be borrowing.'

'Even if they never brought it back?' asked Sid.

'How long is *never*? They might bring it back one day, perhaps hundreds of years later. It'd still be borrowing, only over the long term.'

'A bloody long term,' replied Sid, wearying of the argument. 'Look, we're not equipped to look after a baby. What will you do when it needs changing?'

'Changing for what?' said Titania, taking her eyes off the road and almost going into the ditch.

'No – I mean, it's wearing a nappy at the moment. It'll

need a fresh one sooner or later. Babies do pee, you know. They do the other thing too.'

At that moment the baby made a strange sound like a stoat clearing its throat on a cold February morning, but the noise came from down in its nether regions. It gurgled happily up into Sid's concerned face.

'There, it's done one,' groaned Sid. 'I knew it would.'

'Done one what?' asked Puck.

'A number two. It's filled its nappy. If you insist on keeping the baby, we'll have to stop at a supermarket somewhere and pick up some nappies. And we'll need milk, and a bottle to feed it with, and maybe some bibs. A few changes of clothes wouldn't be out of the question – they are sick over the stuff they're wearing sometimes after a feed.'

'You sound very knowledgeable on the subject of babies, Sid,' Puck said, impressed. 'Have you had any?'

'No, I haven't had any babies,' remarked Sid in measured tones, 'and I don't want any. It's just common knowledge about nappies and bottles. They probably need a stack of other stuff I don't know about. They probably need gripe water and such. My sister had a kid which was always needing gripe water. It screamed its bloomin' head off when it didn't get any. Babies are a lot of trouble.'

'You're in charge of things for the baby then,' said Titania. 'I don't want to do any of that stuff. I just want to cuddle it and love it.'

'I don't want to do it either,' complained Sid, realizing what he'd got himself into.

'It's settled,' Titania murmured, swerving the bus dangerously to avoid a hedgehog crossing the road. The hedgehog looked up as she passed, frowning, not in the least bit grateful for having its life saved. 'I get to hold the baby and kiss its cheeks and rosy-red lips. You get to change its nappy and give it bottles of milk.'

'Flippin' heck,' groaned Sid, falling back in his seat. 'Why don't I keep my big mouth shut?'

'Because you're a rude mechanical, that's why,' replied Puck. 'Oh look – lights. Is that a supermarket, Sid?'

The cactus oruntia was opening, while chickweed and convolvulus closed.

FOUR

Purple Bindweed Opens and Common Nipplewort Closes

THE MORNING-FAIRY WOKE AND KNEW IMMEDIATELY THAT something strange was happening in the land: magical forces, normally fixed and stable when the supernatural beings of England remained in their traditional enclaves, had been disturbed by a sudden movement of creatures in the Midlands.

Morgan-le-Fay knew she had been lying asleep beneath the roots of a thorn tree on the south end of Offa's Dyke for several centuries. The disorder caused by the creatures who had left the pale of their customary habitat had caused her to wake, she being the most sensitive of supernatural beings. And the instant she had become aware, and had formed herself outside the hollow in which her spiritual form had lain, she understood the state of the world into which she had been reborn.

She did not like it.

There were mechanical devices all over the country, spewing foul gases into the atmosphere. There were small, one-bedroomed houses as solidly built as castles. There were huge halls manufacturing goods, great forts that produced massive amounts of power, iron towers that marched across the countryside with metal ropes in their hands, massive dams across rivers, mighty machines that flew through the air – and there were people, people, people, in every corner of the land.

It seemed the world had gone mad while she had slept and was going madder by the moment.

'Can I stand such a world?' she asked herself, as she nestled in the Welsh hills, seeking solace amongst the rocks and stones of her Celtic heritage. 'Surely it would be better to sleep through it, until the end of time?'

Her reply to herself was no, she could not stand it, and the answer was to intercept the magical beings that had vacated their enclave and to turn them around, send them back whence they had come, to the woods of their origin.

The Morning-Fairy set off eastwards, to carry out her night's plan.

Morgan-le-Fay ran swiftly across the land, waking other forces with her mere presence, shaking the supernatural world to its roots with her powerful aura radiating through hill and dale, through spinney, fell and vale.

Any human unfortunate enough to witness her flight saw a tall, slim figure dressed in black, with wild hair (not unlike that of the Sherwood fairies) and wild eyes. The speed of her feet was phenomenal.

It was perhaps lucky for the local inhabitants that few

supernatural creatures had survived until the present day. However, there were some, like the Morning-Fairy herself, who had crawled away to a safe crevice in the Earth's crust, to wait out the destruction of humankind in the hope that there would be something left of the world after these foolish mortals had gone.

As Morgan-le-Fay passed the Wrekin, a strange hill near Little Wenlock in Shropshire, she woke the giant who slept beneath. He rose from the ground with a groan, soil dripping from his face and limbs. In his right hand was the spade with which he had built his last resting place and which had cleft the Needle's Eye, a rock near the summit of the Wrekin that he had hit when swinging at his brother. The two giants had quarrelled and fought with their tools in the time when giants were abroad in the land.

His sightless brother, now imprisoned in Ercall Hill, also woke and cried out for release. Since the Wrekin giant had been the cause of the other's imprisonment, after the second giant had been blinded by a raven, the cries for freedom went unheeded. The Wrekin giant simply went down to the River Severn for a wash, kicking haystacks out of the way as he went, wondering what all those buzzing things were that shot along flat black strips across the land.

People who saw the giant either had apoplexy on the spot, or rushed home to fetch a video camera. Some called the news stations and daily papers on their portable phones, only to be laughed at and cut off. Unless someone was believed within the next few hours, come morning the Wrekin giant was destined to become as infamous and as mysteriously elusive as the black panther on Bodmin Moor, and blamed for a variety of ills.

Morgan-le-Fay did not remain to see what havoc the giant might cause, though she was sorely tempted to do so. It was her wish at that moment that he would pluck machines from the ground, shake out the occupants like pepper from a pot, and eat them by the large, calloused handful.

When she looked back, after crossing several more fields, she saw him standing with his hands on his hips, looking around him with a bewildered expression on his face. She knew what he was thinking: this was a monstrous world in which to wake and perhaps it would be better to go back to sleep until it had changed.

The Morning-Fairy's sights, however, were on the group in the bus, heading south along a motorway. Her sensitive far-sight now told her that another monumental change had taken place in the group's circumstances. There was a human baby in their midst, a very special human baby, the worth of which Morgan-le-Fay recognized at once. Morgan-le-Fay remembered Titania's penchant for human infants and realized at once that the fairy queen had stolen the child from its human parents.

'Well, well,' murmured the Morning-Fairy, 'this is a new turn of events.'

Mortal babies were of course powerful ingredients in any spell. With a human infant Morgan-le-Fay could do many things, especially on midsummer's day, one of the most potent days in the year for magic. With this *particular* child great and terrible sorcery could be performed. The Morning-Fairy wondered if Titania and the fairies knew the full worth of the child the queen had stolen. It was doubtful they did, Morgan-le-Fay decided, since only those like her, closely connected with the infant's pre-decessors, would recognize the ancestry of the child.

39

If Titania could be persuaded to give up her infant, the Morning-Fairy might be able to do something a little more substantial to improve the environment.

There was a problem in that Morgan-le-Fay had nothing to offer Titania, to barter for the child, except perhaps to allow the group passage to the New Forest.

'We shall see how we go on,' she muttered to herself, 'once they're in my hands.'

'A goldfish,' said the police sergeant, feeling that the night was going to be a long one. 'You found a goldfish in the pram where the baby had been?'

The nanny, her face streaked with tears, nodded her head. Her name was Frances Flute and she had been in the employment of Dr Lawrence DuLac and his wife for seven months now, which was the age of the missing child. Dr DuLac, she explained to the police sergeant as she sat in the back seat of the panda car, was a travel writer for the BBC, as was his wife, and the pair of them were at that moment somewhere in the Amazon jungle, unreachable by telephone.

'What are they going to say?' wailed Frances, wiping some of her make-up from her wet face. 'Their poor baby.'

The woman constable on the other side put an arm around the middle-aged nanny and gave her a hug.

'We often find', said the constable, 'that the kidnapper in these cases is a woman with mental problems – a recently bereaved mother, or someone who's not able to have a child of their own. It's not usually a ransom case. Though the parents are quite well off, you say? But not rich.'

'No, I wouldn't call them *rich*,' murmured Frances. 'Just

comfortable – you know?'

'And you saw a young woman touching the baby?' interrupted the sergeant.

'Yes – a pretty girl, but with funny eyes. She seemed a bit queer, if you know what I mean? She had this *look*. On drugs or something, I expect. And her boyfriend had a sort of screwed-up face. They weren't skinheads or punks. They were your sort of black dress, black hair and lace gloves pair – though I actually can't remember *what* they were wearing.'

'Goths, you mean?' said the constable, writing on her note pad. 'I'll put they were Goths.'

'What're Goths?' asked Frances.

'Have you read any of the fantasy writer Storm Constantine's novels?' asked the constable, putting down her pen and becoming a little too enthusiastic for Frances considering the circumstances. 'Well she's a Goth – have a look at the photo on the back of the book next time.'

'I don't think I read that sort of thing,' sniffed Frances, who was a literature prude. 'I like good books.'

The policewoman defended her reading material stoutly.

'Don't confuse personal taste with literary excellence,' she said. 'Just because you don't like the content doesn't mean it's not well written.' She had been involved in these discussions before, with her father.

'Well never mind that,' wailed Frances, 'what about baby Louise?'

The sergeant gave the constable a look which told her to shut up and concentrate on the job in hand.

Around the panda car the police were interviewing the villagers and visitors present at the fête. It was getting late but floodlights had been set up and a tent commandeered as a control centre. The people looked bemused and upset by it all. When the police had arrived, they had been wandering around in a lost state of mind, wondering where the last hour had gone to and why they were feeling so giddy.

The sergeant said, 'You say the baby's name is Louise? The TV crews are arriving. Would you like to go on the news and put out an emotional appeal for the return of Louise? It might work. We've never had any real success with the baby-snatcher, but the general public are alerted to the fact and that often leads to discovering the baby's whereabouts.'

'All right,' said Frances, 'if you think it would help – Mrs DuLac's parents – the grandparents – live near by. What if they see it on the news?'

'We'll have to go back to the house, get a list of all the relatives, and tell them first. Do you have access to that kind of information? Address books? Perhaps we'd better go to the grandparents and get that sorted out?'

'Oh dear,' wailed Frances, 'everyone's going to be so upset – and it's all my fault.'

'Not your fault at all,' said the constable, hugging her again. 'Everyone here has said they fell asleep while the youngsters were dancing. My guess is they used something – some sort of strobe light or something – to make the crowd go to sleep.'

'But what *for*?' cried Frances, suddenly resorting to an anger that bubbled up from deep within her. 'No-one was robbed, were they? Surely they didn't go to all that trouble just to steal one small baby? It doesn't seem possible. Oh, *oh*, I'd like to strangle that girl. I'd like to throttle her with my bare hands . . .'

The sergeant said, 'Now we can't be sure it was the girl.

All right, she's a strong suspect, but we mustn't jump to conclusions. If we start pointing a definite finger, we might get led a merry dance – sorry – and then allow the real kidnapper to escape. We'll follow up the young girl angle—'

'Goth,' interrupted the constable.

'Yes, the Goth angle, but we've got to leave all other possibilities open, do you understand?'

'Just find Louise,' snapped Frances, not yet over her bout of anger, 'before her parents find out. Find her before they . . .'

Something occurred to Frances then, for the first time, and her anger turned to feelings of panic and anxiety. Her voice rose in pitch as she clutched at the police constable's lapels and shouted into her face.

'Oh, my God, they won't harm her, will they? They won't hurt Louise?'

The constable prised the fingers from her uniform.

'In ninety per cent of these cases, the baby is well treated. It's usually a woman – or a girl – who *wants* a baby herself and can't have one. So she treats the child as she would her own. I expect Louise is being spoiled at this minute – showered with toys and things.'

'But, occasionally, it's not a woman wanting a baby?'

The sergeant took over, looking uncomfortable. 'That's true – on very rare occasions, it's a gang or an individual of some kind, wanting ransom money, or using the baby to get at the mother or father, or both, for some real or imagined slight on their character. The latter are often family, so we might run that down pretty quickly. If it's a gang, we'll hear from them sooner rather than later.'

Frances remembered a case where a kidnapped teenager had his ear cut off and sent to his parents.

'They won't – won't cut anything off?' she said, faintly. 'To prove they've got her?'

'I very much doubt it,' said the sergeant quickly. 'It would be a rare case . . .'

'But it could happen? Oh, her lovely fingers and toes. They won't touch her fingers and toes?'

'Extremely unlikely,' replied the uncomfortable sergeant.

'Never been known yet,' replied the constable, more firmly. 'Never heard of such a thing – a baby's finger or toe – nope, never in a million years.'

This was what Frances wanted to hear and she began to calm down a little once it had been said with conviction. She missed the look the constable gave the sergeant, which said basically – you outrank me but you're a prat sometimes.

The constable was not above bending the truth if she felt it would help the victim in any way, over the short term.

'They won't harm her, I'm absolutely certain of that.'

'Thank God for that.'

'Now,' said the sergeant, recovering some of his authority from his subordinate, 'you must have some sort of contact – a telephone number or something – to get in touch with the parents during an emergency? You see, to be frank, an emotional appeal from the child's paid nanny is not as effective as from the parents. Maybe we ought to use one of the grandparents? That's probably better.'

'I love little Louise as if she were my own child,' said Frances in a choked voice.

'Yes, but you see, she *isn't*, is she?' continued the sergeant. 'I know how you feel, but I also know how the public reacts. If they think you've got something to do with it, they'll . . .'

Frances's voice rose in pitch again. 'Something to do with it? Kidnapping Louise?'

'He's not saying you *have*,' said the constable, 'he's saying what people might think, since you were left in charge of the baby, and it isn't really yours – not yours at all in fact – you're an employee. They might think you had a spat with your employer and were punishing him – or her – or something. Do you see?'

'But *you* believe me?' gasped Frances, feeling the nightmare was deepening for her. 'I'm not a suspect?'

'Now you would be the first to say we can't rule anything out at this stage, Miss Flute, now wouldn't you?' said the sergeant gently. 'We have to keep all avenues clear, approach everything with an open mind. If you're sensible you have to see it from our point of view. We might be chasing around in circles, while all the time the baby is at your sister's house or somewhere.'

Frances remembered the case of the parent who had murdered her own children in the United States, before putting out a highly credible and emotional appeal for their return on national television. She felt sick inside. Her whole world had suddenly become a place of darkness and horror.

'I don't have a sister.'

'No, course not, that was an example. Look, don't you worry about anything. Just answer our questions to the best of your knowledge and ability, and we'll get along fine. Now, what was your address before you took up residence with the DuLacs? Local, was it?'

Frances mumbled out her replies, at the same time praying to God that Louise would be found safe and well, preferably within the next hour.

FIVE

*Cactus Oruntia Opens and Convolvulus Linaeus,
Chickweed Close*

OBERON, PUCK, TITANIA AND SID STOOD IN THE
entrance to the all-night hypermarket and gazed
around them, the first three in wonder, the last
one of the quartet in indifference. The brightness of the
lights, the sense of infinite space, the order and neatness
of the aisles and shelves, all had a profound effect on the
Queen of the Fairies and her fellow supernatural
creatures. Here there were sights more beautiful than
they had ever imagined. A pearl nestling in the trum-
pet of a scarlet flower, or a ruby contained by a walnut
shell, could not have surprised and delighted them
more.

Titania said, 'This is truly the cave of Aladdin! Surely here
are all the spices of the Orient, all the perfumes of Egypt, all

the precious oils of India? This is beyond all that is exotic, Sid!'

'Yes, I s'pose it is,' said Sid, realizing he was impressing his captors. Wanting to appear up to the mark, he added, 'I hear they're doing Irish soda bread these days.'

He grabbed a trolley and began wheeling it up the first aisle, followed by the three awestruck fairies.

Oberon found that in here the wild thyme did not blow in the wind, but was contained as dark dust in packets. Here, the scents of eglantine, woodbine and musk-roses were cloying the still air around the cosmetics counters. He learned that the enamelled skins of spotted snakes had been made into wallets and handbags, that thorny hedgehogs had been turned into loo brushes and that a bank was not for growing moss but a place where Sid borrowed money on a thing called an overdraft. Of nodding violets and oxlips he learned nothing – but suspected much.

'Nappies, nappies,' murmured Sid, looking at the signs overhead. 'Be under "Baby Items" I expect.'

Puck on the other hand discovered that he did not need to be a knavish sprite and skim the milk, for there was skimmed milk in plenty available on the shelves. Querns were there too, not for grinding grain, but for milling pepper. The village maidens wearing their green, brown and blue eye-shadow, and their bright red lipstick, were more likely to frighten *him* than he them. Barm was unnecessary, he was told by Sid, since the beer was all canned or bottled, seeming to need no yeast to keep it alive and fermenting.

'Widgets in the bottoms of the cans,' Sid told Puck, 'they do the same job, so I understand.'

Titania walked by the canned fruits, studying pictures

of some of her favourite foods: cherries, plums, black-currants, strawberries, raspberries, lychees . . . Lychees?

'What are lychees, Sid?'

Sid paused and stared. 'Oh, them – you get 'em in Chinese restaurants. I dunno really. Bit like ghostly plums.'

Sid could be quite poetic at times.

'And all these fruits are inside cans such as we see mortals drinking from in the forest?' asked Puck. 'The same cans with which they despoil the world?'

'Yep, it keeps 'em fresh – or rather, stops them from going off. You get meat, fish, pet food, all kinds of things in cans these days. Coke, Pepsi, lemonade, you name it.'

Titania stared at a can of cat food. There was a picture of a white Persian on the label. She thought that food made from household pets sounded ugly. Who would give up their pets for meat? Who would eat their loved creatures? She tried to imagine her pet owl in a can and it made her feel desperately unhappy. These modern people were worse than monsters. They ate their own dogs and cats, the animals that trusted them, protected them, were faithful to them.

There were coloured juices in bottles, some for washing with, others for drinking. They were multi-hued and beautiful to view. There were coloured powders in transparent packages. There were coloured packages with hidden contents. It was all so bright and airy, so splendid in its display.

On the way round Sid put a few items of food in the trolley for himself. The fairies, he knew, would probably not bother to eat until they got to the New Forest, but Sid's stomach almost ruled his life. His first love was real ale: steak and chips romped home a happy second.

Girls *were* in the race, but could not seriously challenge beer and grub, since Sid was one of those young men who as yet viewed the fairer sex from afar – from across the public bar room floor actually – with faint, wistful stirrings and thoughts of engaging with them sometime in the future. Until now he had not met the female who could stir his heart.

Currently 'the lads', television sport and the pub took up the majority of his free time. That was his life before he was enthralled by the fairies of course and one to which he hoped to return after the next twenty-four hours were over.

The group came to the 'Baby Items' counter. Titania let out a yell and grabbed a can of baby food, pointing to the picture of a baby on the front, and squealing about cannibalism. Sid patiently explained to her that they didn't mash babies and put them in cans: the can contained food *for* babies, food they could easily digest.

'Carrot and swede, this one,' he said, doubtfully, as he read the label. 'Yuk! Still, they must know what babies like, or they wouldn't be selling it, would they?'

Sid threw some canned baby food in the trolley, along with a plastic spoon and two plastic bottles complete with rubber teats. Baby powder, baby wipes and cotton wool went in next. Then some soothing-looking lotion. He'd already got a quart of milk and a can opener and was beginning to feel on top of the situation. Then they came to the nappy counter.

Three of the group stared at the nappies with interest, while the fourth member looked in frank bewilderment.

There were rows and rows of them, some in blue packages, some in pink packages. There were nappies for daytime and nappies for night-time. There were double-absorbent nappies and nappies which boasted non-leaking leg-holes. In short, there were nappies stretching the entire length of the hypermarket, looking like stacked rows of war-time stores ready for shipment to a foreign land. Each individual type seemed to have a specific purpose, many of which were either unknown to Sid or were confusing to him.

Sid said in a low voice, 'Is it a boy or girl? There's different nappies for boys and girls, see? When I was small there was just one for both – I think.'

'Why didn't you tell us this?' hissed Oberon.

Sid's voice rose a little. 'I didn't know, did I? I thought there was only one kind of nappy. How am I s'posed to know? I haven't got a baby. It's not so long since they were still using bits of towel and safety pins.'

'Not so long ago they were still using knotted clouts,' muttered Puck, 'but we're talking about *now*.'

There seemed to be lots of different sizes too.

'I thought babies only came in one size,' Sid said, miserably. 'I forgot they grow.'

A woman in a white coat passed them by. Sid stopped her and said, 'We've – I've got a baby, about this big,' he held his palms apart as if bragging about the fish that got away. 'What size nappy do you think we need?'

The woman frowned, staring at the little group.

Sid said quickly, 'It's my sister's kid – she's been took ill suddenly. My brother-in-law's in Saudi at the moment. But I don't know much about babies, see. Which one of these packets do you think I need, for – er – for him?' Sid could be very inventive when the need was on him. He waved a hand at the fairies. 'My teenage cousins,' he explained. 'They don't know much about babies either . . .'

The woman smiled then and asked, 'Do you know how

much the baby weighs? Nappies go by the weight of the infant.'

Sid shook his head wildly.

'Do you know your nephew's age then?'

Sid's head-shaking became even wilder. Then he realized he *should* know the age of his sister's child. He stopped shaking his head and blinked instead.

'Er – a year – it's a year old, I think. Yeah, just coming up to his first birthday – bless him.'

The woman smiled and pointed.

'Then you'll probably need eighteen–forty-two lbs, unless he's a monster, is he?'

'No, he's not a monster,' Titania said, indignantly.

'Fully absorbent,' replied Sid, desperately.

'Night-time, or day-time?'

'Er, what's the difference?'

'Night or day,' the woman continued, patiently. 'The day-time nappies give the babies freer movement, whereas the night-time ones are more thickly padded.'

'Night-time.'

'Well, then, I think you'll be safe with these.' The woman took down a huge packet of blue nappies. 'And I do hope your sister gets better soon.'

'So do I,' said Sid, tossing the packet into the trolley. 'So do I. Thanks very much.'

'You're welcome.'

Sid took the trolley to one of the cash desks and paid for the goods with his own money. He knew the fairies didn't have any money and wouldn't have understood it if they did. It was costing him a fortune, this business of being enthralled, and he only hoped the fairies might make it up to him in some way when they let him go.

When they got back to the bus, the other fairies were in

a state of consternation. The baby was screaming its head off and driving them half out of their minds. Moth was rocking the child in his arms.

'Where have you been?' demanded Cobweb. 'We thought you'd run away to the North Pole!'

'We've been buying nappies,' said Titania, haughtily.

She took the baby from Moth and cuddled it.

Sid said, 'It probably needs changing. Look, I'll make up a bottle. You change the little . . . mite.'

Titania thrust the yelling child into Sid's arms. '*You* change it,' she said. 'I don't know anything about these things.'

Neither did Sid, but he went to it with all the knowledge of a man fully conversant with internal combustion engines.

'If I can strip down motors, I can strip down babies,' he muttered courageously. 'The principle's the same.'

He laid the child on one of the seats. Once he had peeled away the layers and came to the raw baby underneath, the infant began to calm down. He found the sticky tags on the side of the nappy and ripped them away. Then he opened up the nappy itself and a foul smell hit his nostrils.

'Phhhhawww,' he said, reeling backwards as he saw the greeny-yellow sludge in the bottom of the nappy. 'That's disgusting.'

Titania and the rest of the fairies, used to rotting fungi and pond slime, were not so revolted.

'It's a baby girl,' said Oberon, disappointed. 'I thought it would be a boy baby.'

Sid was busy gagging and heaving in the doorway of the bus.

'I can't do it,' he groaned. 'Someone else will have to

do it – I can't.'

Titania peeled away the nappy and folded it, thus covering the substance that Sid found so offensive. Then she proceeded to wipe the infant's bottom with the damp wipes, while the rest of the fairies crowded round, looking on with great interest and admiration.

Then, as if born to motherhood, Titania took up the can of baby powder. When she shook it nothing happened, but by this time Sid had recovered enough to show her how to turn the top so that the holes were open.

Titania powdered the little girl's bottom, put some cream lotion on the sore parts, and took out a nappy.

Whether she and Sid got it the right way round was a secret between God and the baby. However, the nappy did look a little loose once it was on the infant and when Sid held her up, her little legs dangled down through cavernous holes like short, milk-white lengths of rope. There was room for all sorts of stuff to come out around the edges of the holes.

But it was the best they could do.

'I wonder what little girl nappies have in them, that little boy nappies don't?' said Sid, inspecting one of the clean ones. 'This one just looks padded to me. Can't think how they can be that much different from each other. I mean, if there was a sort of hollow bit for a boy's willy, I would've understood, but there's not. Just a big marketing ploy I expect.'

They made up a bottle which the baby took despite the milk being cold. Then Titania fed the infant on carrot-and-swede mash, which to Sid's astonishment it swallowed with gusto. Finally they were ready for the open road again.

Titania reluctantly handed over the child to Swallowtail,

in order to take the wheel of the bus.

She drove the vehicle out of the car-park through the nearest gap, but had to stop sharply after narrowly missing a red, open-topped Mercedes sports car driven by a smartly dressed male accompanied by a female companion in a vanilla dress. The driver of the car hooted in an enraged fashion, shook his fist, then pointed to the word ENTRANCE on a sign above his head. Finally, he pierced the air with a finger and let loose a stream of invectives coupled with the words 'women drivers'. Titania glared, taking offence at these gestures and words, only a few of which she understood.

The fairy queen calmly picked up the sodden nappy on the seat beside her, unfolded it, and tossed it down into the open-topped car. It landed on the driver's lap, its contents squishing forth onto some light-coloured trousers. The man's female companion lurched sideways from him with a revolted expression on her face, grabbing the hem of her white dress and whipping it away from his seat.

'A present from the fairies,' called Titania, and put her foot on the accelerator pedal.

A delighted Puck yelled a parting shot from the side window, 'And it's not vindaloo, either.'

They were soon thundering down the entrance road, swerving around oncoming vehicles.

Sid, to take his mind off Titania's driving, asked Puck, 'Where did you learn about Indian food?'

'At the hypermarket,' grinned Puck. 'There was the cooked-food counter, remember? I saw the labels. It was the same colour as the stuff in the nappy.'

The bus rumbled along the main road, until finally to Sid's relief they came to the sign for the M1.

The stream of traffic on the motorway appeared to

excite, rather than disturb, the fairy queen.

'Sid, look at all those coaches, lorries and cars!'

'Now take it easy, Titania,' warned Sid. 'We don't want to get picked up by the cops. You're driving without a licence for a starter. Then there's the baby. If we get arrested for kidnapping you won't see the inside of the New Forest for a hundred years, I promise you.'

'I'll be careful,' said Titania. 'Watch this!'

She carefully took the slip road up to the motorway and pulled out sharply in front of a car doing seventy in the slow lane. The car managed to whip sideways and streaked past them in the middle lane, its horn blaring. Titania waved and smiled at this greeting accorded her on joining the M1.

'See,' she said, 'I did it ever so slowly.'

The sweat rolled down Sid's brow.

'It's not always a good idea to drive slowly and carefully – there's times when you've got to go fast.'

Titania curled her bottom lip petulantly.

'I never seem to get it right.'

'You're doing fine,' Sid told her. 'Just listen to what I say and you'll be the best driver on the road.'

Oberon asked, 'Are you the best driver on the road, Sid?'

'Isn't everyone?' replied Sid, with an unusual touch of irony.

At that moment he looked in the rear-view mirror, over Titania's head, and saw a juggernaut bearing down on them with its lights flashing. It looked like a truck from hell. He could see the driver's face twisted into a maniacal grin.

'Foot down, foot down,' he told Titania. 'The Devil's on your tailgate.'

SIX

Night-blooming Catch-fly Opens and Smooth Sowthistle Closes

DARKNESS HAD FALLEN.
Sid was fast asleep on the next seat.
Titania felt dreadfully *alone*.

The harsh yellow ribbons of motorway lights snaked over hill and dale.

Now that she had truly left the greenwood back there beyond the villages and lanes, now the trees were far behind her and the wide motorway was stretching out before her, Titania suddenly felt a fear she had never before experienced.

She looked at her fairy features in the rear-view mirror of the bus. Her wild and beautiful hair framed her delicate heart-shaped face, with its silvery complexion. The unnamed terror running riot within her was evident only in the single drop of perspiration running down her cheek like a tiny bead of amber sap. In her dark, far-away eyes was the look that said that she wanted to be in some damp mossy hollow, hidden by bryony vines and surrounded by hoary-topped chervil. She wanted to be where the bark beetles clicked and the woodgrouse sang.

Moth, the navigator called, 'Steer to the left of the cold compass which is our moon, my queen, or we shall be in Nineveh before the first blush of the morning sun.'

'We need to be in the New Forest,' said the worldly Puck, sharing the front seat with Moth.

'Exactly,' replied Moth. 'At any other time, Byzantium, Ophir or Sidon would be fine destinations, but tonight we must keep our course straight for the forest of the south.'

Titania tried to catch a glimpse of her beloved moon, but the harsh, glaring lights obscured its beams.

The panic still played in her breast, but it was beginning to subside.

It helped her to think of her woodland home.

Her cherished oaks and beeches, hornbeams and elms, were far behind her. More importantly, gone was the canopy of leaves, the curtains of suckers, the bracken, the brambled undergrowth and the ivy ground-cover upon which the fairies relied for secrecy in the summer months. In the winter they crawled down rabbit holes and badger sets and slept away the cold time with the animals for company, but this was midsummer, this was the season of delicious dews, rapid rustling growth, shining mornings and warm red evenings.

This particular night was like a dark, scarlet-fringed cloak wrapped around her. The road ahead was prematurely peppered with lights as she drove the bus between the evenly spaced lords-and-ladies lining the motorway.

They amazed her, the clustered lights. They wriggled and dipped and curved and rose, like the shining scales of some giant yellow sea serpent struggling to reach the distant ocean. It was easy to follow the black roadway between, but the way seemed unending. Her pet owl, perched on the bonnet like a motor-manufacturer's emblem, stared straight ahead, the wind ruffling through his feathers.

Morgan-le-Fay had been wrong about Titania not being capable of recognizing the baby she had stolen. Titania's magic, though less than that of Oberon, was certainly strong enough to identify signs of birth. The stolen infant, child of legendary ancestors, was on the seat beside her, fast asleep. The baby had the eyes and nose of Guinevere and the lips and brow of Lancelot. It was a magical child. A child more precious than any exotic baby from the Orient. Under the guidance of the fairies she would grow to be more powerful than Merlin. Her beauty would become more enchanting than that of Helen of Sparta and Prince Paris of Troy combined.

The red tail-lights of a mortal's huge truck suddenly appeared in front of the fairy queen, shaking her out of her reverie. They were in the middle lane and instantly she forgot her fear, swerving the bus around into the inside lane.

'This was well done,' said Moth. 'A plausive manoeuvre, my queen. These avenues of Promethean fire have not blunted your faculties. Hark, I hear the sound of sackbuts behind our carriage, signalling our victory.'

Cars already on the inside lane sounded their horns and the shrieking of brakes was heard. The truck driver's mate looked out of the cab and down on Titania as she passed. He shook his fist savagely and yelled something at her. In the rush of wind past her ear she heard nothing but a strange cursing-word, similar to those she had heard from the driver of the red Mercedes sports car.

'To you also,' yelled Titania back, piercing the air with a finger in the style of the Mercedes' driver. 'You ill-fated, purblind mortal!'

And she added a curse of her own, learned long ago from a grateful banshee who had been lost on the night airs and was looking for the way to a loughside hovel, to which Titania had kindly guided the foul creature without expecting reward. She hoped the curse would work for her. Now that they were outside the forest Titania's magic was weaker than ever. But magic was like electrical disturbances in the sky, it was sometimes available in surges, while at other times it was not much more than a spark. If you caught it on the crest of a surge, however, you could perform miracles.

Titania was lucky this time.

Even as she pronounced the oath she felt the tingle of magic working and knew that at least this time something would happen. The lorry driver's mate disappeared from view, having shrunk to something low and horrible in his seat. In her right wing-mirror she saw that the truck driver himself was looking down at the passenger's side, his mouth open and his eyes bulging.

Mustardseed, staring out of the back window, cried, 'Well struck, my queen. The mortal's face is webbed with fear. See how he stares like the hare starting from his form!'

The truck then swerved, left the motorway and went ploughing through a field into the night, its horn blaring, its lights flashing and its wheels churning up waves of mud. Titania's last view of it was as it came to rest listing to one side, while it sank into the soft turf by a small spinney, its headlights cutting into the trees like two wayward moonbeams.

'What terrible drivers these mortals be,' grumbled Moth. 'Did you ever encounter such lack of skill? You'd think after a hundred years of steering these devices they'd be able to keep on the king's highway, wouldn't you?'

On the seat next to Titania the enthralled Sid woke and turned his star-glazed eyes onto the fairy queen and said, 'You're goin' to have to stop for petrol soon. The petrol gauge's showin' nearly empty.'

Titania's silvery brow wrinkled and she peered down at the funny dials in front of her.

'Which is that one?' she asked. 'Is it the glowing green one, pointing like an arrow to the Dog Star? Or perhaps the one like a purslane flower in seed?'

'None o' them,' replied the youth, 'it's that blooming one, nearly at the bottom. The only trouble is, I've got no more money. I spent the last penny in the hypermarket.'

Puck said, 'Don't worry, Sid – leave the payment to us.'

Shortly afterwards a sign told them there was a motorway stop, showing a cup, a knife and fork, the letters WC and a fuel pump. A show of lights like an island of brightness appeared on the horizon. Titania drove her bus towards this oasis and they soon left the motorway and came to a ragged stop by the fuel pumps. Sid jumped out and began filling the vehicle, while Puck, Oberon and Titania marched into the petrol station where they saw sweetmeats for sale, glossy magazines, newspapers, and a jumble of cheap goods from red bouncing balls to garden hoses to charcoal chips. It was a poor show after the hypermarket.

They confronted the rude mechanical behind the paying booth, whose breath smelled much like that of a hog.

'Ho, sir,' cried Oberon, always ready with a little drama, 'we have partaken of your wares but find we have no coin with which to pay the fare.'

The attendant had a shock of red hair on his head which disconcerted the fairies a little. They found the colour had too much resemblance to the hue found on a certain toadstool which was reluctantly used to ward off venomous snakes in the hot weather. In general the fairies were not fond of toadstool poisons, finding them bad for the skin.

'What?' said the man, looking startled. 'Wass this? A convention of dwarfs?' He stared at their clothes and then at their faces again. 'Who are you supposed to be? Peter Pan, or what? You secondary school kids on an outing? Where's your teacher?'

'Dwarfs? Peter Pan? *Kids*?' cried Oberon, sticking with his dramatic pose. This was one time to relax the rule on not using antiquated speech with modern mortals, if he was to maintain his haughty demeanour. 'You speak strangely, young wight – there are no dwarfs here, nor young goats, but only fairies, descended from the welkin in their new chariot.'

'I'll give you bleedin' fairies, just hurry up and pay and get that old crate off the pumps. Look at the queue that's forming up behind . . .'

Puck then stepped forward and the man blinked, seeing something silvery-green waver before him. The man was beginning to think he had done one night shift too often: his eyes were all of a sudden feeling sore and tired. He fought to keep awake, wondering why the figures kept fading into shadowy shapes. There was a kind of trick of the light which made it hard for him to focus properly on the small forms standing in front of him.

'Wass goin' on?' he said, scratching skin the colour of a griddlecake. 'You tellin' me you can't pay, or what?'

Puck laughed. 'You have it in a nutmeg,' he said. 'We do not have a single groat.'

'I'll call the bloody law then,' said the man, reaching for a black instrument at his elbow.

'Hold!' cried Puck, whipping something out from beneath his jerkin.

The man watched, amazed, as the device which this Peter Pan had extracted from the folds of his coat suddenly began growing. It started out like a marline spike, but with a definite *clack* two wing-like curvatures appeared from the haft and sprang outwards to form the shape of Cupid's weapon. The shaft then expanded, to a slim bronze stock covered in wrought catches and trigger-shaped hooks. There were curliecues and centripetal designs all along the thin central piece, some of which appeared to be in a strange kind of writing, similar to Arabic, but with far more swirls and loops than any earthly language.

From the front of the device a flurry of copper petals suddenly *snacked* into place, making the petrol attendant jump. From the seed-pod of this metal flower came a small spider which scuttled along to the tip of one of the wing-shaped protrusions and then, as the fascinated man watched, threaded a silver line across the instrument from one side to the other. The spider afterwards disappeared into a tiny round hole in the stock.

There were more springings, and clackings and whirrings, as the fantastical weapon continued to sprout points, and parts, and pieces. Needle-thin sights flicked into existence. An exotic golden arrow of miraculous design, with detailed filigree fletching and barbed bee-sting point, sprang from the central casing, its notch automatically finding the silver thread. There was a humming sound as a tiny hook attached to the centre of the silver wire drew the line taut and armed the contraption.

It was finally ready to fire at the mortal.

Elaborate, complex and intricate though the instrument was, with all its projecting augers, flukes, brochettes, gimlets, rowels, goads, caltrops and a single chevaux-de-frise, the petrol station attendant realized it was a crossbow and clearly designed to injure a second party.

'Wass this then?' he roared. 'A stick-up?'

He seemed far from afraid and more than furious. Puck felt the attendant did not quite understand his position, which was possible since he was an ignorant mortal of the very rude mechanical class, not at all in Sid's league. Better to appraise him of the situation.

'This is the most feared weapon of all time,' said Puck. 'Even a noble knight, clad in the most protective suit of armour – metalled from helmet to heels – is afraid of this weapon. The arrow will penetrate a breastplate at fifty yards, will pass through a shield at twenty, will kill a full-grown steed stone-dead at ten paces.

'All men, and women, are afraid of the bow and arrow.

'Yet, this device of death is also the weapon of love, there being little difference between the two states.

'Think of a man in love, who is not in this world but in one of his own, having no contact with the living, who are but ghosts and shadows to him. That man might as well be dead, for he is not in touch with reality, only with some fleeting images of himself and the object of his desire. His situation is surely as dreadful as that of a dead man?

'And none are safe, not even us supernatural creatures.

The arrows of desire penetrate any heart and the owner is lost to love. Even the Morning-Fairy has been smitten by such missiles, though her heart is as black and brittle as charcoal. She too fears the arrows of love and death, powerful though she be.

'Beware then, this most dreadful instrument!'

The other fairies, including the great speaker Oberon, were impressed by this speech.

'Well done, Puck – you surpassed even me,' said Oberon.

Puck tried to look modest, but failed miserably.

The garage attendant, however, was not impressed.

'Get stuffed,' he said.

Clearly this was not a rude mechanical to be frightened easily. Puck's fairy brain quickly gauged how well a robbery might go for them and decided against it. Instead he plucked the arrow from the haft of the fairy crossbow and placed it on the counter.

'Gold,' he said, simply.

The man glanced down at the gleaming arrow. There was a look in his eyes that fairies had seen many times before. It was a strange, greedy glint, awakened immediately by the word that Puck had so wisely spoken. Rainbow seekers had the same obsessed expression as the petrol station attendant.

'What – *real* gold?'

'Is there any other kind?' asked Titania.

They could see the mortal's mind spinning through various slow degrees of elevation, and finally the man said, 'You mean, you're givin' me this in payment for the petrol.'

'Yes,' replied Puck. 'Yours to keep. Worth a king's ransom. You may retire to your cottage in the country.'

'Done,' said the man, snatching up the arrow.

The trio left the man, knowing that at midnight, when the late-flowering dandelion and the creeping mallow closed, the golden arrow would change back into a crooked blackthorn twig.

'What fools these mortals be,' said Oberon. 'Too much time was wasted on that leather-head.'

Puck looked at his king sharply.

He sensed a certain criticism of his methods.

'Think you so, my king? It was not an easy conquest withall, myself having to impress with such clickings and clackings as might wake a corpse. Methinks it was well done, maugre his threat to summon the bum-baily. His intention was to summon some foul creatures of the night to do battle with us, as well as a minion of the watch. You heard him speak of the law! It had twin tines, that word. He meant also the unnatural laws of witches, demons, hobgoblins and gnomes. My eyes detected such amongst the clutter of his merchandise.'

'What?' asked Oberon, shortly.

'Gnomes – red and blue, yellow and white – all ready to spring to life. Gnomes with weapons in their hands.'

'To my eyes,' interrupted Titania, 'they were not so much weapons as little rods with which to fish for perch.'

'*Disguised* weapons,' insisted Puck. 'Methinks you should have cried, my king, "Oh what deviants these mortals be!" '

'Indeed,' sighed Oberon, 'but it grieves me that you employed my precious knobkerrie for your golden arrow. Now I have nothing of Sherwood in my keeping. Let's be on our way south. What did Moth tell us we must do?'

'Follow the Milky Way,' answered Titania.

'Good!' answered Oberon. 'Hi ho, then.'

SEVEN

Late-flowering Dandelion, Creeping Mallow Close

TITANIA DROVE WITH SOME DETERMINATION DOWN THE motorway and for a while everything was fine. The baby was fast asleep, rocking with the motion of the bus. Sid was happy, even though Titania was cutting up drivers with a frequency that would have been the death of anyone but her. It was almost as if other vehicles sensed that this was no ordinary bus, but a juggernaut from Ifurin, the Celtic Otherworld hell, and stepped quietly aside.

Sid was at least satisfied that they were on a true course for the New Forest.

That was before Moth decided the road was not going where he wanted it to go. 'The moonbeams are not as dense here as they should be,' he remarked. 'We must leave the motorway and explore the beauty of the county of Rutland.'

'What's the moon got to do with anything?' protested Sid, seeing his freedom begin to slip further away from him. 'Anyway, Rutland isn't there any more.'

Oberon leapt from his seat and began strutting up and down the aisle, crying, 'They've stolen Rutland? It's those damned Rosicrucians, I'll be bound.'

'No, no,' Sid explained. 'It's still there, only they don't call it Rutland any more – they made it part of Leicestershire – I think. Anyway, it's not there. I think we should stay on the motorway . . .'

It was at that moment Sid saw the blue flashing lights in the distance and stopped in mid-sentence. He told himself that it was probably an accident, that they happened all the time on the motorways. He told himself the police were there in numbers in order to direct the traffic around the wreckage, and possibly carnage, and to keep the traffic flowing. He told himself all this, but he didn't believe it. Deep down inside he knew it was a roadblock, and that the police were looking for a stolen baby and its kidnappers.

'Turn off here!' he yelled, as they came to a motorway services stop. 'Turn off, turn off!'

'Make up your mind,' grumbled Titania, slewing the bus sideways and churning up the grass verge as she took a sudden left turn. 'Now where do I go?'

Sid frantically directed her past the motorway restaurant, to the Shell petrol station beyond. On the slip road past the petrol station was a gate to a field. Sid told Titania to stop the bus and he got out. The gate was a metal one with a chain and padlock, but Sid managed to lift it off its hinges at the other end and open it. Then he directed

Titania through the gateway into the field beyond.

As they bounced across the meadow to another gate which opened onto a lane, Titania said, 'I thought you told us not to drive over fields, Sid. You keep changing your mind about things. You're not very constant.'

'My grandmother must have been seduced by a fairy then,' said Sid. 'Take the direction away from the M1.'

Soon they were cruising unlit lanes once again, until Sid admitted to himself that he was thoroughly lost. He knew the fickle fairies were perfectly capable of losing themselves at a moment's notice, but he had hoped he could keep them on a direct course south. Now they were out in the deep blackness of rural England, with no land-marks around to help. Sid could smell silage and dung. He noticed the occasional light like a star upon the ground, and could hear the swishing of the hedgerow going past, but he searched in vain for signposts.

As any traveller through the kingdom knows, the trouble with middle England is the maze of tracks and roads, unmarked on road maps, which locals think perfectly reasonable but which drive visitors crazy. High banks, thick hedges, drystone walls, all have evolved, grown, been built expressly to confuse the outsider who wants a view of the landscape to find his own location. The lanes seem endless, meander ridiculously and un-dulate irregularly. Crossroads without signposts are frequent. Cottages cloaked in blackness are occasional. Maddeningly, infuriatingly, visitors too often find them-selves in a farmyard just at the point when they expect to meet a main road with blessed lights and traffic. Narrow roads grow narrower until the point is reached where if the vehicle continues it will become jammed as tight as a cork in a bottle-neck. Reversing becomes a practised skill which stands the driver in good stead for the rest of his born days. Overpopulated England becomes strangely empty, with not a soul within a hundred miles of whom to ask directions.

At one point the fairy bus went through a disused airfield which bore a notice ROYAL AIR FORCE HAL . . . the rest of the sign was missing. There was a strong smell of pigs which suggested to Sid that the old hangars were being put to commercial use.

Finally Titania stopped the bus in a leafy lane where the darkness was clustered amongst the trees.

'Where are we?' she asked Sid.

'How do I know?' he grumbled. 'Moth is supposed to be doing the navigating.'

She turned her silvery complexion to face him.

'I thought you said you knew the way to the New Forest?'

'I do,' snarled Sid, only a little intimidated by Titania's frown. 'If you'd let me tell you where to go, instead of Moth, we could be halfway there by now.'

'But we'd be *bored*,' she said. 'And that's worse than being lost.'

'Look, I'm only human.'

'Sadly, this is the case,' Oberon said. 'Sid *is* only human. Listen, what's that . . .?'

A lowing sound, heavy and mournful, had come from somewhere out in the night. It was such a deep, loud sound that it frightened Sid dreadfully, so that his lungs fluttered in his chest like birds. He knew the fairies were capable of conjuring up ferocious beasts and he wondered if they were doing this just to scare him. He was about to protest, when the sound came again: so sonorous and blaring was the cry Sid was convinced it was a monster.

'Is that a banshee?' he asked, fearfully. 'Tell me it isn't.'

'It isn't,' said Titania. 'I've heard banshees and they don't sound like that, they sound more like this . . .' and she let out a scream that made Sid's blood run cold and gave him pains in his eyeballs.

It was then that Sid realized the fairies were just as mystified as he was over the origin of the sounds.

Puck said, 'Our presence appears to have woken some fabulous beast from its eternal sleep – there used to be many in Merrie England, until the infernal machines came and drove them deep down into holes and caves.'

'What?' cried Sid, thoroughly frightened now. 'You mean technology drove them away? What is it then? Is that a dragon or something?'

'Dragon, cockatrice, hippogriff, chimera, gryphon, who can tell?'

'I should have thought you would be able to, being a fairy,' cried Sid in panic. 'Start the bus. Let's get out of here.'

At that moment something came crashing through the trees and stood on the roadway in front of them, preventing their escape. Behind the bus was a twist in the lane just before a humpback bridge over a stream, which made it difficult for reversing. In front of them was the monster. On either side were high banks with trees. They were trapped.

Sid viewed the monster in the headlights of the bus.

'It's *enormous*,' he murmured, in a quiet awestruck voice. 'It's bigger than an elephant.'

The fairies were all staring with as much interest and excitement as Sid, though not with the same fear that coursed through his purblind mortal brain. Caught in the glare of the bus lights, the monster let out another one of its lowing, resonant sounds, making the bus vibrate like a drumskin.

The baby stirred, whimpered, and went to sleep again.

Puck said, 'It's the giant Dun Cow of Dunsmore Heath.'

'Dunsmore Heath?' cried Sid. 'We're on the A45 then. Let's get out of here.'

Puck continued as if Sid had not spoken, 'This savage beast was slain by Sir Guy, Earl of Warwick, in medieval times!'

'If it's dead,' yelled Sid, 'what's it doing out there?'

'We woke it from its eternal sleep,' said Puck, tending to repeat himself, 'and now it's enraged.'

'With us?' Sid cried. 'What did we do? I didn't do anything. What's it doing?'

'It's waiting to be milked,' Titania replied. 'If it isn't milked soon, the pain in its udder will drive it mad – our bus will be crushed. This is the beast that terrorized the medieval countryside, killing men and animals.'

'Right,' said Sid, wildly, 'right. Who's going to milk it then? Who's going to go out there and bloody well milk the sod, eh? And don't look at me this time. I did my bit with changing the nappy. It's someone else's turn. What about Blewit – or Peaseblossom? They haven't done much yet. There's no way I'm going out there, and that's flat.'

'No-one has asked you to, Sid,' said Puck, raising his thin, quarter-moon eyebrows. 'You will remain here.'

'I bloody shall,' said Sid. 'Don't you worry about *that*.'

Sid stared at the enormous beast that blocked the road – and part of two fields on either side – with its ugly bovine body. Its hide looked too thick for arrows to pierce, so any new bow Puck might produce from the folds of his tunic would not be of any use. A battleaxe might do it, in the hands of a competent giant.

'A dragon would've been easier,' Sid moaned. 'How did Sir Guy manage to kill it, the first time?'

Oberon replied, 'The great Dun Cow was once kept in Mitchell Fold, in the county of Shropshire, and its milk supply was inexhaustible, but a witch brought a sieve to the beast and made it attempt to fill it. This so infuriated the monster she broke free and rampaged over the countryside and finally ended up here. Sir Guy killed it with the broadsword of his grandfather.'

'Can't you wake up Sir Guy, then?' said Sid, as the cow ominously took a step towards the bus. 'He could do it.'

'The Earl of Warwick is dead,' answered Puck.

'So was the bloody cow, but you managed to wake that!'

'But the cow is not mortal, fool,' Puck replied.

The beast's eyes rolled in its massive head as it took yet another step towards the lights that were blinding it. It tossed its horns, which were as large as a bull elephant's tusks. It swished its great tail, taking the top off a nearby elm and sending it crashing to the ground. The cud it had earlier chewed and swallowed was suddenly regurgitated and shot from the beast's mouth, hitting the bonnet with a *splat*. Titania's screech-owl took flight and circled the bus making a further terrible racket.

The missile was now a big, green, steaming compost heap perched in front of the windscreen.

The cow let out a bellow of hot damp breath that engulfed the bus and made Sid cough and choke with its fetid stink.

'Someone's got to do something,' groaned the motor mechanic.

Puck cried, 'The church bell! If we sound the bell the cow will think it's dusk and head back to its lair.'

'What church?' asked Sid.

Oberon nodded. 'Sid has a point there, Robin Goodfellow – there is no church.'

'Can't somebody do some magic?' asked Sid. 'You're all good at that – especially you, King Oberon.'

Oberon looked dubious. 'In the greenwood my magic is strong, but out here in the wilderness, who can tell?'

Sid played on Oberon's pride. 'But Titania turned that lorry driver's mate into a toad or something – you're more powerful than Titania, aren't you?'

Oberon turned and smiled at his queen. 'More powerful than *la belle dame sans merci*? It's possible.'

The giant cow moved forward, bellowing, until its great head was over the bonnet of the bus.

'Well?' cried Sid.

Oberon went into a huddle with Puck, mentioning several strange names, and Puck shook his head at most of them, pointing out shortfalls and flaws, until finally they agreed on a creature the like of which Sid had never heard.

Oberon chanted a rhyme in a harsh, guttural and completely incomprehensible language, and when he stopped Sid heard a drumming sound on the summer-hard earth outside.

'What is it?' he whispered. 'What's happening?'

Oberon raised a finger to his lips. The king and the other fairies were staring out of the windows, looking for something that came closer with every thump on the ground. Sid wasn't sure that the fiend or whatever, which Oberon had requested, would not ally itself with the giant Dun Cow and begin attacking the bus from the opposite end. Sid was getting ready to run. He intended to snatch the baby from the seat beside Titania, open the bus door, and take his chances with dashing blindly through the night. It was the best plan he could think of in the time allowed, though he knew it to be a futile one.

The drumming became louder and the Dun Cow lifted its head and snorted fury into the night.

Sid's heart began to race in his chest. He wondered whether he actually wanted to see this terrible creature that had been conjured from the land of nowhere. Perhaps the mere sight of it would give him a heart attack? Perhaps he would go into a shock from which he might never recover? Sid was torn between looking and covering his eyes with his hands. It was like having a huge hairy spider in the bathroom. There was some horrible force in him urging him to look, but he didn't actually want to see the monster.

When it came, hurtling out of the darkness, into the lights of the bus, Sid's heart did indeed stop for a second. Luckily it started up again almost immediately and he knew he was going to live. Even so the cure for what they had outside the bus was ten times more terrible than the problem.

It was a man – or at least in the rough shape of a man – naked but covered in long, grey body hair. A shaggy creature with a ferocious face and, from the look of it, enormous physical strength. Twice as tall as Sid, who touched the top of the last inch in six feet, it leapt out of the darkness and onto the back of the Dun Cow.

The cow, with more bull-like tendencies than the fairer of the bovine sex, reared immediately and roared out her disapproval. She shook like a rodeo stallion, trying to unseat her rider, whose long legs had instantly locked around her neck. The man-thing had her by the horns now and was twisting her head away from the lights of the bus, turning her eyes into the darkness of the surrounding fields. The new creature shrieked in triumph, urging the cow forward with kicks of its horny feet.

'What is it?' whispered Sid.

Oberon replied, 'A kelpie. It used to jump on the backs of horses being ridden by humans, in the days when humans still rode horses. It would take control of the mount and ride the pair over a cliff, or into a swamp, and kill them. I've woken it up from a far-away river.'

'How far?'

'Scotland – it's a Scottish beastie,' said Oberon, proudly. 'I brought it all the way down here along the waterways, to that stream which runs under the bridge. Kelpies are water creatures, you see. Sometimes they are in the shape of a man, sometimes a horse . . .'

Sid gawped at the grisly creature as it savagely wrenched the Dun Cow's head around and set it galloping over the night fields towards some distant stars on the horizon.

'How did you manage that?' Sid asked, impressed. 'If it's from a Scottish river?'

Oberon shook his head sadly. 'Don't you know, Sid, that all the waterways of the world are connected by the ocean? Put a paper boat into Loch Lomond and it'll find it's way into the River Avon eventually. Ask anyone.'

'Oh,' said Sid, relieved to see that the kelpie had ridden the bucking and weaving Dun Cow out of sight and that they were now free to roam the A45 at will. 'Right.'

Titania started the bus again and began cruising along the road as if nothing had happened. At that moment the baby woke. There was a noise like someone treading on a particularly fat toad with a size nine boot. The baby's eyes went big and round as if she was as surprised as Sid. That first sound was followed by a series of similar noises, each a little louder than the last, until finally all was still. A nasty smell filled the confines at the front of the bus.

'She's done another one of those things in her nappy, Sid,' said Titania. 'See to it, will you?'

EIGHT

Scandinavian Sowthistle Closes

THE SCANDINAVIAN SOWTHISTLE WAS ABOUT TO CLOSE and Cobweb was feeling agitated. His rebellion, back in the greenwood, had been unusual: Oberon was such a powerful fairy; the king could have locked Cobweb inside a tree trunk for all time and forgotten him. Cobweb did *not* have powerful magic. Like most of the other fairies in the bus, excluding Titania and Puck, he stood against Oberon as a dandelion stands against an oak. When the Lord of all Magic had been handing out largesse he had used a teaspoon for Cobweb and his fellow fairies, then changed to a bucket when he came to Oberon.

'Not fair,' grumbled Cobweb. 'I don't want to go to this New Forest – I liked the old one.'

'What's that?' asked Mist, a pretty little creature whose looks were in the style of those picture-book fairies with which mortals decorated their children's nurseries. Her favourite flowers were germander speedwell and jack-go-to-bed-at-noon – she loved the blue of one and the yellow of the other – something she never tired of telling her friends. Since fairies recognize one hundred and seventeen different kinds of blues and fifty-nine yellows, she was most particular to point out the superior shades of her flowers. 'What did you say, Cobweb?'

'Nothing,' grunted Cobweb to the female sharing the seat. 'It doesn't matter.'

But it actually *did* matter. Cobweb had never before in his life felt rebellious towards the fairy king. He had suffered any punishment which came his way for mischievous behaviour or disobedience, and had taken it as a matter of course. Now, though, it was as if King Oberon had betrayed the whole fairy nation, small as it was, and was leading them to a woodland which had no Major Oak, was not called Sherwood, and must therefore be a terrible place.

Cobweb brooded. When Sid came back along the aisle to check that his fairy passengers were all right and not feeling motion sick, Cobweb engaged him in conversation. One thing about Sid – or rather two things – was his complete lack of a suspicious nature and his willingness to impart any information he might have to a second party. Sid was actually a very nice mortal, which was why he had been chosen by Oberon to be enthralled by him. The fairies would have hated to enslave a mortal with a nasty nature.

When Sid went back to his seat, Puck asked the rude mechanical the question he had put to him many times before, which Sid again answered with patience.

'The New Forest covers an area of one hundred and thirty square miles of woodland – oak, beech, evergreen – and there's only the wild ponies to share it with. Of course, there's heathland too, but you don't mind that, do you?'

'Heathland's not as good as woodland, but it's habitable,' agreed Puck. 'You can hide in heathland all right.'

Facts, especially of the numerical kind, were not a fairy strong point. Puck furrowed his brow and tried to imagine how big 'one hundred and thirty square miles' made the New Forest. It sounded comfortably large to him.

'And how far is it from Sherwood?'

'It's two hundred miles,' replied Sid, 'but we've covered some of that.'

'So the distance we're going is just a bit longer than the New Forest?' said Puck, his brow furrowing again.

Sid shook his head. 'Square miles are not the same as long miles – you'll just have to take my word for it. The New Forest is a big place. Ninety thousand acres, if that helps you any more than square miles – a third of the size of the Isle of Wight. Big enough for you lot anyway.

'I looked it up in the local library – it's mostly beeches, oaks and birches, but there's also a riot of hawthorn and blackthorn blossom in the season – so the book said – lots of deer of different kinds . . .'

'What kinds?'

'Red, roe, fallow and Japanese – oh, and one other type, a funny name – Mancunian, no – *Manchurian*, that was it. From China somewhere, not Manchester. There's also wild donkeys, as well as the ponies, and somewhere underneath the turf twenty-two lost Saxon villages are buried. William the Conqueror flattened them to make room for more trees to hunt in.'

Saxon. That was a word which smacked of the old days. *Saxon* was a comfortable word, which nestled easily in a fairy's brain. Puck felt at ease with a forest which hid the timbers and hearth stones of old-time Saxons.

'Good, good,' he said. 'And how many wild ponies?'

'About two thousand.'

Puck looked around him, trying to count the fairies on the bus, and then gave up after three.

'Is that more than the number of fairies here?' he asked Sid, swallowing his pride.

Sid raised his eyebrows and replied, 'Tons more.'

'Right then,' said Puck, 'I think I've got a good picture of where we're going. I just hope we get those green misty mornings, when the world looks like it's coming from a place of mystery and magic – and sunlit mornings when the dew sparkles like broken glass on the tips of the clover leaves – and red evenings, when the sun goes down like a huge round ember into the far trees and his sister the moon kisses his hot face on her way up into the welkin . . .'

'I'm sure you'll get all that sort of stuff,' said Sid, who quite liked talking numbers with Puck, but was not so keen on fairy fantasizing.

Sid had told Titania that they had to avoid the motorways now and stick to the highways and byways, which suited Moth's idea of where his navigation should take them.

At one point they crossed under the M1, going westward, and then struck south again. In the open countryside, lit only by the stars, they passed a field where Moth noticed lots of buses like their own were gathered. There were campfires in the field, sending showers of sparks up into the night sky, and people huddled round them. The fires were obviously not needed for warmth, so Moth deduced the mortals were using them for cooking and for social reasons.

'STOP!' yelled Moth. 'Stop the bus.'

Titania slammed her foot on the block of wood stuck to the brake pedal and the bus screeched to a halt.

Sid looked bewildered and Oberon came forward.

The king asked, 'What's the matter, Moth?'

'I think it's time we had a rest,' said Moth. 'There's some gypsies in the field back there.'

Oberon nodded. Fairies had a certain affinity with gypsies. Gypsies understood the country lore and were familiar with herbs and wild flowers, and fungi. They knew the larch burst into leaf between 21 March and 14 April every year. They were aware that a green bird will tell everything a person wishes to know. They knew that the soul of King Arthur migrated into the breast of Cornish chough. They were familiar with the fact that yarrow was a balm for flesh wounds. In short, they had knowledge of the natural world and equally of the un-natural world.

'They weren't gypsies,' said Sid. 'They were travellers.'

'What's the difference?' asked Puck.

'Well, New Age travellers are just ordinary people – I mean, not Romanies, not even tinkers – just a lot of ordinary people on the road. They're into all this alternative stuff. I mean, people consider them a nuisance because they trespass on farmers' land.'

Oberon snorted. 'Land shouldn't be owned, anyway – and if it is, the owners should let others use it.'

At that moment the baby began crying and Titania said, 'I'll need to feed my baby – let's stop here whether they're gypsies or not . . .'

Oberon agreed that a rest should take place.

Titania backed the bus up to the open gateway and then drove slowly into the field. Two men sitting at a fire stood up and came towards the bus. One was a big, rough-looking fellow wearing glasses, the other a smaller, blond-haired man with pleasant features. Sid opened the door and positioned himself in the doorway, looking down on the two men. It was, predictably, the big one that spoke to him.

'What d'you want?'

Sid said, 'Just to rest up for a while.'

The man peered into the bus. 'You travellers? Not police or bailiffs?'

'Do we look like cops?' asked Sid, in a reasonable tone of voice. 'We're just on our way down to the New Forest.'

The blond man said, 'No harm in letting them share the fire, Earl? They could have said they were travellers, if they wanted to join us that bad . . .'

Earl was not to be persuaded that easily. 'If you're not travellers, what are you doin' on the road at one in the morning? Bunch of teenagers? Eh?'

'I told you,' said Sid, 'we're on our way south. These are not actually teenagers – they're short people, see. Adults.'

'Dwarfs?' queried Earl.

Oberon cried, 'We don't like to be called that!'

'Fair enough,' said the blond man, quickly. 'Look, you take your bus over there, then you can join us at the fires. They've got a baby, Earl – it looks hungry.'

Earl grunted and walked away, clearly not too happy with the blond man's decision.

Titania smiled at the fair mortal. 'What is thy name?' she asked, slipping into old-world speech as she began flirting. 'How do they call thee? Dost thou have a sweet-heart? Which of those wenches at the fire comes at thy bidding? All, or only one?'

The young man blushed and looked a little embar-rassed to be addressed by this beautiful young lady in such seductive tones.

'I'm – I'm travelling with my sister,' he added quickly. 'I don't have a girlfriend or anything. My name's Tom Blessing. Look, how old are you?'

'Thirty,' said Titania without hesitating, giving this man the number of centuries she believed she had been in existence. 'Or nearly thirty, anyway.'

Tom Blessing's eyebrows rose on hearing this.

'You don't *look* twenty-nine,' he said. 'You don't look more than sixteen.' Even this was generous.

'Well, I am,' she said a little hotly. 'Would you call me a liar, Tom Blessing?'

'No, no – but you must have the secret of life or some-thing.'

'I have,' she replied.

'Then you won't be out of place here. All these travellers seem to think they've found the secret. Welcome to our camp.'

'We are beholden to thee, Tom Blessing, for your hos-pitable nature and for your friendship.'

'Oh, that's all right,' said Tom, more flustered than ever. 'Come on over and join us.'

Titania parked the bus and the fairies began to troop off and sit around the main camp-fire. They were the object of much curiosity, mainly of course because of their small stature, but also because of their looks. The fairies were very attractive, the males with their nutmeg-brown faces, the females with their silvery complexions. They were a beautiful race, and more than a little passing strange, and many of the New Age travellers stared at them in the firelight wondering if the weed some of them were smoking was responsible for the visions that now paraded before them.

Peaseblossom whispered to one of them, 'We're actually fairies, on our way to a new woodland.'

'Oh *fairies*,' said the spaced-out listener, who was a fortune-teller and tarot-card diviner, 'right.'

She seemed completely accepting of the fact that a bus load of magical little people had suddenly arrived out of the night. In fact the fortune-teller passed on the information to her neighbour, a specialist in aromatherapy and healing with gemstones, who nodded gravely and stared at Peaseblossom without surprise or concern. Fairies. Had a convention of dentists or computer salesmen arrived amongst them the travellers might have raised an eyebrow, but fairies were part of the scene, man. Fairies were cool.

An astrologer was the next to learn the identity of the visitors and he immediately engaged Moth in a discussion about the stars as they related to the signs of the zodiac, to which the energetic navigator responded with enthusiasm, hoping Sid was listening in to see how clever was little Moth when it came to the constellations.

Soon almost everyone around the fire knew that the newcomers were fairies – all except Earl, Tom and his sister Mary – they being more down to earth than the rest of the travellers and therefore unreceptive to such revelations. They might have picked up the whispers, but they failed to hear what was being said, since their mind channels were not as open and responsive as those of the others.

Titania came to the fire and sat next to Tom, smiling at him as she did so. Sid handed her the bottle of milk he had made up and she proceeded to feed the baby with it. Tom looked down at the baby and nodded.

'Boy or girl?' he asked.

'A human girl,' answered Titania, smiling. 'A wonderful, very special little mortal.'

Sid almost choked on the tea he had been given.

One or two of the shabbily dressed women sitting around the fire exchanged smiles. A boy of about eight asked his mother if Titania was a witch, and was shushed. Titania looked hard at the little boy, who suddenly yelled that he'd got pins and needles in his foot. He went off limping towards an old van amongst the buses.

Tom frowned, but was too polite to comment further. 'Oh, right,' he said. 'A girl. Er – what's her name?'

'Pigwidgeon,' answered Titania without hesitation, 'because she's so small and sweet.'

'We call her Piggy for short,' said Sid.

Titania snapped, 'No we don't.'

A dark-haired woman said, 'I've got a little piggy too, haven't I, Harry?'

A small boy by her side, half-asleep, grinned.

Titania proceeded to feed the baby while the other fairies settled down to stare into the flames of the fire. They answered questions if they were spoken to, but did not initiate any conversation themselves. Oberon didn't even reply when he was spoken to, but Puck filled in for him, as if he were a deaf old man, or simple in the head.

Sid jumped up at Titania's request and went to the bus for another can of carrot and swede for Pigwidgeon. Cobweb went with him, saying he wanted to help, but he disappeared into the darkness somewhere before Sid reached the bus. When Sid came out of the bus, he saw Cobweb drifting out of one of the traveller's lorries with a package under his arm.

'I hope he's not nicking anything valuable,' Sid muttered to himself, aware of fairy disregard for the ownership of property. 'I'll wring his neck if he is.'

Cobweb vanished into the shadows and Sid shrugged and went back to the fire with the baby food. Tom was still plying Titania with questions when Sid put the food into her hands. She turned her heart-shaped face, framed by the wild and tangled hair, on Sid for a second. He stared into her perfect tear-drop eyes. The iris ring was dark, while the pupil was silvery-blue. It had taken Sid a long while to notice that in fairies the hues of the two were reversed and that it was the pupil which had the colour and the iris which was black.

Strange eyes – hypnotic, spellbinding eyes – which gave Sid a dizzy feeling when he looked into them. They were the eyes of some incredible, animated doll. Beautiful as they were they frightened and repulsed Sid, though he could well understand why Tom was bewitched by them.

Tom was asking Titania, 'Is Sid your husband? Are you two – married?'

Titania let out a tinkling laugh. 'Sid? No, he's my slave – my husband is that one over there.' She pointed at the small, stocky Oberon, who seemed mesmerized by the fire. 'My husband is the king.'

Tom frowned again, but then his face took on an expression of enlightenment.

'Are you gypsies then? Is your husband king of the gypsies?'

Titania laughed again. 'We're not gypsies, we're fairies,' said the queen. 'I'm Titania . . .'

'And he's Oberon,' finished Tom. 'I get it. You're travelling players. I should have guessed. Why didn't you say so? Do you do any medieval stuff? I love the *Castle of Perseverance*. I'm a writer you know – that's what I'm doing here, with my sister. I'm not really a New Ager – I'm writing a novel based on my experiences as a traveller. But I wouldn't mind trying a play, sometime.'

'I'm sure you would be very good at it,' said Titania. 'You have the right kind of face.'

A woman listening from the far side of the fire, asked, 'What difference does his face make? Surely if he's got talent it wouldn't matter if he looked like a wart-hog, would it?'

'It wouldn't matter if he looked like a wart-hog,' replied Puck, answering for Titania, 'so long as he had the kind of face it takes to write a book.'

Tom said, 'You mean, you believe there are faces for writing books and others not?'

'There's faces for tanning leather, for shoeing horses, for being a sheriff, for being a huntsman, for being a great lover – for everything – including writing books,' said Puck. 'Everyone knows that – at least, I thought they did.'

There was silence for a while after this remark. Titania cooed to the baby, who now that she had been fed was rewarding everyone with brilliant smiles. People round the fire were roasting nuts, or toasting bread. Children were either asleep in a parent's arms, or so round-socketed their eyes were in danger of falling out. One or two of the more awake ones played games around the buses. Music began to blare out from a van. The black-bearded Earl told the music-maker to 'Shut it – the bloody farmers will call the cops and we'll get arrested before we get halfway there . . .'

The music stopped, but other noises continued. The flames from the fires eerily lit the night, producing running shadows and leaping lights. Weary lurcher dogs grumbled in their sleep. The sounds of love came from one of the smaller vans parked at the back of the buses. A child was wailing somewhere, calling for its mother. A sudden breeze blew rubbish across the dark fields, so that paper and plastic ghosts raced over the meadow, chasing each other.

'So,' said Tom, quietly to Titania, while casually tossing a twig into the flames. 'A writer's face – but not a lover's face, I suppose?'

'Thee?' she smiled. 'Thou hast *both.*'

'Oh,' muttered Tom, clearly overwhelmed.

NINE

Yellow Goat's Beard Opens

W HEN SID SUGGESTED IT WAS TIME FOR HIS GROUP TO
get back on the road, Earl rose from a sitting
position and said, 'We ought to get going too –
we want to be at Stonehenge before all the fun is over.'

The travellers began to get to their feet, some of them
dousing the fires, others gathering possessions and carrying them to vans, lorries and buses. Those children that
were awake were reined in and distributed amongst the
vehicles. Sid herded his fairies towards their own bus.
Tom Blessing followed them over, still trying to talk to
Titania.

Sid asked him, 'Haven't you got better things to do?' To
which Tom replied, 'Not really.'

Titania handed the baby over to Swallowtail who

clutched it as if she had been given a treasure.

'Just until we are on the king's highway,' Titania warned.

Tom whispered to her, forlornly, 'Does your husband treat you well – are you happy? If you are, I won't speak to you or look your way again, I swear. But he doesn't seem to pay much attention to you. If you were my wife, I wouldn't let you out of my sight for a second. I would cherish every inch of you. I would adore every moment in your company.'

'Oh, I like you speaking to me, Tom,' she said, smiling. 'I like you to look at me the way you do.'

Tom, heartened, took this to mean she was in a bad marriage and that he stood a chance.

Then Titania got on board and tried to start the engine.

The motor turned over, started then immediately died, and thereafter would not start again. Sid had a go, keeping the accelerator pedal hard down on the floor, in case Titania had flooded the carburettor. The engine churned over, but failed to start, and soon there was a danger of flattening the battery.

Tom, looking on, went to the bonnet of the old bus, to open it, and was confronted by a staring creature.

'Hey,' he yelled, excitedly, 'there's an owl on your bonnet.'

'She's a friend of mine,' said Titania, and made a strange clucking noise. The owl left its perch and flew silently at the small, petite figure of Titania. On the way it swerved towards Mustardseed, whose tunic started moving in various places as if his pockets were about to erupt lumps of lava.

'Keep her away from my mice,' cried Mustardseed.

Titania made another noise, and the owl's flight path

straightened, and she made a landing on the queen's shoulder.

Tom was impressed by Titania's ability to discipline a wild bird, a predator like an owl.

'You've trained her well,' he said.

'I have power over such creatures,' she replied, smiling.

Tom was dreadfully smitten. 'You have power over *all* creatures – including me,' he whispered.

Sid snorted and opened the bonnet of the bus. He and Tom both peered inside, ignoring each other and fiddling with various wires and parts, until Sid said, 'Do you mind? I happen to be a trained fitter, not a Sunday mechanic,' and Tom shrugged and went away, walking around the bus.

The fairies waited impatiently, offering Sid all sorts of advice as usual, none of it relevant to the situation.

Tom came back from his tour and announced that he knew what the trouble was.

'Oh sure,' said Sid, sneering, 'not only do you write books, you're an expert motor mechanic too.'

'No, I don't know as much about engines as you do, probably,' said Tom, 'but I know ants when I see them, and they're all round your petrol cap.'

'Ants?' repeated Sid, thinking this bloke Tom was as bad as the fairies. 'What's ants got to do with anything?'

'That's what I'd like to know,' Tom replied. 'I mean, why would ants cluster around a petrol tank? Ants don't eat petrol – they eat sweet things . . .'

The intelligence dawned on Sid. 'Like bloody sugar,' he cried. 'You mean someone's put sugar in the petrol tank?'

'Looks like it. I ran a finger round the edge of the cap. There were sugar crystals on it.'

'What is the matter, Sid?' asked Oberon. 'Has someone

been feeding our bus sugar?'

'You bet your life they have,' snarled Sid. 'Probably one of these New Age . . .' he stopped in mid-sentence as he remembered an earlier conversation. 'Wait a minute, no, it couldn't have been them. Never mind – we've got to drain the petrol tank now – and the carburettor. Look, Tom, can you give us a hand? Oh, hell, then there's the petrol . . .'

'I've got some spare petrol in my bus,' Tom said. 'You can pay us back later.'

Once the travellers found out that Sid's group was in trouble they rallied round and assisted in draining the petrol tank, cleaning out the carburettor, and refilling the tank with clean petrol. Once the whole process was over the fairies boarded the bus and prepared to leave.

Tom stood in the stairwell and said, 'Look, we're going to Stonehenge via Avebury – why don't you join the convoy in case something else happens? The New Forest is south of there – you can go on after the ceremony tomorrow.'

'What ceremony?' asked Oberon.

'The Companions of the Most Ancient Order of Druids will be there,' said Tom. 'They hold a night vigil.'

Moth said, 'Let's go to Stonehenge!'

The other fairies, including Puck, all looked excited. Avebury and Stonehenge were places of magic. They were naturally drawn to such areas of England, especially at a time like this, spotted double-tongued snakes and thorny hedgehogs notwithstanding. Titania's clamorous owl would point the way, if Moth failed to scent their goal.

Oberon and Titania exchanged looks which Sid did not like.

'Whoa, wait a minute,' cried Sid, 'we don't want to be

sidetracked here – I say we give this a miss and go straight down to the New Forest.'

Tom said, 'But it's on your way.'

'Exactly so,' Oberon said, 'and if we find more sugar in our petroleum then we shall have help at hand.'

'I don't need any help,' cried Sid, sourly. 'I can handle any mechanical problems.'

Oberon put a fatherly hand on Sid's wrist.

'You are a fine rude mechanical, Sid, but you are blowing against the wind.'

'What?' Sid cried.

Oberon walked away, but Puck said, 'The King of the Fairies means that whatever your argument, Sid, we are going to Stonehenge.'

'But why?' wailed Sid.

'Because', replied Puck, 'it is Stonehenge and this is midsummer's day.'

This time the engine burst into life and as the travellers were filing out of the field, Titania fell in behind a beat-up old bus driven by Tom Blessing. Tom waved to her, then when he saw Oberon staring at him, nodded curtly at the little ruler. Oberon ignored the nod, as would any fairy king worth his salt. Poor Tom was beneath Oberon's contempt.

Oberon was a very jealous creature, but not of things like mortals falling in love with his queen. Throughout history he had been used to humans throwing themselves at the tiny, pretty feet of Titania: they could not help themselves. It was flattering to him that his queen was so desirable. Not only was Titania's beauty captivating and unparalleled, she had magic in her pale, silvery complexion. They might for all the world have been worshipping the moon.

93

In any case, Titania was unobtainable. She and Oberon were bound together by preternatural laws far stronger than human love: theirs was a union impossible for earthly creatures to put asunder. It would take a schism caused by earthquakes and volcanic eruptions on a planetary scale to come between the fairyland couple. Before that happened birds would cease to sing; spiders would disappear from the surface of the earth; trees would grow inward, down towards the core; lakes would vanish in steam – in short, the end of the world would come first. Tom did not stand a single chance in the number of stars which light the universe of luring Titania away from her husband and lord.

No, Oberon was not jealous of Tom, but he was jealous of Titania. Once again she had beaten him to a special baby and he had to watch in envy as she coddled it. It was not a fair Otherworld and the king began to hatch various schemes for prising the baby away from Titania. He thought if she became interested enough in this foolish mortal, Tom Blessing, she might forget about the baby and enthral him instead. Tom Blessing was, after all, a pretty young man with his blue eyes and blond hair: almost a substitute for the child. So Oberon decided to encourage the affair, but quietly and without seeming to be concerned either way. If Titania knew what Oberon was thinking, she would cut Tom dead with a cold eye.

Sid moved up the aisle of the bus once they were on their way and part of the travellers' cavalcade.

He stopped beside Cobweb, who was sitting on his own playing some sort of game with a half-hazelnut shell and some dried peas. Sid whispered, 'You did it.'

'Eh?' cried Cobweb, looking up with an alarmed expression. 'Go – go back to your duties, mechanic.'

'You don't fool me, Cobweb. You were asking me about things that would sabotage an engine before we stopped and I told you about the sugar. If I was to tell King Oberon who fixed the petrol, you'd be in trouble, pal.'

'You won't tell him, will you?' croaked a terrified Cobweb. 'Here – you can have this shell – it's precious – you can have it to keep, and the peas too.'

Sid wrinkled his nose. 'Keep your flippin' shell. What I want from you is help to get us away from these travellers. If we stick with them it's going to take longer to get to the New Forest. Maybe we'll *never* get there, and where will that leave me, eh? You help me and I'll keep mum.'

'You sure you don't want these? This shell is very nice,' said Cobweb, holding up a hazelnut husk.

'I don't want your blasted rubbish,' hissed Sid, 'I want your promise.'

'All right, I promise to help you,' said Cobweb, unable to believe he was getting off so lightly. 'I promise, I promise.'

'Good,' said Sid, feeling his intrigue had accomplished something, unaware that of course a fairy's promise is not worth a toad's fart.

After Sid had gone back to his seat, Cobweb continued his game. Whenever Cobweb put the dried pea in the hollow half-hazelnut shell, the pea turned into a diamond – or a ruby – or an emerald – or a sapphire. The game was to guess which type of precious stone the next pea would change into.

'Emerald,' muttered Cobweb.

He was right, it was an emerald.

'Good,' he said, tossing the green stone out of the open window, 'guessed right. That's a good portent. Ruby next time . . .'

The convoy trundled through the night, keeping to A and B roads, rather than using the motorway. The travellers also did not want to come into contact with the police. In previous years they had been harassed by the law, who seemed keen that they should not go near Stonehenge during the midsummer festival. There had been running battles, some of them quite bloody, as the New Age travellers had tried to assert 'their rights' on common land.

Puck was pleased with the way things were going to plan. As a creature who often went among humans to create mischief, of all the fairies he knew mortals best, and he knew that doing mortal deeds, such as driving from one place to another, was fraught with hazards and dangerous possibilities. Puck was a more ingenuous creature than the rest of the fairies and though he played silly tricks on humans, he had an affection for them not shared by the rest of his kind.

Increasingly, though, as the convoy sped south, Puck was aware of another force at loose in the land. This was not a dumb being, like the giant Dun Cow, or the kelpie which had ridden it away into the night. This was an intelligence, sharp and keen, with a definite purpose. Even as it was crossing the landscape, Puck could sense disturbances in the supernatural world, at least a match for their own.

The nature of supernature can be likened to climate and weather: it follows a general pattern, like climate, but in the short term is as unpredictable as the weather. Just as an electrical storm can be started out of season by some unusual activity in the atmosphere, so too can the introduction of a new magical force onto the landscape disturb supernature, causing shock waves to travel through the preternatural world and its inhabitants.

Puck felt these shock waves and turned to look at Oberon. He saw by the look on the fairy king's face that the handsome, glittering Lord of Shadows had felt them too. The other fairies, not quite as sensitive as Puck, Titania and Oberon, were becoming increasingly uncomfortable, and Puck knew they were feeling the changes subconsciously, if not with understanding.

There was not a great deal any of them could do about it though, except wait and wonder.

TEN

Common Oxtongue Opens

L IKE OBERON'S GROUP, MORGAN-LE-FAY WAS DRAWN towards the strong magical magnetism of Stonehenge on midsummer's day. Her far-sight told her that the Sherwood fairies would have to pass near to Stonehenge and she knew that they would be unable to resist the temptation to stop.

She foresaw an opportunity which only came once in an eternity. To be at Stonehenge, where stood the Slaughter Stone, on this particular day of the year, and with a perfect sacrifice to hand – why, the Morning-Fairy could alter the whole nature of time and the universe with such powerful, unfettered magic.

Merlin himself had built Stonehenge, from stones that lay in Killare, Ireland. These were not Irish stones, but had been transported to Eire from Africa by giants. There was the necromancy of a dark continent in those megaliths, as well as the magic of Celtic kings and sorcerers. Four thousand years they had stood on Salisbury Plain and Morgan-le-Fay was now going to put them to use, especially the Slaughter Stone.

As the Morning-Fairy was crossing a rill a figure on horseback came hurtling out of the night. In his right hand was a magnificent sword, heavy-looking with honed edges, its blade covered in Celtic curlie-wurlie designs. Over his shoulder was a bow and quiver full of long arrows fletched with raven's feathers. There was an embossed silver helmet on his head, decorated with hunting scenes, and a dark cloak flowed from his back which flapped like crow's wings in his wake. The rest of him was thick leather strapped around his muscular form by the use of thongs, bronze amulets and pins, and around his waist a massive studded belt.

He was a giant of a man carried by a huge horse protected by flank armour and a unicorn-spiked helmet. The man's face was thickly bearded with clay-red hair. Two bright blue eyes – eyes without mercy or compassion – peered out of the redness. Brutish lips below a straight nose were curled back in a sneer. He was as muscled as a mountain bear.

'Prepare to die,' he yelled, as his mount thundered over the field. 'I shall take thy head from thy shoulders, woman, and feed it to the magpies in the ditches.'

'You shall take nothing from me, Wotan,' spat the Morning-Fairy, 'or do they call you "Grim" hereabouts?'

The ancient hunter, centuries older even than the Morning-Fairy, looked startled and reined back his charger, which came to a halt in front of her. Clouds of steam billowed from the horse's nostrils. The great hooves thumped and flattened the earth on the rill's bank.

'Dost thou know me, woman? How is this?'

'I know Wotan the Huntsman from the days of old, when the land rang with the steel of knights' swords. I am the Morning-Fairy, more powerful than you, my friend. Go your way and slaughter innocents – the guilty are protected by their own infamous deeds of bloody horror.'

'If thou art indeed Morgana, then give me a sign by which I shall know thee.'

Instantly, the Morning-Fairy changed her shape, into that of her long dead enemy, Arthur.

Wotan dismounted from his steed and stood by as she changed back into her womanish shape. The great hunter-god knelt on one knee before her, acknowledging her power. She touched his shoulder and he rose again, towering over her, his physical presence dwarfing her delicate stature.

'Why have I been woken by thee?' asked Wotan. 'Dost thou have some deed for me?'

'You've been disturbed by my presence rather than deliberately aroused. The whole of magical England, Scotland and Wales is stirring because of those Sherwood fairies – they've left the greenwood in search of another home and the world has been shaken to its roots by their movement over the landscape towards the south coast.'

Wotan looked about him in disappointment.

'Does this mean my awakening is only of a temporary nature? When the Sherwood fairies reach their destination, I shall go back into the dark earth again? Is this what thou sayest, oh witch of the wildlands?'

He moaned the words in great despair, wanting to be

part of the living landscape again, wanting to be the hunter on the hill, in the forest, on the plains, killing game with his mighty bow. He wished to return to the times when he was the slaughterer, destroyer of men, whose charger could not be outrun by those of any mortal unassisted by magic. He wanted to be a strong force in the world of men again, not a spirit in the earth and lost to the memory of ordinary men, kept alive only in the pages of dusty books.

Morgan-le-Fay told him it was exactly so. While the fairies moved across the land the magical disturbances would keep some supernatural creatures awake, but once King Oberon and his band reached the New Forest, then all would return to normal once again.

'Unless I can get to Stonehenge at the same time as Titania,' said the Morning-Fairy, 'for she has something which could alter the stability of the world, were it to fall into my useful hands.'

Wotan's eyes widened.

'Something to keep us here?'

'Better than that – something to return us to that time which mortals call medieval Britain – something to rid this stinking place with its foul breath of machines . . .'

A small roe deer suddenly appeared on a rise just beyond the rill, having been drawn to the water to drink. Morgan-le-Fay and Wotan paused in their conversation to watch this wide-eyed, graceful creature picking its way delicately down to the place where the stream widened. It looked around once, then dipped its head to drink, having no knowledge of the two creatures near by – creatures who had no scent.

'Kill it,' said the Morning-Fairy, softly.

Wotan moved with deliberate slowness, unslinging his

bow and removing a long arrow from its quiver. He put the notch of the arrow in the cord and drew back on the weapon. The black barbed head glinted wickedly in the starlight. When it reached the fingers of his left hand Wotan steadied the bow, sighted along the arrow, then let the shaft loose.

The arrow arced through the night air and found its mark with unerring accuracy, pinning the small deer to the bank of the stream through its heart. It let out a last living sigh, then kicked once and lay still. Wotan grunted in satisfaction, pleased to know his skill had not been lost through spending centuries in obscurity.

He turned to Morgan-le-Fay. 'Was the creature a spy? Is that why thee told me to kill it? Is it some good fairy in disguise?'

The Morning-Fairy shook her head.

'No,' she said, coldly, 'I just like to see things die for the sake of it – don't you?'

He stared at her and then laughed, roaring into the darkness and making his mount whinny.

'By the gods of moor and mountain, I do indeed, witch.'

'Now,' said Morgan-le-Fay, 'we must be on our way – I shall sit behind you on the steed. You will carry me to Stonehenge where I shall find Titania. Agreed?'

'Agreed,' said Wotan, gathering the reins of his horse.

Frances Flute had been cleared of any involvement in the kidnapping of her charge and had graduated through a police inspector and was now being dealt with by a Superintendent Jones.

'Look, Miss Flute,' said the superintendent, 'we're doing all we can to find the baby . . .'

'Louise,' interrupted Frances, blowing her nose on a handkerchief already soaked in her tears. 'Louise DuLac.'

'Yes, baby Louise – but you must understand that in the last two or three hours the country seems to have gone crazy. We've been inundated with calls concerning the sighting of giants, ghosts, elves and pixies and God knows what. It's as if the whole population hereabouts has been on hallucinogens or something. It's slowing up operations.'

The superintendent mopped his brow with his own handkerchief, already soaked in his sweat.

'The media,' he continued, 'are more interested in giants than missing babies, but I'm sure they'll get round to us before the morning – after all few people watch television in the early hours of the morning, do they?'

'I was told', said Frances evenly, 'that it's best to catch a kidnapper early – the longer it goes on the less chance there is of getting Louise back.'

'Well, that's true too, of course. We still haven't been able to trace these little people you spoke about – these dwarfs.'

'I didn't say they were dwarfs – I said they were of small stature. They could have been young people, but they seemed too – oh, I don't know – too *mature*, if you see what I mean? In any case, I wasn't the only one who saw them – most of the people at the fête watched them dance.'

'Yes, yes, I understand that, but nevertheless . . . would you like a cup of tea?'

'I've had seventeen cups of tea,' cried Frances. 'I've been swamped with tea.'

'I expect you have.'

A police sergeant came into the room and put a piece

of paper in front of the superintendent. He read it quickly, then looked up at the sergeant and nodded.

'What is it?' asked Frances, anxiously. 'Is it about Louise?'

The superintendent shook his head sadly. ''Fraid not – it's a bunch of New Age travellers on their way to Stonehenge. I'm afraid we've got them to contend with, as well as the missing child. They're liable to do a lot of damage to the monument if I don't draft in reserves as quickly as possible . . .'

'My baby is more important than a load of hippies and a pile of bricks,' shouted Frances, losing her temper. 'You draft in reserves to look for Louise. What harm could a few hippies do to lumps of stone weighing several tons in any case? They can hardly steal them, can they?'

The superintendent said, 'I'm going to hand you over to my sergeant again, now. Sergeant Tomlinson, could you take Miss Flute to the canteen and buy her a cup of tea?' He reached into his pocket and passed a coin over to his sergeant.

'Yes, sir,' said the sergeant, a woman in her forties.

She took Frances's arm and gently persuaded her to leave the chair and walk towards the door.

'You find my Louise,' cried Frances, over her shoulder as she left the room. 'You can beat up hippies at any time.'

The sergeant took Frances along a corridor, down some steps, and into the police canteen. There was chatter going on before they entered, but it stopped almost immediately when Frances followed Tomlinson into the room. Surprisingly, though she had indeed had many cups of tea, Frances felt thirsty and gratefully murmured to her escort that she would like it sweet and strong for once, with just a dash of milk.

The chatter began again, but it was more muted than before, and by the time Tomlinson was sitting with Frances, the room was buzzing again, albeit with fewer obscenities in the air.

Tomlinson put a hand on Frances's own.

'I can guess how you're feeling, love,' said the sergeant. 'I've given birth to three of my own. If anyone tried to kidnap one of them, I would kill him.'

Frances found she wanted to talk to this woman, because she was a woman and, she felt, more sympathetic to her fears.

'You said *him*, but I've been told it's more likely to be a woman who has stolen Louise – a woman with problems.'

Tomlinson said, 'We can't rule out the possibility of kidnappers with financial motives. I understand the DuLacs are rich people. Aristocrats.'

'They have aristocratic *connections*,' said Frances, 'but listen – which would be better for us – Louise in the hands of kidnappers who want money? Or with a frustrated mother?'

'The latter definitely,' said Tomlinson, 'although you know where you stand with a gang of crooks. You pay the money, you get the baby back. They won't want to hold on to the mite for more time than they need to.'

'But aren't they more likely to harm her?'

Tomlinson pursed her lips and looked worried, staring hard into Frances's eyes. 'Are you all right? Are you sure you want to hear all this? After all, we're talking about things that might not happen. I'm no psychologist – I don't want to upset you any more than necessary.'

Frances was firm. 'I've got over the emotional bit. Louise is not *my* baby, after all. I want to know all the possible reasons why a baby would be stolen – and I want to know what the chances are of getting her back soon. I want to have a thorough knowledge of what we're dealing with here, before I have to talk to Louise's parents.'

'You want to try to save your job, I understand that.'

Frances shook her head. 'My job is finished – you think they're going to employ me now? What I want to do is cause them the least pain possible. Now, we were talking about whether kidnappers normally hurt their victims.'

'All right, yes, a kidnapping gang *is* more likely to harm a child,' said the sergeant, sipping her tea thoughtfully, 'but she's a baby. They usually – I'm being very straight with you here – they usually kill their kidnap victims because they can be recognized by them later – but this is a baby that can't even talk, can it?'

Frances shook her head.

'No, I thought so,' said Tomlinson. 'Not at seven months. Well, there's no reason for them to hurt her, is there? Not unless they're psychopaths with sadistic tendencies, and that's unlikely. I think we can be pretty sure, in either case, that the baby won't be harmed at all. It's just a matter of time . . .'

'How about the frustrated mother angle?' asked Frances. 'Tell me about that.'

Tomlinson put down her tea. 'You keep talking about the snatcher being a "frustrated mother" – actually that's not normally the case.'

'But the first sergeant I spoke to . . .'

Tomlinson shook her head. 'He doesn't know his elbow from his . . . look, I've been on a course, that's why I'm on this case. Look, there's supposed to be three reasons why a woman snatches a baby – the main one is to try to patch up a relationship that's gone out of control.'

'You mean, the woman pretends it's *her* baby, in order

106

to bring a wayward man back to her side.'

'That's it,' said Tomlinson. 'Usually she hasn't seen the man for a few months and hopes he'll believe the baby is his.'

'And the second and third reasons?'

'You get acutely mentally ill women, who actually believe the baby is theirs – then you get women who snatch the baby because they have an emotional hole in their lives and need to fill it with something.'

'Well, I suppose that last one is similar to a frustrated mother, isn't it?' asked Frances.

'In a way, but the women aren't usually grieving for their own baby that's died, which is what is usually meant.'

Frances said, 'What about if it's someone completely outside the two types you've mentioned? Someone not a frustrated mother, nor a kidnapping gang – someone with utterly different motives altogether?'

The police sergeant blinked. 'Who would that be? I mean, like what?'

'I don't know,' Frances said. 'If I did I wouldn't be so anxious. But what if it's a baby-selling ring – someone attempting to make a fortune by stealing babies and selling them to parents who can't have their own?'

'That's another possibility, but a remote one,' said Tomlinson. 'It's the kind of thing that goes on in Central Europe, but not in England. There's a baby traffic that goes on in poorer countries, where parents are desperate to find their children homes in a wealthy society. No, I reckon we're dealing with a gang here.'

'Then where's the ransom note?' questioned Frances. 'Show me the ransom note and I'll get it paid.'

'Well, I don't say we've received a note yet,' Tomlinson answered, 'but it's early days. Once the morning comes, we'll learn a lot more. These things have a habit of remaining in the realms of fantasy in the early hours. Nothing seems real.'

'And perverts – she wouldn't be in the hands of a paedophile?'

Frances held her breath, waiting to hear the answer to this one from the candid Tomlinson, a mature woman who knew better than to hide the truth from another of her sex.

'It's possible, but, again, remote. That kind of predator usually doesn't risk a long prison sentence by kidnapping a child – the offence of abusing a child is abhorrent enough to juries, without the added kidnapping charge. No, paedophiles normally prey on inadequate single mothers – mothers whose misfortunes are likely to drive them into unwise relationships – and they groom these women, hoping that by living with them, or even marrying them, they can get at the children. They're monsters, these men, but they know it's easier to get at children in their own home than run the risk of a manhunt by kidnapping them.'

Frances was horrified by the picture the sergeant was painting, realizing it was true.

'They catch these horrible men, though, don't they?'

Sergeant Tomlinson raised her eyebrows and took another sip of her tea.

'We catch them, occasionally – and very occasionally we get them to court – but mostly the "monsters" get away with it.'

'Why?'

'Because juries are reluctant to take the evidence of children, especially very young children – or it's thought the children might suffer more of a trauma by going to court than they would if the man is just sent packing. Sometimes the children are too young to understand – or even too young to talk. It's an ugly business and it's at times like these I wish there was magic in the world, so we could send such criminals to a far-off place and forget they ever existed.'

'I should say so,' said Frances, hotly. 'I should jolly well say so.' She paused, then added, gripping her cup tightly, 'In the meantime I've got to sit here and drink tea while terrible things are happening to my poor Louise. I know I'm not Louise's mother, but I love her just the same. I wish . . . oh, I hope nothing bad happens to her. Please God.'

Tomlinson tried to offer words of comfort. 'Don't let your imagination run away with you – try to concentrate on something else. Are you religious?'

'Yes I am – I'm a practising Catholic.'

'Well, I'm a lapsed Methodist myself, but it sometimes helps, if you have a faith, to use it a bit. Do you want me to take you to a church or something?'

Frances gave a wistful smile. 'I've been praying my heart out ever since Louise went missing. I don't need a church to pray in, not always.' She paused for a short while and then said, 'Do you want to hear a funny story?'

Tomlinson was only too glad to be offered the opportunity to hear about something other than the kidnapping, and nodded enthusiastically.

'Well,' said Frances, with a wry look, 'do you know, I used to live near Stansted Airport and because I'm afraid of flying myself—'

'So am I,' interrupted Tomlinson. 'I usually take a sleeping tablet on a long flight.'

'Right. Anyway, my house wasn't directly in line with the

109

runway but occasionally planes would fly over my roof and when they did I used to pray for the people on board. I used to pray that they would be safe. I did it all the time.'

Tomlinson said, 'That's nice – a bit quirky – but it's nice.'

'Yes, well,' smiled Frances, sadly, 'one day I heard a plane coming in really low, you know? And it didn't sound right – the engines sounded, well *shaky*. I felt in my mind that those people were in real trouble and my heart went out to them in their terror. So I put down the apple pie I had baked and went down on my knees on the kitchen floor.

'I prayed very hard for those poor passengers and for the crew, of course, and do you know what happened?'

'You said it was a funny story, so probably someone came in and caught you at it?'

'No, worse than that – after a while I realized it wasn't an aircraft after all – it was my coffee percolator. I hadn't put the lid on properly and the noise it was making, percolating the coffee, was the sound I'd taken to be a low-flying plane. Funny, eh?'

Tomlinson laughed, causing several heads to turn in the canteen.

'I bet you felt daft,' she said. 'I bet you felt silly.'

'I felt very foolish,' smiled Frances, 'but do you know – it was the best coffee I've *ever* tasted. That makes you think, doesn't it? Eh? There are more things in heaven and earth than are dreamt of in Horatio's philosophy.'

'Right,' said Tomlinson, wondering what in heaven and earth Frances Flute was talking about, and what in the hell this bloke Horatio had to do with anything. 'Gotcha.'

ELEVEN

Hawkweed, Late-flowering Dandelion, Wild Succory Open

TOM AND MARY BLESSING HAD BEEN RAISED AS 'ARMY brats', their father being a colour sergeant in the Welsh Fusiliers. Since the age of nothing they had gone from married quarters to service hired accommodation with barely time to breathe between moves. Tom had been to twenty-two different schools before the age of fifteen. Both had been raised partly in foreign countries and home to Tom was the place he liked best – Hong Kong – even though he was actually born in Aden and spent much of his teenage life in Northern Ireland.

'One day I'll go back to Hong Kong,' he often told Mary, 'when I get enough money together.'

It was a distant dream – and fading fast, for Hong Kong as a British Crown Colony was soon to disappear, into the maw of a mainland China reclaiming its own. It was not that Tom approved of imperialism, but Hong Kong's streets, the New Territories' countryside, had been his playground, and he wasn't sure the Chinese Government would be sympathetic enough to his feelings to allow him to roam at will over old haunts.

Despite the fact that he was travelling with Mary and her boyfriend Earl on this trip, their earlier gypsy-life had given the siblings two opposite desires. Tom wanted to settle down, marry, buy a house and never move again. Mary had permanently itchy feet and wanted always to be on the move, seeing different places, learning new geography. There was an insecurity in both of them and they dealt with it in the ways that suited their personalities best.

In the same way, because they had been saying goodbye to people all their lives, over and over again, they had opposite views on friendship. Tom clung to his friends and never let one go if he could help it. Mary formed only shallow relationships with people, afraid to let herself go or form a deep friendship in the knowledge that it would have to come to an end, so why bother. Mary's boyfriend Earl had fathered her child, a boy named Alex, but Mary's commitment to Earl remained the same – loose and slightly distant.

The other occupants of the bus were all in their set places. Sabre, the English collie, was dozing under the table. Max the cat was lying on the narrow padded seat which ran the full length of the bus's living quarters on the offside. Earl was at present driving the bus, Alex was asleep in a curtained-off section at the back, and Mary felt able to speak freely with her brother.

'You seemed taken with that little woman, Tom. You

better be careful – she's married and all. I heard one of those other pygmies . . .'

'They're not *pygmies*, Mary,' Tom said, admonishing her. 'They're just ordinary people.'

'They're short,' she said. 'I don't want to call people names, but they're not *ordinary*, and I don't know how else to describe them. It's like they're all well-proportioned but only half as big as normal people.'

'You're not so tall yourself, Mary,' Tom said.

Mary was four-feet eight-inches tall. She had a dumpy little figure which made her seem smaller, and though it did little for her height she wore her hair conveniently short. Her personal presence, however, was immense, and at any meeting held by the travellers her quiet, determined voice could alter decisions which had previously seemed rock firm. She was a no-nonsense, sensible woman whose judgements of situations and feelings were unerringly correct.

Mary brought up something else.

'Earlier tonight you said you fancied that woman who came on television – the nanny that's lost the baby.'

Tom's eyes took on a distant look. 'Frances Flute, that's what the newscaster called her.'

'You said she looked the kind of woman you could settle down with, if you could get to meet her and get her to like you. I had the impression it was love at first sight. You seemed quite struck to me.'

Tom shuffled his feet uncomfortably. 'Well, I did think she looked nice – but that was before I met Titania. I mean, there's no comparison, is there? Titania *dazzles*. Frances Flute sort of – well, she seemed a lovely lady, but next to Titania she would be quite dowdy.'

'There's more to a woman than beauty, Tom, you know

113

that – I'm surprised at you. I was quite impressed with that nanny too, but not because of her looks. I think she's handling this crisis over the lost baby extremely well. You could see she was worried, but she spoke in a clear voice without breaking down into tears, and what she said was very moving. I wouldn't be upset if you married a woman like that.'

'You wouldn't be upset if *I* married, but you don't want to get married yourself. Poor old Earl is desperate to tie the knot, but you won't have any of it.'

'That's true, Tom,' said Mary, sitting down at the table with her brother while the bus sped along. 'I'm just asking you to be careful over this Titania. The fact that she's married must make you stop and think about her behaviour – I don't know what she said to you, but if she chatted you up in front of her husband she's not the sort that will settle down with someone like you, is she?'

'And what's someone like me?'

'Steady, loyal and loving, Tom.'

'Boring?'

'It depends on who the other person is, doesn't it? This Titania dazzles, as you say, but she'll get tired of you very quickly, just as she's obviously got tired of her husband. She's a married woman and you're too conventional to overlook that for long. You'll feel dreadfully guilty.'

Tom put his face in his hands and then looked up at his sister.

'Well, that depends, doesn't it?'

'No, it doesn't *depend*. Just because her husband hardly spoke to her round the fire, and didn't seem interested in her at the time, doesn't mean they've got a bad marriage. Earl doesn't pay attention to me all the time – I wouldn't expect him to, and we're not even married.'

114

'It was things she *said* to me, Mary. You didn't hear.'

Mary shook her head. 'Some women play games, Tom. You're such an innocent with women. They'll lead you into hell and leave you there to find your own way out. You be careful – you're a nice person – the world isn't full of honesty and integrity. She might be trying to get back at that squared-off man of hers, or make him jealous, or something. Don't take what she says at face value.'

'I'm not going to do anything silly,' said Tom, 'I've got my book to write.'

'Well, be sure you don't,' said his round-faced sister. 'I don't want to see my brother hurt.' She paused and looked down at the table, before adding, 'Anyway, she's weird.'

'And your traveller friends aren't? Curing illnesses with gem stones? Pressing people's feet to make them well? Homeopathy? Herbs to get rid of aches and pains. T'ai chi in the mornings? Acupuncture? Hypnotism?'

'Those aren't *weird*, Tom – they're just alternative medicines – and t'ai chi is Chinese keep-fit.'

'All right then, what about Earl's tattoos? They're not weird? And Sendal with her astrology and tarot cards? And Goatie and his spiritualism? What about Rosie Zann and her fortune-telling? You're not telling me mediums and stuff like that isn't weird, Mary.'

'You leave Earl's tattoos out of it. He used to belong to a heavy metal band – that's why they look like Satanist symbols. No other reason. He's not really into black magic or anything like that.'

Tom was genuinely surprised. 'Earl's a musician? I thought he was a Hell's Angel?'

Mary giggled. 'He used to be one of those too, but not any more. As for his band, well, I have to admit, when he

115

played one of his records, it didn't sound like music. No, that's cruel, I mustn't say that. The band didn't last long anyway – most of them bought motorbikes and went back to being Hell's Angels again . . .'

'What was this band called?'

'Black Death.'

'Nice,' murmured Tom. 'Sort of has a ring to it, doesn't it?'

'You mean like ring-a-ring-a-roses?' Mary quipped. 'The mark of the plague?'

'Clev-er,' acknowledged Tom.

At that moment Earl yelled back from his driver's seat, 'How about a bloody cup of tea, woman? A bloke could die of thirst up here.'

'Coming,' Mary called back. She poured some of the stewed tea into a saucepan and quickly lit the gas under it. After a few moments it bubbled and she then poured it into a mug. It looked dark-brown and disgusting to Tom.

'He won't drink that, will he?'

Mary replied, 'He'd drink Irish bog water if you told him it was tea. One thing about having a boyfriend with no refinements – you don't need to be a gourmet cook. Chips, over-cooked burgers and beans, all washed down with stewed tea, and he's as happy as a sandboy. And me being a vegetarian, I don't even have to eat the same muck.'

She grabbed a packet of biscuits to take with her.

Mary went through the partition in the bus between the living quarters and the driver's cab to give Earl his tea. It struck Tom that the travellers' buses were like aircraft, with the pilot being serviced by the crew throughout the flight.

Alex stirred in his bunk-bed at the back and Sabre

116

suddenly sat up and pricked up his ears.

'Don't move, dog, or I'll turn you into a mouse,' said a voice near Tom's elbow.

Tom jerked backwards, scraping his chair. 'Uhhhhh!' he grunted, the hair standing up on the nape of his neck.

He turned in shock to see one of the new little people from around the campfire sitting next to him.

'How – how did you get here?' Tom cried.

'Robin Goodfellow, at your service,' said a smiling Puck, bowing. 'Methought to pay you a visit, sirrah. Tis opportunity to do my trickery I seek. Perhaps the drab who left a moment ago has some milk which I can turn sour, or cheese to make watery? Or a hoax? The late-flowering dandelion has opened and the hour has come for this knavish sprite to frolic. What say? Ho! Why do you stare so, mortal? Have you no manners? Art thou a gadfly? Speak.'

Tom hardly heard what was being said to him. He was trying to figure out how the youth had got from one bus to the other without either of them stopping. Had he jumped from roof to roof while the buses were being driven? It was impossible. Then something dawned on Tom: this Goodfellow must have stowed away somewhere, before they left the last camp, and had just emerged from his hiding place.

Tom said severely, 'Don't you know we travellers regard privacy as very important? When you all live in each other's pockets like this, you need to keep your own space. Trespassing on someone else's vehicle is a definite no-no – you'll have to learn that, if you're going on the road for any length of time. Travellers won't tolerate this kind of thing, even if it's supposed to be a joke.'

'Joke?' cried Puck. 'Prithee I'll show thee a joke,

117

friend,' and he turned the sleeping cat into a cushion and promptly sat on it. 'Thus does the watermelon become the moon, or the orange become the sun. Thus does the sycamore seed fall spinning to the earth like a sparrow with a damaged wing. Thus does the dragonfly become a blue dart to pierce the heart of the robber heron, stealing fish.'

Tom stood up quickly, shocked and horrified.

'Hey, that poor cat . . .'

Puck pulled the cat-shaped cushion from under him and tossed it across the bus.

'Poor cat?' he said. 'Know ye not that cats are witches' familiars, and therefore they are the sluts of the animal kingdom? For a morsel of fish they sell their souls to sorcerers, the little trollops. They are greedy, selfish creatures, interested in only their own well-being and comfort. Give me a mongrel cur any day, friend, rather than the Jezebel of domestic pets.'

Tom was staring wildly at the stuffed cat, lying upside down in the corner of the bus, unmoving.

'Mongrels?' he said, distracted.

'Dogs such as this cur,' Puck said, demonstrating his affection for Sabre by giving him a swift kick in the ribs. 'Mongrels like this are worth ten times that of yon moggie, which has no affection for its mistress.'

Tom was now staring at Sabre, who had not moved an inch when kicked by this Robin Goodfellow. Tom bent down and gingerly felt the hound, only to retrieve his hand with a startled, 'Help!' when he touched cold stone. This was some kind of nightmare for Tom.

Tom turned to look at the creature before him. 'How did you do that?' he whispered. 'What have you done to them? Or me? Am I hypnotized?'

'Ah, that is of course a possible cause of your distress,' Puck replied in the tones of a sage, putting his feet up on the table and lacing his hands behind his head. 'To be hypnotized is an unsettling thing, for one has no control over one's own mind. Ecad, I once knew a rabbit that was hypnotized by a stoat thus forfeiting its life. Do you feel that you are about to forfeit your life? Speak up.'

'I – I'm – I'm not sure what's happening.'

'Therein lies a further danger,' warned Puck, 'in being unaware of the situation and the state of the world around one. In the heat of the sun this may be termed *madness*, or *lunacy* under the cold moon. One must remain in full comprehension of that which occurs during waking hours, or one will be beguiled and subject to all sorts of fantasies and frauds. If I were you I would give myself a sharp reprimand and reconsider my position – think on this – if you were the furry humble bee, your hive would be lost to you.'

'Bee?' gasped Tom, feeling giddy. 'What have bees got to do with anything?'

'Go to! Bees are very important creatures,' Puck admonished, severely. 'Without bees there would be no cross-pollination of flowers and blooms, and with no pollination there will be no fruit – no berries, no plums, no rosy apples – and the creatures of woodland and field would starve and die. Have you no heart? Art thou made of stone, like this hound here? Dost thou not care what happens to our woodland creatures? Fie, for shame, sirrah – beg forgiveness presently.'

At that moment the partition door opened and Mary came back into the living quarters of the bus. Tom, still reeling from the shock, turned to her and said, 'He's done something to Sabre and Max!'

Mary stared at her brother and then around the bus.

'Who?' she asked. 'Who's done what?'

Tom turned dramatically and pointed to where Robin Goodfellow had been sitting only to see Max back in his place, snoring gently, twitching as if having an unpleasant dream. Tom then looked under the table and Sabre was there. Tom touched the dog, making Sabre look up sharply. The hound was warm and soft, not cold granite with no life.

'I – I swear someone else was here,' Tom cried. 'He *was*, definitely. One of those – those *people* from the bus behind us. He must have stowed away and then tricked me somehow. Hypnotism – it *had* to be hypnotism. And he talked all this gobbledegook which made my head spin. Look in that cupboard. He's probably hiding there this very minute.'

Mary raised her eyebrows and opened the door to the broom cupboard, only to find it full of its usual junk.

'Well?' she said.

Tom began to shake and he sat down, putting his head in his hands.

'Look, love, you're overtired I think. Why don't you get some kip, eh? We'll be driving for an hour or so yet. You get your head down and have a good snooze.'

'I think I will,' replied Tom. 'I'm going bonkers.'

'No you're not – it's just lack of sleep.'

Tom went to the back of the bus and flopped into the bunk below Alex. He lay back on the hard pillow and stared at the criss-crossing of wire above him, with the thin mattress bulging through the holes. Had he been hallucinating? Tom did not take drugs. He didn't even smoke or drink. Only the odd pint of beer. What had happened back there? A glitch in his brain, or something.

You got weird things like that happening when you were tired. Mary was right – he was stressed and fatigued and that was all there was to it – simple as that.

'Goodnight then.'

The person in the top bunk had leaned over the edge of his mattress to speak to Tom. The upside-down face did not belong to Alex. It was that of Robin Goodfellow.

'Goodnight,' whispered Tom, refusing to be intimidated by this strange state of mind he was suffering.

'Sweet dreams,' said Puck.

'And you too.'

With that the face disappeared.

After a few moments Tom cautiously got out of bed and had a look at the top bunk. Alex, rosy-faced and looking as peaceful and innocent as a cherub, was fast asleep in his bed. Tom stared at the child for a moment, then got back in his own bunk and tried to fall asleep.

It was not easy.

TWELVE

White Water-lily, Naked-stalked Poppy, Smooth Sowthistle Open

'HOW HAS THE PUCK USED THE QUICKSILVER MINUTES that are so precious to such mortal men as we keep in our present company?' asked Oberon.

Puck grinned. 'Methought to pay a visit, to bid our friend Tom Blessing, newly found, sweet and unpernicious dreams.'

Oberon nodded, as if this was quite in order. Puck was a gadabout, a sprite, a fairy with a nervous energy. There was no way Puck could sit on a bus for more than an hour without zipping off somewhere. In the old days Puck would have visited a thousand farms, ten thousand houses and a hundred thousand sleeping souls, all before the shrubby hawkweed and spotted cat's ear opened. His pranks would be talked about over the whole of

Christendom while men went to labour in the fields and women fetched and carried around the houses. Cakes would sink and pasties would have no filling when bitten into. Buckets would have holes. There would be no middle to a loaf of bread, no sharpness to a newly honed scythe, no strength in a waggon wheel recently fitted.

Puck was responsible for all those unexplainable mishaps that seem to occur without signal or warning.

All this was perfectly acceptable to the fairy king.

Sid had also noticed that Puck had been missing and when Puck sat beside him, said, 'I thought your magic was weak outside the greenwood? How come you can vanish like that?'

Puck snorted. 'Well, I can't girdle the Earth three times in a night, but I can hop from bus to bus all right.'

Robin Goodfellow then turned to Oberon again, saying, 'There's a boy, sleeping like a little prince, in a bed with daffodil-coloured sheets. And the mortal who has been bewitched by Queen Titania keeps guard over him. There is a woman, too, sister of the man, and that vulgar rude mechanical who drives the vehicle like a black hearse into the night.'

'A hearse you say?' murmured Oberon, looking up at the bus in front of them.

Sid frowned. He didn't quite understand what Puck was getting at. There seemed to be some sort of hidden message in his words. King Oberon continued to stare at the bus in front through the windscreen. Puck nodded to the King of the Fairies and Oberon pursed his lips.

'You are right, Puck – it is so.'

'What?' asked Sid. 'What's *so*? Hey look, you're not thinking of stealing the little boy, are you? I mean, you've already got me and the baby. How many mortals do you want?'

'The boy is quite beautiful, but we have no need of him,' said Puck.

'Then what?' cried Sid. 'What is it?'

There was noise coming from around the front of the bus now, where fairies were quarrelling about who should hold the baby and for how long. The infant Titania called Pigwidgeon was now wide awake and being passed like a party parcel from fairy to fairy, but not in turn.

The Sherwood fairies had no sense of fairness and would not have dreamed of waiting their turn to cuddle the child. They grappled for her, one after another, squabbling bitterly when they failed to wrench her from another's grasp. Luckily the baby didn't seem to mind all this rough-housing. It was chortling and making squeaking sounds with every tussle.

'Me next,' said Peaseblossom. 'I want a go.'

'You've just had one,' cried Moth. 'Now it's my turn. Give the baby here, Mustardseed.'

Mist said, 'I want it, I want it – I *will* have it – I *will.*'

Swallowtail, currently in possession of the precious bundle, would not let it go at any price and kept turning away, presenting her back to the grabbing hands. As she swung this way and that, she rocked the baby, who giggled gleefully at all this fun. Blewit dashed round the front while Swallowtail was turning away from Mist, and snatched the infant from her arms.

'Got her,' said Blewit. 'Let me cuddle her for a while and kiss her rosy-red cheeks.'

Oberon saw that Titania was becoming distracted by the fracas and not paying attention to the road.

'Put the baby down,' he ordered. 'Now!'

Pigwidgeon was returned to the seat next to Titania and

the fairy queen smiled on her stolen child and then restored her concentration to her driving.

Sid said to Oberon, 'Please, what is it about the bus in front? Tell me.'

Oberon shrugged and said, 'It will crash soon – everyone inside will be killed.'

'WHAT?.' cried Sid. He knew better than to question Oberon's statement. Puck was nodding and in any case there was no reason for the fairy king to tell an untruth. There was nothing to be gained from such a lie.

Sid looked at the red tail-lights of the bus in front. It all looked so normal. The vehicle was only doing about forty miles per hour.

'What's going to happen?' asked Sid, hoarsely. 'How will it crash?'

'When we cross twin serpents of steel a gigantic dragon will come and with its mighty jaws bite the bus in two.'

'Precisely so, my lord,' said Puck. 'It is written on the face of the night in brilliant letters.'

All Sid could see on the face of the night was the haze of yellow street light from a distant town.

Puck said, 'The dragon will come at such speed that nothing might stand in its way. It is a fearsome thing, without conscience – even the sacrifice of maidens leaves it cold. There is no thwarting its intention.'

'Why don't they get out, then? Why don't they escape when the bus gets stuck on the rails?'

'The bus door is pressed fast against the post on which a warning bell is fitted. There can be no exodus. It happens all too fast. The dragon is merciless. This is a sad and terrible thing.'

'We have to stop them then,' said Sid, wildly. 'We've got to stop that bus before it crosses the rails.'

The two fairies looked helpless.

'What can we do?' shrugged Puck.

Sid stared out of the window and saw, in the far distance, a train snaking casually through the night. Its windows were like large scales – bright, opalescent scales – and its blunt nose probed the darkness ahead. He knew instantly that this was the dragon which was about to take the life of the people in the front bus, including a small boy in a bed of daffodil-yellow. Up ahead, Sid could now see a level crossing, the lights flashing and the bell clanging, its barriers beginning to lower.

'They won't cross,' he said relieved. 'The alarm's going.'

'Their bus will fail to stop,' Puck explained. 'The brake things won't work.'

The Blessing bus had taken over as the first in the convoy, since Earl knew the route and had ridden it often as a biker. His navigating skills were good and, the roads being dark at night, the convoy needed someone in the lead who knew what they were doing. Earl was the unofficial leader of this particular band of travellers. He was strong and forthright with his opinions and this loose community needed someone who was confident and assertive.

Titania had slipped in behind the Blessing bus, for reasons of her own.

Strung out behind Sid's bus was the rest of the cavalcade of New Age travellers. If Puck was right, that the bus in front had faulty brakes, it would hurtle over the crossing. Sid had a vision of the bus smashing through the barrier, slewing sideways so that it was bent against the post on the far side, then the diesel engine of that hooting train hurtling into the bus at ninety miles an hour, flattening it like an empty drink can, killing everyone inside, including the boy.

'We have to do something,' cried the enthralled mortal.

He rushed down the aisle of the bus and plucked Titania deftly from the driver's seat, jumping into her place. The fairy queen protested loudly at this rough behaviour, but Sid was already working the controls of the bus, his knees hitting himself in the chin because of the blocks he had fitted for Titania.

Sid began flashing his lights and tried to overtake Earl before the Blessing bus reached the crossing. The other vehicle, however, seemed to speed up and Sid realized Earl thought he was simply overtaking because he was impatient with the convoy leader's pace. The indignant Earl was having none of it and would not let Sid take the lead.

'You bloody fool!' yelled Sid, forced in behind the front bus again. 'I'm trying to save your life.'

Sid tried again and this time he could see Earl's face in the side mirror of the Blessing bus. The man had a determined expression which Sid knew well. The car mechanic read into that countenance a refusal to allow some mad cretin the space to overtake. Earl was sticking to his guns, pressing his foot on the accelerator, roaring along the tarmac of the lonely country lane, not giving an inch.

'I'm not racing you, you flaming idiot,' screamed Sid. 'You're all going to die.'

'Methinks the dolt has raw dung for brains,' said Puck at Sid's elbow.

Sid glanced behind him quickly and saw that all the fairies on the bus were crowded down at the front, watching his driving with excitement in their strange eyes. There was not a gram of fear in them. They were simply soaking up the fever of the moment.

The level crossing was coming up fast. There were only two bends to go. The woods on the left had now disappeared and a grass verge followed the road all the way to the railway line. Sid made a decision. After all, he told himself, this was a matter of life and death. On the next left-curving bend, he suddenly swung the bus onto the grass verge and set about overtaking Earl on the inside.

Sid sounded his horn as his vehicle bounced and leapt over the grass. He managed this time to draw up alongside Earl's bus. Earl blared his own horn in reply. Sid shook his fist. Earl shook his fist back. Gradually Sid's experienced driving took him ahead of the other bus. The gates of the level crossing were coming up frighteningly fast.

Once ahead of the other vehicle, Sid yelled to the fairies, 'Grab the baby! Brace yourselves!' and with that he rammed his foot down on the pedal block, slamming on the brakes of the bus, handbrake as well, and with smoking tyres came to a halt just before the barrier.

Sid stiffened, waiting for the impact of the bus behind – the bus without brakes – hoping his own vehicle would not be shunted through the barrier onto the tracks.

He waited in vain.

All of a sudden he was startled by a tremendous noise in his ears as the train thundered across his line of sight, making his heart claw at his ribs. He could see the faces of one or two night travellers flash past him as they sat staring out of their windows.

Then all was still.

Through the open window he heard the wind soughing over the grasses. There was a pond near by where ducks were settling again after being disturbed by the rattle and rumble of the train. A bus door opened and slammed somewhere.

'WHAT THE BLOODY HELL DO YOU THINK YOU'RE PLAYING AT?' roared a voice in his ear.

Sid jumped again and then looked down to see Earl glaring up at him.

'I – you – you were going to crash through the barrier,' said Sid. 'Your brakes . . .'

'There's nothing wrong with my sodding brakes,' snapped Earl. 'I could stop on a sixpence. You must have bleedin' straw for brains . . .'

'Dung,' corrected Puck. 'Raw dung.'

'You mean,' said the despairing Sid, 'your brakes are all right?'

'They stopped me, didn't they? Otherwise I would have gone into the back of your bus, you maniac. I've never seen such a crazy bastard on the road and I was a Hell's Angel for five years. Don't you know I've got a five-year-old kid in the bus back there? You like to bust up kids, do you?'

'No,' cried Sid, feeling very hurt. 'No – course not.'

He was a hero and he was being treated like a fool. It wasn't fair. He had risked his life and the lives of others to save Earl from certain death. He had taken a calculated risk, coolly and with supreme judgement, and had triumphed over terrible odds. It was *Earl* who had been the fool, not taking notice of his flashing signals, his warning horn, and failing to pull over and let him pass. Sid knew for certain that the Blessing bus would be a horrible wreck if it had not been for his foresight and skilful driving. There was something topsy-turvy about all this. He had prevented a terrible accident: a bloody scene. He wanted recognition.

Sid turned to Puck and the other fairies.

'Tell him,' pleaded Sid. 'Tell him about the crash.'

Puck's face was a picture of surprise and innocence.

'Crash?' said Puck. 'What crash?'

'Ahhhhhrrrggg!' cried Sid, pounding the wheel in frustration.

The other vehicles in the convoy had caught up now. The barrier had gone up and the road invited them to partake of its way ahead. Someone was yelling at Earl to get on the move again. A lorry driver was sounding his horn and flashing his lights with great impatience.

Earl said, 'You better let somebody else drive, mate – you're in no fit state,' and walked away.

Sid was trembling when he stood up and let Titania take the wheel again, but he quickly recovered and rounded on Puck.

'You said their brakes would fail,' he remonstrated.

Puck nodded. 'That's right, they would have done.'

Sid frowned. 'But they *didn't*.'

'That's right, they didn't, but they would have, and they will, once their bus reaches this spot where our bus is standing right at this very moment.'

This sounded like gobbledegook from Puck at first, but gradually the sense of it dawned on Sid.

'You mean, if I hadn't overtaken them, their brakes would have failed just here, before the gates.'

'That's right,' said Puck. 'That's what I said.'

Sid frowned again. 'But they'll pass over this spot in a few minutes, when we pull away.'

'That's right,' yawned Puck. 'That's when their brakes will fail.'

Sid's eyes opened wide. 'Why didn't you tell me this before?' he said. Titania was just pulling away, driving over

130

the level crossing. Sid told her to stop just over a bus length on the other side. When she did so, he jumped out and went to the driver's window to speak to Earl.

'Pull forward a few yards,' said Sid.

Earl raised his eyes to heaven. 'What's going on now? You're bloody bonkers, mate.'

'Just do as you're told,' said Sid, firmly. When he knew he was in the right he could be a very assertive person. 'Drive on a few yards, slowly, and then apply the brakes.'

Earl grunted, but did as he was asked. When he tried the brakes, the pedal suddenly hit the floor, without any effect. Fortunately the bus was going so slowly it just dribbled to a halt. Earl jumped out of the driver's seat and met Sid out on the road. Sid was already under the bus with a small torch he always carried in his overalls.

Earl said testily, 'Well?'

Sid pointed to a patch of shiny liquid under the axle of the bus. 'Hydraulic pipe's cracked – you must have been losing brake fluid for some time now. I – I thought I saw something when you were ahead of us.'

'You saw us losing brake fluid, while we were driving along?' said Earl, incredulously.

'Er – yeah – I noticed it.'

'In the *dark*, while on the move?'

'Well, I've got good eyesight,' muttered Sid.

'You must have flaming X-ray vision,' Earl said. 'You must be bloody Superman.'

They were joined by the curious drivers of the other vehicles now. Tom Blessing came out of the bus to inspect the problem. Fortunately, because of their way of life, there were those who carried spares of almost every description. The vehicles were driven onto the grass verge, to allow other traffic to go past, and Sid changed

131

the broken pipe. Then he drained the braking system completely, before replacing the brake fluid. Soon they were ready to go on the road again.

'I suppose you want me to thank you,' said Earl.

'You don't have to do that,' Sid replied, wearily. 'It's my job – or used to be.'

Earl nodded but grasped his hand. 'Well, anyway, thanks.'

Sid grinned. 'Coming from an ex-Hell's Angel, that's a compliment.'

'You can bet your life on it,' Earl replied.

Before the mechanic walked away, Tom came up to Sid and said, 'You did well there. We owe you our lives. We might have been on the tracks when that train came through.'

'Oh, I think that's a bit dramatic,' said Sid, modestly.

'Yes, I suppose it is,' agreed Tom, infuriatingly, 'but you have to imagine the worst scenario.'

Sid sighed. 'We'd better get back on the road – time's a-wasting.'

With that the hero of the hour walked back to where the fairies were impatiently waiting for him.

THIRTEEN

Shrubby Hawkweed, Spotted Cat's Ear Open

THE CONVOY REACHED THE STANDING STONES AT Avebury sometime after the dawn. The buses drew up in a scattered formation on a piece of common land near to the stones. A gentle mist was weaving over the hillocks where the darkness had lifted earlier, leaving a burnished-bronze light reigning over the landscape. Sheep grazed in the morning's splendour.

It was a hallowed morning, this midsummer's day, full of meaning, rich with signs of God even in this pagan place.

Aromatic wild flowers and herbs perfumed the surrounding countryside: here the wild arum tasting of sacred blood, over there lavender scented with holy garments, near at hand clary sage watching over the world of the quick, in the copse the holly leaf bearing the imprint of the Madonna's grasp, and Mary's milk thistle rustling in the cool shadow of a bank.

Dogwood shrubs proliferated around the ditches and hedges, forbidden ever to become trees, but still struggling towards that end, while the aspen trembled in the morning's breeze, remembering its heresy.

Oberon stepped from the bus into this morning and felt the warmth of the sun, saw the sparkling dew bending the tips of the grasses and heard the songs of the birds.

'This is indeed a day in which nature overflows,' he murmured to himself. 'I shall drink this morning to the full, knowing we are soon to be in our new home.'

The New Age travellers were emerging from their vehicles, also awed by the mystical scene which confronted them. They rubbed the sleep from their eyes and stared around them, at the rugged stones, at the perfect dome of Silbury Hill, at the peaceful grazing sheep, at the soft light falling obliquely through the trees, and they each knew why they had chosen a life on the road, a life which offered them the outdoors.

Mary Blessing walked over to King Oberon and spoke to him.

'This is a special place to us travellers,' she said.

Oberon nodded. 'To us fairies too. This is part of the magical landscape. A place older even than ourselves.'

Mary looked at Oberon strangely and said, 'You really *are* fairies?'

'I have no need to lie,' said the fairy king. 'However, I tell you this on trust, for there are those amongst mortals who would try to exploit us.'

'You're afraid of that?'

'I'm afraid for *them*,' Oberon explained. 'I have no

134

strong wish to harm a mortal, but of course if our liberty is threatened, I would have to do so.'

'The travellers won't tell anyone,' promised Mary. 'They have sympathy for people like you.'

'This is true,' Oberon said, 'for if you tried to speak of us, your tongues would knot in your mouths rendering you speechless.'

Mary did not answer this threat, knowing that anything she said would be superfluous. She stood with Oberon a little longer, imbibing the delicate scents, sounds and sights of the new day, allowing its gentle hues to wash through her mind. Then she found she had a question to ask.

'I thought fairies were docile and meek creatures,' she said. 'I thought you were fragile and feared the clumsiness of human beings.'

'It's true that mortals are clumsy oafs, but we fear them not,' Oberon replied. 'Fairies are not docile and meek – they are savage, uncivilized creatures – Sid has told me this – with no morals, nor any kind of integrity.'

'Perhaps we just don't understand you? Maybe our mind-sets are so different from yours we could never understand you in a million years? After all, fairies are supposed to be a completely different race – an ancient supernatural race – why would we understand beings like yourselves?'

'That is an intelligent answer,' said Oberon, generously.

'But just because we don't understand each other, doesn't mean we can't be friends.'

Oberon shook his head. 'Fairies and humans *can't* be lifelong friends, only casual companions. Our thoughts about the world are too different. You value the metal gold – more important to us, by far, is the gold in the eye of a daisy.'

'But what about *fairy* gold?'

'Fairy gold? You mean our necklaces, bracelets, brooches? These are nothing but trinkets to us. We value them no more than seashells or shiny pebbles. You people however will lie for gold, kill for it, die for it.'

'On the contrary,' argued Mary, 'travellers value more the gold in someone's heart.'

Oberon observed this female through narrowed eyes.

'Are you saying to me that you would walk away from a chest full of treasure?'

Mary said honestly, 'No, I can't say that – but I wouldn't sell my principles for one either.'

Oberon nodded. 'Well said, maid.'

'Money is important to us, I'll give you that, but us travellers don't regard it as highly as some.'

Mary was joined by Earl, leading a young boy of about five by the hand. Mary then took the boy and went off to find water. There was usually a standpipe around a churchyard, for watering the graveyard flowers. It was towards the church this pair headed, leaving Earl standing awkwardly with Oberon, wondering what to say to the squirt.

Titania came out of the bus, her baby in her arms. Mustardseed went off into a spinney, followed by most of the other fairies. Cobweb, that fairy of frailty, scorned the company of his fellows and walked towards Silbury Hill. Puck ran through the standing stones, touching each one, gathering magic into his breast from ancient spirits, turning the spirits into sprites. The travellers lit their gas cookers and the aroma of coffee, tea and toast filled the air around the awakening village.

Tom joined Earl and Oberon.

Oberon said, 'I see Titania over there, sitting on a bank

of grass. A young man like you should be with her, singing madrigals, playing on a dulcimer. Go to, young fellow, grasp your opportunities like nettles for a gentle touch will leave them stinging thy palm.'

'You *want* me to be alone with your wife?' said Tom, astonished and not a little disgusted. 'I will go to her you know, if she wants me.'

'Go to, go to!' cried Oberon, gaily.

Tom said, 'Right, I will, and you've only yourself to blame if something comes of it.'

He left Oberon and Earl together.

As he was leaving, Tom heard Earl say, 'You fed up with your wife, or what?'

Oberon replied, 'My wife is a treasure beyond the imagination of mortals. I adore her.'

Earl said, 'You got a funny way of showing it.'

Tom thought so too, but there was something about Oberon's manner which told him the little man was devious beyond the imagination of mortals. He wondered if he was being used in some way. Not that it mattered, so long as he could look into Titania's eyes once more and receive one of those smiles which made the bones in his legs dissolve.

Titania's bounteous store of smiles opened its doors when she saw him coming.

He said shyly, 'How are you?'

'I am well and happy, and so is my baby.'

Tom frowned and looked worried for a moment. 'I've been meaning to talk to you about that,' he said, looking down at the infant, which appeared to be quite happy. 'I – I heard on the radio that a baby – well, someone's stolen a baby from a village up in the Midlands.'

Titania looked him in the face. Tom could see gold

flecks in her magenta eyes. They dazzled him. Romantic feelings flooded through him. He wanted to hold this young woman the way she held her baby, close to him, treasuring her.

'Yes?' Titania said, daring him to ask the question which was on the tip of his tongue.

Feelings of romance were replaced by feelings of panic.

'Well, nothing really,' he said. 'I just wondered – I mean – can you imagine how the baby's mother feels?'

'Why should I need to?'

'No reason,' he replied, quickly. 'I mean, you love your baby, obviously. How old did you say it was?'

'Just one year today,' murmured Titania, placing kisses on the eyelids of the infant and making it smile. 'Midsummer's day is her birthday. She is Summer's child.'

'A year,' repeated Tom, relieved. 'Well, that's – that's lovely.'

The baby which had been stolen from its nanny, the broadcast had said, was only seven months. Tom thought Titania's child looked older than seven months – much older, in fact. Tom had not had a lot of experience with babies, it was true, but he felt he could tell instinctively if Titania was lying, and her eyes were full of innocence. There was no question about it, this was Titania's child. True, it looked a large infant for such a small woman, but then females of all sizes were perfectly capable of having babies. He didn't like to dwell on the images of women giving birth too much, but it seemed to him that all was in order.

'I hope the mother gets the baby back soon – its name is Louise.'

'This precious little flower of my garden is called Pigwidgeon,' said Titania.

Alarm bells jangled again in Tom's brain.

'Yes, so you said – but – forgive me, why do you keep calling her *Pigwidgeon*? Isn't that what the gypsies call the babies they steal? Or the pixies? I can't remember which – don't they use that word?'

Titania's tinkling laugh filled the morning air like wind chimes in a breeze.

'I call her Pigwidgeon because her face is so beautiful peeking out from her blanket – like a pearl in an oyster.'

Tom said, 'Oh, I see, it's just a term of endearment?'

'Yes,' said Titania, looking into his eyes again, 'my little Pigwidgeon, my cowrie, my pearl – I love her with all my heart, you see, and would not wish her to leave my side for a single moment in the whole of an eternity.'

Maternal instincts were strong in this little lady, thought Tom. She meant every word she said, he could tell that without asking. Woe to the person who ever attempted to steal *her* baby. She would claw the eyes from the thief's head and stamp them into the ground.

'I don't even know *your* name,' said Tom.

'I've told you before, it's Titania.'

Tom laughed, gently. 'Yes – I realize you're a show on the road – but what's your *real* name?'

'That is my real name.'

Tom laughed again. 'All right, you want to stay in role, eh? You actresses! I wish I was more up on my Shakespeare but I'm not I'm afraid. Didn't get a proper education – that is, it wasn't consistent. I changed schools too much. Learned a lot about life, and overseas, but not Shakespeare.'

'But Thomas, you're writing a book. You're just like William Shakespeare. You work the same art.'

Embarrassed, Tom replied, 'Not really – I mean, he's

the bard, and I'm just a hack. I can't do fiction, anyway. Not the right kind of imagination. I write sort of raw non-fiction books, about real life. Actually, I have to confess, this is my first book – the one I'm writing now – about New Age travellers.'

'I'm sure it's quite poetical,' Titania said. 'I believe you have talent, Thomas – a gift.'

He protested, 'Oh, but you haven't read anything I've written yet.'

'It's all in the lines on your face, in your hands, in the way you speak.'

Tom was quite overwhelmed by her faith in his craft, even though he could not bring himself to take her words seriously. He thought she was telling the truth, as she saw it, but he could not believe she had deep enough insight to be able to assess his skills without seeing what he could do.

'Is it? Well, thanks – I hope you're right.'

'Of course I'm right, why would I not be?' she told him, her voice full of confidence.

On the far side of the ring of stones, Oberon was now talking to Earl. They were similar in build, if not in height. The large square Earl was showing the short square fairy king his tattoos. Oberon was clearly interested in the colourful images which included daggers, snakes, dragons, eagles and various banners bearing phrases like DEATH BEFORE DISHONOUR and LOVE WELL, HATE WELL, FEAR NO BASTARD.

'Why do you decorate yourself with these symbols?' asked Oberon. 'Are they for purposes of magic?'

'You kiddin' me?' said Earl. 'Nah, I'm not into the black arts, pal. These are just for show. I had a girlfriend before Mary who was covered in 'em. Funnily enough, Mary's not that keen. She doesn't say nothing, but I know she thinks it. I see her staring at them with a weird look on her face, like she's turning her nose up at 'em.'

'You had another wife, before your present spouse?'

'Mary's not me wife, she's me girlfriend,' corrected Earl. 'We just live together. Yeah, there was this bird before Mary – when I was a Hell's Angel.'

'You are an angel from Hell?' cried Oberon. 'One of the fallen few? Beelzebub, I know thy name!'

Earl frowned, not for the first time losing the drift of this conversation. It was not that Oberon sounded particularly condemning of him. It was just that the little squirt seemed to be grabbing the wrong end of the stick all the time. It was becoming irritating, having to keep explaining the obvious.

'This is nothing to do with Beelzebub whatever – nah, I was in a motorbike gang, you know – a chapter of the Hell's Angels – we used to raise Cain, you know?'

'You brought Cain back to life? You are indeed the Devil incarnate. I fear your magic may be strong.'

'Bloody hell,' muttered Earl, 'why does talking to you make me feel like I've just downed fifteen pints of bitter? Look, all it was – I wore black leathers with HELL'S ANGELS in studs on the back of my jacket. I used to ride a Harley Davidson imported from the States. Me and me mates used to chop a few people now and again for kicks, and we had a few scams going. I wasn't into anything more than demandin' money with menaces though. Fairly tame. Now I can't do nothing – Mary won't stand for it.'

'You are much in love with your Mary,' Oberon said.

'Yeah,' sighed Earl, glancing back at the Blessing bus. 'Shame it's not two-way, if you know what I mean.'

'Ah, your feelings are not requited? I see this in your

face. Yet she is fond of you.'

'Oh yeah, she's fond of me. I mean, we've got a kid – Alex – but if it came to the crunch, she's not that keen on me. I wish she was. I'd give anything.'

Oberon murmured. 'A flower of the bind-around plant has properties which may assist you.'

'Bind-around plant?'

'The periwinkle.'

'Right,' said Earl, having lost his way in the conversation once more. He sighed again. 'If I could only do something useful – if I had some sort of skill – she'd probably think more of me then ...'

The fairy king raised his eyebrows. 'Ah, but you have – I see in you a fine stone mason. It is your vocation, without a doubt. There are many churches which need restoring, even in these ugly times. There are ancient buildings, worked in stone, which have need of such skills. It is an occupation I would recommend to you. You must surely feel at home here, among these rough-hewn stones, products of masons at the beginning of time, when the world was young.'

Earl felt a thrill run through his burly frame. Ever since he'd been a young man he'd been interested in stone carvings, cathedrals, abbeys, priories and castles. He hadn't really known why before today, had been ashamed of his interest which seemed vaguely out of keeping with his position as a biker in a Hell's Angel chapter, and had kept his curiosity suppressed, thinking he would be laughed at by his mates.

He looked around him, at the Avebury stones. Oberon was right: they attracted him with their vibrancy. They had figures inside, waiting to jump out. Earl wanted to go and run his hand over the exterior of the stones, feel their solidity, their cool surfaces. He wanted to study the grain. He wanted to imbibe their mysteries. To touch one at that moment would have been a sensual experience. That was what worried him: that he might be some sort of sexual pervert who got it off in the presence of a lump of rock.

'It concerns you, your love of stone?' commented Oberon. 'Let it not disturb you, for you have it in you to be an artisan, a craftsman of the highest order.'

'I do?' Earl said.

Now that he had time to think about it, he got excited at the idea of wielding a hammer and chisel, cutting stone into shapes. He knew instinctively he'd be good at it. There were images which sprang to mind, which had his hands itching to get hold of some tools: soaring clerestories, high-vaulted ceilings, sweeping arches, flying buttresses! Mary would surely respect a man of craft and vision, if not love him, and indeed Earl knew he would like himself more if he were to perfect the skills of a stone mason.

'There must be night classes,' he said, excited. 'College courses, even? I'll find, next town we go to.'

'You have the sign of the master craftsman in you,' confirmed Oberon. 'Go on, go on.'

'I will,' replied Earl, 'the first opportunity I get. Bloody hell, you actor types are artists, eh – you must know what you're talking about. A stone mason. Shit – that would be something, wouldn't it? Alex would be proud to have a dad who was a stone mason. I could go for that.'

'I'm pleased you have seen your future,' said Oberon. 'Now I must go and find mine.'

With that the fairy king walked back to the bus, to seek Sid and discuss plans for the day with him.

*

The fairies who had gone into the woods were at first intent on imbibing the spirit of the place, soaking up the magic of the stones, drawing to themselves the mystique of the builders of the henge, the enchantment of their shamans. They breathed the air of early hunts during an era when they themselves were believed in and had a voice in the way the world was run. In those times their power had been great, they had been consulted on matters of the natural, they held sway over bog and moor, woodland and wasteland. Large, strong men went in fear of them. Women evoked their blessing for a marriage, a birth, a daughter's future.

Now they were used to captivate the attention of small children and decorate porcelain: they had been so reduced in status as to make them prisoners of the nursery and of gift shops smelling of honey and pot-pourri. No longer allowed in the hearth of the inglenook fireplace, in the recesses of the scullery, in the cobwebbed corners of the coal cupboard, they had been banished to the bottom of the garden, where the compost heap and tangled clumps of weeds were kept, to be out of sight and mind. They were used to delight readers of pop-up annuals, address books and occasional notelets, having been given the gossamer wings of a dragonfly and a flowery, leafy, moth-soft body in the shape of a Hollywood starlet.

Their one sole remaining purpose was to place money under children's pillows in exchange for a tooth, and still most parents failed to entrust them with that task, usurping even this position of employment.

Oberon and Titania's fairies, once inside the trees, shrank to the size they preferred most, and found a flower bell or a soft place under a mushroom, to doze for a while. Though it was light it was not yet their rest time, but the day proper was swiftly coming upon them and they had experienced a tiring journey. They had expected to be in the New Forest before morning, yet here they were in not much more than a spinney and only halfway there, with a bunch of scruffy mortals for company. Still, the oaks and hornbeams made them feel more comfortable by their strong presence, the white poplars feathered the sky over their beds and the elder and alder, the brambles and briars, ran riot around them.

They had not been resting more than a few minutes when they felt a trembling in the earth, and the sound of thunder from the ground.

Mustardseed, ringed by sleeping wood mice, woke with a start and cried, 'What is it?'

Swallowtail, near by, answered, 'It's Gogmagog, I can tell by his tread.'

'Oh, is that all,' sighed Mustardseed, curling up again in the cuckoo-pint. 'I thought it was an earthquake or something.'

In the New Age travellers' encampment the humans were standing with shocked faces, watching the huge giant walk across the countryside, stepping carefully between the roads. Gogmagog was abroad, his massive shoulders blocking half the heavens, his brutish face half-hidden in the clouds. From his great sloping shoulders hung a worn and faded cape, beneath which he wore a linen shirt and cotton breeks. The horny feet were bare and made prints in the earth a yard deep. Every so often a grunt escaped his mouth which spelled, without words, the state of his soul.

Earl, frightened badly for the first time in his life, found Sid in his bus.

'Where's the little bloke?' gasped Earl. 'What the hell's going on?'

Sid, woken from a troubled sleep, glared at Earl, then looked out of the window of the bus at the giant.

'He's asleep somewhere,' he told Earl, grumpily, 'like I want to be.'

'How can you sleep when there's monsters running around the countryside? We'll all be crushed if he comes this way.'

Sid sat up and rubbed his face. 'You won't be crushed – he's stupid, but he's not a savage. He's very careful where he puts his feet, that one.'

'You've seen him before?' cried Earl, surprised.

'No, course not, but they told me he might wake. That's Gogmagog out there. One of the oldest giants in England. He changed into a hill when he couldn't get Granta to fall in love with him. Granta was a fairy. Now can I get some sleep? We've got to be on the road again soon.'

'I think *I'm* asleep – I must be.'

'You're not asleep,' said Sid, with a trace of bitterness in his tone, 'you're just getting a taste of what I've been going through for the last few weeks. The world's going to be topsy-turvy for a while, just until this lot get settled in the New Forest, and we're going to have to put up with whatever gets disturbed in the mean time.'

Earl stared at Gogmagog, who was now standing on the skyline, his hands on his hips, looking into the middle distance. He seemed to be searching for something. There was a glowering look on his face and his bottom lip protruded and hung down like a drooping side of beef.

'He's looking for something?' said Earl. 'What's he looking for?'

'Granta,' replied Sid, 'but he won't find her – she ran off with a wizard about two thousand years ago.'

'Won't he get mad if he doesn't find her?'

Sid shrugged. His knowledge of Gogmagog only went so far. The two men watched as an aircraft went high over the head of the giant, who looked up with an apparent interest.

'It could be a bee or a fly for all he cares,' said Earl.

The giant ambled off in the direction of London, still picking his way carefully among the houses and roads. The strong smell of body odour came wafting over Avebury, engulfing the inhabitants and visitors. Several of the travellers, none too sweet-smelling themselves, held their noses with their forefingers and thumbs.

In the houses, people woke to the sight of New Age travellers parked on their village green for the third year running.

FOURTEEN

*Garden Lettuce, African Marigold Open and Night-flowering
Catch-fly Closes*

HALF-HUMAN PUCK WAS BORN OF A FAIRY FATHER AND A
human mother and had the power to make himself invisible amongst mortals.

His mother had been a milkmaid, but a peasant of such
prettiness she might have been born a princess. Many
peasant girls were pretty in their puberty, but were
overblown or faded by the time they reached nineteen or
twenty, due to the hard life they led scrubbing sculleries
and washing clothes with lye soap, cooking on open
smoky fires, and tending the livestock. Imogen, for that
was the name of Puck's mother, seemed to grow prettier
with her chores.

Buttercups longed to be put under Imogen's delicate
chin and to reflect their bright yellow colour. Violets felt

dowdy when they saw the colour of her eyes. Daisies would have formed chains by themselves, if it meant they could hang in garlands around her slender neck.

There were the sons of gentlemen who stopped their carriages for a glimpse of her crossing a field of wild flowers with her pail in her hand, but they sighed in vain for she would have no more of them than she would farm boys.

There were the daughters of ladies who were green with envy and who would have accepted poverty themselves if it had meant they could adopt the looks of the fair Imogen.

One magical morning Imogen was carrying milk from the house to the village when she was seen in the meadow by a hill fairy called Picantel, who instantly fell in love with her. Picantel changed into a hare and ran between her legs, hoping to catch her attention, but she ignored him. Next he became a bee and flew around her auburn hair, but still she took no notice of him. Finally he flew ahead and took on human form and waited by the stile for her to come upon him.

'Sir,' she said, when she reached the stile, 'you are in my path,' but she blushed pink as she spoke because Picantel had made himself a very handsome youth with curd-coloured skin, long black locks and chestnut-brown eyes. Moreover he affected a manner that was listless and poet-ical, designed to attract females of a romantic nature. His white lace shirt hung open to the waist revealing a smooth bare chest and his trews were tight going down into polished leather boots. His long slender fingers played with a lock of his hair as he stepped aside for this trembling maiden of the vales.

'Please, sir, do not look at me in such a manner,' she

murmured as she brushed close to him. 'I am a virtuous maid and unused to the probing eyes of young men.'

'I want nothing but to worship thee,' sighed Picantel. 'Thou art the most beautiful maid I have ever laid eyes upon.'

'I am *not*,' she replied, with a lowered head, 'am I?'

He took her hand and she went off into the woods with him, emerging much later in the day. The milk in the pail had gone: they had drunk that when thirsty. They had eaten nuts and berries, popping them into each other's mouths. They had lain upon the star moss, under the lacework of the leafy trees, and had made love in the way that only a fairy and a remarkable milkmaid can make love, mingling such passion and gentleness as to startle the heart of the ancient woodlands, which felt it had seen every kind of love in its time.

At the end of the day Imogen bid her lover goodbye and when Picantel asked when he would see her again, she replied, 'Never – I have no further wish to consort with you. Now I shall have a child, one I have no need to share with a man, for my baby will be mine alone to love.'

Picantel was angry with Imogen.

'Thou hast used me,' he said, 'to reach thine own ends.'

'Men have been using women since the beginning of life,' replied Imogen, 'and perhaps even before that. They have picked virgins like bloom-dusty plums and have taken their bite before throwing them away. Now a virgin has taken what she wishes before casting aside the user.'

'I'm no man,' said Picantel, throwing off his disguise and returning to his fairy form, 'I'm a creature of the woodland, moor and hill.'

Imogen laughed. 'You were man enough to want to take your pleasure with me – now be man enough to walk away having gained what you set out to obtain.'

'I want more,' cried Picantel, stamping his foot. 'I want thy love and soul too.'

'Well you can't have them,' replied Imogen, simply. 'They are not for the likes of those who wait by stiles to take their pleasure. My love is for the man who is prepared to share more than an afternoon amongst the bluebells. My soul remains my own, for ever and always.'

With that she walked away, swinging her pail.

'Thou wilt have a child,' he cried after her, 'and no man shall want you after that!'

'More fool him,' retorted Imogen.

And so Imogen had a very special child, one that no other human mother could call her own, a half-fairy boy. That boy she called Robin Goodfellow and he remained her faithful and good companion until she died, old in years but not in looks, many years later. When she had gone, Robin Goodfellow went into the forest and joined Oberon's fairies, becoming the mischievous Puck, who went back into people's houses – houses that did not disgust him with their smells like they upset other fairies, since he had lived in one for the length of a whole mortal life, and played his tricks.

Able to make himself invisible, Puck created havoc in kitchen, bedroom and sometimes even in the parlour, delighting in the chaos.

Now Puck was very useful to the fairy king, being part-human and part-sprite. Oberon had used Puck to capture the indomitable Sid. During the journey south Puck felt it was his duty to watch over the unworldly fairy band, to prevent them from falling into harm. Thus far things were going more or less to plan, given that any such fairy venture into the world of mortals would be bound to have some set-backs, especially those of a delaying nature. Fairies had little sense of time in any case, and they certainly could not follow a given plan or scheme, even if they had proposed it themselves.

The one fairy Puck was especially concerned about was Cobweb, who had gone off by himself after the bus had stopped, seemingly to sulk.

Puck had among his other skills that of pathfinding. He was an excellent scout and a brilliant tracker. Not a bent blade of grass escaped his notice, nor the dust from a moth's wing failed to fall under his attention. He knew the personal scents of every living thing, and many dead things too.

Puck was concerned for Cobweb, who seemed to have got himself into one of those none-too-rare petty moods which caused fairies to rebel.

'I'll see where he is,' murmured Puck to himself. 'He's probably hiding in some wild flower patch hoping someone will come and look for him.'

On a green field behind the Avebury Circle some of the travellers were preparing to remain for a while. A few began raising teepees and benders (a kind of tent made with flexible poles and polythene), while others hauled tarpaulin sheets – 'tarps' as they were known – over flat-backed lorries or used them to extend the backs of trucks.

One or two had real motor caravans and trailers.

In the light of the early morning there were already engine parts scattered on the grass, as the travellers tinkered with their vehicles, many of the parts handmade or modified from mechanical devices nothing to do with road transport. Dogs raced around the field, making it their own. Grubby children played amongst themselves, squealing and running with the dogs.

Puck followed the trail left by Cobweb and found it heading towards Silbury Hill.

Over fields and through hedges, Puck went towards the famous artificial hill where some believed King Sel of the Celts to be buried. When he reached the smooth half-egg hill he searched around the outside for traces of Cobweb, finding not only the fairy's scent, but a foul odour he knew he should recognize but failed to recall. The strange smell aroused primitive fears in Puck, a fairy not used to feeling frightened by anything the world had to offer.

Puck recoiled from the odour, his tiny heart beating fast. He had found the spot where Cobweb had entered Silbury Hill, down a rabbit hole, but that other smell, from some creature Puck had no wish to encounter, was present too. He did not know what to do. He could fetch Oberon and ask his advice, but Oberon was none too pleased with Cobweb at that time and he might well dismiss Puck's fears with an angry wave of his hand. Titania was too wrapped up in her infant girl to concern herself with the missing fairy. Puck realized it was up to him to act on his discovery.

The mischievous sourer of milk and butter, the trickster of the Sherwood fairies, was not one to shirk his duty, and finally he gathered his courage together and made himself small enough to enter the rabbit hole. Along the dark passage he went, winding his way towards the centre of Silbury Hill. The walls of the tunnel were rank with a damp soil odour and rabbit-scent, as well as the other two smells.

Puck, whose sight was good enough to see dimly in the pitch darkness, came upon the body of a rabbit. Although still warm the animal was stone-dead, its mouth open and its eyes glazed. On its face was the sort of expression it might have worn had it encountered a weasel or a stoat in its bed-chamber. Something had scared the creature to death. Once more Puck felt the flutterings of panic in his now tiny breast, but he conquered these feelings and continued along the widening passage until he entered the open recesses of the tomb of King Sel of the Celts.

Here Puck was able to return to his normal size, something he did immediately since outside his woodland home magic was not as easily available to him and was stressful to use.

The tomb added many more smells to those already gathered, including the deep fetid odour that belongs within the trapped air of graves. Had he been wholly human, Puck might have gagged and been sick there and then, but the fairy half of him kept these unwanted motions in check.

He stared around him at stone walls, crawling with half-blind insects, and realized he was in a maze. The path which led to the heart of the hill would have to be found by instinct, but Puck was probably the best maze-solver that had ever lived and he set about the task immediately.

As he neared the centre of the tomb the horrible feeling that he was about to encounter a monster filled Puck with a sense of dread. Still the brave Robin Goodfellow continued in his quest to find Cobweb and finally, after three more turns, he heard the hollow, echoing groans of his lost fairy companion.

Puck then stepped into the centre chamber.

In the middle of the vast high-vaulted catacombs he sensed the presence of two live creatures. Light and air, though in very small proportions, were entering through two narrow vents in the ceiling. Puck's eyes scanned the great inner-chamber, which seemed larger than the external proportions of the hill itself, finding first the husk of the great king himself, lying on a stone altar in the centre of the chamber, then noticing a movement in the hard shadows at the back of the hall, where darkness mated with earth and stone.

Puck took an involuntary step backwards as he saw what was going on at the far side of King Sel's last resting place. A gigantic spider, as large as any human, was binding a creature, whom Puck knew to be Cobweb, with thick silken cords. Cobweb was aptly mummified in the giant spider's nets, unable to move except to roll his eyes and moan through a permanently open mouth. On noticing Puck, the spider paused in its ghastly operations, and regarded the intruder balefully.

'Help me, Puck!' cried Cobweb, plaintively. 'Help me, please!'

Effectively bound, Cobweb was a prisoner of the huge spider, which now stepped away from him and resumed the form of the creature who had lured the fairy into the tomb.

'Morgan-le-Fay,' murmured Puck. 'I thought you were dead and gone to dust.'

The Morning-Fairy smiled. 'Asleep and buried, but not as lifeless as dirt, and hence awakened again by you fairies – the fault is yours. If you had not left the forest and disturbed the supernatural balance of the world, I should still be under that ditch where Merlin had me interred.'

Puck nodded, still keeping his distance, wary of any encounter with this foul sorceress.

'What are you doing with Cobweb?' he asked.

'This?' Morgan-le-Fay poked the mummified Cobweb with her toe. 'This creature came to me asking for power to help him defeat King Oberon. This is a traitor.'

'I asked you what you were doing with him. Why have you bound him like that?'

The Morning-Fairy turned her pale countenance on Puck and he saw the deep hatred in her eyes.

'This world you have woken me to is an ugly place, full of machines and the stench of too many humans. Wotan the Hunter carried me through night on his great horse and I have seen sights that sicken my stomach. This is not a world I wish to live in. It has been corrupted by black tarmac, by oil, by electricity and gas. Things move too fast across the landscape, there is urgency in every breath today's mortals take – they have no time to stand and stare, they are self-seeking, they cover the land with rubbish . . .'

'Not all of them,' defended Puck. 'There are still good mortals out there, who care about the world.'

'Not enough for me,' growled Morgan-le-Fay. 'And there are a few who hold awesome power in their hands – a power called nuclear fission – with which they will one day blow this planet to pieces like a rotten apple and thus creation will all have been for nothing.'

'They have had that power for some time,' agreed Puck, 'but still have not completely *destroyed* the Earth. They are learning with each new day that such a force, wrongly used, will rob their children of their heritage. It's true they despoil the planet, cutting down trees for selfish ends, fouling rivers and seas, destroying the protective veils that circle the earth, dumping inorganic waste in the soil, filling the air with noxious fumes – but they are at last recognizing their faults. They can change – some have already changed – and the world will flower again.'

The Morning-Fairy sneered. 'You are as naive as you always were, Robin Goodfellow. Mortals don't change, except for the worse. This planet is on a downward spiral into the pit of despair, and I plan to stop that plunge.

'I, Morgana, shall return the world to the time of Avalon – Arthurian times – except there will be no Arthur. I shall rule in his stead and never shall I allow the land to fall back into the ruinous hands of mortals. There will be no so-called "progress" into the time of science and technology. Magic will reign for ever supreme.

'The age of machines and devices will not even be a dream, for the age of machines will never arrive – Leonardo da Vinci and his occidental kind, would-be engineers and architects of the Orient – their work will be smothered, buried, forgotten, before it has even started. Man will never set foot on and defile the moon. This I promise you, Robin Goodfellow, as sure as I stand here. Magic, magic, magic, all will be magic – and the fairies will bloom again.'

She seemed so confident that Puck was inclined to believe her, even though deceit was second nature to all fairies. And the world she painted for him was an attractive one. It seemed to him a reasonable course of action, given that the scheme would work, for who among the fairies would not wish a return to the magical times of Avalon? Yet a world ruled by Morgan-le-Fay? Would that be better than the world they had now? Puck was not so sure about that.

'I repeat, why have you bound Cobweb? Why do you hold my friend captive, Morning-Fairy?'

Morgan-le-Fay's eyes narrowed as she stared down at the pathetic, terrified face of Cobweb who had remained wisely calm and quiet during the exchanges between his captor and his friend Puck, obviously hoping for rescue.

The Morning-Fairy then lifted her head and regarded Puck, as silently as she had studied Cobweb.

She was tall for a sorceress, some six feet in height, and of snake-like leanness. Her hair resembled that of magenta-eyed Titania, being similarly wild, but having tangles thick enough for rooks to nest in. It was as red as a rusting sun. Her corpse-coloured face was of course beautiful, but owning a sharp loveliness that could cut through ice. Her startling eyes, with their wan pupils, were cold with lack of compassion and Puck felt uncomfortable under their terrible gaze.

Morgana finally spoke. 'The baby', she said, 'stolen by Titania must be given to me. Today is midsummer, the most auspicious time of the year for spells. At noon when the light of the overhead sun is on my breast I shall sacrifice the infant on the Slaughter Stone at Stonehenge to create such powerful magic as the world has not seen since the times of Merlin.'

Puck gasped. 'You would murder a child?'

Morgan-le-Fay smiled. 'I have killed many infants in my time and still I have not reached such numbers as can be claimed by men and angels. There was Herod, Attila, the Angel of Death, and many, many others. I shall slaughter this babe without a qualm, without a pinprick.'

'But why this particular child? Just to spite Titania?'

'Of course not, you stupid fellow,' snarled the Morning-Fairy. 'Have you not looked into the face of the youngling? Have you not seen what is in her eyes, in her smile, in her countenance?'

Puck shrugged, a little bewildered. 'I've looked – but not closely. She seemed an ordinary infant to me.'

'Titania knew the child for what it was, just as I have recognized it with my far-seeing eyes. This is the progeny of Guinevere's offspring – the descendant of Arthur's queen – a *magical* child, a powerful lifeforce. Guinevere had a son who was unknown to the world, but not to me, nor to Mordred, who went to his grave with the secret untold.'

'Guinevere had a son by Mordred?' cried Puck. 'I don't believe this tale.'

'Not by Mordred, you fool – by Lancelot, of course – an illegitimate child born in the nunnery at Almsebury. This baby which Titania calls Pigwidgeon is a descendant of that bastard boy born to Guinevere. There is such magic in its soul as to shake the foundations of the universe – in the right hands.'

Puck knew now what the Morning-Fairy was planning to do with her captive, Cobweb.

'You want to exchange Cobweb for the baby?'

'I can't go out there and tackle the whole fairy kingdom, especially Oberon, so I've taken a hostage. You can have this excuse for a fairy back when the baby is in my hands. It has to be before noon, or Cobweb will be cut into little pieces and fed to the hawks.'

Puck stared at Cobweb, whose eyes had gone big and round.

'Cobweb has magic too,' murmured Puck.

'I've taken care of that,' laughed Morgan-le-Fay. 'He tried to shrink himself to the size of a mouse when I chased him, but I turned myself into an owl and caught him easily. Now I've stripped him of any magic he might have had – pared him to the bone. He will not escape.'

Puck, enraged by the audacity of the Morning-Fairy, foolishly rushed forward to do battle with the powerful sorceress, crying, 'Titania will never relinquish her baby – she loves it too much.'

'Titania loves only herself,' snarled Morgan-le-Fay, 'and you might need to be taught a lesson, Robin Goodfellow.'

She caught the indomitable Puck with her right hand and prepared to slash across his eyes with the wicked nails of her left.

'An eyeless Puck can speak as well as one who can see,' she laughed.

At that moment a winged, hooked and clawed shape flew between the Morning-Fairy's descending hand and Puck's eyes, parrying the blow. Morgan-le-Fay gave a startled cry and let go of the struggling Puck, allowing him to race into the maze. The wide-eyed phantom which had attacked the sorceress then flashed up one of the air shafts, out of range of her wrath.

Puck fairly flew down the passages which led to the rabbit hole and the safety of the outside world. In this place of death and darkness he was entirely vulnerable to Morgana's magic, but once in the open air, with the birds, flowers, woods and herbs at his disposal, he could at least put up a decent fight against the daughter of Queen Igrayne. He knew she would not dare follow him, lest he summon the other Sherwood fairies, thus outnumbering her.

He found the earthen burrow and fled along it until he reached the sweetness of fresh air.

As he raced across the field, towards the site where the travellers had settled, he realized Titania's owl was at his shoulder, flying alongside him. It was she who had intervened between himself and the sorceress, saving him from blindness.

'My grateful thanks, owl,' gasped Puck, still running

hard. 'I am in your debt.'

The owl made no reply, nor indeed even turned her head, but Puck knew she had heard him.

When Puck reached the travellers' encampment he went immediately to Oberon and told him what had occurred.

'Kidnapped Cobweb?' cried the king. 'We must go to his rescue.'

Peaseblossom, Mist, Moth, and all the other fairies were roused from their beds. The travellers, when they saw the activity, asked what was the matter. Puck wisely refrained from telling them that the kidnapper was the sorceress Morgan-le-Fay but said one of their number had been kidnapped by a woman down by Silbury Hill.

'Bet the police have something to do with it,' said Jug, one of the travellers. 'They'd do anythin' to stop us reaching Stonehenge for the festival.'

The fairies said they could handle it and went off over the fields at an astonishing speed which left some of the travellers with raised eyebrows.

When the fairies reached Silbury Hill, Oberon immediately made himself small and went inside. The others ringed the hill in case Morgana should try to escape. However, a little later Oberon reappeared to say the tomb inside was empty: Morgan-le-Fay had fled taking Cobweb with her. The fairies returned to the site in a dejected mood.

'You lot should be in the Olympics,' said Jug as they slunk past him. 'I never seen anyone run like that before.'

The fairies gathered in their bus to discuss the crisis.

Oberon said, 'Tell me, Puck, exactly what does the sorceress require in exchange for Cobweb?'

Titania was nursing the baby and Puck pointed

dramatically towards the sleeping infant.

'Pigwidgeon!' he said. 'The Morning-Fairy wishes to sacrifice the child on the Slaughter Stone at noon.'

Titania gave a cry and held the baby closer to her breast.

'Take my baby? Never!'

'Why does she wish to do this?' asked King Oberon. 'Is it for some powerful magic?'

Puck nodded. 'To return us to the time of Avalon, except that she says she will rule the kingdom, with Mordred at her side, instead of Arthur.'

Peaseblossom remarked, 'The world *was* a better place then – for fairies at least.'

There was a murmuring amongst the others. Mustardseed and Blewit nodded to each other. Swallowtail, Mist and Moth each gave out separate little sighs. Other fairies shuffled and looked out of the windows at the clear blue skies. Oberon stared first at the baby, then at Titania.

'No!' said Titania, firmly. 'No witch of the morning is going to slaughter Pigwidgeon. She is mine.'

'This is a moot point, my dear Titania,' said Oberon. 'Is the baby yours?'

'It's mine now.'

Oberon said dreamily, 'Think of it! A return to olden times – knights, chargers, castles, acres and acres of woodland and forest, kings and queens, magicians, dragons and monsters, a multitude of fairies, elves, goblins, pixies – it seems to me it would be beautiful.'

Titania's position in the affair kept her sober. She was as much given to fancy as any fairy, under normal conditions, but she had the baby in her arms. She could feel the warmth of it through her leafy dress; she could feel it

162

breathing softly, its rosebud mouth partly open, its petal eyelids closed; she could see the glow of its innocence.

Titania knew that the other fairies longed with all their hearts to be returned to Arthurian England, a feeling so strong it hurt them. They did not belong in the modern world, they were rejected here, forgotten by all except children under six years of age. They had been reduced to a joke, a nursery jingle, a pantomime character. Once they had been taken seriously, were a strong force in the land, and the world had been all woodlands, meadows and rushy streams.

Yet she also knew they were simply dreaming, for even Oberon, the most hardened of all the fairies when it came to dealing with mortals, could not allow the slaughter of an innocent babe to take place.

'You cannot kill the child,' she said to Oberon, 'and I only tell you what you know you feel.'

Oberon snapped out of his reverie and sighed.

'Titania is right. The sum is too huge. The life of that cherry-cheeked child is priceless. Shake any thoughts of returning to Avalon from your heads, my fairy people, for we cannot take my queen's infant.'

Puck said, 'And what of Cobweb? *She* will surely destroy him as she promised.'

'We must do what we can to obtain the release of Cobweb,' agreed Oberon, 'but we cannot contemplate the exchange. We must go to Stonehenge and try to rescue him.'

The fairies all mumured in agreement.

Sid was woken and told of developments. He was told he would be driving the bus in future, since Titania was going to guard the baby every second that passed. Sid told Oberon it would be best if they waited until those travellers who were going on to the Stonehenge festival were ready to move and join forces with them.

'The police will be all over the place,' he said. 'They always are at the midsummer festival. They'll be blocking the roads, trying to keep the travellers out. We've got to remember that Titania stole that baby – the law will mainly be trying to keep the peace and arresting travellers, but they're also looking for the kidnappers of that kid, which is *us*.'

'A point well put, Sid,' Puck said. 'We mingle with the crowds and go unnoticed.'

'Hopefully – that's the plan, anyway,' replied Sid.

On the site outside the travellers had really begun to settle in. Jug had put up his teepee near to the fairies' bus. Jug was a young man, as most of the men were, who said he survived by finding junk and scrap metal and selling it on. 'I get broken TVs and strip 'em down,' he told an interested Sid. 'You can find all sorts of scrap around garages, like old exhaust pipes, and fridges and stuff on dumps. Some people even chuck it away by the roadside. I was always finding bedsteads in ditches. I used to have a flat-bed lorry, but I had to sell that and got the van instead. You can't sleep comfortable in a van, so I made the teepee.'

'But what if you can't find any scrap metal to sell?' asked Sid.

Jug shrugged. 'Do a bit of poaching, pinch a few carrots out of a farmer's field. Nothin' serious, just enough to get by, you know. I got a propane gas cooker I found on a dump – it works OK. You got to use propane 'cause butane freezes sometimes in the winter, when the temperature gets too low.'

'It sounds a hard life to me,' said Sid, looking at the

moth-eaten blankets Jug was carrying into his teepee. 'You must get bloody cold in the winter.'

'Freeze me bollocks off,' grinned Jug, 'but it's better than living in some town or city flat, where the damp's peeling the wallpaper off the wall, and the stink of wet rot's in the air all the time.'

'I dunno,' Sid said, shaking his head. 'You must get sick of mud. Everywhere you look there's mud.'

'Get used to it in the end. Kind of get to live with it. Mud's not dirt, you know. It's mostly clean stuff, like clay and soil. Dirt's different. Dirt is grease and muck you get on a kitchen oven, or the grime you get under your fingernails. Mud's pretty clean stuff, if you're talking about germs and such.'

'But you've always got to contend with the law – don't you get hassled so much you can't stand it?' asked Sid.

Jug nodded. 'The law's not the worst of it. Some of the cops and the council workers are almost human. It's landowners that give us the most trouble. I've been beaten up three times by landowners' lackeys. They seem to enjoy it. You get some lord or other who pinched his land off peasants like you and me, and he thinks he's got a God-given right to it. Honest, they think God gave it to them because they deserve it or something.

'Other blokes, people who came up from nothing, aren't so bad. I once camped on a pop star's lawn and he came out and gave me some cold chicken. Said I could stay there a week, but no more. Well, you got to honour a thing like that,' said Jug. 'So I left at the stipulated time. Another time I was on land belonging to this heavyweight boxer who made a mint with his mitts. Said I didn't have to move right away, but he'd come back in three days' time. I can tell you, looking at that bloke's hands – they was massive – I had the teepee packed and in the van, and was on the road again in two days. He didn't threaten me with words, but you could see by his eyes he was serious about me movin' on.'

'You going to the festival?' asked Sid.

'You bet – there'll be some groups there – the Chumbawumba, Ozric Tentacles, Back to the Planet. Should be good fun. I'll leave the teepee up here, 'cause we're bound to be chased off the site at Stonehenge. Not everyone will be going, so those that stay will watch the gear.'

When Sid had finished his conversation with Jug he was even more convinced he did not want to be a traveller. It was a hard life and authorities and householders all over the country hated your guts. You froze in the winter, got chased from pillar to post in the summer, and you stayed poor. It was not the sort of life Sid, who enjoyed a warm garage and a steady job, would have wished on his worst enemy.

FIFTEEN

*Scarlet Pimpernel, Mouse-ear Hawkweed, Proliferous Pink Open,
Evening Primrose Closes*

THE AVEBURY CIRCLE OF ANCIENT SARSEN STONES, dragged across the fields in neolithic times, stood like solid sentries guarding some unseen secret in their centre. They were of foreign material, Marlborough Downs' sandstone, and some of the old gentlemen weighed more than fifty tons.

Standing proud from the chalky soil, the most interesting part about them was the bits which nobody knew: why they were there standing upright in orderly circles and lines, and who put them there. Had these hidden facts been general knowledge, they would probably be regarded as commonplace and boring. After all, they were just chunks of rock arranged in simple geometric figures.

'A giant must have carried them,' said Puck. 'Probably Gogmagog or some such. He was probably trying to build a hearth for his fire. Nothing more mysterious than that, I'll warrant.'

Sid, who had seen Gogmagog that very morning, did not dispute Puck's theory. Six weeks previously, if you had asked Sid whether he believed in fairies and giants he would have laughed in your face. Now he was a sadder and wiser man, knowing that there was much which lay dormant in the world, but that did not mean it didn't exist.

They were due to be on the road in half an hour and Sid had warmed-up the bus engine, ready for the off. However, some figures had come onto the green from a nearby inn. They were one of those amateur acting groups which came out of the woodwork every midsummer to perform in the open air. There was only one play which would successfully pull in audiences at this particular time of year and this group were preparing to rehearse that very drama.

The posters around the village proclaimed that the actual performance would take place at three o'clock in the afternoon on the green outside the inn.

The fairies decided to watch this rehearsal of *A Midsummer-Night's Dream* by one William Shakespeare.

'That's the one with us in it, isn't it?' remarked Oberon, with a frown on his face. 'I should like to see the actor who's playing *me*. I hope he's handsome and stately, and suitably rakish. In fact I think I'll go over there and speak with him – he might need a few pointers on what it's like to be the *real* fairy king.'

Sid said, 'Er – I don't think they'll take kindly to people in the audience telling them what to do.'

'Nonsense,' replied Oberon. 'They'll never have another opportunity like it.'

Oberon strode off with all the other fairies, over to where travellers were sitting on the grass, watching the rehearsal go through its paces. To the travellers it was free entertainment. Tom was there and he waved to Titania to come and sit beside him.

'Isn't this the play you lot are doing?' he said.

'We're not doing any play,' replied Titania, 'but this should be fun to watch. It may seem incredible to you, Tom, but we have never seen Mr Shakespeare's work. This is our first time out of Sherwood. We know the play well of course – the birds tell us all – but never have we seen a performance with real mortals playing our parts . . .'

Tom was hardly listening at that point because a scene had begun. He shushed her gently as her namesake, a young woman in a white tinselled dress wearing a diadem of ox-eye daisies, was about to be confronted by a rather chubby but personable youth in a jerkin of brown suede leather and a hat with a peacock's feather forming an arch over his head.

'Ill met by moonlight, proud Titania,' piped the youth.

'What, jealous Oberon!' squeaked the girl. 'Fairies, skip hence – I have forsworn his bed and company.'

There was an immediate interruption from the audience. The real Oberon tut-tutted and to Sid's consternation strode out into the middle of the players. He drew himself up to his full height of four-feet, one-inch. Standing off a little way from the girl, he spoke.

'*Ill met by moonlight, proud Titania,*' boomed Oberon, in a majestic and authoritative tone, rolling his eyes and looking incredibly angry.

The girl playing Titania flinched and took a step backward, her cheeks going pale.

'Bert?' whined the fake Oberon.

The youth looked nervously towards a reedy, ragged-moustached man on the edge of the impromptu audience who was obviously the director of this amateur production.

'What the hell do you think you're playing at?' cried the director. 'Who asked you to butt in?'

Puck cried from the audience, 'But he's saying it all wrong. We're just trying to show you how it should be done.'

'And who might *you* be?' squealed the director turning on Puck and clearly getting more frustrated by the second.

Tom shouted, 'They're from the Royal Shakespeare Company – they know what they're talking about.'

'I don't care if they're from the planet Mars,' screeched the director, 'they can just bugger off. This is my production. I say what's what here, not some poncey group of actors from the RSC.'

By this time however, Titania, still holding her baby, had joined Oberon in the midst of the players.

'*I have forsworn his bed and company,*' flung the haughty Titania at Oberon's face and using the word *bed* as if it were some slimy place fit only for slugs and worms.

'*Tarry, rash wanton,*' cried Oberon with immense volume and excess pride ruling his tone. '*Am I not thy lord?*'

The audience clapped wildly and Oberon smiled and gave them a little bow. Around him the players were looking helplessly at one another. Some were as interested in Oberon and Titania as the audience of travellers. The actor playing Oberon looked thoroughly dejected. The

170

actress playing Titania looked annoyed and upset.

'Will you bugger off!' shouted the director. 'Somebody get those sods out of here.'

'Hey,' yelled one of the travellers, 'that's hardly politically correct, is it?'

'We're trying to rehearse a play here,' said the director, almost in tears, taking off his glasses and wiping them on his cravat. 'Please . . .'

Titania turned to the girl who was playing her and said, 'All right, I'll sit down, but make sure you put some venom into your next words – after all, King Oberon has been making love to Phillida and Hippolyta, when he should be back in fairyland with his wife and queen. He's a philanderer and a cheat and he deserves some harsh words.'

'I'll try to remember that,' said the girl evenly, through clenched teeth.

'Quite right,' agreed Oberon. Then to the audience, 'Not that any of it's true of course – I can't even play the pipes of corn, not unless I use magic, which is definitely cheating. You need Peaseblossom if you want sweet music – he is a most excellent player of the pipes.'

Peaseblossom stood up and beamed, before bowing quickly to the crowd and then sitting down again.

Bert, harassed beyond his normal mood of desperation, called for the fake fairies to take the stage.

There were four young women playing the parts of Cobweb, Moth, Peaseblossom and Mustardseed. They were dressed in tight costumes of pastel shades and had little caps like acorn cups on their heads. The one playing Cobweb was small but slim, with shapely legs, and had a very pretty face. She spoke her words clearly and distinctly. She had obviously been taught by her drama coach to stare at one member of the audience while she spoke and the person she chose to look at was Sid. The car mechanic was absolutely entranced by this brave, petite young woman with such mesmerizing eyes.

Every time she spoke her one-word lines, Sid clapped wildly, causing her to smile and blush.

'And I—' said the female Cobweb.

'Oh very good, well done,' called Sid, clapping.

Cobweb smiled and Bert gritted his teeth.

'Hail!' cried Cobweb, a little later.

'Terrific!' called Sid. 'Really good. Excellent.'

Cobweb blushed and smiled again.

Bert said, 'Can we have a little quiet from the watchers please – we are trying to rehearse.'

'I thought the audience was supposed to react,' Tom said. 'I thought that was what the audience was for.'

'You are not an audience,' Bert growled, 'you're a lot of freeloaders getting to watch a rehearsal, which I would appreciate you do in *silence*.'

This speech made no impression on Sid.

When later Cobweb cried, 'Ready', in answer to a question from Bottom, Sid shouted, 'Oh wow, that was great. If I was the director I'd have cast you as Titania – I mean, you're clearly the best actor in the play, isn't she, Tom?'

Tom wasn't given the opportunity to reply.

Bert said, 'Fortunately *I* happen to be the director of this play and not *you*, young man. Kindly take yourself off before I have apoplexy. I can assure you when I have a fit it's not a pretty sight. Now go away or shut up.'

'No need to get huffy,' said Sid, his eyes still on Cobweb. 'It was just a suggestion.'

The young lady smiled again and gave Sid a little wave that made his heart jump like a startled rabbit in his chest.

He was completely smitten. This was a woman for whom he would give up darts and football, probably, if he could get her to go out with him.

Bert's commanding tone took the field again.

'I've had enough of this. Fairies get off the stage – that is, off the grass area designated as the stage. Now, Act One, Scene Two,' cried the director. 'Bottom? Quince? We'll do the fairies later – when we're not being interrupted. I take it we haven't got a bunch of rude mechanicals in the audience, waiting to spring to their feet?'

Oberon and Titania looked around the ring of faces expectantly, wondering if this really was a gathering of Shakespeare's characters, but no-one moved. Titania returned to her place by Tom and Oberon went back to the other fairies. Tom whispered to Titania, 'That was excellent – can't think why that idiot doesn't want a few pointers from you. I would, if I were him. He's a bit stuck up, isn't he? Probably an RSC reject. Got a chip on his shoulder.'

The rehearsal proceeded.

QUINCE: 'Flute, you must take Thisby on you.'
FLUTE: 'What is a Thisby? A wand'ring knight?'
QUINCE: 'It is that lady that Pyramus must love.'
FLUTE: 'Nay, er, faith: let not me play a woman: I have a beard coming.'
QUINCE: 'That's all one: you shall play it in a mask: and you shall speak as small as you will.'
BOTTOM: 'An I may hide my face, let me play Thisby too . . .'

Puck, who loved this part in the play and who had been getting more excited by the minute, could not contain himself any longer. He leapt to his feet and ran in amongst the startled rude mechanicals.

'*I'll speak in a monstrous little voice. "Thisne, Thisne"* – *"Ah, Pyramus, my lover dear, thy Thisbe dear, and lady dear"*.'

When Puck spoke in his 'small voice' he did indeed sound like a mouse squeaking from the hedgerow, yet his voice carried over the whole greensward. The audience clapped wildly. A young would-be actor however came running across and confronted Puck. It being a dress rehearsal the actor was wearing a tattered shift and a cap like a pea pod.

'Look here,' said the actor, whose face had been made-up to look cheeky and mischievous, 'why don't you just clear off? If you want to see the play, come this afternoon, but stop interrupting our rehearsal, or I'll bop you one.'

'Who are you supposed to be?' asked Puck, looking him up and down.

'I'm Puck,' said the youth, 'as you'd find out if you came to the play . . .'

'I'm *Puck*,' replied Puck, 'as you'd find out if you ever came to fairyland.'

'Liar!' snapped the youth. 'I'm Puck – the part was promised me ages ago – and I got it, so there.'

'Want to know how I'm sure I'm Puck?' said Puck.

'How?' sneered the youth.

'Because no self-respecting Robin Goodfellow would wear a silly hat like that!'

The audience roared appreciatively.

The youth went red, snatched off his pea-pod cap and flung it from him. He looked towards the director. 'Bert, honestly! I told you the titfer wouldn't work. Listen to them.'

Bert shrugged his shoulders and rolled his eyes to heaven.

The youth turned again on Puck.

'Look, I mean it, chappie – I'll really have a go at you in a minute. I can be pretty nasty when I lose my temper.'

'Shall I show you what *I'm* like when I lose *my* temper?' replied Puck, ingenuously. 'Watch!'

Puck instantly changed into a six-foot gryphon, with beak and wings, and blood-red eyes. Fire spurted from its nostrils and mouth, singeing the youth's shift. Its tongue lashed out, several yards long, and snatched up the pea-pod cap, delivering it into the mouth behind the monstrous beak. It was instantly spat out again, to land back perfectly on the head of the terrified youth. The gryphon's clawed feet, like those of a gargantuan chicken with hideous talons, stamped in anger as the monster strutted around the hapless actor. Then coming around to the youth's front again, the gryphon flapped its hoary wings, before roaring loudly.

A moment later and the gryphon had changed back into Puck again.

'Now that,' said Puck, 'is *nasty.*'

The youth, the director, the actors and half the audience fled from the scene, leaving a few bug-eyed travellers and Sid and the fairies to hold the green.

'How did he do that?' whispered Tom to Titania, awed. 'How did you do that? Is it an illusion? No wonder you people are from the RSC – that was brilliant. It looked real. Crowd hypnotism, I expect. But brilliant.'

'Yes it was rather, wasn't it?' said Puck immodestly. 'I can be pretty brilliant sometimes.'

'Show-off,' snapped Titania, walking away.

'That was a cheap and easy trick,' snorted Oberon,

striding back towards the bus. 'We were enjoying our-selves, Puck. You always have to spoil things. I shall think of a suitable punishment later.'

'I couldn't think of anything else,' called Puck, clearly deflated by Oberon's reaction. 'Sorry.'

'Hummph,' muttered the King of the Fairies. 'I wanted to get to the bit where I make up with Titania – and we never saw the ass's head. You always spoil things, Puck.'

Tom went to the dejected Puck and put an arm around him.

'Well, if it's worth anything, Puck, I never saw anything like it before in my life.'

Puck breathed deeply.

'Thanks, Tom. I never did anything like it before in my life. Better not do it again, either, or Oberon will put me in a birdcage fashioned from blackberry brambles for a year and feed me stale crumbs.'

Tom shook his head wonderingly. 'You have a funny way of putting things, Puck. I realize Oberon is the leader of your group, but you have a very big part in the play, you know. That means you have a certain amount of power, I would think – who's the producer and director?'

'King Oberon – Oberon is all the things everyone else is not.'

'That's pretty enigmatic,' muttered Tom, taking out a small notebook and pen. 'Do you mind if I put that in my book? I'll acknowledge you, of course – or I would do if you gave me your real name. What *is* your real name?'

'Robin Goodfellow,' said Puck.

Tom laughed and wagged a finger.

'I'm not going to get anywhere with you, am I? Come on, it looks as if we're going back on the road again. Mary's waving to me. Let's get our skates on.'

The fairies piled onto the bus and found their seats, acutely conscious of the fact that one of their number was missing. Sid was upset with Puck for chasing away the actors before he had time to speak to the young woman playing Cobweb, but Sid had long since learned that it was pointless being annoyed with Puck. Puck was as thick-skinned as a rhinoceros and simply shrugged off criticism.

Sid had removed the blocks from the pedals and was soon weaving amongst the other travellers, anxious to join the now smaller convoy heading down the A361 towards Stonehenge. The pull of Savernake Forest, below the River Kennet, came strongly from the east. As they were leaving the field a woman came hurtling out of the inn and began hammering on the side of the bus with the flat of her hand.

Sid stopped and she stepped in front of the bus in a determined manner.

'I want you to know,' she said, shouting furiously, 'that you've ruined the village play. No-one will take part in it now and the Townswomen's Guild is deeply upset. I refuse to move until I get an apology. Oh, if I could just get my hands on one of you . . .'

'Sorry,' said Sid, through the side window. 'OK?'

'Not good enough,' she cried. 'One of those creatures has to come out here.'

'Creatures?' muttered Oberon, raising his eyebrows.

'We've got to do something,' said Sid, to the fairies. 'I can't just drive over her.'

Oberon turned and studied his fairies, then said, 'Mustardseed – this is a job for you, I think?'

Mustardseed was the most bashful of the fairies, but he obediently rose and went to the door of the bus, opening it and stepping down. The woman rushed round and confronted him with her arms crossed under her bosom. She was a formidable female, the kind whose jaw frightens horses at point-to-point races and whose strident tone startles babies.

Now even Pigwidgeon was beginning to winge.

'Well?' she boomed, bearing down on poor Mustardseed.

The sound of her voice panicked not only Pigwidgeon, but also the mice in Mustardseed's pockets. They began swarming out and over his body, running from one safe haven to another, disappearing up trouser legs, down necklines, into shirtsleeves, around lapels. There appeared to be thousands of them and the woman's eyes opened wide. She recoiled violently, which gave Mustardseed the courage to find his voice and make his apologies.

'We're very, very contrite,' said Mustardseed, leaning forward intently. Then overcome by a sudden unusual flush of truthfulness, 'Or would be, if we knew how to be.'

The worst over, he shyly picked a mouse out of his hair and put the end of its tail in his mouth, letting it dangle like a yokel's piece of straw from between his teeth. The mouse swung like a wriggly pendulum before the woman's eyes. She murmured something faintly about Mustardseed being mad, at which point he opened his mouth and let the mouse sky-dive onto the hem of her billowing dress, where it clung.

The woman finally found her full voice and ran off screaming in the direction of the inn, dropping the mouse in her panic and allowing it to rejoin its friends.

Mustardseed said, 'Rude!', calmed his mice and then climbed back into the bus.

'I think you said that very well,' Titania told him. 'I

'couldn't have put it better myself.'

'That's right,' said Mustardseed, feeling pleased with his efforts. 'Nobody could.'

The bus trundled out of the field and onto the road.

At Stonehenge the Most Ancient Order of Druids had kept their usual all-night vigil during the longest day of the year, coming out of the circle of stones in their white robes looking like bleached nuns at sunrise on mid-summer's day.

The police had kept the 'hippies', who flocked around the Bronze Age site where sun-worshipping ceremonies had taken place four thousand years ago, at bay. There were benders, teepees, old buses, flat-topped lorries, vans and various other forms of traveller homes scattered across the surrounding fields. The place looked like a refugee camp for the people of a displaced nation. A 'festival' was in progress, with stalls for every kind of prophet, fortune-teller and alternative science known to the modern world. The atmosphere was blue with incense smoke, the landscape teeming with dogs and children. It was wild and chaotic. It was Stonehenge on midsummer's day.

The Slaughter Stone stood apart and away from the main two rings of sarsen stones but was within the circle formed by the Aubrey holes.

Morgan-le-Fay, disguised as a bent old woman, carried Cobweb on her back bundled up like a pack. He was gagged and bound so tightly he was unable to move. No-one recognized him as a living creature, since no part of his flesh was showing through his binding rags and his head was locked firmly between his bent-double legs, while his arms were wrapped as further bonds around his shins.

179

With her staff to help her hobble along, the Morning-Fairy looked like a hag from a medieval leper colony, out begging for coins. Even the travellers were startled by her appearance and stepped hastily out of her way as she crept between them.

When she reached the outer perimeter, a sentry in blue, seemingly unarmed like the rest of his fellow soldiers, stepped firmly in her way, though he was clearly revolted by her appearance.

'That's far enough, lady. No-one goes onto the site. What are you doing out here anyway? You should be at home. There might be trouble later on.'

'Trouble?' she cackled. '*I'm* trouble.'

The blue sentry seemed prepared to be very patient with her at this stage.

'Look, we're going to have to clear these fields soon and it could get quite nasty. Some of these hippies regard their vehicles as sacred and we have the devil's own job to persuade them to move. A few heads might get cracked. I wouldn't want one of them to be yours.'

'Your mother would have something to say, young man, if you attacked a little old woman.'

Morgan-le-Fay tried to push past the man, who blocked her way with his body.

'Lady, please,' he pleaded, 'don't make me arrest you. You wouldn't like it in the van with a load of smelly hippies. They've got disgusting habits, some of 'em.' A lurcher dog came hell-bent out of the mass of travellers and tried to bite the blue soldier's leg. Morgan-le-Fay whacked it on the rump with her stick, sending it yelping back whence it came.

'There,' she said, 'I helped you – now you have to let me pass, like any chivalrous knight.'

'I don't have to do any such thing. The site is out of bounds to all civilians, now the druids have finished. Come back another day, dear – when this lot have gone. Who brought you anyway?' He craned his neck to look over the heads of the crowd, which he was well able to do, being about six-foot six-inches in height.

'Wotan the Hunter fetched me here,' she said, 'but he has since returned to Wales.'

The sentry peered suspiciously into the Morning-Fairy's strange-looking eyes.

'Hey, are you on something? Maybe we ought to take you in for a bit – for your own protection. Has anyone offered you drugs? Have you taken something from these hippies?'

'No-one has given me anything,' snapped Morgan-le-Fay, becoming annoyed with the obdurate law-keeper. 'I have everything I need on my person.'

'What's in the pack?' asked the sentry. 'I might have to search you if you don't go away.'

'A fairy,' answered Morgan-le-Fay with a smile. 'A captive fairy. I'm going to cut out its heart on the Slaughter Stone if I can't get a baby to take its place. What do you think of that, mortal?'

The man winced. 'Strewth, you're a gruesome old cow. You must be on something. Look, if you're here to earn a bit of dosh telling fortunes or whatever, you'd better go and do it. I'm getting pissed off with you – now haul your bony old backside away to the other side of the field, or I warn you I'll run you in.'

Morgan-le-Fay realized she was not going to get past this particular soldier to reach the Slaughter Stone and rejoined the milling travellers. There seemed to be noise, ordered confusion and activity everywhere. The Morning-

181

Fairy had once visited Ifurin, the Celtic Otherworld, through the doorway of the Green Chapel, and it was not unlike the scene around her now. The same schematic chaos had presented itself to her eyes and ears then and she had quickly retreated back to the real world.

Here she could not escape the cacophony which seemed to come from dull-blue battle horns, placed high up on posts, with wires leading from them. From these flared objects issued sounds like those which came from the bull roarers of wild northern English tribes when they ravaged the south. The peasants who listened and danced to these sounds were not that much different from the serfs Morgana remembered, being similarly grubby and offensively familiar.

'Out of my way, dolt,' she growled at a figure who blocked her way.

'Who are you calling a dolt, you old bag?' retorted the man.

'Yeah,' said a sleazy-looking woman at his side. 'What makes you so special?'

'Turning strumpets like you into frogs,' muttered Morgan-le-Fay, brushing past the pair.

But it wouldn't do to attract attention to herself at this stage. She would settle with this lot once the world was back in time, when she was queen of all England. Then the frog population of the local ponds would increase ten-fold. Then darkness would descend upon the lives of these warty rustics, who would hang in droves from the natural gallows of oaks. Until that time, which was only a few hours hence, she had to suffer their obscene presence in the land.

Morgan-le-Fay was also incensed at the number of machines which littered the fields around the sacred site of Stonehenge: horseless chariots with rusting bodies smelling of oil and spirits. These would satisfyingly be spiralled into the void once the baby's bloody heart was in her hands, dripping red fluids onto the Slaughter Stone. The conical and rounded tents she did not mind. These were familiar and reminded her of a joust.

The litter, though, was not a thing of her time. In her day the peasants wasted nothing, for poverty was such that even if there was waste food it was given to the hogs. Here chunks of bread were thrown to the ground. Meat cakes covered in a substance that looked suspiciously like blood were half-eaten and tossed away. Pale sausages smeared with yellow pus, coloured ice on sticks, frozen white whey skimmed from milk – all these were carried and eaten, some to be discarded only partially devoured, as if the world were a place of plenty and no want existed amongst the poor.

Paper was precious in her day and only used by the monks. Any scrap metal would have been quickly gathered and melted down: refashioned into some useful item like a cooking pot or warrior's mace. Here on this field was a whirlwind of paper, a profusion of abandoned metal objects. This later world was a place of ugliness far worse than the dirt and squalor of the land in which Morgan-le-Fay fell asleep.

The one familiar aspect which Morgana found comforting was that the dogs still shit anywhere and everywhere.

The smell of their dung and urine helped overpower the awful stench of engine oil.

As she wandered amongst the heaving throng, she could not help thinking that King Oberon would surely persuade that sow's orphan Titania to hand over her stolen baby. After all, thought the Morning-Fairy, even Oberon must want to get back to the time of the forests. Looking around her now, Morgana grieved at the bareness of the landscape. England had been stripped clean of woodland and forest. Only a few scrubby spinneys decorated the ridges. She wondered if Scotland and Wales had suffered the same deforestation, and hoped they were still tree-bearing lands.

From a distance came the rumble of thunder.

Surely, thought Morgan-le-Fay, looking up, we're not going to have a storm? The sky was almost cloudless, with a light baby-blue backdrop. Yet the growl of the thunder became louder and louder, until at last a black object flashed across the heavens like a metal dragon at blinding speed. Morgan-le-Fay was stunned. What was this magic? More terrible machines no doubt, but with such power! Perhaps there were still witches and magicians in this new world, with forces at their command which had never been available in the time of hatted and booted cottages with their thatched roofs and sarsen stone foundations?

She shrugged and hoisted her bundle higher onto her shoulder.

These things would pass, very soon now.

The immediate thing now was to find a way to get to the Slaughter Stone and await the coming of Oberon. What she had to do was get these peasants to riot and to overwhelm the soldiers in blue. Then, in the confusion, she could slip through the sentries' ranks and get to the stone.

'Are we going to let the king's lackeys keep us from our rightful ground?' she screeched at the mob around her. 'Let us storm them – they are but few and unarmed, while we are many and have good flints to use as missiles!'

She picked up a nodule of flint from the field and prepared to fling it towards the nearest soldier.

A small boy, licking a piece of coloured ice on a stick, regarded her with some favour.

'Yeah, let's chuck a few stones,' he said, picking up a pebble.

A woman grabbed him by the arm and shook the stone out of his grasp.

'Jimmy, put that down. You start throwing stones at policemen and they'll run us off. They're just looking for an excuse to bring in the riot police and wade into us like they did last year.'

'Aw, mum . . . this lady . . .'

The woman turned furiously on Morgana.

'You should know better.'

With that she dragged her young child away into the mob, who had taken very little notice of Morgan-le-Fay's incitement to violence. There was too much noise going on to notice one old woman, even if she did have a voice to match one of those war trumpets on the posts. Morgana would have to do a great deal more than just shout if she was going to rouse more than a seven-year-old to action.

A drunk young man came up to her and interrupted her thoughts.

'You doing tarot or crystal? Tell me fortune, misses – what's me future?'

'Short,' snapped Morgan-le-Fay, 'you're going to die when your liver explodes in one week's time.'

The young man swayed and went pale.

''Ere, you're not supposed to say things like that – you're supposed to cheer me up, tell me I'll win a fortune.'

'Just don't bother to make your bed next Wednesday morning,' replied Morgana, pushing past him.

At that moment a crow hopped near to her and cocked its head on one side.

'Well?' she said. 'What have you found out?'

There was another man sitting on the ground with his back against the wheel of a large tin box. He was burning some weed wrapped in paper and inhaling the smoke. His pupils were dilated and his face bore a far-away expression. He stared at Morgana when she spoke to the crow, then turned his attention to the bird.

The crow said, 'Oberon is not going to force Titania to hand over the baby – the fairies are coming to rescue Cobweb.'

The Morning-Fairy was furious. She could feel the rage bubbling up inside her, like volcanic lava gushing from a vent. So they thought they could fool Morgan-le-Fay, did they? Well the stupid oafs would find their precious companion in pieces when they found him. Cobweb was not the youngling of Guinevere and Lancelot du Lac, but she could create a certain amount of magic with the ritual slaughter of the fairy. Perhaps she could drag this ugly world back a couple of centuries at least.

'Go back and find out what they plan to do next – I shall find another place for my ministry!'

'I obey,' cried the crow and took to flight.

Morgan-le-Fay strode from the field, heading towards another, lesser known site of magic.

The man who had been smoking looked open-mouthed at the burning weed in his hand, then at the departing crow, then rolled his eyes in satisfaction.

'Good ganja,' he murmured, dreamily.

SIXTEEN

Field Marigold Opens and Purple Bindweed Closes

B Y THE TIME THE FAIRIES AND THEIR FELLOW TRAVELLERS neared Stonehenge there was a strong cordon of police around the festival, discouraging further would-be participants from entering. Officers from the Wiltshire and other forces had gathered in strength to the north, south, east and west. There was an unofficial order to beleaguer New Age travellers and keep them away from Stonehenge. Many had already reached their destination of course, in earlier days, but now the time had come to close the doors on further travellers.

Earl was driving the lead vehicle and he jumped out when confronted by the roadblock. Jug joined him a few moments later. You could see in the faces of these two men that they rather enjoyed a dispute with the police.

They were certainly not intimidated by authority, as Sid was, and they regarded the baiting of policemen as something of a harmless sport. It was all part of the game. The police hassled them, they made it as difficult as possible for the police. Everyone respected that stance.

'You can't obstruct us,' said Earl, 'this is a free country. You want to interfere with the rights of a citizen to go about his lawful business, go to some South American country, where they have death squads. You'd like that, you lot, wouldn't you? Power, that's what it's all about, ain't it? Well you haven't got it here – let us through.'

The inspector in charge of the cordon sighed and shook his head. He was not fond of being out in the field, literally out in the field, and would rather he was sitting behind a desk shuffling papers from tray to tray, and supping a nice hot coffee when he felt like it. Duties like this one were a burden on his family, friends and to his love of comfort.

'I have to consider the safety of the public. There's already too many people in those fields. If we let in any more the situation will constitute a hazard. Turn round and go back where you came from.'

'We demand to enter the festival,' cried Jug. 'You got no right to keep us out. This is an infringement on our liberties – I'll take this up with my MP. We're the bloody public – it's up to us to decide whether it's safe or not. Ain't you heard of free will?'

The inspector's face hardened. 'Take it up with the Tinker's Union for all I care, son. You're not coming in and that's that. And I warn you, if you don't turn those vehicles around I might have to ask my constables to board them and search them for illegal substances.'

Earl nodded. 'Oh, like that is it? Harassment. We got

nothing to hide, but you still ain't getting on board. These are our homes see – you can't enter a home without a search warrant.'

'Don't test me,' snapped the inspector. 'My constables are ready to do their duty.'

The constables concerned were not looking at all comfortable on hearing their inspector's remarks, since many of them had heard stories about boarding travellers' vehicles: stories of shrieking women defending their homes with brooms and shovels and dark tales of savage German shepherd hounds, of children with dirty teeth who bit them on the legs, of rats and cockroaches, of wild men with unlicenced shotguns.

'I hear they teach their dogs to go for the goolies,' one constable whispered to another. 'They stick 'em onto you while your hands are busy searching.'

The second constable winced and his hands automatically went down to protect his valuables, much in the same way that footballers do when forming a wall to stop a free kick from going in the goal.

'Button up, Jameson,' snapped the inspector to the first constable.

'Sir.'

The music from the festival floated over the heads of the policemen and whetted the musical saliva glands of the travellers. They wanted to be in there, joining in the fun. They could smell the hot dogs and burgers. They could hear the laughter and shouting. The attitude of the police was, as usual, very high-handed in their opinion.

Earl said, 'Doesn't sound like a riot's going on to me.'

'I didn't say there was a riot in progress,' answered the inspector pompously. 'That's what we're trying to prevent.

189

If we swell those numbers any more, there *might* be a riot. It's my duty . . .'

'Right,' snapped Jug, 'that's it – I'm drivin' through. You better get those coppers out of the way or they'll get run over. They're blocking the queen's highway. That's against the law that is. We could prosecute.'

'All right, I've had enough of your lip, sonny,' growled the inspector, pulling on some leather gloves. 'Men, search the vehicles!'

Sid, in the vehicle behind Earl's, began to panic.

'Oberon,' he whispered. 'If they inspect the bus they'll get a close look at the baby. They might recognize her. We can't let them get too near her. We'll all be arrested for kidnapping!'

A nervous-looking constable came to the open doorway of the bus and peered in.

'I've got to search this vehicle,' he said. 'Er, you got any dogs on here?'

'Dogs?' said Puck, turning to look at the King of the Fairies. 'Have we got any dogs?'

Oberon raised his eyebrows, gave a low whistle, and stared down the aisle of the bus.

To the constable's horror, out from under one of the seats slunk a huge beast which resembled a dog in form, but which was like no breed the constable had ever encountered before. Everything owned about its person was enormous: its paws were like dinner plates, its haunches would not have been out of place on a bull, its neck was ridged muscle which rippled as it walked. The coat was dark coarse hair, like the bristles of a stiff yard broom. On top of that it had three huge heads and three terrible sets of sharp teeth. Its hackles were raised as it stepped forward, a low menacing growl in the back of its throat, its six eyes glowing like red headlamps.

'Sarge?' squeaked the constable, his face a horrible pallor. 'Can you come here a minute?'

A sergeant came up whispering, 'What is it, they got firearms or something?' Then he saw the hound and he stopped short in his tracks.

'What the bloody hell is *that*?' he croaked. 'Is that a *dog*? It's a bloody mutant.'

The hound snarled and slavered, saliva dribbling on the floor of the bus. Its several lips curled back to reveal gigantic fangs. All six ears flattened against its heads as it hunched on the floor halfway down the bus.

'Down Cerberus,' said Oberon in a quiet, commanding voice, 'good dog.'

Titania, holding a wide-awake Pigwidgeon, reached out with her free hand and patted the hound from hell on the back.

Cerberus snapped and snarled by way of answer, but at the policemen, not at the fairy queen.

'I ain't going in there, Sarge,' whined the policeman. 'Definitely. I'd leave the Force, first.'

'I don't blame you, son,' said the older man. 'I'm not going in there either. I'm calling in the riot squad. That thing needs to be put in a zoo. That comes under the Dangerous Dogs Act, that does.'

'S'not a pit bull terrier,' remarked Sid, gathering courage from their cowardly behaviour. 'It's just a house pet.'

'A bloody pet?' cried the sergeant. 'You got to be joking – that animal is a savage, dangerous beast – and what's more it's got three bloody heads. How can you call it a house pet? It's a monster.'

As the sergeant was peering through the doorway, a tiny

demon, not much more than six-inches high, jumped from within the thick hair of Cerberus and flashed across the floor of the bus, to hide beneath a seat. The sergeant blinked and rubbed his eyes. A chill came up from the base of his spine to freeze the back of his neck and lift the nape hairs.

'What was that?' he gasped.

'What?' asked Oberon. 'What is it you saw?'

'Well, it looked like – I dunno. Something red and horrible – like a bloody cooked lobster running on its hind legs.'

'There's no lobsters in here, Constable,' said Sid. 'I can guarantee that. Not cooked ones, anyway.' Sid dimly remembered some of his English literature from school. 'Not like them crabs hissing in the pot that greasy Joan keeled – that's from one of Shakespeare's plays,' he added proudly.

Puck remarked, 'Those were *crab apples* I believe Marian had hissing in her bowl, Sid, not seashore crabs.'

'Oh,' said Sid, genuinely surprised. 'You know I never knew that – I thought they was, you know, like crabs from Leigh-on-Sea.'

'I'm not concerned with cooked crabs,' said the frustrated sergeant, realizing he was getting nowhere.

'Nor uncooked, I suppose?' remarked Puck.

The inspector, aware that no-one had yet boarded the bus, came over to the doorway.

'What's going on here, Sergeant?' he asked, brusquely. 'Why isn't the constable searching the bus?'

'Sir, they've got a wild animal in there – it's – well, frankly it's *horrible*, sir.'

'Nonsense, man,' said the inspector, stepping up onto the first step of the bus.

Cerberus growled in stereo – or rather in triphonia – the sound rolling from mouth to mouth.

The inspector froze and the blood drained from his face leaving it a deathly wan colour. 'Shit!' he said, quietly.

Sid said, 'Do you mind? There's ladies on board.'

'Queens, in fact,' said Titania, standing up and putting the gurgling Pigwidgeon astride the back of Cerberus. 'And you're upsetting our house pet.'

Pigwidgeon gripped the hair on the cheeks of the fabulous beast and tugged them like reins, chortling to herself, while the inspector stared at Cerberus, a lump in his throat as large as a Granny Smith.

'That child's in danger,' whispered the inspector hoarsely. 'That beast is a killer.'

'Nonsense,' said Puck. 'It's as tame as anything. We have suckled lambs on the teats of Cerberus. She has kept kittens warm in the winter with her coat.'

The inspector was in a quandary. Clearly the deformed beast before him was as savage as any wild animal he had seen, yet to the occupants of the bus it was tame and gentle. He stepped down to the ground and said, 'We'll do this bus last – search all the other vehicles first.'

'Yes, sir,' replied the constable, relieved. 'Willingly, sir.'

On the other vehicles, there was trouble with dogs, with men and women wielding brooms and shovels, with children, with rats and cockroaches, but no-one actually produced a shotgun and threatened the lives of the law officers.

Finally, not finding any illicit or illegal substances, the inspector was faced with letting these few vehicles go on, or arresting the occupants. A long line of traffic had built up behind the travellers. Ordinary drivers on their peaceful way across the Wiltshire plains, were sounding their horns, confronting the constables themselves, and generally making the situation more difficult for the inspector.

'Get on,' he said, waving Earl through the cordon, 'and don't cause any trouble or I'll come down on you like Salisbury Cathedral, you hear me?'

A big cheer went up as the travellers passed through the line of police, the constable who had been ordered to search the fairies' bus grinning from ear to ear. Titania held Pigwidgeon's arm and flapped it giving the officer a little wave. He waved back. He was whole and he was relieved. He would live to search another day.

The convoy thundered on and into the fields where the festival was reaching fever pitch. The travellers drove across the chalk meadows, joyously churning up the surface soil with their wheels, and found places to park their vehicles. Tom Blessing immediately came running round to the doorway of the bus to help Titania alight, only to be confronted by a severe-looking Oberon.

'Sorry,' said Tom, ducking aside.

Oberon got down, followed by the rest of the fairies, who immediately became the centre of the festival's attention. The festival travellers instantly saw that this was a fantastic little group of people, possibly from some circus or other, and were far less reserved than other members of the public when it came to asking questions.

'What country you from?' asked one new traveller.

'From the Country of the Young,' said Puck. 'Or if you prefer – fairyland.'

'Fairyland?' grinned the youth. 'Wow!'

Oberon said, 'We're looking for a woman bearing one of our number – she has him in thrall.'

Women and men shook their heads. They had not seen such a woman, nor anyone similar to the little people before them, in or out of thrall.

Titania said, 'My owl said she's disguised – as an old woman with a bundle on her back.'

Still there was no response from the crowd. There were plenty of people in disguise here today. As for old women, well there were fortune-tellers, tarot-card readers, Indian-silver sellers, ear-nose-and-nipple piercers, tattoo artists, acupuncture specialists, gemstone healers, foot massagers, spine walkers, spiritualists, mediums, and a thousand other kinds of alternative medicine practitioners and soul menders, many of them old women who might carry backpacks.

'Which way is the Slaughter Stone?' demanded Oberon.

A dozen fingers obliged him with a direction.

Oberon strode off, followed by his little band, leaving Sid in charge of the bus.

The group went first to the edge of Stonehenge, then finding no-one out near the Slaughter Stone they began scouring the crowd, with the owl flying overhead, seeking their enemy. The search was in vain. They could find no trace of Morgan-le-Fay and Oberon wondered if she had given up her idea of murdering Cobweb, for some other plan.

'She would not kill him just anywhere,' he murmured to Titania. 'It would have to be a ritual slaughter, for she would waste magic without the trappings.'

'The Morning-Fairy is not one to waste magic,' agreed Titania, hugging her baby to her breast. 'If she's not here, she must be in some other place where her power can be increased with the death of Cobweb.'

'Call down the owl,' said Oberon. 'We need to have a meeting!'

The fairies gathered in a corner of the field away from the mainstream of travellers. The owl flew this way and that, making sure there were no rooks or crows near by who might be agents of Morgan-le-Fay. King Oberon summed up the situation as he saw it.

'We must find the Morning-Fairy, wherever she is, and chase her from these sacred sites. If she is still within reach of a magical spot at the stroke of noon, then she may carry out her threat to sacrifice Cobweb. You must all spread yourselves and search the surrounding country-side.'

'But,' said Swallowtail, 'we must go on foot – we are unable to summon enough magic to fly.'

'What about you, Puck,' asked Oberon. 'Can you still fly?'

'Not very high and not for long periods,' confirmed Puck. 'I can hop from place to place, that's all.'

King Oberon nodded. 'Then we must rely on the owl, though her sight is excellent only at short range. We can't expect her to see over long distances. We need a tall, ami-able creature, someone who can see over vast distances, someone with a head higher than the ridges and trees, someone with no malice who might wish to save a fairy. It's a pity Gogmagog has gone in the direction of London – we could have used him, even though he's as stupid as an ox . . .'

'There is someone,' Puck said. 'He lies to the south east.'

'Then send the owl for him,' said Oberon.

Puck called in Titania's owl and gave her instructions.

She set off in silent flight towards the figure Puck had told her about, with instructions to guide it to the fairies.

'In the meantime,' Oberon said, 'we must find somewhere to rest our heads, for we are all feeling weary. Sid, drive us to a great wood, where we can find cowslips' bells in which to lie and dream of yestercentury.'

Sid looked at the Ordnance Survey map which he had spread out on his knees.

'No big woods around here – can't do it,' he said.

Oberon stamped his foot. 'I'm getting tired – I always get bad tempered when I get tired. We need somewhere to sleep, Sid.'

'What about the bus?' said the worried rude mechanical.

Moth cried, 'We've been on the bus for long enough – we can't sleep on the bus – it stinks of mortals.'

Sid said huffily, 'There's no need to be offensive.'

Titania, almost asleep on her feet, snapped at Moth.

'Leave Sid alone, he's trying his best.'

'Not best enough,' grumbled Peaseblossom. 'I hate the bus – I wish the bus was dead.'

Mustardseed sniggered. 'The bus isn't alive in the first place – you're thinking of a horse and carriage.'

'Half of which isn't a living creature either,' retorted Peaseblossom.

Oberon held up his arms. 'Stop it, be quiet, you fairies. We're all unhappy for Cobweb. It makes us fatigued to fret over one of our number, we are so few in any case. Sid, we *must* have somewhere to sleep for an hour. Somewhere which does not disturb our slumber with its odours of the modern world – somewhere with the scent of bygone times.'

Sid opened a tourist map of the area and spread it on the ground in front of him.

'What about Longleat House?' he questioned.

'A *house*?' cried some of the fairies. 'A house will be worse than the bus.'

'Not necessarily,' replied Sid. 'This one is an old mansion, with a park and woodlands full of azaleas and rhododendrons, overlooking a valley. It says here the house was built in 1568 for Sir John Thynne, an ancestor of the Marquess of Bath, and still has lots of old furniture in it. If you can't find somewhere in the woods, maybe an old four-poster bed or something, eh?'

Oberon sighed. 'If that's the best you can do, Sid, we shall have to accept it. Take us to Longleat. Once we've had an hour's rest, we shall be ready to do battle with Morgan-le-Fay. Onward.'

Sid led the way back to the bus and loaded the fairies on board. He drove them out of the chaotic festival, towards Longleat House in the west. The A303, leading to the A36, on this side of Stonehenge was relatively quiet. Sid was able to get them to Heaven's Gate, the half-mile walk through woodlands landscaped by Capability Brown, before Oberon's temper worsened.

'Sid,' said Puck slowly, as they drove to the car-park, 'there are lions here – I can smell them. And leopards, and panthers. Are we to be eaten by wild animals while we sleep, Sid? Will you have us swallowed whole?'

'You don't have to go into that section of the park,' said Sid. 'They're not allowed to stroll around just anywhere. You can find a place outside the fence.'

'I shall go into the house,' said Puck, 'and find a quiet inglenook. You may keep your four-poster beds, Sid. They are for human forms to rest upon. Give me a good sooty chimney, or warm scullery cupboard in which to lay my head.'

'Under the rhododendron bushes for me,' murmured Titania. 'I can't take the baby there, Sid. You will have to keep her here on the bus.'

Pigwidgeon was awake and almost ready to be fed.

'Please change that nappy thing again – she feels damp underneath,' ordered Titania. 'And afterwards you may rock her to sleep in your arms and you may kiss her just once on both cheeks.'

'Thanks very much,' said Sid, sarcastically. 'I'll look forward to that treat, especially since she has a snotty nose at the moment, and it seems to have spread.'

Once the fairies had scattered to their various resting places, Sid found some biscuits and lemonade in his food cache at the back of the bus, and ate them. Then he fed and changed Pigwidgeon, before going out and lying on the grass outside, letting the hot wind waft over him. Pigwidgeon lay beside him under the shade of an old hornbeam, her eyes gradually closing, until she was sound asleep.

Sid listened to the murmuring of insects, the whisper of the leaves above. The morning was gradually getting hotter under a hard blue sky with little cloud visible. A pale weak moon which had kept her frail grip on the heavens, even though the sun had taken his rightful place, finally disappeared from sight. Near by some running water tinkled over stones and swished between bull rushes. A buddleia gathered to itself butterflies: red admirals, tortoiseshells, peacocks, speckled woods and cabbage whites. The sweet smell of old grasses, littered with granny's bonnet, entwined with the breeze.

Sid woke a little later, his head muzzy, with a desire to go to the toilet. The lemonade had found its way through to his bladder and he needed to empty the latter urgently.

The toilets consisted of two semi-detached wooden shacks near the entrance to the car-park. He got up and staggered to them, then relieved himself, before returning to the grassy patch by the bus where he had been having such pleasant dreams.

He was later awoken by a rough hand shaking him, to find Oberon standing there.

'What?' said Sid, rubbing his eyes, seeing Puck half-covered in soot, and Moth with pollen dust on his shoulders. 'Are we ready to go?'

Titania, standing beside Oberon, looked stricken.

'Where is my baby, Sid?' she cried. 'What have you done with my beautiful Pigwidgeon?'

The baby! Sid looked around him wildly.

'She was – she was right here on the grass next to me – she was here asleep. I only left her once . . .'

'You *left* her?' shrieked Titania, looking more formidable than an army of terrorists in her distraught rage. 'You left my baby to be stolen?'

Sid stood up and shook in his boots.

'Maybe – maybe it was some other fairies? Maybe it was the police? Maybe the real mother found her?'

There was a roar not too far away from where they were standing.

'Maybe it was eaten by a lion?' said Blewit, unhelpfully.

Titania wailed, pulling frantically on her wild hair in a frenzy of grief.

'The lions are locked in,' said Sid, 'definitely. It wasn't a lion that took her, I guarantee that.'

Blewit wasn't going to have her theories brushed aside without a fight. 'Maybe some other wild creature then – perhaps an eagle? Eagles can fly over fences – it might have been an eagle.'

'Shut up, Blewit,' said Sid. 'You're making things worse than they should be.'

Titania cried, 'What could be worse than having my baby stolen? My dear, sweet baby with her cherry-red lips, her rose-petal cheeks? Why have you let someone steal my little Pigwidgeon, Sid? How could you?'

Sid began to gather his indignation together. He knew he had been in the wrong, but he had forgotten about the baby when he went to the toilet. His head was buzzing from lack of sleep and he couldn't be expected to re-member he was supposed to be minding an infant. He wasn't a nanny, he was a garage mechanic. That is, he didn't *mind* looking after children, but they couldn't expect him to be responsible for their whereabouts, when they themselves had gone off to find places in which to sleep.

'It's not *your* baby, for a start,' said Sid. 'She belongs to someone else – her mother and father – and perhaps you realize now how *they* must have felt when you stole her from them? After all, you've only had her for a few hours, while her mother carried her in her womb for nine months and has brought her up ever since.'

Titania's beautiful heart-shaped face, as delicate as that of a porcelain doll fashioned by a toy maker for the daughter of a French Sun King at Versailles, screwed itself into the countenance of a witch.

'I don't care about mothers suckling their young,' she said, stamping her foot. 'I left the mother a changeling – she should be satisfied with that.'

'A goldfish,' said Sid, laconically. 'I'm sure she was really pleased about that – I mean, fair exchange, init – a goldfish for a baby?'

'A *dead* goldfish,' murmured Puck, who had enough

201

human in him to understand what Sid was talking about.

'It was alive when I put it there,' snapped Titania. 'There wasn't any water to put it in.'

Oberon said quietly, 'Perhaps Morgan-le-Fay has the baby after all? She may have followed us to this place and waited for Sid to drop into his deep slumber, then stole the baby. She is a devious sorceress. She will murder the child without a thought for its mother.'

'Well,' said Sid mournfully, 'if we see the Black Knight and his squire come riding up that road we'll know she did.'

Oberon cried, 'We must search the grounds for my queen's infant – each must take a different point of the compass – then we must all be back here before the red sandwort opens. Hie thee hence, fairies – search the park!'

The fairies shot off in different directions.

Puck went towards the section where fifty lions roamed free. It had been a long time since he had seen any beast larger than a fox or a badger. In the old days there had been the snorting of boars and the baying of wolves, but now the only sound was that of the roar of traffic. Puck liked the beasts of the field and the birds of the air: they gave colour and excitement to the world.

He came to a high fence and skipped over it. Inside there were not lions but two cheetahs, lying almost camouflaged in tall grasses. They regarded him through half-closed eyes as he approached their languid forms. Having recently eaten they were not driven to the hunt by their hunger, but they would not have touched Puck, nor any fairy. They simply fixed their golden uninterested eyes on the intruder and watched him as he circumnavigated their nest in the grass.

'Ah, the cat who can run faster than antelope,' said Puck, appreciatively. 'Thou has wings on thy heels, like the speedy messenger, Mercury. Yet I think I can best you in a race over the landscape. What say you?'

Neither cheetah, it seemed, was eager to voice an opinion.

Puck continued on his way, realizing, as he walked on, that mortals remained in their cars in this part of the park. They regarded him through puzzled eyes, as they wondered whether he was a keeper or a lunatic out for a walk. Puck covered a lot of the park in a very quick time, without coming across Morgan-le-Fay or the baby. He met many different types of animal, including a giraffe up whose neck Puck shinned in order to have a viewing platform over the whole park.

He saw nothing to give him hope. Finally, coming to a pride of lions, some seven of them, Puck sat down for a rest amongst them, running his fingers through the dusty dark mane of the largest male. Cars began to stop and video cameras whirred. Soon there were enough vehicles around that spot to attract the attention of the keepers, who came out in a Range Rover to ascertain why all their visitors preferred to halt in the same place and were taking so many pictures.

When the horrified keepers saw that someone was amongst the lions, they used a loud hailer.

'WALK TOWARDS OUR VEHICLE, SIR! SLOWLY AND CAUTIOUSLY.'

Puck rose and strolled casually over to the Range Rover.

'Good sirs,' he said to the boggle-eyed occupants, 'these lions are but pussy-cats to such as I. I have lost my true love, Thisby, and sought to find her amongst their kind. Alas and alack, there is no sign of her. Now canst thou tell me whether or no the red sandwort has yet opened his flowery head, for I must at such a time be with my king.'

They would have dragged him into the Range Rover if he had not skipped back to the lions.

Then one of the keepers loaded a dart gun and got out of his vehicle to approach the lions warily.

Puck felt it was time to leave, before one of the lions, or the keepers, did something regrettable. But there was too much of the showman in Puck to go without a final gesture. He went to the nearest lion, a brute with a magnificent mane, and gripping its jaws, opened them wide.

'Thisby? Thisby? Are you there?' called Puck, into the dark depths of the lion's throat. 'Thy loving Pyramus awaits without.'

The lion retrieved its head from Puck's tiny hands and shook itself like a ruffled cat.

Puck then began running towards the perimeter fence, which he leapt with astonishing ease, leaving the occupants of the vehicles staring after him with wide eyes.

Having made his way back to the bus, Puck found a dejected band of fairies gathered around Sid. The rude mechanical was preparing himself for his own execution. There was talk, from Titania, of handing him over to Morgan-le-Fay in exchange for Cobweb. Sid had tried to run, but of course being still enthralled he made no progress, simply turning in a wide circle to end up back where he started.

'All right, it was my fault,' he admitted to Titania, 'but I'm just as upset as you are . . .'

As he was talking, Peaseblossom gave a shout, and pointed.

The fairies all stared to see Tom Blessing, crossing the grass car-park, with the baby in his arms.

Titania ran to him. 'You found my little Pigwidgeon,' she cried. 'You rescued my baby.'

Tom went bright red with pleasure and handed over the infant to Titania's waiting arms.

'I found her alone on the ground next to the bus – I thought you'd all be arrested. I thought the baby had been abandoned.'

The moment Tom spoke the words he saw from the reaction of Sid and the fairies that he had done the wrong thing. They had thought he had caught the baby-stealer and had rescued the child. Now they realized that *he* was the thief, though he had taken the child with the best intentions.

Titania stiffened. 'You took my baby, from *here*, where Sid left it? You removed my child? I was out of my mind with worry. How could you do this to me, Tom? We thought Morgan-le-Fay had her and was going to kill her.'

Tom looked very uncomfortable. In an instant he had gone from conquering hero to child-snatcher. His heart shrank within him under the terrible gaze of Titania. He wanted to crawl away somewhere and hide himself.

He tried to defend himself.

'Well – the baby was just lying there. I followed you all here in my sister's bus, but I lost you at the entrance. When I came looking for you, I found Pigwidgeon on the ground, with no-one else in sight. If I hadn't taken her, someone else might have done.'

'Tom must have got here just as I left for the toilet – it wasn't his fault, it was mine,' said Sid.

But Titania was unforgiving of mortals who made her feel bad, whether it was their fault or not.

'I realize now what an ass you are, Tom,' she said. 'I

never saw it before, but I see it now. You are a fool and an ass and I shall never forgive you.'

Tom stared at her in despair.

SEVENTEEN

Red Sandwort Opens and Yellow Goat's Beard Closes

PUCK WENT WITH TOM IN HIS BUS AS BOTH VEHICLES WERE driven back to the festival site. Tom was utterly miserable and hardly said a word. Puck, being half-human, was aware of the emotions running through the young man. Of course, Puck had never felt love himself, not romantic love – he was too much fairy and too little mortal for that – but he had a greater understanding of such things than the rest of the fairy band and he was capable of compassion in mortal terms too.

'Never mind, Tom,' he said. 'Queen Titania snaps at everyone from time to time. She's an imperious creature, with a quick temper and given to moods. I should think next time you see her, she'll be smiling at you.'

'I won't hear a word against her, mind,' said Tom,

207

gloomily, staring at the road ahead as he steered the bus. 'I don't think she's imperious.'

'As you will, as you will, but I think I know her better than you – better than most, except my King Oberon.'

'That's funny, isn't it, them being married and playing opposite each other in the *Dream?*'

Puck saw very little humour in the affair, but he let it pass.

'And there's something about that baby – something which I feel Titania keeps hidden from me,' added Tom.

Puck stared sharply at Tom, who took the look to mean he was overstepping the bounds of propriety.

'What say you, friend?' asked Puck. 'There is some secret concerning the infant?'

'Exactly,' Tom said. 'I mean, it takes after her, doesn't it? It's got her eyes,' Tom mused. 'And Pigwidgeon's lips are the spit of Titania's. But I can't see any of Oberon in the little mite – do you – do you think its possible . . .' Tom hesitated.

'What? What is possible, my fine companion?'

Tom ran the fingers of his left hand through his blond hair, clearly nervous.

'Well, you won't be angry at what I'm going to say next, will you?' he asked.

'Depends,' said Puck. 'If you are about to call me a Tartar, then I shall be vexed.'

'No, I wasn't going to call you anything. I was going to suggest that perhaps – perhaps Oberon is not the father of Pigwidgeon.' Tom glanced sideways at Puck. 'It seems to me the baby has none of his features, after all.'

Puck sighed, leaned over and whispered in Tom's ear.

'Tis true,' he murmured. 'Oberon did not conceive the child – it was another father who lay with the mother.'

Tom looked triumphant. 'I knew it,' he said, thumping the wheel with his fist. 'I knew he couldn't be the father. He's very cocksure of himself, that one, but I always felt he wasn't capable of producing such a beautiful child. How can Titania bear to be with him? Do they still – you know – share a bed together?'

Puck sighed again. 'Oft times they sleep in different places, she in a bed of rose petals, he in the hollow of an old oak.'

'Do they argue a lot – or is it one of those sulky marriages, where they hardly ever speak?'

'Both, both. Sometimes they quarrel over the children – at other times they go their separate ways, neither touching nor speaking, not even to dance together.'

'Children?' Tom said, throwing a quick glance at the mischievous Puck's innocent face. 'I thought – I thought the baby was Titania's only child?'

'She had another, an Indian child, which Oberon wanted for his own henchman.'

'Indian child?' cried Tom, astonished. 'You mean she had an Indian lover who .... oh,' it finally filtered through the murkiness of his mind, 'you're talking about the *play*. I wish you wouldn't do that, mix up fiction with fact. Are there really other children?'

'Where?' asked Puck.

'Oh, never mind,' said Tom, irritated with Puck's games. 'Anyway, you're sure Oberon isn't Pigwidgeon's father?'

'Absolutely. I know it for fact.'

'Well, if she's had one lover, the father of her child, then it won't be so difficult for her to accept me, will it? It also means there's less of a bond with Oberon. And Oberon seems to neglect her constantly. I'm sure she 'can't put up with that for too long.'

'She never puts up with it,' said Puck. 'She is a demanding creature, Queen Titania.'

'I wish you wouldn't keep criticizing her,' said Tom, 'I don't like it.'

'As you will,' sighed Puck, finding a dead spider under his seat and plucking off its legs one by one. 'As you will.'

Back at the festival site things were getting out of hand. The police had decided the situation was becoming dangerous, with too many 'hippies' pouring in, and they had decided to clear the area. Bulldozers were lined up all down one side of the field. The order was given for these vehicles to move forward, sweeping the travellers back to the counties from whence they had come. The chief constable didn't mind where they went, so long as it was out of Wiltshire.

Just a few minutes earlier, before the order was given, Alex had gone running off with Sabre into the crowds, thinking he saw a friend. The dog returned without him. Mary began to get frantic.

'Earl!' she cried. 'I've lost Alex.'

Earl came out of the bus with a sandwich stuck in his mouth. He saw the bulldozers moving forward, across the landscape. Some of the travellers were already beginning to panic and their lorries and vans blocked the exit to the fields. Others were cutting the wires of fences, in order to get out more quickly. Still more were being harassed by police with riot sticks.

Windscreens were being shattered out of sight of the cameras; there were confrontations between groups of travellers and police; dogs were running amuck, trying to find their owners, imbibing the sense of fear and panic in

the air and responding with barks and bites when someone got in the way of their terrified search.

'OK, darlin',' he said. 'I'll find him. You get the bus
over to the far corner of the chalk meadow. We'll drive
over bloody ploughed fields into the next county if I have
to.'

Earl ran into the mêlée, shouting Alex's name. All
around him there were running battles and confrontations. A policeman approached him with a drawn trun-
cheon. The policeman did so warily: Earl was a big man,
with brutish looks, and it was obvious that anyone who
took him on would not find the job easy.

Earl cried, 'I'm looking for my son – there are kids
here, you know – you ought to think about their safety
before wading in like this . . .'

The policeman pulled up short. 'They're gathering any
loose children at the paddy wagon.'

'Right,' said Earl, heading that way immediately.

Some of his travellers saw Earl and shouted to him, asking him what they should do.

'Get the hell out of here,' cried their leader. 'Go back
to the Avebury site. Me and Mary will meet you there
later. You haven't seen Alex, have you?'

His people shook their heads and Earl continued with
his search. When it became obvious that he would only
run into Alex by sheer good luck, he climbed a marquee
pole that had been left standing. He had just begun
surveying the crowd from the top of the pole when it was
pushed over by a group of travellers and police,
struggling with each other down below.

The pole toppled like a felled tree and Earl was thrown
from his perch and landed heavily in the dust. For a few
moments he lay there, winded, wondering what had

happened. He was soon back on his feet however, having ascertained there were only bruises and no broken bones, and was weaving in and out amongst the thick crowds, shouting, 'Alex? Alex?'

After a few more futile searches of abandoned tepees and benders, Earl noticed Sid's bus weaving its way along the main road beyond the fence. Earl was becoming desperate now. Alex was only five years of age. Earl ran to the roadway, leapt the wire fence, and flagged down Sid's bus.

Sid leaned out of the window.

'What's the matter – what's going on over there?'

'Oh, as usual it's got out of hand,' said Earl, impatiently. 'Look, I need your help. I've lost my son. Can you and your pansy friends give us some help, or what?'

'Well, they might do, if you're a bit more polite,' said Sid. He was unsure whether Oberon would object to being called a pansy or not. After all, the woodland fairies seemed to revere flowers, so he might even be pleased. 'Where'd you last see him?'

Earl gestured impatiently. 'He's in the middle of that sodding lot, somewhere. Come on, get a move on. I'm worried he'll be hurt.'

Sid turned and told the fairies what was the problem and then parked the bus on the grass verge. The fairies poured out of the bus, all except Titania who stayed to look after her precious baby, and onto the battlefield. The fairies knew what Alex looked like from their stay at Avebury, when Alex was running around the site with his pals. Now they zipped amongst the milling people, skipped between bulldozers, dashed around buses, lorries and vans, until finally Swallowtail saw Alex sitting in an empty trailer attached to a van being driven out of the field at high speed.

The van's driver had no back window in the cab and relied on his wing mirrors to see what was going on behind. There was no way he could see the small boy from his position and probably had no idea he had a passenger. Alex looked terrified, clinging onto the edge of the trailer, being bounced dangerously high when the vehicle hit bumps. No doubt he had climbed into the trailer to hide from the fighting. At any moment he might be thrown out of the trailer and into the path of some other vehicle.

'There he goes,' cried Swallowtail to Earl. 'In the back of that thingy!'

Earl followed the line of Swallowtail's arm and saw his son's white face above the edge of the trailer. He looked around him quickly and saw a motorcycle chained to a fence post. Earl ran over to the machine. He hugged the fence post and ripped it from the ground, pulling it through the chain which now dangled from the handle-bars.

'Hey!' yelled a big man nearby. 'That's my chopper!'

Earl saw the man was a Hell's Angel, come down to Stonehenge looking for some action in the wake of the midsummer festival, no doubt. Earl held up his arm, showing his tattoos.

'Earl Royal,' he yelled back, 'All-England Chapter. I need your chopper. I'll bring it back.'

The Hell's Angel shook a fist at Earl and began running towards him.

'I'll tear your head off your shoulders, nobody touches my hog, you bastard.'

Earl ignored this threat and started the bike, roaring out of the field onto the road in pursuit of the van and trailer. He very soon overtook the van and signalled to the driver to pull in. The driver, a thin-faced youth, threw up two fingers at Earl.

'Pull over, you dickhead,' cried Earl, 'you've got a kid in your trailer.'

But the wind took his words away and the driver was now concentrating on beating Earl to the next set of crossroads.

Earl tried to wrench the headlamp from the front of the bike as he sped along, so that he could throw it through the windscreen of the van. As he was doing this he felt some arms curl around his waist. He swerved the bike in alarm, startled by this new turn of events. Next he heard Puck's voice in his ear.

'Get close to the other person, so that I can jump from this machine into the box.'

'Wha . . . how did you get there? I didn't see you get on,' cried Earl, into his slipstream.

'Do as I say,' said Puck.

'You're crazy, you'll kill yourself.'

Nevertheless, Earl had little choice in the matter. The van driver clearly thought he was being chased and was not going to stop or be caught if he could help it. Alex was crouched down in the back of the trailer, shivering with fright. Something had to be done. He drew up alongside the trailer again and to his astonishment Puck seemed to flip from the pillion to land in the middle of the trailer.

Puck then patted the crying little boy on the head before climbing over the top of the cab and hanging his head down over the windscreen to look into the van driver's eyes.

The man was so startled he slammed his foot on the brake hard, which sent Puck sailing through the air. Puck did a triple somersault, going with the momentum, but mostly for effect. The fairy landed deftly on his feet, did a little twirl, and held up his arms for the non-existent applause.

'Gramercy, thank you,' he murmured.

Earl had halted, jumped from the bike, and was hauling the van driver out of his cab.

'I ought to – didn't you know you had a kid in your trailer, you idiot? What did you think I was after you for? Do I look like a cop?'

'I didn't know – I didn't know,' cried the driver, holding his hands up in front of his face.

Earl shoved him aside without hitting him, an act which took a considerable amount of Earl's will-power to achieve. He saw that it was not the driver's fault. Earl had lived a violent life until he had met Mary and it was difficult to put those days behind him. But he was learning to put his reason before his fists in such matters at last.

Then the father and son were reunited. Earl hugged Alex to his chest, the small boy smothered by the big man's arms.

'I was scared, Daddy!' wailed Alex.

'I know, I know – but it's all over now. Let's get back to Mummy, eh? She's worried about you.'

Alex sniffed and nodded.

Puck came to them.

Earl stared at Puck. 'That was some feat. You a circus performer, or what?'

'I think I must be a what,' said Puck, 'because I've never been to the circus.'

'Well, I owe you one,' said Earl, gratefully. 'You ride pillion with Alex. We've got to get back to Stonehenge.'

They all climbed aboard the chopper, with Alex between Puck and Earl. Puck was beginning to enjoy the motorbike. He hated the smell of the oil and petrol, but that wasn't so evident when they were going at high speed. Although he would never let Oberon know, Puck was thrilled by the ride on the modern machine, with its roaring engine. After all, he argued with himself, it made the fresh air fresher. If one had to choose a vehicle at all, it would be this motorbike, rather than Sid's smelly bus.

They reached the site and Earl rode the motorcycle straight across the field, on which knots of festival people and police were still struggling, weaving in between these groups. The Hell's Angel to whom the hog belonged, was nowhere to be seen, so after his passengers had alighted, Earl propped the bike up against the fence and left a note telling the owner if he wanted compensation for the loan to come to Avebury.

Mary Blessing came out of their bus and gathered her son into her arms.

'Thank God you're safe,' she said. Then to Earl, 'Where was he?'

'In a trailer on the back of a van – we had to chase it on the chopper. I couldn't have done it without that Puck guy – he did this jump from the sickle to the trailer – I've never seen anything like it. He's some kind of aerial athlete – he must be.'

'You chased the van on that motorbike? Who does the bike belong to?'

'Some other guy.'

Mary frowned. She knew Earl as well as he knew himself.

'You didn't hurt the van driver?'

Earl shrugged. 'Nah – I wanted to – but it wasn't his fault. Just scared him a little. Didn't touch him really.' Earl chuckled. 'I'll bet he checks his trailer before he goes out next time, though.'

Mary stroked Alex's hair, then looked at Earl.

'You're a good man, Earl,' she said, with an unusually gentle tone in her voice. 'You had no thought for anything but finding Alex, did you? I saw you climb that pole. You could have been killed.'

'What?' Earl said. 'He's my son, you know.'

'I know,' she replied, a soft light in her eyes, 'but that doesn't make you any less a man. I'm proud of you, I want you to know that.'

'Ahhh,' said Earl, waving her words away, but he felt as if he had a warm loaf of bread in his chest.

'And I'm proud of you, too,' she said to Puck.

'Ahhh,' said Puck, 'it was nothing any other hero wouldn't do, especially one as courageous and ingenious as me.'

Earl pulled out a couple of fence posts and flattened the wire so that Mary could drive out of the field. Then he climbed on board the bus. He called to Puck, 'We're going back to Avebury.'

Titania had come to meet the other fairies but Oberon asked her if she would go with Earl and Mary in their vehicle.

'We have to hunt the sorceress,' he said. 'It would be better if the baby were well out of her reach.'

Titania agreed.

The bus then trundled over the field beyond, towards a roadway in the distance, the sunlight flashing from its windows.

EIGHTEEN

Star of Bethlehem Opens

'THE PAST IS A NICER PLACE, THEY DO THINGS BETTER there,' said Oberon.

The fairies were now waiting in a layby for the return of the owl, sent on her mission to the south-east. Oberon would have liked Morgan-le-Fay to return the world to the Dark Ages. He saw great merit in this scheme, but of course he conceded that a baby's life was at stake and nothing was worth the deliberate murder of a child, especially the daughter of the descendant of Guinevere and Lancelot du Lac. Neither did he want any harm to come to Cobweb, despite that fairy's recent rebellious attitude towards the King of the Fairies.

'Powerful magic requires powerful ingredients,' said Puck. 'I know the Morning-Fairy was taught her arts by the greatest magician of all time, Merlin, but still she has her limitations. Yet it is as you say, my lord, we cannot sanction the harming of a mortal infant, but the daughter of Igrayne and Gorlois has a heart darker than that of any fairy, being mortal herself and subject to the sins of mortals.'

At that moment the screech-owl returned. They heard her cry from far off and then saw her flying towards them. She had company. With her, marching over the country-side, was the Long Man of Wilmington, a chalk giant from Windover Hill, his thin spindly legs carrying him in great strides over the landscape, helped in part by the two staves, one in each hand.

The Long Man was a skeleton, a muscular outline in chalk and mortar, with a blank face. The wind blew through his form, through which could clearly be seen the countryside over which he had marched that morning. Birds dived through his chest, arms and legs, while the owl occasionally rested on one of the staves, replenishing her strength. The Long Man was a white two-dimensional towering figure. He strode confidently over the landscape in blind awareness, knowing his path because he was part of that path, part of the chalk downs, part of the green plains, part of Mother Earth.

When the Long Man reached Salisbury Plain the fairies scrambled up his legs and climbed to stand on his two-hundred-foot-high shoulders. From here they could see over the whole of Wiltshire and some of the surrounding counties. The Long Man, having collected his passengers, then began to make a systematic search of the county, striding over hedges and along ditches, his great staves thudding on the hard June-baked ground around the site of Stonehenge.

'She has to be close by,' said Oberon. 'I feel it in my fairy bones.'

There were over a dozen eyes up there, searching for a sign of the Morning-Fairy, but they were relying more on their sensitivity as fairies. They were like deer on high ground attentive for the faint scent of the wolf, using the height of the Long Man to cover a greater distance on all points of the compass.

The hour was rapidly closing on noon, the opening of the ice plant, and Cobweb had to be found before the time of the vertical sun. Morgan-le-Fay did not make idle threats. Cobweb was in danger of being obliterated by the woman who had destroyed her half-brother, King Arthur.

Mist sensed a ripple in the atmosphere to the north-east.

'Tally-ho!' she cried, pointing out the direction. 'Morgana lies over there!'

The fairies began shouting all at once.

'Which way?'

'Over where?'

'I feel it, I feel it!'

'Yes, yes, the Morning-Fairy and Cobweb!'

The lithe, active figure of Puck scrambled about along the Long Man's chalk shoulders, over his head, down his upper arm and up his forearm, to the top of the left staff, on which perched Titania's beloved screech-owl. Brown-skinned, willow-muscled Puck, nervous energy smoking from his dusky body. Aromatic Puck, smelling variously of forest bark and leaf mould, whose woodland odours grew stronger when he was in a state of agitation. His dove-feather eyes, in shape and colour, glittered with the excitement of the chase.

Puck was afraid of the Morning-Fairy, yet he knew she

was also afraid of him. They were powerful creatures of the landscape, each frightened of the other's Earth-given potency. She had gathered strength over centuries from the dark and ancient dirt of Offa's Dyke, while he had drawn his puissance from the forests and the stony outcrops of the lighted world. If he had to be matched against her, champion against champion, Puck was ready for the fight – but he was scared, he did not deny that to himself – he was afraid. Oberon might match himself against Morgana, or he might choose a champion from amongst the fairies, in which case Puck knew it would be him, for the others – Peaseblossom, Mist, Moth, Mustardseed, Swallowtail, Blewit – were not combatants.

'Woodhenge!' cried Oberon. 'The sorceress chose Woodhenge for her slaughter ground. See, she flees – she has seen our coming – she runs from the place – and Cobweb is left on the altar.'

It was true, from their vantage point on the tall chalk giant they witnessed the dark shadow of the witch escaping across the landscape, her load lighter now that she had dispensed with the bundle that was Cobweb. Her shape was not human, but that of a nebulous thing, a shade flitting through the grasses, a sudden wind that lifted the reeds on the ponds, an ambiguous pattern of movements. The fairies watched her go, unable to follow at such a speed, happy to let her run if it meant that Cobweb was saved.

Puck, for one, heaved an enormous sigh of relief. He would not have to fight.

'To Cobweb, brave Cobweb!' called Puck, from his seat on the staff. 'On, on!'

At that moment, however, as they were crossing the corner of Salisbury Plain, whistling things began to whizz past their heads and explode upon the floor of the plain.

'Ordnance! Artillery!' cried Mustardseed. 'It's the Civil War, revisited upon us innocent fairy folk. Ho, where are the Cavaliers and Roundheads? Witness, gunpowder and ballistics! *Roaring Meg* bellows at us. See, see, the flashes of the guns! We are under attack.'

Shells were falling all around them then, but the magnificent chalk giant did not pause in his stride. Missiles went through his hollow form, arced over his shoulders, went into his empty face and out the other side, without causing him the least concern. It would have to be an accurate shell to strike the thin white lines of *his* figure. He cast a tall but outlined shadow, with no substance on which to fix a target. The Army field guns and tanks of Salisbury Plain had no slings and arrows with which to fell a chalk giant. These were empty gestures, hopeless manoeuvres.

'On, on!' cried Puck. 'To Woodhenge!'

The chalk giant continued his long strides until out of reach of the guns. Finally they were at Woodhenge. The fairies slid down the Long Man to the ground below and found a cocoon, a mummified figure which, once they tore away the white mesh of fibres, revealed a frightened Cobweb.

'Am I saved?' cried Cobweb. 'Is this my king I see?'

'It is indeed, brave Cobweb,' replied Oberon. 'Your fairy friends have come to your rescue at last. How do you feel? Has the sorceress harmed you in any way?'

Cobweb felt along his limbs, down his slim body, between his fingers and toes.

'I am whole and I am free. Gramercy.'

The fairies clustered around their Cobweb, kissing him profusely, stroking his fine hair, welcoming him back into their number. There were fairy tears of joy and there was fairy laughter. Cobweb was safe once again.

Oberon could not help remarking, 'See what becomes of rebellion and sulking!'

The Long Man of Wilmington was thanked and sent on his way, back to his home in the chalk hill. Tall as the pylons, he went off over the dusty fields, crossing roads with mighty strides, fording rivers and splashing through brooks. A giant drawing in white, a walking outline of a murder victim, he was seen by police and travellers alike as he passed the rock beams of Stonehenge on his journey first south, then east. Then the geometric figure was gone, into the haze of the noonday heat, his twin staves rippling in the warping tendrils which twisted from the earth.

'He could have carried us to the New Forest,' said Moth, 'instead of going in that bus.'

'It would be too long a journey for us to sit upon his shoulders all the way,' answered Oberon, 'and we first have to fetch Titania and her baby.'

The owl was despatched to bring Sid and the bus, which, when it arrived, had Sid remonstrating with the fairies for expecting him to know what the owl's screeches were intended to convey. They were surprised, first at his annoyance, then at their own assumptions. Being fairies they had forgotten Sid was mortal and did not speak with birds.

'It's a good job I saw *Lassie, Come Home*,' he said, 'and guessed she wanted me to follow her.'

The fairies boarded the vehicle, then set off for Avebury.

Morgana was incensed by her failure to thwart the fairies,

but realized that Titania and the baby were not with the main group. She followed the scent of the baby and the trail led her back to Avebury. She knew the fairies would soon be back with Titania and so she remained near Silbury Hill, where she enlisted the services of the Green Man.

'You will do my bidding, do you understand me?' said the Morning-Fairy, harshly. 'Whatever loyalty you feel towards the fairies, they cannot protect you from *me*.'

The Green Man had awakened that very morning, finding himself in a world almost shorn of his beloved deciduous woodlands, replaced only in part by conifers. The world was still very green, but even the old grasses were gone – the cocksfoot, reed canary, quaking, false-brome, black and tufted hair – these were rare now. The world was full of timothy grass, favoured by the farmers, which covered the landscape. The hedgerows, too, were few and far between, with copses only in boggy places where the farmers could not grow their crops. The Green Man loved secret places in the wood, where rotten logs grew fungi and thick ivy flourished, but the open landscape was devoid of such hidey-holes.

At Morgana's bidding the Green Man had emerged from Ryhope Wood, which some call Mythago Wood, one of the last enclaves of a lost forested England. He felt betrayed by what he found outside the only few acres of primal woodland the island had to offer and wanted to go back there soon, to fall asleep again for another few centuries, in the hope that things would change. This was no place for him, out here where agoraphobia might smother his primitive brain and cause him untold misery.

'I understand you,' said the Green Man.

When he remained completely motionless, the Green

Man was likely to be mistaken for a stunted hawthorn tree, or a weathered tor, or an ancient blackthorn shrub. He was grey-green and craggy, pitted and striated. Bits grew from him like foliage from rotten logs: cauliflower-fungoid shapes of various hues. The ants, the wood lice, the beetles were all unaware that he was not vegetable and sap, but flesh and blood. Spiders made webs between his eyelashes and earlobes. Only his soulful eyes were likely to give him away, staring out from deep pits like the holes left by tree knots, bearing a mixture of sadness and solitude.

'What must I do?' he asked.

'You must steal the baby which the Queen of the Fairies is keeping from me,' hissed Morgan-le-Fay.

'And if I cannot?'

'Then you must take the fairy Cobweb. It grieves me that those fairies should be so triumphant. If I again snatch Cobweb from under their noses, they will be forced to acknowledge my superiority. What they take from me, I can swiftly take back. However, the baby is the first priority.'

The Green Man nodded in his misery.

'How will I capture Cobweb, if I cannot take the baby?'

'You must give him this dedoction made from magic plants,' replied the Morning-Fairy, 'which will cause him to become a shadow. Roll the shadow up like a black tapestry and bring it to me. I shall then let you go back to the wood.'

The Green Man stared at the phial of black liquid.

'It will not kill him? I wish no murder.'

'This is not a death potion,' snapped the witch. 'It's simply a temporary prison. If no further drug is administered, the victim will return to his normal shape after a few hours. Spare me your conscience, Green Man.'

The Green Man regarded the midnight face of Morgana. Its beauty had not been worn away by the ravages of age, but torn from her visage by acts of evil. The eyes were still clear and bright, but hard as flints. A countenance without grace, eyes without compromise. Ambition and avarice had shaped her features and the sculptures of greed and a lust for power are not attractive pieces, being without warmth.

It was true that the Green Man could look into her heart and see love there, but it was not love of fellow creatures, but love of self, love of Morgan-le-Fay.

'Go now,' she said, aware that she was being scrutinized. 'Fetch me my prey.'

The Green Man slipped away into the folding hills, down the lanes of purple shadow, along the secret furrows, cryptic in his movements, silent in his going.

NINETEEN

Ice Plant Opens and Field Sowthistle Closes

TITANIA HAD GONE OFF SOMEWHERE TO A VILLAGE SHOP, to replenish her baby supplies. Earl had gone with her because Titania had professed an ignorance of money. She had produced some gold coins rather mysteriously from somewhere on her person, none of the humans were sure where because she didn't seem to have any pockets, and these coins seemed to be antiques of some kind. On one side they bore the head of some exotic warrior-woman ruler of an extinct African kingdom. On the reverse side of the coin was a snake's head with a sun in its widened jaws.

Tom had told her to hold on to the coins and said he would loan her ten pounds for groceries. Titania had thanked him with her wide bright eyes, and her wide bright smile, and had then asked Earl instead of him to accompany her to the shop, leaving Tom feeling deflated.

'She's playing games with you,' said Mary. 'Thank goodness Earl isn't one of those men who are impressed by fluttering eyelids.'

'You hope,' said Tom.

'No, I know Earl and his feet are firmly on the ground.'

The tone of voice she used made Tom look at his sister.

'You sound – oh, never mind.'

'What?' asked Mary.

'Well, you've got a very, I don't know, *fond* sound to your voice, when you talk of Earl. You're usually very matter-of-fact about him.'

Mary smiled. 'The more I learn about Earl, the more I find him fascinating.'

'What? That's the *last* thing I'd say about Earl – that he was *fascinating*. I find him stolid and unimaginative.'

'That', said Mary, 'is what I find fascinating about him.'

Tom snorted. 'You always said you only stayed with him for convenience, that he had done you a favour by fathering your child, but you didn't trust any man. Going by the sound of your voice you'll be telling me you've fallen in love with him next.'

Mary began tidying up the bus. She shrugged.

'Anything's possible,' she said.

Tom stared at her for a while, then nodded. 'Well, I'd like to see it. I mean, Earl's not exactly the man I would have chosen for you – being your brother I think you're too good for him – but there's nothing terrible about him. I trust he didn't murder anyone while he was a Hell's Angel – they seem to be fond of burying axes in each other's skulls – but apart from that I would like to see you settled and happy.'

Mary replied, 'That's very nice of you, Tom, allowing me to choose my own partner for life,' but there was no rancour in her tone.

'You know what I mean, Mary,' he said. 'You're my sister – you're all I've got – and I'd rather see you married to a prince than a prizefighter. That's only natural, surely?'

'Prizefighters make good solid husbands. Princes tend to be rather spoilt. If you want the best for me, Earl's probably the man. If you want me to have a flighty time, wear lots of jewels and go to parties, then probably a prince would be the best thing. I don't want jewels and parties – I want something warm and comfortable and a stable, ordinary family life in which to raise my son.'

Tom looked around the bus.

'You call being a traveller a stable, ordinary family life?'

'Just because my house has wheels, doesn't make it any less valid than one resting on concrete foundations.'

Tom didn't agree, but he didn't say so. He was no traveller, having joined them only for the duration of his book, his normal abode being a flat in Camden. His sister seemed to be more contented than he was however, and he couldn't criticize her lifestyle if his own brought nothing but unsettled feelings of dissatisfaction.

Mary and Tom then watched the twelve o'clock news on TV, on which the distressed face of Frances Flute had once more appeared, asking for the person or persons who had stolen her employers' baby to return it.

'I know that person must be someone who loves children,' said Frances, 'otherwise why take a little baby?'

Since there had been no ransom note, the police had ruled out kidnapping, and were left with child-snatching. Out there somewhere, said a senior police officer, there was a man or woman who wanted revenge on the DuLacs

229

for some reason, or who needed desperately to have a baby – so desperately they had stolen what could not be achieved by other means. Perhaps it was someone who had been turned down for adopting a child? Or someone whose child had just died? Or someone who felt incomplete without a baby to look after? Or someone who was mentally ill and in a confused state?

Clearly the policeman did not agree with Frances that whoever it was must necessarily love little babies.

'What a shame,' said Mary. 'I do hope they find whoever it was soon.'

A fuzzy picture of a baby some five months old appeared on the screen, with apologies for its poor quality.

'She's very pretty, isn't she?' Tom said, in a dreamy tone.

'What, that little baby?'

'No – Miss Flute – the nanny. I think she's quite attractive.'

'So you said before,' answered his sister, 'but this Titania woman seems to have eclipsed her.'

'Well, yes, but one's here in the flesh, while the other's just a face on TV. I mean, how am I supposed to get to meet Frances Flute? I can't just write to her.'

Mary raised her eyebrows. 'Why not? She's human like everyone else. If she's already got a boyfriend, then she won't answer, will she? If she hasn't, then she might, and so long as you don't rush things, you could get to meet her sometime, really get to know her.'

'You're right,' said Tom, slamming a fist into a palm. 'It's just that under Titania's gaze I feel bewitched – she hypnotizes me with her beauty. Beauty isn't everything though, is it?'

Mary shook her head. 'That's what *I* said, earlier.'

'Well then,' said Tom, 'I'll put Titania out of my mind – she's a married woman after all. I can't think what came over me. I've never been the adulterous sort. You must admit it was quite out of character, sis.'

'I was worried about you.'

'Worry no more. Your brother has come to his senses. I'll write to Frances Flute, via the BBC, and hope she answers my letter. If she doesn't, well hard luck, but I can't go around chasing other men's wives, can I?'

At that moment Titania appeared in the doorway to the bus, with the baby in her arms.

'Hello, Tom,' she said in her silvery voice, 'we've got the groceries. I bought this little hat. Do you think it makes me look too – what's that word I heard? – frumpy?'

Her heart-shaped face was framed by a Paddington Bear hat, which made her look like a vulnerable, delicate flower. Titania smiled, her gold-flecked magenta eyes captivating the fickle Tom oh so easily in barely an instant. Tom was swept away on a flood of romantic passion, which threatened to drown him, and his former resolve was now driftwood.

'Oh no, not too old-fashioned – you look – you look *stunning*. I've – I've never seen anyone look so – so incredibly beautiful.'

'Well, now,' said his sister, laconically, 'there's a revelation.'

Tom could not be put off by his sister's attitude.

'Would you – would you come for a walk with me, while you're waiting for your people to arrive?'

'Of course I will, Tom,' said Titania, plonking the baby in Mary's arms, 'if your sister doesn't mind looking after Pigwidgeon for a short while.'

'She won't mind,' said Tom, steering Titania down the bus steps and not even looking towards Mary. 'She likes babies.'

As they walked away from the bus, towards a distant copse, Titania slipped her fingers into his palm.

'Would you mind holding my hand, Tom?' she said. 'In case I trip on this rough ground.'

Tom's hand closed covetously around Titania's slender fingers. Touching her soft skin filled him with such ecstasy it was difficult not to shout in joy. He wanted to yell his delicious feelings to the world. Containing himself with difficulty, Tom simply savoured the tender emotions which flowed through his whole being.

The thought of having Titania alone to himself filled his heart to the brim with happiness. How could he have compared Frances Flute to this angel by his side? It was simply ludicrous. His stupidity, he decided, had been prompted by his sister. He was in love with Titania, would die for her, would kill for her, would compromise anything in the world for her, including his honour, his integrity, his honesty.

'I don't think your brother-in-law likes me,' said Titania, 'nor your sister.'

'Oh, Earl's not my brother-in-law. They're not married. And you shouldn't worry what he thinks. He's a rough sort of bloke – not at all used to women like you.'

'What sort of woman am I, Tom?'

'You're – you're superior to every woman I've ever known. You have looks, intelligence, and I should say breeding. I expect you come from an aristocratic family, don't you? What's your real name?'

'You must call me Titania, Tom, and yes, you're right – I am from a noble house.'

'I thought so,' said Tom, triumphantly. 'And you like me? That's astonishing. I'm just an ordinary sort of man. I mean, I couldn't even dream of having a woman like you, could I? Not seriously? Eh?'

There was a plea in these questions, but Titania chose to ignore it.

'But your sister doesn't like me either.'

'She doesn't understand you, like I do. She thinks you're flirting with me, leading me on. She doesn't like married women who play around.'

Titania showed a flash of temper.

'Who's she to talk of morals – unwed, yet bedded by that crude, uncultured man? If she were a maid instead of a strumpet and a trollop, I might heed her words.'

'Here, steady on, my sister's not a trollop,' said Tom, feeling things were going a little too far. 'She's a nice person – she just doesn't choose to get married.'

Titania squeezed his fingers and looked up into his eyes.

'You're so loyal, Tom. Your sister is lucky to have you as a brother. I have no brother to protect me. I have no-one who cares for me like you do for Mary.'

Tom wanted to shout ME, I care for you, but it was too early for that.

'You – you have your husband.'

'Oberon? He's too busy with his own affairs – and besides, he's always trying to steal my babies.'

'Steal your babies?' cried Tom, astonished. 'How many have you got?'

'One at the moment,' replied Titania, and Tom recalled the conversation about the Indian child.

'Oh, right. But why would he want to do that? I mean, Pigwidgeon's his baby too, isn't it? At least, in name, if not in fact.'

Something occurred to Tom which gave him hope.

'Here, you're not wrangling over custody are you? You two aren't getting divorced?'

'No, Oberon would never let me divorce him. We are to be together always. It is the natural law.'

'Well, the law these days says you can get divorced in six months if you put your mind to it.'

'Tom,' said Titania, 'you really care for me, don't you?'

They had reached the edge of the wood by this time and Tom's mind was buzzing with a kind of miserable happiness. He had the woman he adored by the hand, leading her into a wood, where he could be romantic and tell her all those things about her that he loved, yet she was someone else's wife and that made him desperately unhappy. She was unobtainable: he had to persuade her to make herself obtainable.

'Oh, Titania,' he said. 'You know I do.'

'Thank you, Tom,' she said, and with a tinkling laugh, she let go of his hand and skipped off into the wood.

'Wait,' he called. 'Where are you going?'

'To get some rest,' she called back. 'I'll be back soon – wait for me.'

Tom hung around on the edge of the wood for about ten minutes and then allowed his temper to rule his finer feelings. He stomped back to the bus where his sister was feeding the baby. Tom sat down and began fiddling with some typewritten pages of his book, but his sister could see he was upset and asked him what was the matter.

'She just flitted away into the wood, after first making sure that I was in love with her,' he complained. 'Why would she do that?'

'*La belle dame sans merci*,' said his sister, enigmatically. 'I know something you don't know, but I can't tell you.'

'Why? Why won't you tell me?'

'Not *won't* – can't. My tongue's tied.'

'Oh well, have it your own way,' said Tom irritably.

At that moment Earl entered the bus with young Alex in tow. The big man wiped his boots on a piece of coconut matting that was already thick with mud and dirt. Little Alex copied his father's actions with a serious face, which made Mary smile a little with fondness for both of them.

'There's something going on down in the village,' said Earl. 'A lot of bawling and shouting.'

'Oh, God,' Mary replied, 'you don't think one of the travellers has upset the people down there? If we get a vigilante group coming round, I'll go mad. The last time that happened there was a fight and the police managed to get a court to rule against us for riotous behaviour.'

Earl nodded grimly. 'They start the trouble and then we get the blame.'

'A vigilante group?' said Tom. 'That sounds like a Western film or something.'

'You get gangs of youths taking up cudgels on behalf of the community. Once some of these village thugs think they've got right on their side, they'll wade into the travellers with no thought for women or kids. Earl, chain Sabre outside, where they can see him. They'll think twice about wrecking the bus if there's a dog guarding it.'

'They'd better not try wrecking *my* bus,' said Earl, hotly. 'I'll bust a few heads first.'

'That's what they want you to try, and in any case, they can throw mud and bricks without coming near you.'

Earl nodded. 'I guess you're right, Mary – you usually are. OK, I'll put Sabre on a long rope, so he can bite the backside off any villager that comes within sixty feet.'

'I think we should get ready to move, don't you?' asked

Tom. 'I'm not so keen on this place anyway. Why don't we follow Oberon's lot? They're talking about going down to the New Forest.'

Earl said, 'We all know why you want to go with Oberon's crew, don't we?'

'If you mean Titania, say so.'

'All right,' Earl growled. 'I mean Titania. Personally I don't know what you see in the little minx. She's just fishing for compliments all the time. A right little . . .'

'And I suppose you're impervious to women like her.'

'Immune, pal. I've had the inoculations.'

Mary laughed at this and Tom felt sulky, but he left it at that. It was pointless arguing with a bluff Yorkshireman like Earl, who had an answer for everything. Tom buried his face in his work and tried to blot out thoughts of Titania and, as always, when he was out of her presence, his efforts at purging her from his feelings were fairly successful.

The Green Man returned to Morgan-le-Fay with a roll of black shadow under his right arm. He handed it over to the furious sorceress, who stamped her foot in frustration.

'You didn't get Titania's baby?'

The Green Man was apologetic. 'I followed her into the woods where she fell asleep on a bed of star moss. There I searched for the human child, but found none. Perhaps she has given it to someone else?'

The Morning-Fairy shook her head. 'Titania would never willingly give her baby away. She must have guessed I would still be after it and hidden it somewhere. Did you search all the hollow logs, all the clumps of wild flowers, all the reed beds in the area?'

'Everywhere,' confirmed the Green Man. 'All I found

was a dead pigeon in a patch of herb robert.'

'It might have been the baby, disguised. What did you do with it?'

The Green Man looked shamefaced. 'I ate it.'

Morgana looked at the Green Man steadily, as if wondering whether to give vent to her foul temper.

The Green Man said, 'It was all rotten – I like rotten things – it must have been lying there for days – it was crawling with blow-fly maggots. She would not have disguised her baby as a *rotten* pigeon, would she?'

'Probably not,' conceded Morgan-le-Fay. 'So you've brought me someone else?'

The Green Man nodded. 'You asked for Cobweb. I found him talking with other fairies, at the back of that village church over there. When I heard one answer to the name of "Cobweb" I waited until I heard that one say, "I have to go for a pee – does anyone else want a drink while I'm there?" They all said "no" and I followed him to an inn. When he came out of the inn, he had a drink in his hand. By melding with the foliage above the path back through the churchyard, I was able to let some droplets fall from the phial you gave me into the drink. He took one sip at the corner of the path around the church and he was mine, to roll into the tapestry I now give to you.'

'You did well,' said Morgan-le-Fay. 'I release you.'

The Green Man bowed and then was gone, into the brown-green world around Silbury Hill.

Morgana knew that the fairies were heading for the New Forest and she decided she would go there too. She wanted them to witness the death of Cobweb. This time there would be a forest to hide in afterwards and she would not have to flee across open country. She would wait on the greensward close to the edge of the New Forest, there she would change Cobweb back into his normal shape and then slaughter him before the eyes of his fairy companions. Then she would escape into the darkness of the forest, which she understood was large enough to hide regiments of witches, even from the sharp noses of woodland fairies.

Once again Morgan-le-Fay confined herself to ley lines, crossing the countryside quickly, but not swiftly enough for her designs. Eventually she entered Berkshire and felt the vibrations of a supernatural being through the ground. This county was the home of Herne the Hunter, whose attraction to Windsor Great Park in the old days had been the deer with whom he had an affinity. Now he simply appeared from time to time, shedding his antlers, going into velvet, becoming the great stag for yet another season's rutting.

The shaggy figure of Herne, mounted on his fire-breathing horse, was not as bloodthirsty as Wotan the Hunter, once having been a good human and hanged by a king. The antlers had been bound to his head as a magical remedy for serious wounds received from a deer, and became fixed there, to remain part of Herne after his untimely and unwarranted death on the gallows. Herne was a stalker, a forester, a hunter by necessity rather than for the sake of sport, and was therefore a true huntsman. He never killed for gain or gamesmanship, only for food. Herne despised those who tracked and slaughtered animals for its own sake and he was no friend of Wotan, whose bloodthirst was slaked by the kill.

Morgan-le-Fay called for Herne the Hunter and he came reluctantly to answer her bidding.

'What do you want, Morgana?' he asked.

The sorceress looked up at the magnificent figure astride his black, smoking horse. Herne had appeared in a sunlit glade, naked astride his charger, his shaggy body still dripping with earth mould. Ribbons of old ivy hung from his antlers. In his hand was a hunting bow, a quiver of arrows on a back as hairy and muscular as that of an Angus bull. His wolfish face, with its coarse dark bristles, held two peat-brown eyes. His demeanour was that of a wronged man, out to cause havoc on the royal hunting grounds, punishing those who had descended from the king who took his life.

'What do you want?' demanded Herne.

'I need a ride to the New Forest, hunter,' said Morgan-le-Fay. 'You must help me.'

'Why must I help you?'

'Because those from whom I flee are of royal blood – the king and queen of fairyland.'

Herne's mount snorted, sending sprigs of fire flicking out towards Morgana, who backed a pace.

'You yourself are of royal blood,' boomed Herne. 'Your father was a king and your mother a queen.'

'That wasn't my fault,' snapped the Morning-Fairy. 'I didn't ask to be born into a noble house.'

'Nevertheless, you are of royal lineage and therefore an enemy of Herne the Hunter.'

He withdrew an arrow from his quiver, put it to his bowstring, and drew back. He let fly the shaft, which hissed through the air, pinning Morgana to the ground by her gown. A look of pain went through her eyes. When she pulled angrily on the dress, her hem ripped around the stitching and the gown bled from the wound. Her garments had been on her so long they had become part of her, hence they had not rotted into the earth of Offa's

Dyke. The wound could just as well have been in one of her limbs. Morgan-le-Fay spat acid on the ground in front of Herne's horse, causing the earth to hiss and burn with an acrid smell.

Herne was not in the least concerned by her anger. True hunters and woodmen have been killing witches since the beginning of time: there exists an enmity between the two which even the silken, persuasive Morning-Fairy could not dispel.

'Begone, sorceress,' said Herne. 'Find your help elsewhere.'

TWENTY

Common Purslane Opens and Proliferous Pink Closes

THE FAIRIES SET OFF ONCE MORE ON THEIR JOURNEY towards the New Forest. Some of the New Age travellers decided to go with them and formed a small convoy, which also included the Blessing bus. The New Forest had some good sites and the children liked the wild ponies and donkeys: travellers found the New Forest area more interesting than old quarries or common scrubland.

As Jug said, 'It's what the travelling life's all about – living on the edge of the old world.'

Tom was happy about following the beautiful Titania, of course, and Mary didn't object, but even Earl was becoming attached to the group which he and Tom still thought were travelling actors. Earl especially liked Puck, who he saw as a man like himself, a lapsed Hell's Angel.

Puck travelled with the Blessings and Earl for the first part of the journey.

Moth was back navigating again and since the travellers were in no hurry to get anywhere fast, he was given license to take his own route to the New Forest. Moth did not like main roads and the scent of blossom took him directly south from the A303 down the A3084 to the Wallops and Whiteshoot Hill. They passed through Over Wallop, then Middle Wallop, before taking a byway to Nether Wallop, where Titania drove directly to the church and stopped the bus.

Tom asked Puck, 'What have we stopped here for?'

'King Arthur,' said Puck. 'He's buried here in the churchyard.'

Tom wrinkled his brow. This did not seem at all likely. Tom didn't know where King Arthur *was* interred, though he was inclined to put the site somewhere in the West Country, like Tintagel, but he was sure it was not in this tiny country churchyard. The theatre group was yet again producing a mystery for him to puzzle over. It was getting to be frustrating.

The fairies all piled out and trooped into the graveyard, where the stones lay at all angles as if planted by a maladroit giant. There were one or two semi-famous people buried in the graveyard – a prime minister, two scientists, a composer and a novelist – but the fairies marched straight past these to a gravestone in the corner wedged between the drystone wall and some strong-smelling elderberry shrubs.

They stopped by this headstone which bore the words:

ARTHUR TRUMBLE

BORN 1903 – DIED 1987

SADLY MISSED BY HIS WIFE AND DAUGHTER

Here they removed their caps and stood silently regarding the tomb of this person who seemed to be a nobody.

Tom was right behind the fairies and he read the words on the stone with some bewilderment.

Had the inscription read: ARTHUR PENDRAGON, KING OF THE SILURES, FELL MORTALLY WOUNDED IN THE BATTLE OF CAMLAN, he would have been surprised but satisfied.

Earl, Jug, Tom, Mary and Alex joined the fairies around the grave and Jug asked who was buried there.

'Arthur Trumble,' said Puck in a reverent tone.

'Yes, we can read that,' replied Tom a little irritably, 'but who was he? An actor?'

Oberon shook his head. 'No – I believe by profession he was a salesman.'

Tom raised his eyebrows at his sister, then something occurred to him.

'What did he sell – costumes for the stage?'

'Ladies underwear,' whispered Puck. 'He was a very simple man. He travelled the whole country and learned very little about other people. He was not very good at his job.'

'Yet – yet you seem to revere this man? Why are we standing around this grave talking in hushed tones, paying our respects to a man who sold women's underclothes and wasn't even very good at that?'

'To us, this man was the most important mortal to grace the British Isles for many centuries,' replied Puck, sternly. 'Please keep a deferential tone to your voice.'

It went quiet for a time, during which Swallowtail let fall

243

a silent tear, which trickled down her pale cheek.

Mary sighed and said to Puck, 'All we want to know is, why you think Arthur Trumble is worth grieving over?'

Oberon put on his cap at this point and so did the rest of the fairies. They left the grave in good order, filing back to their bus. Puck again joined the Blessing group and finally explained the reason for the halt.

'During his lifetime,' said Puck, 'Arthur Trumble planted some 3328 trees – mostly ash and oak trees, which he loved, but also hornbeams, elms, sycamores, poplars, and others – one a week from the time he began his job as a salesman, until his death. To us he was a king – the King of Tree Planters.'

'That's very laudable,' said Tom, still not really understanding. 'I mean, I suppose his job took him all over the place and he planted these trees as he went.'

'Correct,' said Puck. 'It was an act of the most precious kind. The world owes Arthur Trumble a great deal. Just think what a better place the Earth would be if every person planted a tree a week!'

'I don't know about a *better* place. It would be a bit difficult to get around, with all those trees. There wouldn't be anywhere for people to live.'

'Precisely!' said Puck, his point having been made.

'Well, that aside,' Tom said, 'why should a bunch of actors worry about having lots of trees around? I mean, that was no ordinary ceremony out there. You people are really fond of this Arthur, that's obvious. But what puzzles me, is why you should care? If you were a bunch of gamekeepers I could understand – but not the acting profession.'

'I know,' muttered Mary, 'but I can't tell you.'

'And,' Tom continued, 'if his selfless act of planting so

many trees was his life's work, why doesn't it say that on the gravestone? Why didn't his wife and daughter tell the world what he'd done?'

'They didn't know,' replied Puck. 'Nobody knew. That's why he's such a special person. He didn't do it for fame or fortune. He did it for *us*. Arthur Trumble was taken to see *A Midsummer-Night's Dream* when he was twelve and for the rest of his life he devoted a little time every week to making sure there would be *some* trees left for us.'

Tom was getting exasperated. 'What has planting trees got to do with Shakespeare and actors? I don't understand.'

'I understand,' said his sister, quietly.

'You keep saying that,' yelled Tom, 'but you won't tell me what you mean by it!'

'I can't,' said Mary.

'You keep saying that, too!'

'Don't yell at Mary,' cried Earl from the driver's seat. 'You'll frighten Alex.'

At the end of the conversation, Tom knew little more about the business than when he first started asking questions, and he let the matter drop. He suddenly became aware that the convoy had taken a sharp right turn and was heading, not south where the New Forest lay, but west into Somerset. Not for the first time was he perplexed by the group who had joined them yesterday evening and were now leading the cavalcade.

'Where are we going?' he cried to Earl. 'Where are they taking us?'

Earl shrugged and laughed. 'Puck? What's going on?'

Puck tuned in to his fairy brothers and sisters and found Moth's electric mind.

'We're going to Annwn,' Puck replied, after a moment.

245

'It is midsummer's day, after all. It would be a pity not to visit Annwn while we're so close. I haven't seen it for over a thousand years.'

Tom thought Puck was using an hyperbole.

'Annwn?' he queried.

'Hurray!' cried Alex, who had just woken up. 'We're going to Annwn.'

Tom took a grubby-looking, dog-eared road atlas from a makeshift bookcase. He pored over it for a few moments, before shaking his head.

'I can't find any *Annwn* on here,' he grumbled. 'Point it out to me, Puck.'

Mary, who knew exactly what Puck was talking about because she read Janet and Colin Bord books by the bushel, pointed to Glastonbury for him.

'There,' she said, 'that's where Annwn is – Glastonbury.'

'Glastonbury?' called Earl. 'That's good. You're right – mystical midsummer's still with us. Hey, you blokes are on the same wavelength as us travellers. Glastonbury's one of our favourite spots. Are we still going to the New Forest later on?'

'We've got to get there today,' said Puck.

Tom threw up his hands. 'You've got to get there today, yet you take these diversions? It's crazy.'

Earl called, 'It's not crazy, Tom. You don't understand road people. We don't travel in straight lines . . .'

'Unless they're ley lines,' corrected Puck.

'. . . . yeah, unless that. What we do is follow our instincts, our hidden natures, don't we, Mary?'

'Earl's right, Tom. That's why we're travellers, despised by the rest of the community in Britain, hated by the landowning class, scorned by the police. If we were

246

ordinary people, we would go *straight* to the New Forest, at eighty miles an hour, probably on the motorway. But we're not – we're oddballs, alternative-lifestyle people. We let ourselves be distracted by bees and flowers, by sunsets, by magical places like Glastonbury.'

Tom shook his head. 'I don't know – well, anyway, it'll give me something to write about in my book. What is this Annwn place, anyway? A theme park?'

'A fairy realm,' replied Puck. 'The home of the Tylwyth Teg. Do you believe in fairies, Tom?'

'Of course not – that's for six-year-olds,' scoffed Tom.

'Then you can't come with us,' said Puck, 'for the entrance to Annwn is on Glastonbury Tor.'

Alex squeezed next to Puck, who was sitting on a bench that ran down one side of the bus.

'Can I come?' he whispered. 'I believe in fairies.'

Puck put his arm around the five-year-old. 'Of course,' he replied, smiling.

Alex was looking into Puck's face from about six inches away and he shook his little head.

'Sometimes', he said, 'you seem like an old, old man, Mr Puck – when your smiley face crinkles up – and sometimes you seem just as young as me.'

'That's because I am.'

'Which one?' asked Alex.

'Both,' replied Puck.

'Don't be rude to Mr Puck, Alex,' said Mary. 'You mustn't call people old.'

'But I am old,' grinned Puck. 'You mustn't have him telling untruths – mortals shouldn't do that.'

Then Puck said to Tom, who was shaking his head still, 'King Arthur is at Glastonbury.'

'What?' cried Tom, astonished. 'Arthur Trumble is

buried there, too?'

'Not Arthur Trumble,' admonished Puck. 'King Arthur of the ancient Britons. The remains of Guinevere are there too – Pigwidgeon will be glad to see them. They are her ancestors – well,' he admitted as an afterthought, 'one of them is – the other is sort of step-ancestor.'

'What a lot of rubbish you do talk, Puck,' grumbled Tom. 'I never know what to believe of you.'

Mary said, 'It's thought the Holy Grail is in the Blood Well at the bottom of the tor.'

'Not that old story?' said Tom. 'Now why would the chalice used by Christ at the Last Supper be at the bottom of a well in England?'

'Joseph of Arimathea brought it here,' Mary told him.

'So I've heard – you'll be telling me next it was the fairies who persuaded him to leave it at the bottom of a well, where it could not be seen or cherished by anyone. Why didn't he put it in his church? It's a precious sacred object. It should be on display, not being used by frogs and toads at the bottom of a deep hole.'

'Tom, Tom,' said Puck, 'you really don't understand these things, do you? Once the grail has been found and put on display, it will lose all its magic, all its mystery. While it's still unobtainable, it's the dream of every knight errant to find it. Once it's been found, it's lost.'

'Once it's been found, it's lost,' snorted Tom. 'Riddles, Puck, riddles. What does that mean?'

'It means,' said Mary, 'that when someone finds the grail, it will be a five-minute wonder, then it'll be stuck in some museum somewhere and forgotten. It'll be lost to us for ever, because we found it and made it an ordinary object.'

'Oh, you've joined the clever brigade too, have you?'

'Now don't be unkind, Tom – that's not like you,' said Mary. 'You're just upset about something.'

Delicacy prevented her from speaking about Tom's infatuation for Titania in front of Puck.

'All right, all right, I give in,' said Tom. 'We're going to Glastonbury, whatever I think about it. But I don't want to be made a fool of, you know. I think you're playing some game with me, all of you – trying to make me look a fool.'

'You're doing very well at that by yourself, Tom,' said Mary, primly. 'You don't need any help from us.'

Glastonbury Tor stood on a ley line over twenty miles long, between Butleigh church and Brockley church, which added to the attraction of the place for the fairies and the travellers alike. The buses arrived at the back of the tor and swept into a field without a gate. There were already several flat backs, teepees, benders, buses and vans parked in the field, with children running around chasing dogs and dogs running around chasing children. Cooking was in progress on primus stoves, adding the rich aroma of wild rabbit, cabbage and carrots to the country air. The cabbage and carrots were from two nearby crops and the rabbits had been caught using the lurchers who were now practising on children.

'If travellers could only learn to control the amount of rubbish they leave around,' said Tom quietly, looking at the trash around the site, 'they might receive a little more goodwill from local people.'

But he had said this many times before and still the travellers managed to drop litter all around the field, making it look unsightly, and giving the local authority some ammunition. Where there was rubbish, residents argued, there would be rats and other vermin. The travellers were their own worst enemies at times.

Oberon called the fairies together.

'We must climb the magical tor,' he said, pointing to the hill with the ruin on its crest. 'To visit our cousins on this fine midsummer's day.'

Tom, sensing that something really important was going on, asked to be part of the expedition.

'What's this about cousins?' he asked.

'You don't believe in Annwn, so what is the point in explaining it all to you?' said Puck.

'All right,' Tom replied, 'convince me, Puck. What is Annwn? A fairy realm, right?'

Puck pointed to the top of the tor.

'Up there,' he said, seriously, 'is an invisible gateway leading directly to the heart of Wales. Therein is a realm called Annwn, where the Welsh fairies have their home. Actually the gateway comes *from* Annwn, but of course gateways have a two-way purpose. Fairies do not have a separate land – they live amongst you ordinary people – but they do have their own names for the places where they live.

'They also have these special gateways, located in places of great spiritual significance, which lead directly from fairy realms. This enables them to visit places with mystical atmospheres, like Glastonbury, without crossing vast distances.' Puck sighed. 'I wish there had been one in Sherwood, so we could have gone straight to the New Forest, but unfortunately Sherwood does not have any direct paths to other woodlands.'

'Are you telling me that you're actually fairies – not just travelling actors?'

Puck pointed to Oberon. 'There stands the King of the Fairies,' said Puck. 'Do not doubt it.'

'And there, the queen?'

'That is indeed Titania, Queen of the Fairies.'

Tom shook his head in disbelief.

'Well,' said Puck, 'we must be off now – see you when we get back. Come Alex, take my hand.'

Mary stepped forward and said anxiously, 'You're sure he'll be all right, Puck?'

'I shall guard him as if he were the child of an Arabian prince,' said Puck. 'He shall be more precious to me than all the treasures of Africa and India combined.'

'*Please* can I go?' pleaded Alex. 'I want to see the fairies.'

Puck's assurances were not exactly the kind Mary wanted to hear, but she could see Puck was serious about looking after Alex. It was an opportunity she did not feel she could deny her young son: a trip to fairyland at five years of age. Such a visit was golden, to be cherished in later years. If she stopped him from going, she knew she would regret it later, when they were recounting their times with Puck.

'You can come too, Mary,' said Puck, 'if you wish.'

'No,' Mary said, 'I'm too old. I would expect it to be one thing and it would be another. I would be disappointed and that would upset you. You take Alex.'

Oberon and the rest of the fairies were already quarter way up the tor and Puck ran after them, with Alex holding his hand. Titania was carrying the baby in her arms, helped by Cobweb on one side and Mist on the other. Tom watched them climbing up the steep slope.

Mary came and stood by his side.

'That character Puck tried to tell me they were fairies,' said Tom. 'Can you believe that?'

'Tom,' replied Mary, 'for a writer you're an awfully unimaginative man.'

'You believe it?' cried Tom in surprise.

'I was told by Oberon, at Avebury, but I was not allowed to pass it on. Now that you've been told, it seems I can talk to you about it. Yes, I do believe in them. After all, what are fairies but another race of people? Why shouldn't they exist? They clearly *do*.'

'Yes, but *magic* and all that?' scoffed Tom.

'Just another science, different from ours. You believe in the atom, though you can't see it – and the infinity of space. Why is it so difficult to believe in fairies then?'

The fairies were now three-quarters of the way up the hill. Tom was struggling with himself inside. The writer in him was marvelling at the idea that not only fairies might exist, but that he, Tom Blessing, had met them and had the opportunity of visiting a fairy realm, if he could only get himself to believe in what he was doing.

Mary was a traveller, she believed in astrology and future gazing and a host of other things of a mystical nature. He was, it was true, more down to earth. It was harder for him to take this fairy stuff on board. But the more he thought of missing such a wonderful opportunity because of narrow-mindedness, the more he overcame his disbelief.

Finally, he shouted, 'Wait!' in panic, and ran to the tor, climbing up its steep slope like a monkey, horrified that the fairies would enter Annwn without him, and this marvellous adventure would be lost to him for ever.

It was a hot, sweaty scramble up that hill, with a bright sun stuck like a badge on a hard indigo sky.

When he got to the top he was gasping for breath, gulping down air in short, strained draughts. He looked around him, wildly, unable to locate the fairies. They seemed to have gone to one side of the tor once they reached the top and he scrambled over the grassy knoll in the same direction.

He found Puck and Alex, waiting for him.

'Where are they?' choked Tom. 'Have I missed it?'

'No, I heard you,' said Puck. 'I stayed back for you – here, take my other hand, Tom.'

Tom did as he was told, finding the small hand strangely calloused and rough. Then he took a step forward and found himself walking on a narrow rocky path up a mountain. He stopped short, suddenly, staring about him. It was true, there was a gateway to Annwn, and he had passed through it. There were rugged hills and stony outcrops all around them, with stunted trees and tufted grass sprouting from fissures in the rock. The sky was a wishy-washy colour, misted over like pale-blue glass, while a dim yellow sun shone through the haze weakly: a pathetic heater for such a high, cool world.

On one side of him was a sheer drop of several hundred feet, while on the other was the mountain up which the narrow winding path, not much wider than a goat track, twisted and curled around boulders and escarpments. Below, in the valleys, was rich lush vegetation, narrow streams twisting and turning, and green pockets filled with sheep.

'Where are we?' he moaned, letting go of Puck's hand.

'Wales,' said Puck. 'Annwn. Realm of the Welsh fairies – the Tylwyth Teg and the Bendith Y Mamau – some good, some bad.'

Alex said, 'I don't like bad fairies – they're wicked.'

'There are bad ones?' said Tom.

'Oh yes, the Bendith Y Mamau, but they don't live in this part – they're over that way somewhere.' Puck gestured towards an horizon, over the next mountain, far from the path up which they were walking. 'At least – they used to be.'

'That's comforting,' muttered Tom. 'Where are the others – Oberon, Moth and Swallowtail?'

'They're all up ahead, can't you hear them?'

Soon the sound of chatter reached Tom's ears and he was shocked to hear they were talking a more archaic English amongst themselves, now that they were not conversing with humans. He felt a little humiliated at being fooled, all this time, into thinking they were actors. He complained to Puck about this, but Robin Goodfellow had little sympathy.

'We didn't pretend to be actors – *you* decided that on your own.'

'True,' said Tom, feeling even more upset, 'but it was a natural assumption.'

'For a mortal,' grunted Puck, 'but then mortals be such everlasting fools.'

The air was freshly scented with the perfumes of tiny alpine flowers. Small, unidentifiable birds danced gaily between the rocks, like quick insects, too swift in their movements to be seen clearly. They twittered in a distracting manner. Flies flicked from one plant to the next, in search of food and shelter.

Old granite towers stood on corners, split away from the main thrust of the mountain, to form tempting climbs for the agile and adventurous. Brows of gneiss loured over the pathway occasionally, as if glowering at some distant offensive object down on the plains. The occasional gnarled tree sprang from a soil-filled crack to overhang the path.

'How much further?' panted Tom, when they came to a stream like a zigzag flash of silver shooting down the mountainside.

At that moment they rounded a steep corner to find a plateau on which stood the Sherwood fairies. Around them, emerging from hiding places in the rocks and from under the roots of crooked trees, came an even smaller race of beings, which Tom guessed were the Welsh fairies. They were talking a language he recognized as Welsh, having been to North Wales many times as a child.

'*Dydd da*,' said one of them to him, '*Mae hi'n gymylog heddiw. Ydych chi'n siarad Cymraeg?*'

Tom recognized some of what was being said.

'Good day to you. Er – clouds, did you say? No, I don't speak Welsh, but I understand a little.'

'*Beth ydy'ch enw chi?*'

'My name? Tom. Tom Blessing.'

'*Croeso!* Welcome, Tom Blessing.'

'Thank you.'

Finally, one of the residents spoke in full English, clearly directed at Oberon.

'Who's this then?' said the individual, haughtily. 'Someone come to call, have they?'

'Tis I, Oberon, King of Mommur,' said that royal personage, 'and Queen Titania. Here too are the fairies late of Sherwood Forest, and the renowned sprite Puck, also called Robin Goodfellow. We have come to give hearty greetings and good morrows to our cousins, Gruffydd of Cymru and Betsw-Y-Coed, King of Annwn, and Blodwyn-the-Beautiful, Queen of the Tylwyth Teg, and all the fairies of this handsomely rugged landscape on midsummer's day.'

'Oberon and Titania, is it?' said a female fairy. 'Now there's posh for you.'

There was a reserve in the air, which Tom felt quite strongly. It was as if two opposing forces had come together to size each other up, each waiting for the other to make the first move. Tom had no knowledge of the history of these two sets of fairies, but he guessed it was similar to that which held for the English and Welsh peoples. Perhaps wrongs had been done, to one side or the other, which called for mistrust and aloofness? Perhaps the past was not a happy place and it was time to close old gates and open new ones?

Suddenly, Titania took a step forward and held up the baby.

'Behold!' she cried. 'The descendant of Guinevere and Lancelot du Lac!'

Pigwidgeon giggled and let free a windy-puff.

There was an awed 'Ahhhhh!' from the Welsh fairies, who then rushed forward and crowded around Titania and Pigwidgeon, some reaching up to touch the child's small feet. They were clearly quite overcome by the sight of the infant. To Tom, it was as if the baby Jesus had suddenly been produced at a meeting between Catholics and Protestants, and all differences between the two had melted away in the face of this uniting symbol. Pigwidgeon was a special child, obviously.

Pigwidgeon took all this fuss and adulation without another murmur, though she was clearly enjoying herself.

Once the ice had been broken, the fairies on both sides fell into each other's arms chattering so swiftly Tom could not follow the conversations. Some revealed their inner excitement by doing a little jig. Others threw their caps in the air. If there was a history of wrongs, they were quickly forgotten, and natural goodwill prevailed.

'Who's this then?' said Gruffydd, pointing to Tom. 'This is no fairy, is it? Nor a child, eh?'

He turned to smile at Alex.

'We welcome the chatter-charm of children, for they are the keepers of our castles and have saved our sanity these past few sad centuries. Such cherished babes are bonnie beauties, chock-full of bounteous innocence. This older, bolder, brave little child a chortle-cheeky chit, to be treasured as a trove tucked tight on a toddy-tappers' isle.'

Now he whirled to face Tom.

'This is no kite-carrying child though, but a man in magnitude, one of those thre'penny-eyed, thin-lipped louts forever lapping bonnyclabber with long lissome tongue, staggering homeward soppy-gaited with stout and stale cigars, sicking in the shallows, falling silly in the stream and waking woeful in the noon heat with hammering head and regretful never-again, oh-never-ever-again heart.'

Puck said, copying Gruffydd's accent, 'This is Tom, look you – he's a mortal man. Got lost on his way to chapel, so he did! Can't seem to find his way down the mount-ain.'

Gruffydd glared at Puck, then after a moment burst out laughing.

'That Robin Goodfellow,' he said. 'He should be locked up. A terr-ible fellow, so he is.'

Gruffydd moved closer to Tom and regarded him with such a severe face that Tom began to shake a little in fear. These were not ugly creatures around him, but they were quite bizarre and eerie. He could feel the magic in the air, smell it like a strange gas. There was a power there which he would be helpless to resist, should it be directed at him with malice.

'Come with the Sherwood fairies, have you?' said Gruffydd. 'Come to see the Welsh, eh?'

'I – I'm a friend of Puck,' stuttered Tom. 'We – we're

fellow travellers.'

'Got an eye for Titania, too,' said Blodwyn. 'Any fool can see that.'

'No! Not at all,' cried Tom, horrified. 'Friends, of course, but nothing more than that, I assure you.'

'Get away with you,' laughed Blodwyn. 'You're smitten, man. She's got you trailing around after her like she does with most mortal men. It's written all over your face.'

The fairies all burst out laughing, delighting in his discomfort. Angry with this treatment, Tom wanted to pick up stones and scatter the fairies like crows, but some inner alarm warned him that it would be his last act if he did. These were not people, they were fairies, and as such they did not have the morals of mortals, they had their own codes. He might be pushed off the edge of the rock, to become another victim of the mountain. He wondered how many climbers' fingers these creatures had prised from handholds, when they had felt violated or wronged by mortals.

These thoughts helped him to remain calm and pleasant under their ridicule.

Pigwidgeon chortled and distracted the Welsh fairies once again, as they swarmed around Titania like bees, wanting to touch the magical child.

'Is that baby really the descendant of Guinevere and Lancelot?' whispered Tom to Puck. 'That must mean that as the parents of Pigwidgeon, either Titania or Oberon is a great-grandchild of the offspring of the two lovers. I never realized there was such a child. I don't remember it from the stories.'

Fortunately, his first question did not require an answer from Puck, being more rhetorical in nature, but Puck did say that just because there were no *written* stories about an illegitimate son or daughter of Guinevere and Lancelot, did not mean they did not exist.

'Oral tales get lost,' said Puck. 'Not all of them survive to go into books.'

Tom said, 'That makes sense.'

There was a general party atmosphere and the Tylwyth Teg began bringing out fairy food, from cracks in the rocks, small caves and hare forms. Most of the sweetmeats were unrecognizable, at least to Tom, but he identified mushrooms and toadstools, could smell honey and brine, saw cakes of packed diaphanous green hair which must have been made of weed from streams, witnessed algae and lichen being scraped from rocks and patted into lumps.

Even the Sherwood fairies had their offerings, bringing out of their pockets acorns, chestnuts, hazelnuts, and other woodland fare. Mustardseed's wood mice leapt from his pockets and rushed to a slab of rock where crumbs had been scattered for them. Soon the fairies were tucking in, while Oberon held court, explaining why they had used the Glastonbury gate at this time.

'Our beloved Sherwood has taken on a shrunken look,' he told King Gruffydd. 'Only the Major Oak has kept us locked to the forest until now. 'Tis well for you Welsh fairies that you need no trees for your homeland – the rocks and hills suffice to keep your ways secret from mortal eyes. A place where rugged Welsh fairy husbandry is possible. We English fairies need our forest, in which to gather food, eat and sleep, a canopy of leaves for our heads.

'Yet we have found such a place, on the edge of the sea, where my kingdom may yet flourish again, and where Titania and I may keep our cryptic manners and survive until the end of time, when all will crumble together, dust to dust.'

'Oberon, I'm pleased for you,' said Gruffydd, taking a mouthful of waterweed cake. 'But you mustn't think the Tylwyth Teg have it all too easy, mind. Our land has shrunk as well and we're crowded in on each other, like sprats caught in a net, and some of us don't get on too well together, see.'

At that moment, as if to prove his words, some creatures appeared on the top of the rocks behind the feast. They sat there, hunched against the wind, staring down with wicked, greedy little eyes, on the scene below them. They were not happy folk, Tom could see that, being different again from both the Welsh mountain fairies and the woodland fairies.

'The Bendith Y Mamau,' muttered Puck, seeing them. 'Ugly creatures.'

They were indeed unpleasant to look at, being stunted and misshapen. Puck told Tom this was the result of inbreeding. Unlike the woodland fairies, who lived for ever and did not need to reproduce, the Bendith Y Mamau bred and died like humans. Over the many centuries their worst features – long noses, skinny knock-kneed legs, big-knuckled fingers, pointy chins and beetle brows – had become even more exaggerated.

These intruders were not greeted by either the Welsh or the English fairies and they were left to sit in a ragged line on the rock, staring down at the feast. They spoke Welsh in a high-pitched tone, their sharp eyes watching every crumb that disappeared down a fairy throat. They fidgeted and fussed with themselves, playing with their buttons, or straightening their caps. However, Tom was pleased to see these strange creatures made no attempt to crash the party, because he felt instinctively there would be a battle. He wasn't worried for himself, but there was Alex to think of.

At that moment, Alex chose to speak. 'Bad fairies,' he said, pointing to the Bendith Y Mamau. '*Wicked* fairies.'

On hearing his voice, the Bendith Y Mamau suddenly perked up, their necks craning, until they caught sight of little Alex, hidden amongst the Sherwood fairies.

There was sharp chatter amongst the Bendith Y Mamau then, as they pointed to the child. They seemed to be getting highly excited and Tom didn't like the look of things. He nudged Puck, who nodded and motioned for Tom to keep calm.

One of the Bendith Y Mamau fairies dropped down from his perch with a plop onto the feasting place. He eyed the now silent and watching Welsh and English fairies warily. Slowly, he edged his way towards Alex, and stopped within touching distance of the child.

'Puck?' said Tom.

'Quiet, Tom – don't move.'

Alex stared wide-eyed at the corpse-coloured fairy, with its bald, bumpy head and grotesque features. However, to his credit he did not move nor cry out. He simply watched and waited, while the creature eyed him up.

'Boy,' said the Bendith Y Mamau in a thick accent. 'Little human boy.'

Then he reached out, ever so slowly and touched Alex on the face, stroking his cheek.

Alex drew back at this contact and looked at Puck.

'Enough,' said Puck to the intruder.

The Bendith Y Mamau smiled, a wide slit opening his face.

'*Bad* boy,' he laughed, shrilly. '*Wicked* boy.'

261

Then he threaded his way back through the lines of Welsh and English fairies, their faces like stone, until he could be helped up the rock-face by his companions. Once he was back on his perch the feast began again, the chatter and the laughter ringing out, and the Bendith Y Mamau started hooting and whistling to each other, scratching their feet and pulling their ears, making a spectacle of themselves.

'What was all that about?' whispered Tom to Puck.

'The Bendith Y Mamau like to steal children who can talk and walk – they drain the child's beauty and use it on themselves like a mortal woman's cosmetics. It works for a while, then the beauty fades from the fairy thief as the child grows to adulthood. Finally, they let their grown captive go and he or she is returned to the real world. Usually they become misfits in society, not knowing how to act and not having had any human contact for so long. They spend the rest of their lives ragged and hungry, squatting on street corners and down railway tunnels, staring at passers-by.'

'Stolen by fairies. That's terrible,' said Tom. 'We mustn't let them near Alex then!'

'They won't dare take Alex, not with all of us here. There would be a horrible fight and fairies would tear each other in two. They wouldn't risk that.'

Despite Puck's assurances, Tom spent the rest of the meal, at which he ate nothing, in a state of trepidation. To take his mind off the Bendith Y Mamau, he asked Puck how many different types of fairies existed.

'Only two or three, now – most clans have disappeared,' said Puck. 'There were many sub-species, like the Bendith Y Mamau, but of course there were the non-fairy races too: boggarts, bogies, gremlins, leprechauns, trolls, brownies, goblins, hobgoblins, pixies, elves, gnomes. Then there were the wood spirits, like the leshy, and the wasteland spirits, like the wendigo, who enjoyed leading people deeper into trouble, until they were thoroughly lost.'

'You must see the leshy, if you're forest fairies.'

'Not any more,' sighed Puck. 'They're all gone. You can't lead a human into a forest which isn't there. How can you lose someone if they can find their way out of the trees in less than an hour?'

'Was there any way a human could stop it happening, if he was becoming lost?'

'Certainly,' laughed Puck. 'There are always antidotes – you put your clothes and shoes on back to front – that bewilders the leshy, because they don't know whether you're coming or going, and they run away.'

Finally, the feast was over, the talking was done, and Oberon said it was time they left for Glastonbury.

Tom felt immensely relieved. He had visions of going back to Mary and telling her that her son was now a prisoner of the Bendith Y Mamau, an uncouth and unpleasant group of Welsh fairies, who were going to steal his looks. *That* would have been a very happy task, wouldn't it? Mary would have killed him and fried his liver for breakfast.

'We'll go first, shall we?' he said to Puck. 'Let's keep Alex between the two of us?'

Puck agreed this, but they left by continuing along the path around the mountain, instead of retracing their former route. When Tom complained that they were going the wrong way, Puck told him that if they returned the way they had come, they would end up in the heather of the Isle of Skye, via a Scottish gate. Tom shrugged his shoulders, perplexed by fairy orienteering, and did as he was told.

As they disappeared around the first bend, the Bendith Y Mamau hooted and jeered, calling, 'Little boy, little boy, come with us! We've got nice presents, nice toys. Come and eat ice cream, little boy. Come and play all day . . .'

'Don't listen to them, Alex,' said Tom.

Soon they were out of sight and sound of the hideous creatures and Tom relaxed a little. It was as if they had been in the midst of a savage primitive tribe, who might attack and kill them at any moment, and with every step they trod further and further away from danger.

Finally, Tom walked through the shadow of a tall rock and found he had left the goat track and there was meadow grass underfoot. When he looked down, he could see the travellers' site below, with Mary waiting anxiously outside their bus. Tom waved and pointed to Alex. Mary waved back, the warmth of her smile reaching them even at that distance. They had been to fairyland, and they had survived!

While Tom and the fairies were in Wales, Earl took himself off into town, to buy groceries. On his way to a small supermarket he passed the Job Centre and on an impulse went inside. There were a few desultory characters going from one set of cards to another, glancing in a depressed manner at offers for employment which were in the main unpleasant manual work which was underpaid. They were for jobs like cleaning public toilets, washing dishes in a café, shelf-filling in a supermarket. The pay was a pittance in every case.

Earl went straight to a desk where a woman with a grey cardigan was going through cards, writing something on them, then filing them in a box.

'Excuse me,' he said, 'are there any openings for stone masons?'

The woman looked up at him and blinked.

'Stone masons? What do you think this is, the eleventh century? They're pulling churches down, not building them.'

She was not being nasty: she was just stating a fact.

Earl shrugged. 'Surely there's restoration work going on, somewhere? Not *all* the cathedrals are perfect? Give us a break – have a look through the cards, would you?'

She blinked again and then did as he had asked her to do.

'No,' she said after a while. 'No stone masons required. I've got one here for a carpenter. The council needs someone. Pay's not good though.'

'Nah, I'm not even trained yet. I want to do it – stone masoning . . . masonry? Anyway, I want to do it, whatever it's called.'

'Oh, you want retraining. You have to go upstairs for that – the Employment Training Centre – it's on the door.'

Earl went upstairs and found the door marked EMPLOY-MENT TRAINING CENTRE and went inside.

There was a man this time, looking bored and depressed.

'I want to be a stone mason,' said Earl. 'You got any courses for that?'

'None whatsoever,' said the man.

'You haven't even looked.'

'I don't have to. I know there isn't a course, because I was asked about it the other day.'

Earl was astonished. 'Someone else wants to be a stone mason.'

265

'No, there's a stone *carver* who works on the other side of town. His business is expanding and he wondered if he could get an assistant from a training school. I looked through the books, but there's no training scheme for stone masons. Just about everything else but that particular trade.'

'But that's what I want,' blurted Earl. 'I want to learn. Do you think he'd take, like, an apprentice or something?'

The man shook his head, bleakly. 'It sounded to me as if he wanted someone who was already skilled at the work. I told you, his business has taken off. People are clamouring for Green Men and Aphrodites to put in their garden. The well-offs don't want plaster or concrete ones – they want authentically carved figures. They want something by an *artist*. It seemed he was pushed to fill his orders and wanted someone straightaway.'

'Can you give me his number, please? I'd like to try him, if I could. You never know.'

The man nodded and took out a pad. 'I hope I've still got it,' he said, rummaging through some papers in his piled-high in-tray. 'I don't think I threw it away.'

Eventually he came up with the number and Earl phoned the stone carver. The artist was adamant at first – he didn't want to have to train someone – he needed a young Michelangelo right away – someone who would be useful to him. However, Earl pleaded with him, said he had wanted to be a stone carver ever since he could remember, needed to be taken on. The man sighed and told Earl to come and see him, giving Earl an address. Earl went round there.

The sight of the virgin sandstone and limestone blocks filled Earl with excitement. There was fine yellow dust everywhere, which entered his nostrils and sent his blood racing round his head. The faint damp scent of sedimentary rock and igneous stone was in the atmosphere. This was where men and women cut the unspeakable, created chaos out of order, turned raw substances into strange and frightening figures, eerily beautiful. Here the stone became copies of Man's dreams and Man copied the Creator. Here the wild imaginings and nightmares of the mad crawled slowly out of solid blocks and became shapes for the sane and ordinary to behold.

Horrible gorgons, angels, monstrous gargoyles, Green Men, fantastic fairies, ogres, cunning-looking gryphons, mermaids, sea gods and land gods.

A craftsman in a leather apron with a chisel and hammer in his hand met him in a courtyard full of images – characters chipped from granite – effigies with bits of copper pipe stuck in their mouths like cigarettes – heads with curly hair, blank eyes and strong faces. He knew he had come home. This was his heaven. This was the place he was intended to be. It was written on stone.

The man, whose name was Joseph Wright, looked Earl up and down and said, 'I want a worker, not a biker.'

'I'm not on the cadge, honest,' said Earl. 'I really want to be a stone mason. They don't have masons any more – at least not around here – so I thought you could help me become a stone carver. That's the same thing, isn't it?'

'As near as damn it,' said Joseph. 'Look, I'm not much older than you.'

'But you have all the skill. I need the teaching.'

Joseph put his hands on his hips and stared at the ground. When he looked up, Earl knew he was going to be taken on. His heart jumped in his chest.

'You won't regret this,' he said, taking Joseph's hand and pumping it.

'I hope so, Mr Tattoos and Hell's Angel jacket.'

'Aw, that's all behind me. I'll shave the beard. I'll even get a haircut if you want. I'll wear something different.'

Joseph said, 'You don't have to do all that – except the last bit – you'll need to wear overalls. Stone dust gets everywhere – in your nose, ears, mouth and hair. Everywhere. When can you start?'

'Next week?'

'Look,' said Joseph, 'if we're going to do this thing, it's got to be *now*. I need someone to do the rough work on various projects. If I get you going now, we could have a system going in a week or two. Tomorrow morning, here, seven o'clock sharp. You live locally?'

Earl didn't want to tell him he was with the travellers, having loaded enough on the man already.

'No – just came into town. Know any lodgings?'

'Mrs Salwood's looking for someone.' He gave Earl a phone number. 'You tell her I sent you. She gives meals too. You got any money?'

'Only a bit,' Earl replied.

'Well tell her I sent you then. She's good for a month, then you'll have to settle up with her.' He stared hard at Earl. 'I hope I'm not making a mistake.'

'No mistake,' said Earl, firmly. 'This is the start of a beautiful relationship.'

He left Joseph Wright and collected the shopping. He felt as if he had just smoked something strong. He was on a high. Mary would be so proud of him. He was going to work, for the first time in his life, and he didn't even know what the wages would be. He hadn't asked. He didn't care. He was going to carve with his hands, just as Oberon had predicted, and become a man who worked with stone, an artist.

Cathedrals and churches. Theatres and playhouses. Museums, concert halls, art galleries and opera houses.

On the way back his head was full of flying buttresses, soaring clerestories, stone pillars, pinnacles, entrance archivolts and tympanums, triforiums, lace-like quatre-foils and cinquefoils, pilasters, cornices, barrel vaults, cushion capitals, piercing spires and formidable towers.

He didn't know the names of all these workings in stone, but his racial memory enabled him to see them in his mind's eye, and he was ready to begin cutting and shaping them, hewing and scraping them, boring and sanding them – after he'd made a few garden statues, of course.

When he told Mary, she did not jump for joy as he expected, but stared at him in disbelief.

'But Earl, we're travellers. We don't settle down in one place.'

'Don't you see, Mary, this is something I've got to do. It's – it's my destiny. Oberon looked at my hands and told me I was a stone mason – and he was right. Even the thought of it makes me feel good, deep down in my stomach. I'm a stone carver, Mary. It's in my blood. I want to cut and shape and make – make *art*.'

Mary looked miserable. 'I think I understand how you feel, Earl, but this wasn't what we agreed to do.'

'You wouldn't want to live in Glastonbury?'

'Not for ever – no I wouldn't.'

Earl said passionately, 'It won't be for ever, Mary.' He gripped her by the shoulders. 'Just until I'm sure I'm good at it. Then we can go on the road again. I've got to give Mr Wright some years – he's passing on his craft to me, after all. He's a master craftsman, and he wants to make me into one too. It's what I have to do, Mary.'

'And what will I do?'

'Anything you want. We'll work it out. If you want to be a lawyer, fine. If you want to be a businesswoman, great. If you want to sell charm bracelets on the street corner, that's OK with me. Whatever you want. We'll share looking after Alex. He should be going to school now, anyway. Mary, please.'

Mary shook her head. 'I'm sorry, Earl, I'm not ready to give up travelling yet. It suits me, this life. You'll have to do this thing, this settling down, alone.'

Earl felt his guts screwing up tight into a ball.

'Mary, I love you more than anything else in the world.'

She stared at him bleakly. 'But you'll leave me, won't you, Earl, to do this job?'

'It's not just a job and it'll be you who's leaving me – I *have* to be where the work is. I can't go back on the road now. I went into town to fetch groceries and I came back with a whole future in my hands. Mary, Mary – please stay with me. I'll make it right for you.'

She shook her head sadly and turned away from him.

'You can't love me, Earl, or you'd stay with me and Alex.'

'That's not fair, I'll miss both of you so much I already feel as if my insides have been strip-mined. When I've done here I'll come looking for you both. You may change your mind.'

'I'll probably have a new man by then,' she said cruelly, knowing it would hurt him.

Earl gave a sigh. 'If you do, he'll be a good bloke, Mary, because you're a treasure yourself. I'll go now. I'll probably be staying with a Mrs Salwood.' He gave her the telephone number. 'If you want me in an emergency, you can contact me there. I'll come, whatever time of day or night. And I want to see Alex sometimes – he's my son. I'll get a bike and come down to the New Forest as soon as I can. We'll work something out. Goodbye, Mary.'

She didn't answer and he turned and walked out of her life.

Mary stood and stared at the empty doorway and burst into tears. Oberon was passing by at the time and he came to see what was the matter. Human tears did not move him emotionally, but he was curious and wondered if he could help the person in distress.

'You weep, young woman?'

Mary dried her eyes and turned away, she did not like telling strangers her problems.

'It's all right.' Then something stirred her anger. 'This is partly your fault – putting such ideas into Earl's head. Now he's gone off on a foolish jaunt.'

'Not so, not so,' replied Oberon. 'If there were ideas there, they were of his own making. Such architecture of the mind cannot be constructed by an outsider, they are formed within and are erected there by the owner. Outsiders can only point to their existence and remark upon their stature.'

'Well, you told Earl he could be a stone mason.'

'And that is foolish?'

'He's never held a tool in his hand that wasn't to do with fixing a motorbike. How can you think he's going to be able to make statues? That's silly fairy talk.'

Oberon shook his head. 'Fairy talk is never silly. I saw what I saw, in his hands. He has the mark of the craftsman, the artist in him. You will regret you called it silly

271

when he becomes one of the most gifted stone carvers in all England. You will see his work and gasp at its beauty – I tell you this in friendship, not because I wish to be right, or because I want you to forgive me.'

He paused before adding, 'I have no need of those human frailties and weaknesses. I am King of the Fairies – I see what I see and I sometimes tell what I see. You cannot change a person's destiny in order to keep your world safe and secure – an unchanging, reliable world. I wish you well, madam, and now I must go.'

'And what do you see in me? Or is that too much to ask?' she said, bitterly. 'A woman's future?'

He stared at her before turning to leave – as he left he called over his shoulder.

'You are aware of what you are, what you want to be – unlike Earl you do not need a fairy king to tell you what you already know.'

And it was true. Mary did know what she wished to do. She wanted to be a family therapist. There was that within her which required her to give something of herself to the community at large, while at the same time earning a living. Money was not at the top of her agenda, nor recognition for her services – if they had been, working for social change would not be the right path – but she did want a profession which was respected within itself and by its clients.

She had read about family therapy and wanted one day, when Alex was a little older, to take a degree course.

But this was just a dream, which she had never taken seriously, which might have fallen by the wayside if Earl had not followed his aspirations.

'I don't know,' she said to herself, upset by the sudden turmoil in her life. 'I'm not ready yet. Why couldn't Earl have waited for a better time? It's all too much at once.'

She stared out of the bus doorway, at the children running and laughing around the site, and wished things had not been brought to a head so abruptly.

TWENTY-ONE

Purple Sandwort Closes

THE FAIRIES, HAVING NOW VISITED THEIR WELSH cousins, the Tylwyth Teg, struck south-east, towards Sherborne on the A37. Mary and Tom followed them, along with the usual retinue, including Jug.

In the last twenty hours there had been sightings of giants and other fantastic creatures roaming Britain: radio and television stations were choked with excited reporters breathlessly pointing out huge vaguely human shapes on the horizon. Given this upsurge in supernatural phenomena and the open-minded kind of people the travelling life seemed to attract, the existence of fairies had quickly become an accepted fact amongst the members of the convoy.

There were reports on the radio of a dragon terrorizing

the countryside around Norton Fitzwarren. This was a particularly ugly dragon, having been spontaneously generated from a pile of dead bodies, and the fairies suspected it might be the work of Morgan-le-Fay, up to her old tricks. She would expect the fairies to send someone to fight the dragon, but Oberon was not falling for this one.

'I will not have my henchman Sid risking his life, fighting decomposing dragons with only a monkey wrench for a weapon,' said Oberon. 'We need him to drive the bus. I won't send him and that's my final edict.'

'I should think not!' cried Sid from his driver's seat, alarmed. 'Don't even think about it. Anyway, it'll rot away before too long, won't it?'

They all agreed it probably would. Besides, there were other monsters, all over Britain, raising their horrible heads and frightening their neighbours. Sid couldn't fight and destroy them all.

There was a three-headed giant called Red Etin, running around loose at Duns in the Scottish county of Borders, only one of a thousand or so giants which had awoken. There were phantom dogs all over the country and the odd dragon or two in various locations. There was a monster worm at Lambton in Durham, squishing its way through the lanes and streets and frightening the cattle. There were boggarts, house fairies, running all over Hothersall Hall at Ribchester. A buggane (a particularly horrible type of goblin, Oberon explained) was trying to pull down St Trinian's Chapel at Crosby just outside Manchester. In Hinckley church in Leicestershire the tombstones were bleeding. The radio was full of such news and the stolen baby was hardly mentioned any more.

At Trent Barrow the convoy stopped because Moth,

Swallowtail and Blewit wanted to look for King Arthur's sword, Excalibur, in the pool which had collected in Trent Barrow earthwork.

'If I find it,' said Blewit, searching amongst the reeds, 'I shall be King of all England.'

Moth said, 'You'd have to be *queen*!'

Mary, the feminist coming out in her, took Blewit's part.

'If she wants to be king, why shouldn't she?' said Mary. 'Why does it always have to be a *man* who's king?'

Moth became exasperated at this.

'Because kings are male and queens are female, that's why.'

'Typical,' snorted Mary. 'So Excalibur can only be found by a man?'

'Well, would you want the Lady of the Lake to be a man, then?' Sid cried, taking Moth's side. 'That would be just the same thing, wouldn't it? Having a great, hairy, muscular arm come out to grab the sword when it's chucked back in the water? A few tattoos would be nice, wouldn't it?'

'Doesn't have to be thick and hairy,' said Drone, Jug's girlfriend. 'Could be nice smooth-armed youth – maybe Italian – an arm like a woman's, but a man's.'

'Oh, yeah, great,' snorted Jug, getting in on the argument, 'an Italian Youth of the Lake. I can see the legend holding up under that one.'

The debate was gathering fuel and getting nice and warm when suddenly Swallowtail gave a yell and pulled out a long, slim metal object from the water. She flourished it above her head, crying, 'I'm king of the Britons!' but it turned out to be an old aluminium bicycle pump, a difficult symbol with which to unite the Britons around her banner in order to defeat evil and instate good throughout the land.

Oberon and Titania were, of course, very famous fairies, and the travellers felt rather privileged and special to have with them Shakespeare's own band of little folk. They felt sure that when it became public knowledge, there would be a road novel written and a film made of the erratic journey.

When the caravan stopped to rest on the A3030 just past Sherborne, the travellers began discussing amongst themselves which film stars would be cast to play their particular role. Everyone agreed that Holly Hunter would make a great Titania, but there was a dispute over who should play Oberon and Puck.

'Dustin Hoffman and Tom Hanks are both short,' said Drone. 'I think Hanks to play Puck and Hoffman to play Oberon.'

'Nah,' said Sid, 'the other way around.'

'I think Tom Cruise would do for me,' said Jug. 'I mean, we're more or less the same height.'

Sid snorted. 'Tom Cruise is too good-looking to play you – 'scuse me, but you're not exactly a pretty boy, Jug.'

Jug had particularly craggy facial features.

'No, but they can do special effects. You could make Tom Cruise craggy quite easy,' argued Jug.

'Why would they want to? Why not use Charles Bronson?'

The fairies were very interested in all these arguments, even though they had no idea who were the film stars being talked about. Cobweb was especially concerned about who would be the actor to play him, since he had a very dramatic role in the whole affair, having being kidnapped and subjected to humiliating and painful treatment.

'Who would play me?' he asked, excitedly. 'Who would play the brave Cobweb?'

The group looked at Cobweb and there was much chin-stroking and head-scratching.

'That's a tough one,' said Jug. 'I mean, you're sort of thin and nobbly, ain't you? If Twiggy was around, I'd say she was the best bet, but I don't know really.'

Drone said, 'Maybe special effects could make up some sort of scarecrow – an automaton or something. You know, a machine like CP30?'

'There was a man inside CP30,' argued Jug.

'Jimminy Cricket!' said Sid. 'You know – a cartoon character – they can do that these days – mix cartoons in with real people. They did it in *Roger Rabbit*, didn't they?'

While the group was talking two giants suddenly appeared, up from Melcombe Horsey way. They each held a huge boulder which first one, then the other, threw over the heads of the travellers and fairies. The rocks went arcing through the sky and landed with two separated thuds in the field half a mile away. One of the giants yelled, 'I won that one.'

'Even if you did,' said the other, 'I'm still two up.'

'You are not!'

'Am so!'

The monstrous men stepped carefully over the group of fairies and humans, to continue their argument a little further on.

'What was all that about?' said Sid.

'Stone-throwing contest,' replied Puck. 'Giants are always doing things like that – weight lifting, stone throwing, tossing the caber, hammer throwing – they always need to be proving their strength. It's the only thing they've got – they certainly haven't any brains.'

'Where do those two come from?' asked Jug. 'We would need big John Wayne to play one of them, and then we'd have to blow him up ten times his real size.'

. Puck said, 'They're the same giants who threw stones from Nordon Hill to Henning Hill. One of them lost the last contest, a few centuries ago, and has been lying in his grave ever since. They say he died of disappointment at being the loser. Now we've got him up again.'

'Will he stay up?' asked Jug.

'No,' Puck answered. 'When we reach the New Forest and make it our own, all the giants and supernatural creatures will go back to the places from whence they came and Britain will return to its normal state.'

The group went back on the road again, heading down the A3143 towards Piddletrenthide, Piddlehinton and Puddletown, passing on the other side of the hill from the Cerne Abbas giant for the sake of modesty and decorum.

When they reached Dorchester, they turned towards Wareham Forest, drawn by the scent of trees. Sid let them out for a while, to wander amongst the woodlands, then gathered them back in again to continue their journey. They went through Poole and Bournemouth, then Christchurch, before Sid took another wrong turn and ended up at Milford on Sea outside a hotel called The Compton, which seemed to be full of strange people hotly discussing a subject called science fiction.

The travellers, Tom, Mary and Alex included, brewed some tea and were happy to look at the sea from two fields away.

Oberon and Titania, and Puck and the rest of the fairies, wished to see the ocean at close quarters. Some of the fairies had flown over salty waters on their way to Oriental climes – Puck, Titania and Oberon – in the days

279

when their magic had been powerful enough to make such journeys, but they had never been on a beach before now. They crossed some fields to stand on the high bank of pebbles which protected the land from the Atlantic's fury. Oberon, who had seen some terrifying sights in his time, was overawed by the size of the waves and the vastness of the watery desert which lay before him.

'The land of the mermaids,' he murmured. 'Methinks they are welcome to it, Puck.'

'Indeed, my lord,' agreed that sprite, 'I would not live under the waves for all the world.'

'If you had all the world,' argued Sid, 'you wouldn't *need* to live under the waves, Robin Goodfellow. Your logic's a bit skew-whiff.'

Puck said scornfully, 'Logic? What has that got to do with anything, Sid? Not even mortals take much note of logic – they live by their perceptions and feelings.'

Sid thought about this one and conceded Puck was right as he studied The Needles off the Isle of Wight.

Titania sat on a lonely patch of sand which she found amongst a billion pebbles and played with Pigwidgeon for a while, showing the infant how to make a fairy sandcastle. Her efforts were architecturally fantastic, as one would expect of a fairy, and seemed to be founded not on solid ground (which would be logical) but on the flimsiest excuses for pebble pillars. It was a marvellously elaborate castle balanced on several drystone columns through which the sea washed without disturbing the structure. Children out walking along the natural sea wall came to watch as Titania's hands produced a miracle from the Milford beach.

'Wow!' said one ten-year-old. 'You must be brilliant.'

'I am,' replied Titania flashing him a famous smile. 'I

am absolutely brilliant.'

Once the fairies had tired of the sight of the sea, though they never got over the wonderful smell of the brine – a clean, salty scent which seemed to clear their lungs of the traffic fumes – they wandered in groups back to their bus. The people who had been talking science fiction inside and outside the hotel went by them on the way, still talking intently about their subject. The fairies greeted them as they passed with a 'Ho' and a 'Good morrow', which was returned in kind. The fairies sensed an affinity with these creators of futuristic fiction and were not too proud to acknowledge the connection.

The bus at last went north, towards the New Forest, passing through Lymington.

As the fairies drew closer to their destination, followed by their traveller friends, they were aware of the presence of Morgan-le-Fay. The sorceress had arrived ahead of them and had woven an invisible barrier around the forest with her powerful magic, thus effectively stopping them from entering the forest. When the convoy halted on the edge of a green, beyond which the fairies could see the magnificent woodland to which they had been travelling over the last many hours, they witnessed wild ponies frolicking in and out of the trees.

It was maddeningly close, this paradise, but as yet unreachable.

'What's the matter?' asked Jug. 'Why don't we go inside?'

'We cannot,' replied Oberon. 'The witch is here before us – she prevents our passage with an invisible wall. You may pass through it, but we fairies cannot.'

'Then let's get rid of the witch,' Jug said. 'You lot can do that, can't you?'

With a sinking heart, Puck said, 'One of us must fight Morgan-le-Fay in single combat – the winner will be entitled to exclusive use of the New Forest. If – if we lose – we'll have to find somewhere else to live.'

'Well, can't you bargain with her?' asked Drone. 'Don't you have anything she wants?'

'Yes, we do,' said Titania, clutching her baby, 'but she's not going to get it.'

The fairy queen hurried away from the group, back to the bus, where Sid sat at the wheel. She held the baby close to her breast as she went. The other fairies watched her go and then got back to discussing their plight.

Titania boarded the bus and sat down in a seat near Sid. For a few moments she played with the happy Pigwidgeon, dangling a ribbon for the child to clutch. Then the fairy queen began crying softly. Sid became alarmed.

'What's the matter?' he asked. 'What's wrong?'

'Sid,' said Titania through her tears, 'you must return my baby to its mother, before Morgan-le-Fay gets her claws on the darling little infant. My Pigwidgeon. I shall miss you desperately, but you must go with Sid. Take her, Sid, and return her to her mother, quickly.'

Sid began to get a little hot and bothered.

'Here wait a bit,' he said, anxiously. 'I don't know her mother – I'll have to leave her somewhere.'

Titania looked at him sharply, her bright eyes penetrating his inmost thoughts.

'You cannot abandon her,' said Titania. 'The Morning-Fairy might find her.'

'Then what am I supposed to do?' cried the unhappy rude mechanical. 'I can only hand her to the police.'

'Then do that.'

'But they'll arrest me – for taking her in the first place.

You don't know what you're asking. Don't forget I was with you when you took her, and in the hypermarket. They'll throw me in prison for a hundred years.'

'Then you must go to gaol, Sid,' said Titania, heartlessly. 'The baby must be returned.'

'O Lor,' Sid said, miserably taking Pigwidgeon into his arms. 'What a bummer.'

Titania rained kisses on Pigwidgeon's face before calling her pet owl to her shoulder and walking away.

Oberon came over to Sid and said, 'If I were you, Sid, I would give the police another man's name,' and Oberon turned and nodded at a man standing on the edge of the green.

'Him? His name?' said Sid. 'You sure?'

'It will all work out for the best if you do,' said Oberon. 'Believe me.'

TWENTY-TWO

Dandelion Closes

S ID DROVE DOWN TO LYMINGTON WITH THE BABY ON THE
  seat beside him. His mind was in a turmoil. He was
  convinced the police could connect him with the
kidnapping and while he did not want to remain
enthralled for the rest of his life, he was also chary about
spending a few years in jail.

He glanced down at Pigwidgeon, who was playing with
her toes, trying to remove the knitted shoes Titania had
placed on her feet and tied with pink ribbon.

'You're a liability, that's what you are,' groaned Sid.
'I've got to think of something. I don't want to spend time
in prison. I didn't pinch you – *she* did.'

Despite what Titania had said to him, Sid was tempted
to just leave the baby on the steps of the nearest police

284

station. He would have carried out his plan if he didn't suspect that Titania would know exactly what he had done. She seemed to be able to read his mind. When he saw the blue lamp of the village police station come into view, he decided to do as Titania had bid him – but he was going to lie.

He stopped the bus outside. There was a ditch with water flowing along it. Sid took some mud and rubbed it into his face until it was good and dirty. Then he went back into the bus and found the woollen hat he always wore when he worked under cars. He pulled this down over his ears and left only a thin line of dirty skin above his eyebrows. Then he pulled on an old anorak, zipping the collar up so that it covered most of the lower half of his face.

A look in the mirror told him he would be hard to recognize if they came looking for him again.

He picked up Pigwidgeon and, with his heart beating fast, Sid entered the police station.

There was a woman sergeant behind the desk and no-one else in sight.

''Scuse me, ma'am,' said Sid in a throaty voice, 'I found this baby.'

The sergeant looked up from her paperwork and stared.

'You found a _what_?'

'Baby,' said Sid, unable to resist teasing her. 'If no-one claims it after six months, is it mine to keep?'

The sergeant, a stocky woman in her forties, stared hard at Sid.

'Joke,' he said. 'Here, take it.'

He put Pigwidgeon on the counter. At that moment there was a sound like someone stepping on an overripe orange. This was followed by a horrible smell. Pigwidgeon wore a satisfied smile on her face.

The police sergeant took a step back, wrinkling her nose. Sid shrugged.

'Filled her nappy,' he said, apologetically.

'Is that your wife's child?' demanded the sergeant. 'You trying to get rid of a baby? I suppose she told you to leave it on the steps? We can't take babies in here.'

'Why did you think it was my wife's child?'

'Because you knew she's a baby girl. How would you know that? Unless you've been peeking. Did you bring the baby straight here, or what?'

This was going to be harder than Sid had first envisaged.

'No, you don't understand, I heard on my radio about that baby which has gone missing – you know, from up in the Midlands somewhere – and I thought it might be this one. It's – it's got *pink* laces in its booties,' Sid said in a whisper, 'it *must* be a girl, mustn't it? The baby that's missing is a little girl, isn't it?'

The sergeant's eyes opened wide. 'Louise DuLac, the baby stolen from its nanny?' She grabbed Pigwidgeon as if she expected her to run away. 'What makes you think this is baby Louise? Where did you find her then?'

Pigwidgeon, or rather Louise, was now gurgling in the sergeant's arms, feeling the soft substantial bosom beneath the starched shirt pressing against her warm body. This was more like it. The fairies were nice, but flat-chested and angular. Sid was unintentionally rough. This lady however had some nice soft layers about her person. Pigwidgeon liked the feel of her and snuggled in deeper. She added a bit to the package already in her nappy and sighed contentedly.

Sid saw the expression on the sergeant's face and decided he would like to go as soon as possible.

'Er, we – we found her in a clump of bushes, just outside the New Forest. We think her kidnappers abandoned her. They do that sometimes, don't they? To stop from getting caught? I would, anyway.'

'Willie!' yelled the sergeant.

A door opened at the back of the room and a constable entered, sipping a mug of tea.

'Put that down and take this baby,' ordered the sergeant. 'Call Nottinghamshire. Tell them there's a possibility we've found the baby Louise stolen from that nanny – Miss Frances Flute. I'll take a statement from the man who brought this to our attention.'

The sergeant was quietly excited now. If this *was* the baby Louise this would be a big coup for her. She didn't want to give too much credit to Sid. It was true this scruffy herbert had walked in and plonked the baby in her lap, but there were ways of wording these things which would cut out unnecessary third parties. The sergeant could make it sound as if Sid was simply an instrument of well-ordered police planning – her planning – which had been successful in locating and finding the child.

When the media descended on the police station, the sergeant would refuse to give Sid's name to them, on the grounds that it was invading his privacy or that enquiries would be prejudiced by so doing. That would help focus all the attention on herself, she being the only other party involved in the discovery. There was Willie too of course, but Willie wasn't very pushy and wouldn't mind being left in the background. He was only twenty.

The young constable called Willie reluctantly put down his mug of tea and took the baby.

'It stinks,' he said, screwing up his face.

'She needs changing, that's all,' said the sergeant. 'You'll have to do it. Police constables should be prepared for all emergencies.'

'Like Boy Scouts, eh?' suggested Sid.

'What do I put on her?' whined the constable, holding Louise at arm's length.

Sid said severely, 'Use a bit of initiative, man – use some towelling from the toilet or something.'

'Do as he says,' ordered the sergeant, then whirling on Sid, she asked, 'By the way, what *is* your name?'

Oberon had prepared Sid for this question.

'Tom Blessing,' he said, without a twitch. 'I'm – I'm a New Age traveller – that's why I'm so dirty. We're camped out on the green by the New Forest.'

The sergeant frowned. 'Trespassing?'

'No – and anyway, even if we were, we wouldn't have found the baby if we hadn't been there, would we? You've got us to thank for that. I expect you'll get a lot of praise, being the police station that found the stolen baby. If this *is* the right baby, which seems logical to me. I mean no-one else has reported a stolen kid, have they? No, well, it's *got* to be her, hasn't it? Stands to reason.'

'You finished?' said the sergeant as the constable went through the office door into the recesses of the building, presumably in search of some towelling before he called Nottinghamshire Constabulary, to find out if he had the right baby or not. The sergeant wrote down THOMAS then looked up and asked, 'Any middle name? Do you know your National Insurance Number? Got a permanent address?'

'No, no, no,' replied Sid.

She wrote BLESSING.

Willie poked his head around the door, still holding Louise well away from his shirt front.

'They're flying the nanny down here now,' he said, excitedly. 'They asked me about a birth mark and I found one on her leg. It matches up. This is baby Louise all right. Well done, Sarg!'

The sergeant seemed to swell to twice her original size and she allowed herself a sly smile.

'Thanks, Willie,' she murmured.

'Promotion in this, eh?' Sid suggested.

The sergeant looked at him and frowned. 'Do you have any means of identification, Mr Blessing?'

'What, on me?' said Sid, panicking. 'No, not really.'

'You have a driver's licence, for that bus out there?' questioned the sergeant, pointing with her pen.

'Oh, that – yeah – in the cab. I'll go and get it,' he said, walking quickly out of the station before he could be stopped.

He ran to the bus, jumped in, and started the engine. A moment later he was roaring along the road towards Milford on Sea. The sweat was pouring down his face. There was something the matter with the bus, too. The engine bonnet was open and bouncing up and down. Someone had opened the bonnet and left the catches off.

'Bloody kids,' cried Sid, feeling the world was against him. He stopped the bus, jumped out, secured the bonnet, and then got back in again to continue the journey.

Every so often he glanced in one of his wing mirrors to ensure he was not being chased by a police car. Everything seemed clear. It had only been a small police station and there had been no squad cars visible. Of course, they would probably put a call out to all cars already on the road, to watch out for him. It wasn't as if he were easy to miss, driving a wacking great bus.

Something stirred in the back of the bus.

Sid pulled over, stopped the bus with a screech and whirled, crying, 'Who's there?'

'*Ble mae'r plant?*' said a shrill voice.

'What?' cried Sid, startled not only by the strange language but by the horrible tone of the voice. 'Who is it?'

'*Ydy'r plant wrth y tŷ?*'

Sid gulped and stared at the back of the bus.

Eventually, two strange-looking shapes emerged from behind the back seats. They were covered in dirty oil. They sneered at Sid with ugly wizened faces.

Their skin was a sort of sickly shade of green, covered in warts and growths. Their nostrils were wide and flared, very red inside. They had no lips at all, to hide the pointed grey teeth, and their eyes seemed lidless, with jaundiced whites. Tufts of coarse hair stuck up from the top of their scalps. Thin stick-like limbs, seemingly crooked, poked from their shapeless garments and a tall scrawny neck enabled their heads to swivel like that of an owl. Their bare scabby feet were enormous, with long finger-like toes.

Sid had never seen such horrible creatures before in his entire life. He looked out of the window. There was gorse scrubland on either side of the road, guarded by one or two Scots pines looking as shattered and lost as always. In the near distance ahead was Milford sea front. He wondered if he should make a break for it and run, but there seemed little cover for him, at any point of the compass.

'Who are you?' he quailed.

'We are the Bendith Y Mamau,' snarled one. 'Don't you

know your Welsh fairies, mortal?'

Sid remembered that Tom had told him about these creatures, after coming back from that fairy realm on Glastonbury Tor.

'What do you want?' asked Sid, as they closed on him, robbing him of the choice of flight. 'I haven't got anything.'

'We want the little boy, Alexander,' grinned one of the fairies. 'We want to take him back to Annwn. And any other little children who might be around.'

Sid was horrified. 'You can't do that.'

'We can and we will, you stupid mortal,' snarled the second Bendith Y Mamau. 'If you refuse to assist us, we shall destroy you instantly.'

'Instantly?' croaked Sid.

'You will not have time for a last breath,' confirmed the speaker. 'A small pile of dust will be all that remains.'

Whether they could do this thing to him or not, Sid remained seriously afraid. Their breath, and other things about them, smelled awful. He had no experience of such terrible beings and he had to take them at their word. His brain worked feverishly. He could see Milford strand from where he sat, some way ahead, where the promenade ran alongside the beach.

The wind had increased in strength in the last half an hour and there was a churning sea, jumping and leaping. Giant rollers were driving obliquely, coming in from the south-west, surging madly towards the strand as if it were a battle front. The tide was now fully in and as they arrived the waves were hurling themselves over the car-park, washing it down with a mixture of green water and white froth.

The sea thundered and hissed in as the tall dark-green

waves crashed over the promenade and then retreated, clawing at pebbles, rattling them in the backlash as if they were marbles in the pocket of a young child.

Sid studied the monstrous waves on the far side of the car-park and tried to think what he could do to get rid of these ugly creatures. He was in as much turmoil inside as the ocean appeared to be between the Isle of Wight and Milford on Sea. One thing was certain, Sid couldn't take these horrible excuses for living things to where they could lay their hands on Alex. That was unthinkable.

'I'm not feeling very well,' he complained with a groan. 'I feel quite ill.'

'Turn this chariot round,' snarled one of the Bendith Y Mamau, 'or you will certainly perish.'

Sid said, 'I can't turn the bus here on this road – it's much too narrow.'

'Then find a place to do it, stupid!'

Sid nodded and drove the bus slowly down the main road to the car-park, entered it and turned round on the wet surface, so that they were facing the exit. He turned off the engine and sat perfectly still, the sea water swilling around the tyres of the bus, washing over the hub-caps.

'What's the matter now?' snapped a Bendith Y Mamau. 'Why aren't you making the chariot go?'

'It has to rest from time to time,' lied Sid, desperately trying to stall them. 'It won't go again until it's rested. It gets very tired, working so hard.'

Far away, in the distance, Sid could see a squad car cruising the neighbourhood, crossing the main road and into a side street as if searching for something.

'He's right,' said the other fairy. 'You remember it stopped a few times before.'

So they had been with him since leaving Glastonbury.

Sid glanced at the dirty oil on them and remembered the loose bonnet on the bus.

'You were hiding in with the engine!' he gasped. 'You were under the bonnet!'

The Bendith Y Mamau laughed. 'It was hot in there – but we like it to be hot, don't we?'

The other one shrieked with laughter, as if his companion had made a hugely funny joke.

'Hot and tight – not much room,' added the second fairy, with a further shriek.

The police car crossed the main road again, three streets ahead, appearing and disappearing amongst the bungalows.

'Listen,' said Sid, the perspiration running down his neck and tickling his back. 'Listen, I really am sick. How about one of you two driving the bus? I could teach you in a few minutes. How about it?'

'Drive the bus? You mean, work the chariot?' cried one. 'Is it possible?'

Sid could tell the idea had excited them. Unlike the Sherwood fairies, these creatures seemed to thrive on the smell of petrol and oil. They had obviously enjoyed their ride, cramped up as they must have been under the bonnet with the engine, from Glastonbury to Milford. He guessed the idea of driving a machine appealed to them. They were like children, eager to have a go at something they thought they could master within a few minutes. If he could get them to drive out of the car-park, the bus would be apprehended by the police before they got a few hundred yards up the road. The next pass the police made they would be bound to spot the bus, being that much closer to the car-park.

Outside the bus, the sea continued to thrash the

promenade and car-park with its flails, leaving rivulets of white running along gutters and down drains.

'Shall I show you?' asked Sid. 'Who wants to drive my bus?'

'Me!' snapped one of the fairies. 'You next!'

He pulled Sid by the collar, hauling him from the driver's seat and jumping into it himself. The other fairy snarled and then sulked for a minute, before saying in a surly voice, 'Halfway there, I get to make the chariot go,' but his companion wasn't listening. He was turning the wheel this way and that, at the same time making engine noises.

'Here's what you do,' said Sid. 'You start the engine . . .'

Sid turned the key and the motor roared to life, causing the fairy to leap from the seat.

When he saw his friend making a move towards him, however, he threw himself back into it again.

'What next?' he growled.

'Press down on that pedal there,' pointed Sid, 'with your right foot.'

The fairy put his left foot on the accelerator and gunned the motor, revving it wildly.

'Next?' cried the creature excitedly.

Sid decided to forget about the clutch: after all the bus was clapped out anyway.

'You have to push that stick there backwards and forwards, until it jams tight,' said Sid. 'The bus will go then.'

The second fairy said, 'I'll do that,' and grabbed the gear stick with both hands, twisting on it to make it grate and crunch.

Blustery shoulders of wind came in over the ocean, driving the high-topped rollers before them. A tea kiosk standing on the edge of the promenade vanished occasionally in a cloud of hissing, lashing, white spume, to reappear dripping and flecked as the sea sucked back its liquid whips. The same waves had gathered in strength and were crashing around the bus now, lapping over the tops of the wheels, splashing the windows with salty water and ruining the visibility.

Sid, his heart drumming fast, edged towards the doorway. The police car had appeared from a side street, as Sid had predicted, and was now coming down the main road towards the car-park. The two policemen were staring intently at the bus. Sid stood on the top of the bus steps and edged open the door while the fairies were struggling with the gears.

'It won't go in,' shrieked the second fairy, incensed, wrestling like mad with the gears which screeched and scraped making an appalling noise, while the first fairy continued to gun the motor, racing the engine until it sounded as if it were screaming for mercy, and reached out with his right hand to help his companion with the obstinate stick.

Suddenly there was a loud CRUNCH as the gear stick finally found a slot in the transmission.

Sid jumped through the open doorway into the misty sea spray that hid the car-park.

Even while he was still in the air, the bus shot backwards into a high wall of water that was rushing in to swamp the tarmac. The fairies had found reverse! Sid was aware of the bus disappearing into the green and white whirlwind froth as it went over the edge of the promenade and into the swirling ocean. The water hissed and boiled. Shingle flew as if fired from shotguns as the bus wheels, still spinning when they hit the beach bottom, showered the police car as it entered the car-park.

The squad car's windscreen shattered instantly and the vehicle slewed sideways to a halt.

Sid rolled away towards a concrete litter bin and managed to slip behind it before the two policemen jumped from their vehicle and ran to where the sea was inhaling its water and pebbles. The great green monster had swallowed the bus whole and nothing could be seen of either it or its occupants. Then another wave came in, smashed down in front of and over the policemen, and threatened to draw them to a watery grave too. They struggled back to their car, soaked to the skin, their faces the colour of wholemeal flour.

Sid crawled away, Indian-style, into the garden of a nearby bungalow. Once there he went round the back, over the fence, and made his way to the main road again. There he hung around a bus stop, hoping that a bus would come along to take him back to the New Forest. He had been there twenty minutes when a Shogun driver took pity on the soaked and miserable Sid and offered him a lift to Lymington.

Sid got in the back seat of the Shogun, aware that he was wet through.

The car driver was an elderly tweedy woman with a voice like a sergeant major's.

'Ought to get out of those wet clothes soon, young man – catch your death.'

'Yes, thanks – you're not going through the New Forest, by any chance? I'm – I'm camping there,' said Sid, shivering.

'Matter of fact, I am,' bellowed the woman. 'Thought you wanted Lymington. Easily drop you in the forest.'

'Thanks,' murmured Sid.

'Got caught by a wave, did you? Dangerous. Should

keep off the sea front in blowy conditions. Could be swept away – lots of people have.'

'Yes, I suppose they have.'

The woman was quiet for a while, then bellowed, 'Bit of a hullabulloo back there. Seems a bus went into the sea.'

'I hope no-one was hurt,' said Sid, trying to sound sincere.

'No idea,' bawled the woman. 'Couldn't wait around and see. Police had it all in hand. Bus is lying under the water – has plenty of air in it – they've got time to get people out. Tragedy if they don't, but Milford's rescue services are second to none.'

'I hope so,' said Sid, hoping not. He wanted to be given as much leeway as possible to get away from the New Forest. It was time to be set free by the fairies. He wanted to go home now. He deserved his freedom.

The woman dropped him on the edge of the green in the New Forest and Sid went to Titania to dutifully report all that had happened to him.

'Well done, Sid,' she said. 'Now we must deal with Morgan-le-Fay. She must be defeated here and now, on this green, if we are to enter the New Forest.'

'Puck will fight her in single combat?' asked Sid.

'Not Puck,' replied Titania, 'me. I shall fight the sorceress. It shall be between the two of us.'

'You?' cried Sid. 'But what if you lose?'

'Then you will remember your Titania with sweet thoughts,' she said, smiling wistfully. 'Won't you, Sid?'

TWENTY-THREE

White Spiderwort, Field Bindwort Close

ALTHOUGH THE SKY HAD BEEN CLEAR AND BLUE, AS BE-
fitting a midsummer's day, a vermilion storm
began to move across the heavens, grumbling in a
deep thunderous voice. It was like no storm the travellers
had ever seen before. Ominous and threatening clouds
like great columns of dark red smoke formed over the
heads of the spectators and combatants alike. The sun disappeared into the murk, swallowed by a crimson deeper
than itself. Woodlands thickened and grew gloomy and
the inner roseate darkness of their souls crept out onto
the green, turning the bracken to bloody feathers, changing single trees to red silhouettes.

Toad and adder took refuge in their hiding holes.

The wind dropped and became still.

Out of the forest came the dreadful Morgan-le-Fay, a rolled shadow in her left hand.

She stood just beyond the pale of the trees, dressed in dark purple, her eyes glinting with anger.

'I have here,' she said, holding up the shadow, 'the living form of Cobweb, your fairy compatriot. You will now all be witness to his destruction. I shall pierce his brain with my fingernail and fling him back into some unknown time and place – into a dungeon wherein he shall languish for ever – or until such time as you shall find him.' Her eyes glinted with scorn, as she added, 'Do not be optimistic, for I have secret prisons in places beyond even the scope of your dreams.'

'Nay!' cried a voice, stepping forward out of the crowd of fairies and travellers. 'You have no fairy in your hand, but a mortal, for I am that Cobweb of which you speak!'

The Morning-Fairy's eyes at first showed puzzlement and then flashed with fury as she recognized Cobweb. In an instant she had unrolled the shadow in her hand and restored it to its true form.

It blossomed like a quickened flower into a young woman.

The small, slim-figured woman stood there, dressed in a pastel-coloured stage costume. Her brown hair was cut short in an urchin style. An attractive round face was set with intent blue eyes and a small pert nose. Her hands and feet were delicate leaf-like objects, almost as beautiful as those of any fairy. The small, sweet mouth was partially open, no doubt in surprise, as she trembled like a poplar sapling in a breeze.

'Where am I?' she wailed. 'What is this place?'

Crimson shadows from the clouds swept over the meadowland changing its aspects by the moment. A sudden wind rushed in from the stillness of the woods, winnowing the litter left by the travellers around the parked vehicles. A weasel with a fiery breast stood on its hind legs, on the edge of the forest, as if trying for a better view.

'It's the girl from the play, at Avebury,' cried Sid. 'It's the lass who played Cobweb.'

'A *mortal*?' shrieked Morgan-le-Fay, staring at the young woman in revulsion, studying her attire and her general demeanour. 'What good is this – this *rustic* to me?'

The shrill sound of Morgana's voice triggered the young woman into action. She let out a startled cry and then turned like a panicking wild faun, running for the woods. The Morning-Fairy did nothing to stop her. Morgana came from a time when the life of a peasant wench counted for very little, when the death of a serf was cheap and such hostages worthless. Certainly Oberon and the fairies would not be interested in such a girl, whose garments and bearing spoke of poverty and low-breeding. The maid was useless to the sorceress.

The young woman disappeared into the woods, thrashing through the undergrowth like a hindered deer, and then all was still once again.

Titania now stepped forward, out into the gloomy waste where Morgan-le-Fay was gathering her wrath.

'Leave our forest, witch,' said Titania, 'or this fairy queen will strike you down!'

The Morning-Fairy stared for a moment at the diminutive form of Titania and gradually a grim smile came over her face.

'What manner of creature are you, who thinks you can destroy Morgan-le-Fay?' said the sorceress, slowly. 'I shall tear you into little pieces and throw the scraps to the wind, do you hear? Kiss your Oberon goodbye, woodland waif, for his eyes shall not behold your form ever again.'

She held up her left hand, first finger extended, from which sprang a slim, wicked-looking spike as sharp and deadly as any stiletto.

A similar blade grew from the same finger of Titania's right hand.

'No magic,' said Titania.

'No magic,' agreed Morgana.

In the manner and keeping of fairies and sorcerers, the pair of them lied.

'Good God,' said Tom Blessing, standing next to Sid. 'Stop them, someone.'

But not a soul moved, not fairy nor traveller. Oberon remained still, his face like stone. Puck glanced quickly from Morgana to Titania, then he sighed deeply. In the forest, in the grasses, it seemed that every living creature was alert, listening, waiting. The red darkness deepened, so that only vague shapes could be seen, the details hidden under the folds of cardinal shadow and shade.

To the travellers, it appeared that two scarlet scorpions, carapaces glistening, were circling each other warily. The tails of these creatures were arched above their bodies, curved and terrible stings protruding from the tips. On the hair-thin point of each sting was a tiny drop of viscous liquid which gathered the light to itself. Pincers locked with pincers, as a dozen spiny legs fought for a grip on the surface of the world, and each other.

'Oh Lord,' whispered Tom, as shocked and pale as any of the petrified people there watching, 'don't let her be hurt.'

The combat was long and terrible.

Tail-stings flashed in the dimness of that scruffy patch of turf, stirring the vermilion colours of evening. The sounds made by the two warriors were eerie and sickening, belonging not in the mouth of a known creature but in the throat of some strange barbaric beast. The smaller of the two combatants was disadvantaged by height, but she was swifter. They fought at close quarters, neither giving ground.

As the struggle continued, deeply into the hour of closing white spiderwort and field bindwort, the turf began to heave under the feet of the watchers. It was as if an earthquake were taking place to coincide with the bloody battle. Narrow chasms appeared all round the area, making an island of the greensward. Peat hags burst into view like quickened pustules on putrid flesh. Tongues of foul gas licked from cracks in the soil, filling the air with nauseous fumes. Hillocks folded in on themselves and rocks sprang from the turf as needles of gneiss.

While the two figures moved back and forth, their weapons stabbing the air, their screams of frustration and cries of fury becoming ever louder, the thunder came from above, crashing down on the heads of mortals and fairies, shocking everyone with the force of its blows.

This only served to intensify the struggle between fairy queen and sorceress. Sinews strained to snapping point, tendons were taut as bowstrings, muscles tore and carapaces creaked and cracked. Backwards and forwards danced the pair of scorpions, the onlookers unable to separate favourite from foe they were locked so tightly together, knitted intricately into each other's forms like two filigree figures. Then two delicate dancers became one contorted multi-legged image which appeared to be devouring itself. It was an ugly sight, not meant for the eyes of either fairy or human.

To the watching travellers it was a nightmare, a terrible

nightmare, which seemed to worsen with every second.

In the distance, the sea could be heard roaring out its disapproval.

'Stop this!' cried Tom Blessing, running forwards, unable to contain his horror any further. 'Stop this!'

But mayhem and murder once begun needs more than human words to force it to a conclusion. Tom tripped on the heaving ground, went sprawling full-length on his face. Vines whipped from secret creases in the earth, pinning him to the heather, holding him fast from harm. He struggled there, whimpering, trying to claw his way to his feet, but being forced down by a power beyond the natural.

Trees crashed in the forest, one falling dead with every stab of a sting.

A light appeared in the heavens – the moon had come out, peering through the dusk – shining on the scene.

It was at this moment that a final blow was struck and a brain was pierced, the body containing it, the soul enveloping it, all cast into oblivion.

Sorcerers do not die, any more than fairies do, but they can be destroyed in the time they inhabit: they can be hurled backwards or forwards, into another time, another place. Morgana had already spent centuries in a ditch, a similar punishment for a former offence. Titania had once, long ago, been locked in the trunk of tree, until Oberon found her again and released her. Now one of these two combatants had been flung far away, immured somewhere beyond the sight and sound of the world, an imprisoned spirit beneath some underground sea, or at the bottom of a closed disused well, or buried in the heart of a mountain.

One had been defeated, the other, victorious.

In the dimness it was difficult to tell who stood in the victor's spot.

Oberon, King of the Fairies, knew instantly, however, and ran forward to embrace the victor.

'My dear Titania,' he said, his eyes shining, 'you are indeed a formidable opponent for any sorceress!'

'Am I, my Lord?' she laughed, restored to her former fairy shape, her terrible wounds closing themselves, healing by the moment. 'Am I your dear Titania?'

'You are my queen,' he said, stepping back and bowing gallantly, 'and I your servant – for today at least.'

She let out a sweet tinkling laugh that chilled Tom's blood and made him realize, at last, that she was not a human being like himself, but some ethereal creature of the night, a dangerous, *different* being with alien ways.

The light of the world returned to normal, the blood draining from the sky, the red thunder clouds hurrying back over the horizon, the Earth righting itself. A tattered cheer went up from the travellers as they saw it was Titania who remained amongst them and not the sorceress. Tom walked away, hurried away, back to the Blessing bus, there to hide and tremble in the solitude of familiar surroundings.

Sid went to inspect the ground where the fight had taken place, to find a large circle of smouldering earth where the grass had been scorched. Clearly the battle had been more fierce than the spectators had imagined. The mechanic then went over to Puck.

'I didn't like that much,' he confessed. 'I'm not one for this violence stuff.'

'It happens rarely to fairies,' Puck said. 'I am not so fond of battle myself.'

Sid said, 'Hadn't we better go and look for that girl, the

304

one who ran off into the forest? She looked a bit scared. I wouldn't want anything to happen to her.'

Puck agreed and called everyone together.

'Now that my queen has defeated the witch,' said Puck, 'we are free to enter the New Forest. The barriers have gone and we have no more need to stand out here in the world of mortals. But before we leave you I must ask you all to help search for the maid mistaken for our own Cobweb. Fairies and mortals alike, I think we should find this wench and restore her to her own people, at the village of Avebury.'

There was a general assent and they went into the forest, in bands of three or more for comfort, having seen something strange enough to invade their dreams for many nights to come. In each of the human hearts was a dread they could not even identify or explain. It defeated all words. They carried with them hellish visions, images locked in their cerebrums, sounds they hoped they would never hear again, and they wanted to be busy for a while to keep the scenes at bay.

They went through the darkening woods, calling for the young woman, though they had no name.

'Hallo! Where are you? Don't be afraid, we've come to help you. Hallo! Hallo!'

Sid was especially anxious to find the young lady who had smiled at him during the rehearsal at Avebury. He had felt an affinity with her that had never entered into his relationships with women before. They had always been to him not worth the trouble. He disliked women, generally, because they tended to laugh at him for being what he was – unfashionable, sometimes untidy, fond of darts, fond of snooker, fond of football, not fond of dancing – but this one seemed different. And even if she wasn't, it didn't seem to matter. Her smile had melted his insides like warmed butter: turned them to a runny yellow. Somehow he had to be the first to find her, so that he could be gentle, caring, understanding.

It was not to be.

In fact it was Oberon himself who found the creature, nestled exhausted and asleep in the crook of a great oak root, her soft breath unsettling old leaves.

The sweet maiden's face captivated even the fairy king.

Oberon studied her for a few moments.

Her eyes, closed in slumber, were gently touched by Oberon's fingertips. Her pink cheeks were stroked by a caring hand. Her confused mind was explored by Oberon's own, and he came to an understanding of her innermost needs.

She murmured in her sleep, as if disturbed by his wanderings through her dreams.

Oberon went back to the green, to where the Blessing bus stood, and called on Tom.

'Come, good gentle,' said the fairy king, 'I have a maid for thee who will match, in small part, mine own Titania.'

He led the pale and questioning Tom to a glade and pointed to the sleeping young woman.

'There,' he said, 'wake her and mayhap you will receive her everlasting gratitude. Unless,' and here Oberon stared hard at Tom, 'you can think of a better man to open her eyes?'

So saying, he left Tom staring at the sleeping form of the pretty young woman, his mind in turmoil.

Tom continued to look down upon the woman, not moving for a very long time, even when he heard Oberon's distant hallooing, calling his fairies to his side. Then she moved slightly in her rest, flinging a sleepy arm over an oak root. Tom at last went into action, hoping he was not too late.

Tom ran quickly out of the forest, back to the green, where travellers were regrouping having been told that the young woman had been found. On the edge of the crowd, talking with Jug, was Sid. He looked as if he were feeling a bit flat and Tom guessed he knew the reason why.

'Sid,' said Tom, 'come with me.'

'Eh? What for?' asked the surprised Sid.

'Just come with me,' Tom repeated, 'and I'll explain when we get there.'

He led Sid into the forest and to the glade where the woman lay, still nestled in the roots of the oak.

Tom said, 'You can wake her yourself, Sid – good luck,' and left Sid standing there.

Sid gazed upon the form of the young woman and decided she was the most divine creature he had ever laid eyes on. She had the sweetest face, a pretty nose and mouth, nice soft-looking hair. He couldn't see her eyes, but he knew them to be adorable. He wanted to shower her face with kisses right now, but he knew that to be immoral and possibly even illegal. You didn't kiss a perfect stranger while she slept, no matter how pure your intentions might be.

In any case, he was just a greasy car mechanic. This young lady was obviously a princess or something: a duke's daughter at the very least. She would find him ugly, boring and downright unromantic, besides him being, well, pretty much one of the lower classes. What was it the fairies called him, a *rude mechanical*? They didn't mean *rude* as in ill-mannered or coarse – he knew that –

they meant he was your basic craftsman, a worker without refinements.

He sighed, wistfully. Well, he had to do something. He couldn't stand here all day just staring at her. That didn't seem right either. Sid leaned over and gently shook her shoulder, the touch of her doing electric things to him.

The young woman opened her eyes – a startling blue which took Sid's breath away for a moment – and then she linked her arms around his neck and hugged him to her breast.

'Oh,' she cried in his ear, 'has she gone?'

'Has who gone?' asked Sid in a strangulated voice, trying to maintain his balance under this attack.

'That *horrible* woman? Has she gone?'

'Oh, Morgana – yes, they've sent her to hell, I think.'

'A very suitable destination,' said the girl, firmly.

For a moment the young woman seemed happy to clutch Sid to her, obviously deriving some comfort out of the act. For his part Sid was happy to let it happen, except that his legs were beginning to develop pins and needles, jammed as they were against the tree roots. He was in an awkward position, trying not to fall completely on top of the young woman, while at the same time not wanting to appear churlish by pulling away. Eventually, she let him go and sat up properly.

'Where am I?' she asked.

'Well, New Forest I'm afraid,' said Sid apologetically. 'Sorry about that – you were kidnapped by that – by Morgan-le-Fay.'

'The New Forest?' cried the girl, her eyes opening even wider and making Sid's heart do a flip-flop. 'The flipping New Forest? In Hampshire? That's miles away.'

'Yes – as I said, you were kidnapped.'

She stared frankly into Sid's eyes. 'And you rescued me – you lovely man.'

Lovely man? Sid's head swam. 'Well, me an' a few others, of course.'

'I don't remember anything really,' confessed the young woman. 'Can you help me up? I'm a bit cramped.'

Sid did as he was asked, putting his arm around the very narrow waist, while she put a slim bare arm around his neck and shoulders. She was remarkably light, as he imagined an angel would be. The jerkin she was wearing for the play was exceptionally short and revealed her long slim legs, encased in sheer lustrous tights. Sid was glad he couldn't see her legs any more, in his position as her crutch, because they had been doing funny things to his stomach. He had actually wanted to cover them up with his jacket, but he knew this would have been regarded as a rather foolish act.

'My name's Jennifer,' she said, as he helped her hobble along through the ferns. 'What's yours?'

'Er – Sid – Sidney.'

'Sid,' she repeated, as if savouring the name on her tongue. 'It suits you.'

He didn't know what that meant. It might be that the name 'Sid' was associated in her mind with the gardener's son at her parents' mansion.

'Jennifer's nice,' he said. 'It's sort of – well – nice.'

She rewarded him with a dazzling smile which almost knocked the legs from under him, thus rendering him pretty useless as a rock on which she could build her strength.

He half-carried her towards a woodland path alongside which was spread an uncharted ocean of bluebells. Hawker dragonflies were darting through shafts of sunlight. A pair of pigeons thrashed their way out of the branches above, making enough noise for a squadron of eagles. It was an entrancing little walk, which Jennifer seemed to appreciate, because she continually made oohing and aahing sounds.

Sid did not want their walk to end. He had this fair damsel by the waist, her silky-soft arm around his neck, and so far as he was concerned the rest of the world could go to hell in a bucket, as long as he could assist Jennifer on an eternal journey to a destination on the other side of infinity. This was heaven and he was in it. You could forget darts and snooker, or football – for the time being, anyway.

'What will you do now?' he asked her, as she limped along beside him. 'Take the train back to Avebury?'

'I haven't any money,' she said with dismay in her voice. 'Only a couple of pounds.'

Sid nodded. 'Oh, that doesn't matter – I can lend you some. In fact I was thinking of hiring a car. Would you like me to give you a lift back to Avebury? I wouldn't mind, honest, I quite like driving.'

'Oh, you are an angel,' she said. 'Would you? That would be really good of you. You like driving then?'

'It's sort of my job,' said Sid. 'I'm a car mechanic – I work in a garage.'

He expected her to shrink away from him on hearing this, and say something like, Errrghh, *really*? A grotty car mechanic. My God, what am I doing clinging to your neck like this – you might have some epidermic disease caused by constant contact with grease and oil.'

Instead she said pleasantly, 'What a great job. I love cars, don't you? My dad's a fanatic about his Morris Minor. It's even got a name – Wilf. He's always tinkering with the engine, but it never seems to run smoothly. I bet you could really sort out something like that, couldn't you, being a professional and all.'

A professional! And all! Sid's heart was full.

'What does your dad do? Is he local gentry?'

Jennifer let out a fuzzy little laugh. 'Gentry? I should say not. He's a primary school teacher. Due for retirement soon. My mother's dead. I never really knew her. My dad raised me. He thinks I'm the bee's knees.'

'So he should,' said Sid, fervently. 'What do you do? For a living I mean?'

'I'm a barmaid at the moment, but I'm waiting to go to nursing college. I've been for all the interviews and such. I know it's not well paid and all that, but it is a good profession. I've still got old fashioned romantic ideas about nursing. It's probably silly, but I still think Florence Nightingale was a wonderful person.'

'Florence Nightingale,' said Sid, enthusiastically. 'She was an angel that woman – caring for all those soldiers in the Boer War.'

'Crimea,' corrected Jennifer, almost apologetically. 'They're easy to get mixed up though.'

They had reached the edge of the forest by this time and were about to go onto the green. Sid had the feeling that once they were amongst people again, things would be different between them, less magical. So he took the opportunity of striking while the relationship was hot.

'Listen,' he said, anxiously, 'I don't suppose you'd want to come out with me sometime – on a date I mean?'

She cuddled his arm and gave him one of those lead-melting smiles.

'Of course I would. I think you're really nice. I've thought so ever since I saw you watching me do the rehearsal for the play. You were watching me, weren't you?'

'Like a bloody hawk,' laughed Sid, happily. 'I couldn't take my eyes off you. I've never felt like this about a girl before. You missed your play you know.'

'That's all right, I only had about two words to say – anyone could have done it.'

'Not with your flair,' said Sid, gallantly. 'You were just right.'

She kissed him on the cheek and they went out onto the green, to be greeted by mortals and fairies.

TWENTY-FOUR

Julap Opens and Common Cat's Ear Closes

THE FAIRIES, EXHAUSTED, BEGAN TO SAY THEIR GOODBYES to their companions of the road. Puck called them 'friends'. Cobweb remarked that the fairies had never been so close to mortals before and certainly had never called a human 'friend'. He said it made him feel funny inside and he didn't know how to explain it.

'It's called love and affection,' Mary Blessing told him, smiling. 'You'll get used to it.'

Titania went to Tom and gave him one of those wistful smiles which sent his spirit spiralling up into the welkin. He stared into her strange eyes and there was a lump in his throat. It robbed him of speech.

Finally he managed to say, 'I was afraid for you, but I knew you'd win. You win at everything.'

'I didn't manage to keep my baby.'

Her petulance on stating this reminded Tom of how much of the child was in Titania. She was at one and the same time the most wise person he had ever met and yet the most immature and puerile of creatures. An infant and a sage in one form. It required a sort of double-thinking from Tom which he was only just getting used to.

'That's because it wasn't yours. Now you're going back to the forest, I suppose?'

'Yes, my fair and lovely Tom – are you not going to wish your Titania a fond farewell?'

He found these words rather ironic.

He replied, 'Yes, my unfair and incorrigible Titania. Actually, you're not *my* Titania – nor anyone else's, are you? You don't belong to anyone.'

'None of us do, really, Tom, but we like to think we are loved sometimes.'

'You mean the fairies?'

'I mean fairies *and* mortals, Tom. But you will miss me, won't you? I know I captivated you. You will think of me sometimes. You must.'

Tom sighed. 'I'll never forget you. You'll haunt my dreams, though I don't suppose you'll give me a second thought. You simply bewitched me, Titania. Nothing is real around you fairies. You're like soft lights glowing in the dark, intangible, hardly even there at all. You can't be touched, physically or emotionally, because there's no substance to you – you're ethereal, ephemeral creatures. You're a sudden passing breeze, a quick current in the stream, a flash of sunlight on the forest floor, there and gone, leaving no trace of yourselves behind you.'

'Why, Tom,' Titania laughed, 'that's quite poetical.'

He gave her a wry smile. 'I am a writer, after all.'

'Yes, yes you are – you're a brilliant writer.'

Tom said, 'Hmmm. You fairies have a way of convincing us mortals that half-truths are really whole. Off you go then – and good luck. We'll try to see to it that the New Forest doesn't shrink like Sherwood did, but I can't make promises for the rest of the human race.'

'Thank you, Tom.'

He bent down and proffered his cheek, but she kissed him lightly on the lips. Tom was stunned by the honeyed taste of the kiss and the impact it had on to his heart. He was glad he was young and fit. He watched the fairy queen as she skipped lightly over the grass, towards the edge of the forest, hardly even touching the ground.

'*La belle dame sans merci*,' he murmured, the pain of loss swamping him. 'What do I do with the rest of my life now?'

Mustardseed, his neck and shoulders flowing with excited wood mice, overheard this remark and came to Tom, saying, 'Oh, that's all sorted out, Tom, don't you worry,' and then he too was gone, into the lengthening shadows of the forest, leaving Tom wondering what on earth he was talking about.

The sound of Peaseblossom's flute began to drift through the evening. It was at one and the same time both a melancholy and a happy sound, depending on the mood of the listener. Mist, Swallowtail and Blewit were taking their leave of Jug and the other travellers.

Jug said, 'See ya. Don't do anythin' I wouldn't do – not without checking first to see if the law's around, ha, ha. I s'pose you fairies know all sorts of mushrooms to eat, don't ya? And plants and stuff. I bet you get high all the time. I guess you know stuff that's legal, eh?'

The female fairies, who had no idea what Jug was

talking about, agreed with him enthusiastically.

'Well,' said Jug, 'maybe I'll come look for you someday, when I'm feeling a bit flat. Maybe you could cheer me up with some of those plants and things. Yeah, one day I'll come and pay you a call, eh?'

'You'd be most welcome, Jug,' said Swallowtail.

Then the fairies were gone, in amongst the brambles.

Sid, standing with his arm around his newly found love, was having his free hand shaken by little Moth. Sid had now been released by Oberon and was free to go home. He was sure things would never be the same again.

'You're the best rude mechanical I've ever met,' said Moth, generously. 'We made a good team, didn't we? You with your bus and me with my navigating. You thought I wouldn't get us here, I know, but you see us fairies have a way of sniffing the wind, following a moonbeam, chasing a shadow, which leads us to where we want to go in the end – it might be a longer way round, but it's very accurate and sure.'

'Oh, I don't know,' lied Sid. 'I thought you knew what you were doing.'

'Have a good life with your bride,' said Moth, causing both mortals to blush furiously. 'And many babies.'

'Well don't you come stealing 'em,' warned Sid, laughing. 'I know you lot.'

'Only the first one,' said Moth.

Sid's smile left his face and he stared hard at Moth.

'Only joking,' Moth said. 'Bye, Sid.'

And he too was gone, into the networks of ivy.

Oberon, the King of Shadows, was one of the last to leave the green. Mary Blessing was by him, holding Alex's hand. Oberon stared at the boy.

'Goodbye, mortal child – keep you safe.'

Alex nodded, looking up at his mother.

'And you too, woman – keep you happy,' said Oberon. 'It might be, you know, that you could postpone your travelling just for a while, until your man is skilled in his art? What do you think? Once the gift is common in his hands, you could both return to the road. The nature of his work will no doubt take him here and there, wherever the restoration of ancient buildings is taking place, and in that way could you travel. You might join him at Glastonbury for a year or two, until he is ready to take his hands elsewhere?'

'You just can't resist matchmaking, can you?' said Mary, a little smile around the corners of her mouth.

Oberon smiled too. He made a gesture with his tiny hands. 'It's in my nature,' he said. 'And where I see love going to waste I want to gather it together and encourage its owners to make use of it. Think about my words.'

'I shall,' Mary replied, seriously. 'I think you've convinced me.'

'Are we going to see Daddy?' asked Alex, catching on very quickly to the conversation. 'Are we, Mummy?'

'It looks like it,' said Mary, grimly. 'Well, goodbye, Oberon – and good luck.'

'There's my luck,' said Oberon, pointing to the gregarious Puck, who was darting around, shaking hands, whispering in the ears of any mortals not strong enough to resist his social intimacy. 'Good and bad.'

'I'll be back,' Puck was crying. 'Don't leave your pies out on the window-sill to cool! Watch for my footprints in the porridge! Be sure to blame me if the milk is sour! Goodbye, goodbye, keep you well and safe, keep you happy.'

Then Oberon took Puck's hand and the pair of them

strolled into the soft evening light in the forest together, into the world of conifer and decidua; into the world of the darting damsel fly, the bull finch and the wild pony; into the world of toads and toadstools, adders and blind worms; into the world of bracket fungus and woundwort – home at last.

A screech-owl took to the air from a fence post on the edge of the road, flew like a silent missile across the green, and plunged into the darkness of the woodland.

Tom Blessing went back to his sister's bus to find her crying.

'What's the matter?' he asked. 'Is it the fairies? Because they're leaving?'

'Don't be daft,' Mary said, 'I might miss my man but I'm not one of those silly emotional types that cry at the end of a holiday. I'm missing Earl, that's all. Listen, let's go back to Glastonbury tonight and surprise him.'

'This is a sudden change of heart, isn't it?'

'Yes – Oberon convinced me that I was being selfish. Actually, I'm not really convinced, but I don't want to live without Earl, so I'll go along with him until he's qualified – or whatever it's called amongst stone masons – and then I'll persuade him to move round a bit.'

Tom shrugged. 'Sounds like a good compromise to me.'

At that precise moment there was a rapping on the door of the bus. Tom opened it to find a smartly dressed attractive-looking woman standing there. He felt he should know her but couldn't come up with a name. She seemed nervous and his first thought was to put her at ease.

'Hello – can I help you?' he asked.

'I wanted to find someone who knew Tom Blessing.'

He was a little taken aback. 'Why, that's me.'

She looked shocked, retreated. 'You can't be. The police said you were in a bus under the water. They chased a bus – it went into the sea. They said the person who gave his name as Tom Blessing must be drowned by now . . .'

'Gave his name as Tom Blessing?' repeated Tom, utterly confused. 'To whom?'

'To – to the police – when he handed in Louise.'

Comprehension flooded Tom's brain. 'Baby Louise!' he cried. 'You're Frances Flute – the nanny of the stolen baby. I saw you on television. I was racking my brains trying to think where . . . so the person who handed the baby – Louise – over to the police gave his name as Tom Blessing. I'll kill that Sid when I get my hands on him.'

'I beg your pardon?' Frances said. 'I'm sorry – you mean, it was someone called Sid who handed Louise to the police. It must be this person Sid who was drowned then – though they haven't recovered the body yet.'

'I guarantee that when they dredge that bus out of the tide it will be empty. I saw Sid only a few minutes ago. He obviously managed to get out of the bus before it went into the waves.'

Frances looked relieved. 'Are you sure? You think he jumped clear?'

'Positive,' replied Tom.

Frances looked around her. 'Well, where is he? I'd like to thank him for – for handing in Louise – even if he did have something to do with stealing her. I mean, I've been through a dreadful time, but it's all right now. The baby is with her grandparents. Is Sid around?'

'Gone,' Tom said, knowing Sid was probably in Jug's

teepee, but realizing he would be in trouble if found by the local police. 'Left a few minutes ago.'

Frances appeared to be disappointed, but then rallied and smiled.

'You seem to know a lot about it. Was it you travellers who stole her?'

'No, nothing to do with the travellers. It was another group of people. I could explain . . .'

'Well, anyway, it's all academic now. I don't suppose we'll get enough proof to prosecute and I believe Mr and Mrs DuLac wouldn't want any more publicity. Their faces have already been given huge coverage over the media. Louise is safe, that's the important thing.'

Tom stepped down from the bus and took Frances's arm.

'Look, have you got time for a short walk in the forest? I'm not actually a traveller – that's my sister's bus – I'm writing a book . . .'

Frances allowed herself to be steered across the green towards the trees.

'You're a writer? I wondered why you said "whom" instead of the usual "who" a little while ago. I mean, one doesn't like to be patronizing, but I spoke to some other travellers before you and they couldn't string two sensible words together. They appeared to be deliberately obstructive when I was asking for Tom Blessing – for *you* that is. You don't seem like a traveller at all. You seem a little more refined. That sounds a bit snooty I suppose.'

It pleased Tom that she found him *refined*.

'Oh, the travellers are all right,' said Tom. 'They're OK really. They probably thought you were someone in authority – they hate authority. It's the one thing that makes them clam up. They just have different priorities to us. I mean their hearts are pure enough. Listen – are you married or anything? Or going out with anyone?'

They had reached the line of the trees by now and she turned. In the evening light her eyes looked misty and quite enchanting. He knew instantly he was in love with her, though he wouldn't tell her so, not yet. It was too soon for words like that. That was for the fairies, that instant love, not for people. People needed time to grow towards each other, share each other's thoughts, give to each other, take from each other.

'How about it – do you have someone?' he asked, realizing he was not getting an answer.

She shook her head slowly. 'Living with a family, as I do, one doesn't get to meet many men. It's not like an office job. Are you going to ask me out then? I'd like that.'

'Yes, I think I am,' Tom said, emphatically. 'In fact I know I am.'

At that moment Tom could have sworn he heard a tinkling laugh, coming from amongst the bluebells in the forest. He looked sharply at Frances, wondering if she had heard it too. She showed no signs of having done so.

'On second thoughts,' Tom said, 'perhaps we'd better not walk in the forest after all. Let's get a lift to the nearest restaurant and I'll tell you all about how Louise was abducted when we get there. Do you like Indian food? I love it. Otherwise there's Chinese – or even Italian at a pinch, though I can only take so much pasta . . .'

They walked back across the darkening green, towards the travellers' encampment, their arms linked.

On the strand at Milford they had just hauled the bus from the sea and were watching it empty onto the car-park, the water pouring from the open doorway.

Watchers steeled themselves for the first sight of the drowned man.

However, to everyone's amazement, the bus proved to be empty and one of the frogmen, who went down to attach lines to the vehicle under water, now said he definitely remembered seeing two shapes swimming away from the bus when he was hooking a hawser to the bumper.

'I didn't think anything of it,' he said. 'I mean, I thought they were fish. After all, they were *outside* the bus, not trapped in it – yet now I come to think of it, they seemed to have come from the vehicle . . . '

The director of the operations shook his head, thinking his man was being fanciful, that the stress of the job had got to him somehow.

'The two policemen who *thought* they saw a man at the wheel, before the bus slipped into the sea, must have been mistaken,' he said. 'I mean, anybody dead or alive who came out of that bus while it was under water would've been washed up onto the strand straight away. Why would anyone swim out to sea? It doesn't make sense.'

And that, so far as he was concerned, was that.

In the New Forest, the fairies were now invisible to mortal eyes. The King of Shadows strolled blissfully through ferns and bracken, a broad canopy of leaves and branches above his head, soft mats of humus beneath his feet. He missed his Major Oak it was true, but the old tree would not remain there for ever, it had to fall some day, and King Oberon of the New Forest fairies would not have to witness its demise.

'All's well that ends well,' he said. 'And such a journey

as we had is not a thing to be forgot. My dear Titania had, for a time, a human babe with special ancest'ry, and we ourselves of wide adventures had surfeit. Still, I am not sad that all our travels are now done and we can rest in peaceful harmony within this newly planted wood – a babe itself next to our Sherwood home – much of it being but a thousand years from birth and not yet out of swaddling bark. We shall enjoy our gambolling in these leafy glades, amongst the creeping mallow and the ivy spreads, drinking from the cuckoo pints and feasting on the best of toadstool bread . . . . hark, I hear the footsteps of my hero, Puck. Sublime Titania comes this way as well!

'Ho, my queen! And Puck, my faithful servant, what?'

'The fairies call for you, my lord,' said Puck, 'the witenagemot has now begun.'

Titania took him by the hand. 'Yes, come, my husband, come to join our first wassail under the beeches of this greenery we now call home. We miss your company, good lord – how can we dance without the King of Shadows showing us the steps?'

Oberon smiled and allowed himself to be pulled by the hand, through the bluebells and other wild flowers with which the woodland walks were trimmed. In the near distance he could hear Peaseblossom's pipes, spilling out sweet music, and the voices of his other fairies, raised in joy. The bonnyclabber would be ready to quaff, his feet were itching to dance, and merriment was the tone of the evening.

All was indeed well that had ended well.

Sid was driving north-west, with Jennifer at his side. He had told her most of what had happened to him, over the last week or so, and he waited for her comments. She said she envied him his time with the fairies but could understand that it hadn't all been fun. She asked him to sum it all up in one sentence as truthfully as he could.

'The truth? It's been a nightmare,' said Sid, 'but I came out the other end with *you*, so it's not been all bad.'

'I should say not,' she smiled, hugging his arm. 'He's a bit of a matchmaker, that Oberon, isn't he?'

'Just a bit,' laughed Sid.

They were silent for a few moments, warm in each other's company, then Jennifer said, 'What about all those giants and dragons and things – will they go now?'

'They should have all gone,' said Sid. 'They'll all be back in their lairs or whatever.'

'You're sure about that?'

Sid remembered what Oberon had told him, about the supernatural beings being vanquished, sent back to the place from whence they had come, once the fairies were in the New Forest and established in their new home.

'Positive – if there's any of them left I promise you I'll fight them myself – to prove my honour.'

She laughed and snuggled into his side and they drove on into the night, the lights of houses falling away beside them, the country road winding in and out of spinneys, through dark tunnels of trees whose branches touched over the highway.

As they travelled through one such leafy corridor Sid thought he saw a green knight, a giant of a man on horseback, cross the road in front. The figure had his great helmeted, bearded head tucked under his left arm. The green face flashed a grin at Sid, before the mounted warrior disappeared into the foliage on the other side of the ditch.

'Did you see that?' cried Sid. 'Did you see it?'